SANDITON

Kate Riordan is a British writer and journalist. She has had three historical novels published by Penguin in the UK: *The Girl in the Photograph*, *The Shadow Hour* and *The Stranger*, which have sold in excess of 150,000 copies and been praised for their atmospheric evocation of nineteenth-century England.

SANDITON

Kate Riordan

GRAND CENTRAL
PUBLISHING

NEW YORK   BOSTON

Sanditon © 2019 Red Planet Pictures
"Sanditon" television series © 2019 Red Planet Pictures Limited. All rights reserved.

Cover copyright © 2019 by Hachette Book Group, Inc.
Cover photography © Red Planet Pictures

Grand Central Publishing
Hachette Book Group
1290 Avenue of the Americas, New York, NY 10104
grandcentralpublishing.com
twitter.com/grandcentralpub

First published in Great Britain in 2019 by Trapeze, an imprint of The Orion Publishing Group Ltd. Carmelite House, 50 Victoria Embankment, London EC4Y 0DZ. An Hachette UK company.

First US Edition: December 2019

Grand Central Publishing is a division of Hachette Book Group, Inc. The Grand Central Publishing name and logo is a trademark of Hachette Book Group, Inc.

This book is published to accompany the television series entitled Sanditon. A Red Planet Pictures Production for ITV co-produced with Masterpiece first broadcast in 2019.

MASTERPIECE® is a registered trademark of the WGBH Educational Foundation. Used with permission.

Sanditon is available on Blu-ray and DVD. To purchase, visit shop.pbs.org.

Sanditon is a Red Planet Pictures production for ITV co-produced with MASTERPIECE in association with BBC Studios Distribution.

© Red Planet Pictures 2019

The PBS Logo is a registered trademark of the Public Broadcasting Service and used with permission. All rights reserved.

The publisher is not responsible for websites (or their content) that are not owned by the publisher.

Library of Congress Control Number: 2019951950

ISBNs: 978-1-5387-3468-1 (trade paperback), 978-1-5387-3469-8 (ebook)

Printed in the United States of America

LSC-C

10 9 8 7 6 5 4 3 2

For Morris and Jenny

Foreword by Andrew Davies

In the last year of her life, Jane Austen embarked on a new novel, a bold departure from anything she had done before.

Of course, she provides us with a spirited young heroine and a fascinatingly complex and moody hero, but the setting is new, and the Parker brothers embody a new kind of Jane Austen character: they are men of affairs, entrepreneurs, men who want to change the world they live in and leave their mark on it. You could say it's a bit like *Boardwalk Empire*: Tom Parker is trying to develop a sleepy fishing village into a fashionable seaside resort. He's mortgaged his property to the hilt, borrowed from all and sundry, and now he's transforming Sanditon before our very eyes.

Young Charlotte Heywood comes to stay and falls in love with Sanditon and the whole enterprise. It's a different world for her, with a fascinating cast of characters: the eccentric and endearing Parker family; Lady Denham, the rich and domineering patroness; Sir Edward Denham and his step-sister Esther, whose relationship seems a little too close; Lady Denham's protégée Clara, the poor relation, who has something clandestine going on with Sir Edward – and Miss Lambe, the heiress from the West Indies, Jane Austen's first black character! Mix in a few quarrels, schemes and misunderstandings, a couple of balls, and a bit of naked sea bathing (for the men) and we have a fascinating set of possibilities.

The Regency era, when we set our story, saw a huge explosion of holidays for pleasure and for health reasons, both at seaside resorts and inland spas – and a great entrepreneurial spirit of 'If we build it, they will come.' Men like Tom Parker were making vast fortunes – just as many were going bankrupt from misjudging the market. And resorts like Sanditon were attractive to visitors because they were places where you could meet new people, goggle at celebrities, create a new personality for yourself, fall in love – anything was possible.

So far, so wonderful – but Austen's 60-page fragment only offered enough story material for half of the first episode of what I hoped to develop into a returning eight-part series. Cue lots of research into the Regency era, and lots of imaginative brain-cudgelling. Lots of meetings with producers – executive producer Belinda Campbell and producer Georgina Lowe – and lots of jolly lunches. ITV wanted to go into production quickly, and there wasn't going to be enough time for me to write all eight scripts, so once the overall structure was set, we agreed that I would write the first three episodes and the last. From here on, everything happened bewilderingly quickly: Olly Blackburn, the director, and Grant Montgomery, the production designer, outlined their vision for the show, and soon we were casting established stars like Anne Reid, Kris Marshall and Theo James, as well as exciting newcomers Rose Williams and Crystal Clarke as our heroines Miss Heywood and Miss Lambe.

At the time of writing this foreword we are halfway through filming, and I am thrilled with what we have achieved: a period drama that feels utterly fresh and modern – Jane Austen, but not as you knew her.

Chapter One

1819

It was a spring day that whispered of a fine summer to come, the flowers chancing to open themselves up and the mild air scented with possibility. On the green slopes above the tiny hamlet of Willingden, Charlotte Heywood was leading an assortment of her brothers and sisters on a walk. The rain of the previous days had prevented any exercise and, as the eldest of twelve lively offspring, she was excessively glad to be out of the house.

The walk undertaken, but none yet willing to go back indoors, they decided to take their rest in the long grass. The gentle countryside rolled away from them in all directions, peaceful and luxuriously green. It was so wonderfully quiet – the children becalmed after their exertions, the bright birdsong only distant – that Charlotte could hear the soft breeze sighing through every blade of grass. She ran her free hand through it, marvelling at its springiness; the other hand occupied by the gun tucked expertly into the nook of her shoulder.

She was just wondering how she might occupy herself for the rest of the day when a small movement caught her eye. Just below the gathering of Heywoods were two rabbits, white tails flashing as they nibbled the clover.

In a single, fluid motion, Charlotte stood up, shifted her grip on the gun, and took aim.

'Look!' cried her sister Alison at the same moment, gesturing towards the rabbits, who immediately turned tail and vanished into the scrub.

Charlotte, much irritated, was about to make a cutting remark when something more diverting caught her eye. Two horses, the sweat on their flanks visible even from this remove, were struggling to pull a carriage up the steep and twisting lane that served as Willingden's only road. That anyone should attempt this was so unusual that all the Heywoods were soon on their feet, to better observe the spectacle. As they watched, the carriage, which had already slowed considerably, began to list, then lurch, and finally toppled over on to its side with a resounding crash.

Charlotte hitched up her skirts. 'Quick, Alison! Quickly, boys!'

As they hurried down the hill, more Heywood children – alerted by the racket – poured forth from the house as though there might be no end to them. None could hide their glee at this unexpected turn of events for Willingden was a very out-of-the-way sort of place. What was surely a misfortune for the occupants of the carriage was already proving great entertainment for the younger Heywoods.

When Charlotte reached the bottom of the slope, the coachman was already up and busy trying to calm the distressed horses. There was as yet no sign of the carriage's occupants but as she drew closer, the door, which was now facing skywards, opened up. A gentleman's head and shoulders emerged. He looked about him with keen, darting eyes, as though enthusiasm and interest might be mustered even from the most alarming incident.

'Here we are!' he cried, with admirable cheer. 'No harm done! Give me your hand, my love,' he said to his yet unseen companion, who was still ensconced in the stricken carriage. 'We'll soon have you out.'

Without further delay, Charlotte scrambled up on to the carriage to offer her assistance.

Her sister, always more mindful of propriety, was shocked. 'Charlotte, what are you doing?' she exclaimed.

'Steady!' said Charlotte, ignoring Alison and addressing the carriage's female occupant. 'Take my hand.'

The lady, with Charlotte's help, pulled herself clear and landed very tidily on the road, her fair hair only slightly disarranged.

'Thank you,' she said, smiling, her demeanour quite as good-natured as the gentleman's now she was rescued. 'You are very kind, and very brave to risk yourself.'

Charlotte smiled back, dark eyes sparkling. 'Not at all, ma'am, this is the most exciting thing to happen in Willingden for years.'

'There we are,' said the gentleman from his precarious perch above them. 'Neat as ninepence!' But he spoke too soon for on leaping to the road himself, landed awkwardly and turned his ankle. He cried out, face blanching, but after a deep breath attempted to rally, saying bravely, 'It's nothing, nothing at all.'

But indeed it was not nothing and when he tried to put weight on it, he grimaced in pain.

'Give me your arm, sir,' said Charlotte, with the usual good sense that made her the secret favourite of her father's. 'Our house is close by.'

He took it gratefully. 'Thank you, my dear – what kindness! I see we have fallen amongst friends.'

*

Mr and Mrs Heywood were fetched from their various quarters and, as people entirely contented with their quiet corner of the world, were very glad to welcome the newcomers to it. The gentleman introduced himself and his wife as Mr Tom and Mrs Mary Parker. They had been in London and were on their way to their home on the Sussex coast when the fateful turn was taken towards Willingden and its impassable lane. Already the accident had passed into amusing anecdote, at least for Mr Parker, and once he was settled in the Heywood drawing room, his leg elevated on a cushion and a reviving dish of tea drunk down, his customary spirits were almost entirely restored.

The Heywood children, who were much taken with the strangers, had stationed themselves around the room like so many cats, and were now absorbing the Parkers' every gesture and word with wide eyes.

'This is really so kind of you,' said Mrs Parker, smiling gamely round at them and trying not to count.

Mr Parker gave Charlotte a rueful look. 'We were in search of a physician, you know. For Sanditon.'

She was confused. 'Is Sanditon a relative, sir?'

'No, no, a place! And what a place!' He smiled, the gleam of a rare enthusiasm in his eyes. 'I am amazed you have never heard of it. Sanditon is, or very soon will be, the finest seaside resort on the whole of the south coast.'

Charlotte's mind filled with pleasant images: soft sand, glittering water, the saline breeze in her hair. The strange restlessness that had lately begun to infect her peaceful days was stirred anew.

'I should very much like to see it, sir,' she couldn't help saying, shocking her sister Alison all over again.

4

Sensing a kindred spirit in his young rescuer, Mr Parker asked for various trunks and cases to be brought in. Only a little scuffed and muddy from the lane, one of these contained Mr Parker's precious architectural plans for the numerous improvements that were steadily transforming Sanditon from an unremarkable fishing village into a resort of the first water.

A card table was brought over to where the invalid was propped and the drawings spread across it.

'You see, Miss Heywood: here is the Crown Hotel, the shops, new terraces here, the cliff walk – and the new Assembly Rooms here!' He pointed them out, triumphant.

Charlotte felt as though she could almost see them. 'Do you plan to have dancing there, sir?'

Mr Parker was most gratified by her interest. 'We shall be holding our first ball next week!'

'And you are really building all this?'

'I am! Well – causing it to be built.'

For the rest of the day, Charlotte remained in Willingden only in body. Her mind had flown south to alight at Sanditon. The book of poetry she took to the upper pasture to read might have been written in Greek for all the attention she paid it, and when, as the dusk crept in, she went as usual to the stables to lunge her faithful old horse, she did not see the stars coming on above her, though the air was wonderfully clear and they were especially bright. Though she did later notice the moon, silvering the water in the bowl on her washstand as she undressed for bed, she did not admire it for itself, only for the astonishing fact that the same moon also illuminated the sky over Sanditon.

Her reverie persisted into the next day, when she was obliged by her mother to walk into the village for some trifles she would have forgotten if she had not been handed a list. She wandered home, scarcely seeing the farmhands and fields she had known all her life, her lively imagination quite occupied with the question of what a fashionable seaside resort might look like, and how she herself might be transfigured by such a place.

Her father calling out to her brought her back to herself. He was signalling to her from the open window of his office. Going inside, she found him puzzling over a thick ledger, a large pile of bills at his elbow.

'Come and have a look at these figures; see if you can get them to balance for me.'

She stood behind him and ran her finger down the column of black-inked figures.

'So what's the news from Willingden?' said Mr Heywood. 'What's going on in the world?'

'Nothing at all,' replied Charlotte mournfully.

'Good,' said her father. 'That's the way we like it.'

Charlotte permitted herself to roll her eyes a little, though with great affection. She was quite unlike her parents, dear as they were to her. If it wasn't for her father's annual journey to London to collect his dividends, he would happily never stir from Willingden again. To him, Willingden *was* the world. Once she might have agreed; now she couldn't think of anything more stifling.

'There,' she said, suddenly spotting his mistake. 'You forgot to carry one.' She picked up the pen and neatly corrected the sum. 'All done.'

Mr Heywood patted her hand. 'Good girl.'

Some days passed in quiet fashion, as they were wont to in the Heywood household. The weather turned chilly on the third afternoon, the wind coming from the east, and a fire had to be laid in the comfortable sitting room. Charlotte was ensconced in the corner, pretending to read her book, while Mr Parker once again expounded the many virtues of Sanditon to Mr and Mrs Heywood. Since the Parkers' unexpected arrival, it had become apparent to even the youngest Heywood that Mr Parker's up-and-coming resort was his life's purpose and passion. Indeed, it had been observed by more than one person of his acquaintance that it was as good as his religion.

'Indeed, Mr Heywood,' he was saying now. 'I insist that you must come and sample the delights of Sanditon without delay.'

Mr Heywood smiled but shook his head implacably. 'You must forgive me, sir. I make it a principle never to go more than five miles from home.'

Though some version of this conversation had played out before, Mr Parker was no less aghast. 'But for Sanditon, sir, for Sanditon with all its charms, you must make an exception!'

'My husband is ever the enthusiast,' put in Mrs Parker, with the endearing mix of pride and apology that characterised her role as Tom Parker's wife.

'And nothing wrong with that, madam,' returned Mr Heywood with an affable smile, 'but he cannot tempt me.'

'Then one of your daughters, perhaps?' said she. 'In return for your kindness?'

Charlotte sat up, almost dropping her book. The movement caught Mrs Parker's eye, who gave her a nod that was so silently encouraging it could not be mistaken.

'Papa – might I go?' she said in a rush.

'Really, Charlotte!' Her mother turned in her chair, shocked at her forwardness.

'Forgive my eldest daughter's presumption, Mr Parker,' said Mr Heywood.

But Mr Parker waved his hand dismissively. 'Nothing could delight us more, Mr Heywood. Of course Charlotte can come and stay for the season or for as long as she likes, can she not, Mary?'

Mrs Parker gave Mr Heywood a smile of the utmost sweetness. 'If you permit, we would be very happy, sir.'

Charlotte's father puffed out his cheeks and turned to his wife. 'Well, what do you think, my dear?'

'I think it very kind of Mr and Mrs Parker, and if Charlotte is so *very* eager—' another reproving glance here –

'I am, Mama.'

'Then . . .'

But Charlotte's father was not yet satisfied. 'Sanditon, I understand, is not yet fully-fledged, as it were, as a seaside resort? It is, ah, in the process of *becoming* a resort of public entertainment?'

Mr Parker turned to him eagerly. 'Exactly, sir, and I have sunk all my resources into the enterprise!'

'Quite a risky one, I imagine?'

'If you had seen the situation, sir, you would not doubt. Sanditon is a very jewel of a place.' His eyes shone with the conviction of a true zealot. 'I am absolutely convinced: if we build it, they will come!'

That evening, Mr Heywood asked Charlotte to accompany him fishing. Though, to her great delight, he had relented and given permission for her to go to Sanditon, he was not yet easy in his mind.

'My dear—'

'Yes, Papa?'

'Just a word, my dear. Just a word.' He hesitated, apparently searching for the right ones. 'These seaside resorts can be odd places. No one quite knows who anyone else is, where they come from and what they are up to.'

Charlotte wasn't sure how to respond. She was suddenly gripped by the fear that her father would change his mind.

'That sounds . . . stimulating,' she said carefully.

Mr Heywood sighed. 'Yes, well, I suppose it is. But, ah, the normal rules of conduct tend to be relaxed, and sometimes altogether flouted.'

'But if I am with Mr and Mrs Parker nothing bad can happen, can it?'

'Just – just be careful, that's all.'

'Careful of what, Papa?' Her father was looking uncharacteristically ruffled by now.

'Everything!' he said, throwing up his hands and scaring away a shining trout, which disappeared into the depths of the dark water. 'I know you understand me. You're a good girl, and can tell right from wrong.'

Charlotte, somewhat baffled, nodded her head and hoped that would be the end of it.

Chapter Two

The Heywood family gathered to wave the Parkers and Charlotte off in their newly mended carriage. The latter was in such high spirits at the thought of the adventure ahead that there was room for neither apprehension nor sadness. The world, or at least Sanditon, awaited her. Even the unsatisfactory contents of her wardrobe, now packed into a trunk and strapped to the back of the Parkers' carriage, could not dampen her mood.

The long journey to the coast gave Mr Parker ample opportunity for further describing Sanditon's singular appeal. As the view beyond the carriage window changed, the villages more populated and the roads wider and busier than any Charlotte had seen, he kept up a flow of conversation so ceaseless that it was as though the resort's success depended on it.

'Now we are coming near!' he cried after some hours, interrupting his own lengthy description of the new Assembly Rooms. 'Do you feel a difference in the air, Miss Heywood? I am of the firm belief that sea air is better than any medicine or tonic! And look: there is the sea itself!'

They crested the hill and it appeared before her, a bolt of fine blue satin rolled out for her approval.

'Oh yes!' she said reverently. 'There it is.'

'Doesn't it make your spirits soar?'

'Tom, you can't expect Charlotte to be as excited by a glimpse of salt-water as you are,' broke in Mrs Parker.

'Stuff and nonsense,' he retorted. 'I'll wager that within a few days, she'll be as keen as mustard on it!'

'Indeed, Mrs Parker,' said Charlotte. 'I am eager to see everything! Oh, what a pretty house.'

Her eye had been caught by a snug-looking place, its garden, orchard and the surrounding meadows quite lovely.

'Ah, that's our old house,' said Mr Parker dismissively, his gaze still fixed on the road ahead. 'I grew up in that house, but it wouldn't do – too sheltered, no sea view . . .'

'I was very happy there,' said Mrs Parker wistfully, twisting around in her seat to see the old, cast-off house fade from view.

'I know you were, my dear.' He patted her leg absently. 'Now, we are just coming up to Sanditon House, Lady Denham's place. She is the great lady of the town, you know. Very rich, and very much involved, as I am, in the future of Sanditon as a first-class bathing resort. There, you see it coming into view now.'

As Charlotte admired the large house of grey stone in its extensive grounds, Mr Parker turned to his wife. 'Shall we call upon her this very minute, my dear? I should like Miss Heywood to meet her and I have business matters to discuss with her.'

Mrs Parker gave him a reproving look. 'Before seeing our own children, Tom?'

'No, well, perhaps you are right.' He cleared his throat. 'Indeed, you *are* right, always – Trafalgar House and the children it is!'

The carriage now entered the resort itself. It made a most fascinating study of the pace of change, with an ancient church and a row of low-slung cottages giving way to buildings that were far younger than Charlotte herself. As they continued, passing along what was evidently the high street, with its cluster of shops and a hotel with a jutting portico, the point where old met new was striking. It was almost as if Mr Parker's vision of Sanditon was an advancing army; the original buildings knowing themselves beaten and beginning the downhill retreat towards the old harbour and the sea.

It must be said that Charlotte was rather too overcome to muse on the ruthless march of progress. Sanditon was so much more than Willingden could ever hope to offer that she could only stare.

'Here we are, Miss Heywood!' said Mr Parker, with no small amount of pride. 'This is civilisation indeed!'

The carriage rolled on, past more shops. In one carefully-dressed window, Charlotte's eye fastened upon a pair of blue shoes. Indeed, she was far from Willingden now. The shops soon gave way to grand houses that as yet waited unoccupied, 'Rooms to Let' signs sitting hopefully in their large windows.

'Excellent!' cried Tom, as the carriage came to a stop. 'Here we are.'

They had arrived at Trafalgar House, a large, handsome place of pale stone in the new style. Compared to the soft lines and weathered face of Charlotte's own dear home, it was startlingly symmetrical, every stone square-cut and flaw-less. As she stepped down from the carriage, the gleaming front door was flung open and two small girls ran out to greet their parents. A toddling boy followed, and finally a nursemaid carrying a round-eyed baby.

'Well, here we are!' exclaimed Mrs Parker happily, bending to embrace them. 'Have you been good? Say how d'ye do to Miss Heywood.'

The girls curtsied prettily and the boy put up a small hand to be shaken.

'This is Alicia, Jenny and Henry. And the baby is James.' Charlotte beamed round at them all. 'How d'ye do?'

The introductions made, Mr Parker, who wished always to be doing the next thing to whatever he was currently engaged in, ushered them inside.

While the servants carried in the luggage, Charlotte was drawn to a large portrait in the hall. Its subject, a dark-haired gentleman of unusually handsome features and powerful bearing, seemed to regard her with approval as she approached.

'That portrait is of Sidney, my younger brother,' said Mr Parker, joining her. 'We're expecting him here from London in time for the ball. We're counting on his help to make Sanditon fashionable!' He smiled affectionately up at the likeness.

Somewhat distracted by the picture, and rather surprised that the two Mr Parkers should look so different, Charlotte cast around for something further to say. 'And er . . . what is his occupation?'

'Ha! Very good question. What would you say, Mary?' He turned to his wife, who was taking off her hat. 'He's a man of affairs, a man of business! Importing, exporting: he is here, there and everywhere. You can ask him yourself when you meet!'

Mrs Parker came over and touched Charlotte's arm. 'Let me show you your room.'

Upstairs, she was shown into a lovely room, light-filled and spacious.

'I hope you'll be comfortable here.'

'Thank you – I'm sure I shall.' She found herself blushing. 'I have never had a room of my own before.'

Mrs Parker squeezed her hand gently. 'Come down for tea as soon as you've settled in.'

Chapter Three

After Charlotte had changed out of her travelling clothes, she went to the window to admire the view from her new room at Trafalgar House. It was a sight quite unlike the one she was used to from the old bedroom she shared with Alison. Though some older, timber-framed buildings remained, others had obviously been cleared and replaced by a haphazard assortment of unfinished buildings that gaped open to the sky. Beyond this confusion lay the sea, vast and inviting in the sunshine. *I am here*, she thought, smiling to herself. *I have arrived*.

It was only on the stairs that she felt a tug of apprehension. Below her, she could hear voices. One was Mr Parker; the other, rather loud and commanding, belonged to a lady.

'A governess and her school,' she was saying, with evident dissatisfaction. 'Is that really the best we can muster? And what about the rest of our houses?'

'They will be taken up soon enough, Lady Denham, mark my words,' replied Mr Parker, a note of desperation dampening his usual buoyant tones.

'So you keep saying, but by whom?' she retorted. 'You promised I would see a *quick* return on my investment'.

'I assure you the ball will change everything! My brother Sidney is bringing a crowd of his most well-connected friends. Once they spread the word of Sanditon's delights, we will be overrun!'

The lady harrumphed. 'From what I know of your brother, I won't hold my breath. And if this ball is so vital, why have you not been here to arrange it? Instead you hare off in pursuit of a doctor we have no need of and return with nothing more than a sprained ankle and another young lady! What is the use of that? We have enough young ladies here. Unless she brings a fortune with her. Does she?'

'Miss Heywood is a very charming—'

He happened to pause as Charlotte, who had been discovered loitering nervously by a servant, was shown into the drawing room. Mrs Parker was sitting next to her husband, with the newcomer – a stout, keen-eyed lady of fifty or so years – opposite them on the best chair.

Catching sight of Charlotte, Mr Parker stood.

The lady followed his gaze and fixed Charlotte with a gimlet eye. 'Ah! So this is the young lady?'

'Lady Denham, allow me to present Miss Charlotte Heywood.'

She dropped a curtsy, at which Lady Denham nodded her approval.

'Very prettily done, my dear.'

Mr Parker gestured towards a young woman Charlotte had not yet noticed, who was sitting in a patch of sunlight by the window. She was extremely pretty in a doll-like way, with bright golden hair and round blue eyes.

'Lady Denham's ward, Miss Clara Brereton.'

Charlotte smiled at her, glad to meet someone of about her own age.

Lady Denham was still inspecting Charlotte closely. 'Well, she's a fine, healthy-looking girl, though nothing remarkable as to looks,' she continued, as though Charlotte was deaf or else impervious to criticism. 'What is your father, Miss Heywood?'

'He has a small estate in Willingden, ma'am,' she said.

'And farms it, I suppose. That won't do any more. Land's not what it used to be. Industry and enterprise; that's the future!'

'Indeed it is,' murmured Mr Parker.

Charlotte smiled with all the good manners Lady Denham apparently wanted.

'How many brothers and sisters have you?'

'Eleven, ma'am.'

'Eleven!' Lady Denham was scandalised. 'You will need to marry well. And no doubt they've sent you to Sanditon to find yourself a fortune.'

Charlotte's smile was growing rather fixed. 'Not at all, ma'am.'

'Lady Denham, I . . .' Mrs Parker tried to interject.

'Nonsense, of course they have!' Lady Denham continued, as though her hostess had not spoken. 'No shame in that. I married very well myself, though I brought thirty thousand of my own to the match to Sir Harry Denham.'

'No children, ma'am?' ventured Charlotte.

'We were not blessed – Sir Harry was elderly and in poor health. And now, do you see, everybody is waiting for me to shuffle off this mortal coil so they can have my money! What do you say to that, Miss Heywood?'

'If you have no direct heirs, Lady Denham, I suppose you can leave it where you please.'

Lady Denham clapped her hands. 'Ha! Quite right! You're a sharp one, Miss Heywood. But all my relations think they have a claim on it! The Breretons – I was a Miss Brereton – Miss Clara over there is but one of many Breretons; and then there's Sir Harry's nephew and niece, Sir Edward Denham and Miss Esther. All of them hoping to do well by my demise!

But there is one thing they all forget.' She leant forward conspiratorially. 'And that is that I have no intention at all of dying!' She smiled triumphantly. 'For a good many years, that is. And so my advice to all of them is that they must fend for themselves. Now you go and sit down with Miss Clara. Mr Parker and I have matters of business to discuss.'

Charlotte did as she was told. When Lady Denham had resumed her interrogation of Mr Parker, Miss Brereton said in an undertone.

'I'm afraid you must have found Lady Denham rather rude.'

Charlotte searched for words that were both truthful and civil. 'She does seem very . . . direct.'

Her companion widened her eyes. 'She is. But I am very grateful to her for taking me in.' She gave Charlotte another sweet smile. 'I am the very poorest of poor relations, Miss Heywood.'

'Charlotte, please – and may I call you Clara?'

'Of course. How do you like Sanditon?'

'Very much, though I have seen very little of it.'

'Do you plan to try sea-bathing?'

Charlotte's eyes glittered. 'I want to try everything there is to try. Do you care for it yourself?'

'I confess I haven't been in the sea yet, though Sir Edward has been extolling its health-giving properties to me.'

'Perhaps we could enjoy, or endure it, together?'

'I should like that very much.'

Charlotte was about to reply when a strident voice rang out. 'What are you talking about over there?'

'Sea-bathing, Lady Denham,' said Clara meekly.

'Excellent! Nothing better for a young woman's circulation.' She looked at Charlotte. 'Our bathing machines at Sanditon are the best on the whole of the south coast.'

Just then, the sound of the front door closing out in the hall signalled that someone had arrived.

'I wonder who that can be now,' said Mrs Parker. 'We are expecting Mr Parker's brother and sister, but their health has been so uncertain . . .'

'Sir Edward Denham and Miss Denham,' announced the footman, and in they swept: not the ailing Parker relatives but Lady Denham's niece and nephew. Sir Edward fairly gleamed with good looks and the sure knowledge of them. His sister Esther, on the other hand, was rather pale and aloof, her expression as she looked around the room considerably less amiable than her brother's.

'I thought we might find you here, Aunt!' said Sir Edward. 'We have been taking the air, and I thought to tempt you all out on to the cliff walk—'

It was then that he caught sight of Charlotte, and rather ostentatiously lost his train of thought. 'Ah, I beg your pardon.'

'Let me introduce you to our guest,' said Mr Parker. 'Miss Heywood.'

'Delighted.' He took her hand and bent low over it, all the while gazing deep into her eyes. 'Enchanted to make your acquaintance, Miss Heywood.'

Charlotte found herself somewhat flustered. He was indeed a remarkably handsome man.

As it was such a fine day, Mr Parker – who had never knowingly missed an opportunity to demonstrate Sanditon's charms – eagerly suggested they take a walk on the cliffs. He led the way, Mrs Parker's arm in his, followed by Lady Denham, who was flanked by Clara and Esther. Charlotte found herself appropriated by Sir Edward.

'So, Miss Heywood,' he said, in solicitous tones. 'What do you say to this prospect?'

'Very picturesque, sir.'

'It's so difficult to find the words to describe the majesty and power of the ocean,' he continued, with a sweeping gesture. 'Do you remember Sir Walter Scott's lines on the sea? So powerful and moving . . .'

'No,' Charlotte interrupted. 'I don't recall him writing anything about the sea.' She gave him a mischievous smile.

He laughed. 'Neither do I, come to think of it. I do remember his lines on Womankind, though. "O, Woman, in our hours of ease, uncertain, coy, and hard to please . . ."'

Charlotte wasn't sure whether to blush or laugh. 'I'm not sure I should like to be described so, Sir Edward.'

'Would you not? No, you are right. There is nothing uncertain or coy about you. But hard to please? I think you have more discrimination than to be easy to please?'

'Perhaps. But hard to please sounds so disagreeable.'

'And you are certainly not that.'

Now she did blush and cast around for something innocuous to say. 'I – I hear you're an advocate for sea-bathing?'

'I am. Miss Heywood, you must experience it. The bracing shock of the first plunge! And then the incomparable feeling of freedom and lightness, the ocean bearing you up when you give yourself to it fearlessly, the delicate play of the currents over your naked limbs. Nothing can give such a sense of well-being!'

Charlotte, somewhat shocked, found herself at a loss for what to say next, especially when she caught Esther Denham's cold gaze on her. Fortunately Lady Denham was her unlikely saviour.

'Come and walk with me, Miss Heywood!' she demanded.

Now he was abandoned, Esther swiftly took her brother's arm.

'I see you are enjoying yourself,' she said to him in a sarcastic undertone.

'Just making a newcomer feel at home, sister.'

'Perhaps you might find time to focus on the task in hand?' She gestured at Clara.

Meanwhile, Lady Denham was talking to, or perhaps at, Charlotte.

'Esther there has been trying to persuade me to have her and her brother to stay at Sanditon House for the season, but I have no fancy for having my house as full as an hotel.' She sniffed. 'My housemaids would be wanting higher wages, for one thing. They have Miss Clara's room to put to rights every day as it is. And Sir Edward, you know, has done very well by me. When Sir Harry died, I gave him his gold watch.' She glanced sideways at Charlotte. 'What do you think of that?'

'Very kind indeed,' said Charlotte dutifully. And when that didn't seem enough: 'Very handsome!'

'I didn't need to, you know. It wasn't in his will. But he's a good young man. How do you find him?'

'I find him very elegant and' – she wondered how she might put it – 'very . . . spirited.'

'And very well to look at?'

'That as well.'

'Yes, he is very well to look at, very pleasing to the young ladies, and no doubt he'll sow some wild oats, but he *must* marry for money!' She gave Charlotte another meaningful look. 'A handsome young fellow like that will go about smirking and paying girls compliments, but he knows he has to marry a fortune. You do understand me?'

Charlotte lifted her chin. 'I understand you perfectly, ma'am.'

'Yes, I think you do. You're a good, sensible sort of girl. What we need at Sanditon is an heiress. If we could get a young heiress sent here for her health! And if she was ordered to drink ass's milk, I could supply her – and then, when she got well, have her fall in love with Sir Edward. But these young heiresses are in very short supply, I find. And then there's his sister, Miss Esther. She must marry somebody of fortune too. It's no use them looking to me for money for it is all tied up in great projects, as they well know!'

As Lady Denham rattled on, Charlotte saw two figures approaching on the cliff path ahead of them, one a lady of about thirty with pink cheeks and general air of liveliness and the other a very portly gentleman in his twenty-something years.

'There you are!' the lady cried out in their general direction. 'Are you surprised to see us? How d'ye do? How d'ye do?'

Mr Parker turned to the others. 'My sister, Miss Diana Parker, and my brother, Arthur. What a pleasant surprise!'

'Yes, we have all of us been very ill,' said Diana with great solemnity. 'Almost at death's door, haven't we, Arthur?'

If her brother Tom's religion was Sanditon, Diana's was her and Arthur's state of health, and the innumerable perils the world presented to it. Arthur, a man whose natural indolence benefitted from his sister's horror of dangerous exertion, shook his large head gravely. 'I thought I would never leave my bed.'

'But we have rallied, as you see,' Diana went on, 'and came to call on you as soon as we arrived. We were told you were on the cliff walk, so we decided to brave it and surprise you!'

Arthur squinted suspiciously at the clear sky. 'I wish we hadn't now. Damn chilly breeze. I think I might have caught my death.'

'Then we must get you both indoors without delay,' cried Mr Parker.

'Our lodgings are nearest,' said Arthur. 'Come and take tea with us there. And let's all of us for God's sake get out of this howling gale!'

Soon enough they were ushered into the rather overheated house the two siblings had taken for the season. Arthur rushed to the fire and held his hands up to it, as though he had lately emerged from a blizzard.

'You see we made sure of a good fire,' said his sister. 'Poor Arthur feels the cold so. Oh!' She brightened. 'We have seen Miss Lambe, who is said to be a great heiress, with a fortune in the sugar trade. Her party arrived in two hack chaises: Miss Lambe, her maid, her governess, and two Miss Beauforts.'

'What does she look like?' said Mrs Parker eagerly. 'Is she pretty?'

'To be truthful, we only caught a glimpse of her back as we went into the house, but the whole party looked very fine and respectable. To travel with her own maid, that speaks of riches, does it not, brother?'

He nodded. 'It does – and I hope she sets a fashion, and all the rich young heiresses flock to Sanditon to spend, spend, spend!'

'Come and sit by me, Miss Heywood,' said Arthur. 'Warm yourself, you must be as chilled to the bone as I am.'

Charlotte suppressed a smile. 'Thank you, but I don't find the weather chilly at all.'

He gazed at her in admiration and wonderment. 'What a constitution you must have! I like the air, you know, as much as anyone, but it doesn't like me. My nerves, you see. My sister thinks me bilious, but I doubt it. If I were bilious, wine would disagree with me, but it always does my nerves good. Do you know, the more I drink, the better I feel. I often wake up in the morning feeling very groggy, but after a few glasses of wine I'm right as rain. That is quite remarkable, don't you think?'

Charlotte was not sure that she did. 'You don't think regular exercise . . .?'

'Regular exercise? I wish my nerves were up to it, Miss Heywood, indeed I do, but strong wine is the only thing that does me any good at all. Though I can take a little toast with butter on it – no more than six or seven slices, though. Let me toast some for us now. A little bit of toast won't do us any harm. Will you let me toast you a slice or two?'

She nodded her assent.

'With plenty of butter, that's the secret. Toast with no butter is an abomination; very bad for the coats of the stomach.'

She stifled a laugh. 'I will try to remember that.'

He took up the toasting fork and speared a slice of bread. 'If I were to be shipwrecked on a desert island, with nothing but hot buttered toast and port wine, I should be quite content, you know.'

Now she did laugh openly. 'I can't imagine quite how such a circumstance would come about.'

'No, I suppose not. But if it did, I'd be a happy man!'

They smiled at each other. Charlotte liked him: though at first meeting he had seemed rather an oaf, she suspected this was in part for everyone's amusement, including his own.

'The barometer is set fair,' said Mr Parker from the far end of the room, where he was tapping the glass. 'I propose a sea-bathing party tomorrow!'

Arthur caught Charlotte's eye before turning back to his toast.

'Madness,' he muttered.

Chapter Four

The next day dawned fine and perfectly clear, just as the barometer had promised. The occupants of Trafalgar House descended to Sanditon's beach straight after breakfast, where they met Mr Parker's brother Arthur, Miss Clara Brereton and Sir Edward Denham. Though it was still quite early, the sand was already thronged with people, from promenading ladies and excited dogs to children on donkeys being led up and down. It was such a happy, lively scene that it immediately sent Mr Parker into raptures.

'Here we are,' he cried jubilantly. 'A perfect day as I promised you! But this is where we must part company. Ladies, you see the bathing machine awaits you. We men must go further down the beach.'

Charlotte eyed the row of bathing machines he was gesturing towards. Despite the flamboyant sea creatures that writhed along their wooden sides in red and gold, they were little more than horse-drawn wagons with doors at front and back. As she, Clara and Mrs Parker approached them, her excitement was tempered with apprehension. She was rather afraid that taking off her dress to bathe almost naked in the sea was precisely what her father had been struggling to articulate in his warning to her.

'Two of these will accommodate us all,' said Mrs Parker, apparently quite unperturbed. 'Unless any of you prefer to be private?'

Charlotte and Clara exchanged shy glances.

'For myself, I should be glad of your company,' said Charlotte.

Clara nodded eagerly. 'And I.'

'You can show us the right way to go about it,' said Charlotte to Mrs Parker. 'I must confess I feel a little nervous.'

'Oh, you'll soon get in the way of it, won't they, girls?' She addressed the last to a pair of remarkably sturdy women who, from their muscled legs and leathery skin, were obviously old hands at sea-bathing. 'We go swimming almost every day, in the season,' Mrs Parker continued. 'Here we are – it's quite private. We can change without being seen.'

Once the carts had been led down to the water's edge, Mrs Parker entered one with her daughters Jenny and Alicia, while Charlotte and Clara shared the other. They helped each other undo the many buttons of their dresses and then moved gingerly towards the door. Cool fingers of sea air blew right through the diaphanous muslin smocks Mrs Parker had lent them.

Charlotte turned to Clara with a nervous smile. 'It's now or never.'

Taking the strong arm of one of the bathing ladies, she stepped into the water, which was so shockingly cold that a gasp bubbled out of her. Another splash and gasp told her Clara was in too. Turning to each other, they burst into peals of laughter.

Some hundred yards up the beach, the gentlemen had already shed their clothes in the tent provided for the purpose. In the water, a great many men and boys were already shouting and larking about.

Arthur, who had not yet changed, regarded them dubiously. 'I think I shall just watch, and look after your clothes.'

Tom Parker frowned. 'I'm disappointed in you, Arthur.' Wearing not a stitch of clothing between them, he and Sir Edward strode manfully towards the sea.

Arthur, who had been growing increasingly hot in the sun, didn't want to be so excluded. 'Oh, damn it all!' he suddenly expostulated and began tearing off his own clothes. Before he could change his mind, or Diana's voice in his head could cry caution, he barrelled into the water, displacing an impressive amount of it into the air.

'Well done, Arthur!' cried Tom, as the younger Parker passed him and continued swimming towards the open water at a speed that suggested his life depended on it.

'Good God,' remarked Sir Edward, most astonished.

Mr Parker gave him a knowing look. 'My brother is a very unexpected man.'

Further up the beach, Charlotte was enjoying the water immensely. She could just feel the sand at the sea bottom if she stretched out her toes.

'This is delightful, isn't it?' said Clara.

'Yes, wonderful!' A couple of familiar figures in the near distance caught Charlotte's attention. 'Are those the men over there?'

'Yes. Yes, I think so.'

She risked another look towards the men. She hadn't been sure at first but, yes, it looked as though they had removed their shirts, and possibly everything else. Despite the chill of the water, she found herself blushing. 'Do they really have no clothes on?' she said shyly.

Clara gave her an unexpectedly mischievous smile. 'None whatsoever.'

She thought on this for a distracted minute and, when she glanced over again, couldn't help exclaiming. 'Clara, the men are getting closer!'

'And what of it?' she replied, and began to swim towards them, leaving Charlotte staring after her in shocked surprise.

Chapter Five

Much to everyone's comfort and pleasure, the weather the day after the bathing party went on just as fine. Charlotte couldn't help smiling to herself as she went downstairs after dressing. Sanditon was proving to be everything she'd hoped it would be and a great deal more. Here, her mind strayed again to the exhilaration of her swim. As much as she missed her family, Willingden and its quiet rhythms seemed like a thousand years ago.

Mrs Parker and her daughters were already seated at the breakfast table when she got there. Mr Parker, for his part, was pacing agitatedly.

'It's too bad. It's really too bad!'

'It's nothing to worry about, really,' said Mrs Parker soothingly.

'Nothing to worry about? No word from him, and the ball only a day away? Good morning, Charlotte,' he said, as she took her place.

Mrs Parker continued to smile with great patience. 'You know Sidney always leaves everything to the last minute, dear.'

'But does he realise the paramount importance of this occasion?'

'Is it really so very important?'

'Of course it is! Of *course* it is. Sanditon's first ball!'

'Sit down and eat your breakfast, Tom.'

'I can't. I'm too . . .' Too distracted even to finish his sentence, he marched from the room.

It was only after breakfast, once the two ladies had set forth for Sanditon's shops, that Mrs Parker confided in Charlotte. The sun was so bright on the water below that Charlotte had to shield her eyes from it.

'My husband has two wives, Charlotte,' said Mrs Parker with admirable fondness. 'Myself and Sanditon – and I'd hesitate to say which of us he cares for most. Marriage is very much about making allowances for the other person, as I am sure you'll find out for yourself.' She laughed softly. 'And life with Tom is at least never dull.'

'But – forgive me – he was comfortably situated,' said Charlotte in her plain-spoken way. 'He had no need to throw himself into all this speculative activity?'

'Yes, indeed. I had no idea what I was letting myself in for when I fell in love with Tom. But here we are.' She gestured to the activity going on around them, from the new-built houses to the respectable visitors promenading past them.

Charlotte smiled. 'There is something thrilling about that, don't you think?'

'Thrilling. But exhausting.'

They were by now outside Heely's, the shoe shop. The blue shoes she had seen before were still displayed prominently in the window. At close quarters, they were even more glorious.

'Now what do you think of those?' said Mrs Parker.

'Oh, they're lovely,' Charlotte breathed.

'I think you would look very well in them at the ball,' said Mrs Parker. 'Shall we go in?'

Despite her protestations, the shoes were soon tried on and pronounced the perfect fit. Charlotte could hardly believe her good fortune. They were already halfway back up the hill to Trafalgar House when she realised hers was the only purchase.

'You didn't buy anything for yourself!'

Mrs Parker waved her concern away. 'I no longer need to put all my charms on display, and Tom likes me well enough in any old thing. He's very worried that if Sidney doesn't come and bring a friend or two there won't be enough eligible young men for you young ladies. But you wouldn't be too proud to dance with a clerk or a shopkeeper, would you?'

'Indeed, I would not. I love to dance, and I'll stand up with anyone who will partner me.'

'Excellent! And I hope the mysterious Miss Lambe and her friends are of the same agreeable frame of mind. Oh, look, here is Miss Denham.'

Esther Denham greeted them with a chilly smile. 'Mrs Parker, Miss Heywood. Well met. I was growing sick of my own company. Could I persuade you to walk a few steps with me?'

'I have things to see to at home,' said Mrs Parker, 'but Charlotte?' She looked expectantly at her.

'Gladly.'

'So, what do you think of us all so far?' said Miss Denham when they had found a bench upon which to take their ease.

Charlotte hesitated, rather intimidated by Miss Denham's cool manner. 'It's . . . always pleasant to make new acquaintants.'

'Very prettily said, and you don't mean a word of it. I saw Lady D. haranguing you the other day. What was she talking about?'

'Well, her money mostly.'

'And how we are scheming to get it, no doubt. She talks of little else. She's a mean, miserly old monster.'

Charlotte couldn't bring herself to disagree. 'I did find myself feeling a little sorry for Miss Brereton.'

But Miss Denham snorted derisively at that. 'Oh, *she* has no need of your sympathy. She is well enough, basking in the warmth and luxury of Sanditon House, while Edward and I shiver in the damp and cold of Denham Place. If she succeeds in her object, which is of course to get everything herself, I swear I'll poison her.'

Charlotte was shocked, and could only hope that she was being teased. 'I'm sure you don't mean that.'

'You wait and see. And your hosts?'

'I am very fond of them already.'

Miss Denham gave her another withering look. 'Mr Tom Parker is a monomaniac who is well on the way to ruining himself and his family with his crazy schemes.'

'You don't really think that?' Charlotte felt rather indignant. 'I think his ideas are admirable.'

'Wait till he bankrupts himself. I have nothing against his wife, indeed I feel very sorry for her. His brother is a buffoon, as no doubt you've noticed for yourself, and as for Sidney . . .'

'I have not had the pleasure yet.'

'Very unsteady and unreliable,' pronounced Miss Denham. 'I advise you to be on your guard.'

'Thank you,' Charlotte said weakly. She didn't know how to respond to this barrage of disparagement.

'All in all, I think you may come to regret ever setting foot in Sanditon,' continued Miss Denham. 'I know I do.' She turned to face the water, which looked particularly dazzling from their vantage point, the sun glancing off the blue like scattered gold. 'Look at that view,' she said despondently. 'Sea. Sky. Isn't it all unutterably dreary?'

Charlotte could only stare at her in astonishment.

*

The day wore on in pleasant fashion but, over a luncheon of cold meats, Mrs Parker turned to Charlotte. 'Lady Denham has been asking me why you haven't been to call on her yet, my dear.'

Mr Parker spoke before Charlotte could. 'The reason is that whenever we set out to call on her, we meet her on the way and she comes back and takes her tea here. I have been thinking of sending her a bill.'

'Well, however that may be, I promised her that we would call this afternoon. I hope that suits you, Charlotte?'

She nodded. 'It suits me very well. I have been looking forward to seeing Sanditon House.'

When the meal was finished, Mrs Parker and Charlotte set out on foot together once again. A mist had rolled in from the sea, casting the town in a strange and spectral light.

'What sort of carriage is that?' said Mrs Parker, as one approached.

'It's so hard to make out through the haze. I think it's open. Are there two horses or four?'

Mrs Parker peered again and then straightened. 'Charlotte, I do believe it might be – yes, it is! It's Tom's brother, Sidney!'

She began waving and a man in the carriage waved back. He pulled the horses to a stop, handed the reins to the servant who was sitting next to him, and jumped down.

'Mary! Well met.'

He pulled his sister-in-law into an affectionate embrace, giving Charlotte an opportunity to study him at close quarters. He was quite as good-looking as his portrait, with a marked air of ease and fashion. But when he stepped back from Mrs Parker, he gave her only a cursory glance.

'New maid?'

'Sidney, this is Miss Charlotte Heywood. She's our guest at Trafalgar House.'

He took Charlotte's hand and made a half-hearted bow. 'Miss . . .?'

He'd forgotten it already. 'Heywood,' said Charlotte primly.

'Miss Heywood,' he repeated, though he was already looking off into the distance, as though something more diverting would surely be found there. Charlotte was stung but resolved not to care.

'Are you on your way to Trafalgar House?' said Mrs Parker smoothly. 'You'll stay with us, of course.'

'No, I've taken rooms at the hotel. My friends will be joining me there. Of course I'll come to see you – this evening, if you will. And tomorrow evening is the famous ball, is it not?'

Mrs Parker shook her head. 'Tom has been in such a state about it. You will do all you can to help, won't you?'

His jaw tightened almost imperceptibly, though Charlotte caught it. 'Tell him he has nothing to worry about – all is in hand. You're on your way to Lady D.'s?'

'We are.'

'Then I won't keep you. Miss Heywood.' With another cursory bow, he jumped back up beside the driver and the carriage moved off.

Mrs Parker turned to watch them disappear into the gauzy air. 'He is so good.'

Charlotte elected to say nothing but her companion caught her doubtful look.

'He has so many concerns and yet he always manages to come to Tom's aid when he's in need. He can be abrupt and inattentive, as he was just now with you, but he has a good heart.'

'I am glad to hear it,' said Charlotte with asperity.

'But I do worry about his own happiness,' Mrs Parker continued. 'I should like to see him settled, but I fear it's not in his nature.'

They walked on, the ground rising beneath their feet. At the brow of the hill they stopped to recover.

'Here we are,' said Mrs Parker, slightly out of breath. 'This land all belongs to Sanditon House.'

'It's a fine park. It complements the house very well.'

And indeed it did. The house was very large yet did not overwhelm the landscaped parkland that surrounded it. Nature seemed to cradle it perfectly. It was quite the most impressive house Charlotte had ever visited.

'Lady Denham is very proud of it,' said Mrs Parker. 'There are deer, though they're very shy. You can sometimes see them over there, on the other side of that fence.'

She gestured off to the side and Charlotte went over to look, standing on tiptoes to see over it. About twenty yards away, something white caught her eye, half-obscured by foliage. Looking more closely, she saw with surprise that it was Clara Brereton, sitting on the grass. She was accompanied by someone and . . . yes! It was Sir Edward Denham. She peered closer still; there was something strange about their stances. They were markedly close – almost entangled together. Clara's arm seemed to be moving and Charlotte couldn't work out whether she was fending off Sir Edward, or . . . Unsure what she was witnessing but suddenly certain that it was a private matter she was not meant to have stumbled upon, she retreated and trod on a stick, which was old and brittle and snapped loudly. Both figures on the grass turned at the noise and Charlotte hurried back to Mrs Parker.

'Did you see any?'

Charlotte shook her head, slightly breathless, her cheeks hot. 'No, for a moment I thought I did, but I . . .'

Mrs Parker smiled guilelessly. 'As I said, they're very shy.'

Mr Tom Parker strode into his study, his countenance openly anxious now that Mary and Charlotte had left him alone with his thoughts.

'You look concerned, Tom. Anything I can help with?'

The familiar voice made Mr Parker's head snap up and his brow unfurrow. His brother Sidney was seated at his own desk, a drink in hand. His worried heart gladdened at the sight of him.

'Sidney! I have never been so pleased to see anyone.' He pulled him into a warm embrace.

'You didn't doubt I would come?'

His elder brother faltered for a moment. 'No,' he eventually managed. 'No, no! Not for a moment. You are here now. That is all that matters.' His face clouded over again. 'But you are not alone? I had hoped you might bring some friends with you?'

'Rest easy, brother. I have done just as you asked. As we speak, Lord Babington and Mr Crowe are habituating themselves to the charms of the Crown Hotel.'

'Splendid, splendid! I knew I could depend on you, brother. Between them and our heiress, even Lady Denham must concede that we are well on our way to becoming a fashionable destination.'

'By "heiress", I take it Miss Lambe has arrived in Sanditon?' For the first time his expression grew sober.

His brother was surprised. 'What do you know of Miss Lambe?'

Sidney picked up his glass and drained it. 'A good deal more than I'd like to.' He raised a smile. 'Come, have another drink with me.'

When Mrs Parker and Charlotte reached Sanditon House, the footman informed them that Lady Denham would be with them shortly. Left alone in the imposing entrance hall, Charlotte couldn't help but gawp open-mouthed. If a visitor had been in any doubt of Lady Denham's wealth on the approach, they would know it for certain here.

Lady Denham bustled into view. 'Mrs Parker, Miss Heywood, forgive me. I have been trying to find Miss Clara. I can't think where the girl's got to.'

As Charlotte and Mrs Parker followed Lady Denham into the drawing room, she felt her cheeks colour again. She knew exactly where Miss Clara was, and who she was with. Fortunately she then looked up and the enormous room before her banished all other thoughts. It was nothing less than extraordinary, almost every item in it black and gold. A gilt statue of Neptune dominated one end of the enormous room while the walls were painted from floor to ceiling with mythical creatures of the sea and towering angry waves. A gigantic chandelier glittered above floor tiles depicting a giant serpent, curled as if poised to strike. Charlotte's mouth dropped open in astonishment. It was more like a pagan temple than a mere drawing room. She did not believe herself sophisticated enough to judge, but in her heart she thought it rather monstrous.

'Well, sit down, sit down,' said Lady Denham, with a gratified little smile. She had noted, and happily misread, Charlotte's apparent awe. 'Higgs will bring us tea. So, Miss

Heywood, I hear you have had your swim. How did you find it?'

'Very . . . invigorating, ma'am,' Charlotte managed to say. 'I hope to make a regular thing of it.'

'Good, good. And did you drink the sea water as well?'

'Well, not on purpose!'

'Ah, you should, you should! I take half a tumbler of it every morning. Where is that girl, I wonder?'

Just at that moment, Charlotte, who was facing the open door, saw Clara dart past in a state of some dishevelment.

'Well, never mind her,' continued Lady Denham, who had noticed nothing. 'Are you looking forward to tomorrow's ball?'

'Very much, ma'am.'

'I was a very fine dancer once upon a time. But my dancing days are over now. Ah! Here she comes, the rascal!'

Clara hurried in looking flustered, her eyes feverishly bright.

'Where have you been?' exclaimed Lady Denham. 'I have had the servants all over the house looking for you!'

'Forgive me, Aunt. I was – walking in the park.' She glanced at Charlotte and, reddening, looked away in confusion. Evidently she had seen her in the park.

Lady Denham, apparently oblivious to this awkwardness, gestured towards the piano in the corner. 'Well, you can play for us as penance.'

'I have had the instrument brought over from Denham Place,' she confided to Charlotte and Mrs Parker. 'Miss Esther has neither the taste nor any gift for music. Clara, on the other hand, plays very tolerably. Well, sit down, girl, and demonstrate your talent!'

Clara played the piece well, her only fumble occurring when she looked up, and again caught Charlotte's questioning eye.

Chapter Six

The following evening brought the event that had dominated Mr Parker's thoughts for weeks. By the time they reached the Assembly Rooms, he was in such a stew of excitement and frayed nerves that Mrs Parker had to lay a steadying hand on his brow.

Charlotte, dressed in her best and the new blue shoes which were now her dearest possession, had none of Mr Parker's dread and almost all of his excitement. Although, in truth, and to a Londoner's jaded eye, it was little more than a country dance, to Charlotte it seemed the very height of sophistication.

Mr Parker's attention to his dress had made them rather later than planned and the high-ceilinged room was already busy with guests and humming with conversation and laughter. Charlotte was so occupied in absorbing the general scene that she failed to notice an exchange between Sir Edward and his sister Esther, who were side by side playing cards at one end of the room, Sir Edward running his hand lingeringly up Esther's gloved arm. If she had seen Esther briefly close her eyes with illicit pleasure as the hand inched upwards, she would have been no less shocked than she had been in Lady Denham's deer park.

Sir Edward only removed his hand when Mr Parker cleared his voice and called for the room's attention.

'Lady Denham, ladies and gentlemen,' he began. 'Let me welcome you to our first ball of the season. Our committee has agreed that there will be no standing on ceremony here – if a lady wishes to be introduced to a gentleman, or vice versa, I will be happy to do the honours. Let good fellowship prevail, and I hope you have all come prepared to dance! Mr Cromarty?'

The conductor of the band struck up and the guests began moving naturally into couples, ready for the first dance.

Mr Parker, flushed from his speech and the festive air which augered well for the rest of the evening, was ecstatic to see his brother enter the room. Even better, he was accompanied by the two promised gentlemen, who looked precisely the sort of quality Sanditon needed to attract.

'Sidney!' he exclaimed, beckoning them all over with a smile. 'There you are. Make yourself known to these ladies over here.'

Sidney obligingly joined them, his companions in tow. 'Miss Heywood, Miss Denham, Miss Brereton,' he said. 'Let me introduce my friends: Mr Crowe and Lord Babington.'

'Our friend has assured us of good sport here,' said Mr Crowe suggestively, his eye roving over the ladies. 'Shall we find any?'

Esther regarded him haughtily. 'I believe there's very little shooting in the neighbourhood, sir.'

'I wasn't thinking of shooting,' he said with a grin.

Charlotte frowned in confusion and then, a little understanding dawning of what he was angling at, found herself blushing yet again.

The slightly better-mannered Lord Babington noticed her discomfort. 'My friend was thinking of dancing, I am sure.' He smiled kindly. 'Could we persuade any of you young ladies to dance with us?'

'I'm sure you could, sir,' said Charlotte gratefully. But then, just as she was sure he would lead her onto the dance floor, he moved to take Esther's hand instead, leaving Clara with Mr Crowe and herself with Sidney Parker.

The dance afforded only momentary opportunities for conversation and though her partner seemed content with silence, Charlotte could not help but try.

'Your brother will be very pleased with you, Mr Parker,' she said, as they drew close.

'I hope he will. Babington's a good fellow, and what's more he's a friend of the Prince Regent. Now if *he* could be tempted to come to Sanditon . . .'

'The general rejoicing would be unconfined, I imagine,' replied Charlotte drily, before being whirled away from him.

'Sanditon's reputation would be firmly established,' he said, when they came together again.

'And you care about such things?' she said, slightly breathless by now. She wasn't sure if it was the pace of the dance or Sidney Parker's intimidating air.

'For my brother's sake I do,' he said.

At that moment, the music ceased. Mr Parker was ready to announce the entrance of a new group of guests.

'Mrs Griffiths, Miss Julia Beaufort, Miss Phillida Beaufort and Miss Georgiana Lambe.'

Intrigued, especially by rumours of Miss Lambe, the crowd turned as one to inspect the strangers. Like them, Charlotte couldn't help staring: not only was the heiress beautiful and very finely turned-out, but she was also darker-skinned than anyone else in the room. As the crowd began to murmur at this novelty, the word 'negress' audible from at least one quarter, Miss Lambe looked on proudly and somewhat wearily, as though this had happened more times than she cared to remember. Her gaze eventually settled on Sidney, who went forward to greet her.

'Georgiana, delighted you could join us.'

If Charlotte was surprised the two knew each other, she was more taken aback when Miss Lambe chose not to reply. Instead, the mysterious heiress threw Sidney an icy glare and simply stalked away.

The music struck up again, and Charlotte had just turned to face Sidney when Sir Edward stepped between them.

'May I have the pleasure?' he said.

Sidney, who was still frowning after Miss Lambe, gave way without demur, leaving Charlotte no choice but to accept.

'You're looking very lovely this evening,' Sir Edward said, once they were alone.

'Thank you, sir.' She did not quite meet his eye.

His air of supreme confidence faltered a little. 'I would like to . . .' He stopped and then tried again. 'What you saw yesterday afternoon – what you thought you saw . . .'

The dance moved them away and when they were brought back together, Charlotte concentrated on her blue shoes. 'It was none of my business.'

'But I am anxious that you should not get the wrong impression,' he pressed. 'Miss Brereton – Miss Brereton was distressed, and I was endeavouring to comfort her.'

Charlotte knew her cheeks were growing hot again. She wished he would stop. 'You have no need to explain yourself to me.'

'But – you promise you won't speak of it to others?'

Charlotte looked up at that. 'Do you really think I would?' she said reprovingly.

'No, of course. You are altogether too good, too pure in heart, to gossip.'

With that, thankfully, the music parted them again and he was forced to say no more.

On the other side of the dance floor, Sidney found himself face-to-face with Miss Lambe.

'Mr Parker,' she said stonily.

'How do you like Sanditon?'

'Little you care,' she spat, moving off down the line of dance partners before he had a chance to reply.

'You mistake me,' he said, when he had caught up with her, her escape hampered by the other dancers. 'I have your interests very much at heart.'

'Then you should have left me where you found me,' she said furiously.

He sighed. 'Believe me, I wish I could have, but duty dictated otherwise.'

'Damn your duty,' she said, dark eyes flashing. He was relieved when the dance spun her away again.

In another part of the room, Lady Denham had engaged Mrs Griffiths in conversation about her young charges.

'Miss Lambe is from a very wealthy family in Antigua,' said Mrs Griffiths confidingly. She was enjoying the attention the heiress had brought her immensely. 'Very wealthy indeed, and she would be *even* more so had her father not ended his business there and set his slaves free before his death. She came to England to complete her education and has been in London for some time.'

Lady Denham absorbed these confidences with interest. 'And the other girls? Equally advantaged, I hope?'

'Not quite, but the Beaufort girls are very genteel. All three are quite ready to enter society, they just need a little guidance and to be chaperoned.'

'Good girls, are they?' said Lady Denham, leaning closer. 'Need to keep a sharp eye on 'em?'

'Oh, they're delightful girls but,' and here Mrs Griffiths paused, 'well, they are *girls*, you know, and young men being what they are, one needs to be constantly vigilant.' She lowered her voice. 'Between you and me, Lady Denham, I understand there was another reason for removing Miss Lambe from London.'

Lady Denham nodded sagely. 'Hmm. Doesn't surprise me in the least. What's her fortune?'

'A hundred thousand pounds,' she breathed, in reverent tones.

'Ah,' said Lady Denham, the light of an idea beginning to glow in her eyes.

Behind her, Arthur Parker, who had been idly eavesdropping on this conversation while enjoying his third pork pie of the evening, inhaled a piece of pastry and almost choked. Spotting Miss Lambe on the other side of the room, he loudly cleared his throat and strode purposefully towards her, arriving just as a slow waltz began. He led her onto the dance floor with surprising grace. He didn't appear to hear his sister, Diana, calling after him to be careful.

Charlotte was sitting out the waltz. In truth, her beloved new shoes were pinching slightly. Clara Brereton appeared from nowhere and sat down beside her.

'Can we speak?'

'Of course,' she replied, with some trepidation.

'I saw Sir Edward talking with you. Was he – did he speak about – yesterday afternoon?'

'Yes, he did.'

'And what did he say?'

'He said you were distressed and he was doing his best to comfort you.'

Clara's blue eyes flared. 'How dare he say that!' Apparently almost overcome, she took in some deep breaths. 'If I was distressed,' she said, once she had mastered herself, 'it was his conduct that distressed me.'

'Oh.'

'He was . . . forcing his attentions on me.'

'Oh!'

Clara turned to Charlotte. 'He is not to be trusted, and *you* should be on your guard against him too. I say this as your friend. He has no conscience and no sense of what is proper or decent. I believe he intends to ruin me in Lady Denham's eyes.' Her eyes filled with tears.

'How shocking! But why would he do that?'

Clara dabbed at her eyes. 'Because she favours me, of course. He fears she will favour me over him in her will. But he sees every girl he encounters as fair game.'

'I have heard there are men like that.'

'Well, there are, and he is one of them. It has been my fate to meet with more than one of his kind. You come from a happy and loving family, I expect.'

'I do.'

'Mine was not, and I am so grateful to Lady Denham for rescuing me from it. What you saw yesterday afternoon . . . I was obliged to . . . do something I didn't want to do, in order to avoid something even worse.'

Charlotte had never felt less sophisticated. 'I don't understand.'

'No, of course – I shouldn't have—' Clara had suddenly understood that Charlotte really *didn't* know what she had seen. 'You won't say anything to Lady Denham?'

Charlotte shook her head, still mortifyingly confused. 'Of course not. But shouldn't Sir Edward's conduct be exposed?'

'How could it be, without involving my disgrace?'

Mr Crowe approached at that moment, cutting Clara short. 'Miss Brereton, can I tempt you back onto the floor?'

Quite abruptly, as though the conversation with Charlotte had never taken place, Clara put her hand in Mr Crowe's and stood. 'Very happily, sir,' she said with a pretty smile.

Even more confused now, Charlotte watched them walk away, Clara smiling and simpering as though she hadn't a care in the world. In need of some air to gather her wits, Charlotte went towards the balcony. She hoped to find it deserted but Sidney Parker was already there, apparently deep in thought.

'Oh, I beg your pardon.'

'Not necessary.' He smiled at her, the first proper one he had bestowed on her. It quite transformed his face. 'A penny for your thoughts, Miss Heywood.'

She sighed. 'I was thinking how very hard it is to make people out.'

He was amused. 'And did anyone in particular provoke that thought?'

She glanced behind her, at the heaving throng on the dance floor. 'Oh, people in general. I like to amuse myself by observing and trying to make conclusions. But in a place like Sanditon, where strangers mingle freely, it is hard to form a reliable judgement. People can be so difficult to interpret, don't you find?'

'Some people can,' he said heavily, but noticing her questioning look continued more lightly. 'And what have you observed about me on our small acquaintance?'

She smiled. 'I think that you must be the sensible brother of the three.'

'And what makes you say that?'

'Well, I may be mistaken, but it seems to me that your younger brother Arthur is of a very contrary nature, alternately over-lethargic and over-energetic, while your elder brother Tom could be called over-enthusiastic. I am afraid that despite his good nature, he neglects his own happiness and his family's in his devotion to Sanditon. Don't you agree?'

There was a silence. When Sidney spoke again, his voice had grown cold. 'Upon my word, Miss Heywood, you are very free with your opinions.'

Charlotte was flustered; she had spoken freely, as was her way. 'I beg your pardon – I did not mean to . . .'

'Upon what experience of the world do you form your judgements?' he interrupted her.

'I – I . . .'

His lip curled. 'Where have you been? Nowhere. What have you learnt? Nothing, it would seem. And yet you take it upon yourself to criticise. Let me put it to you, Miss Heywood: which is the better way to live? To sit in your father's house with your piano and your embroidery, waiting for someone to come along and take you off your parents' hands? Or to expend your energy in trying to make a difference – to leave your mark; to leave the world in a better state than you found it? *That* is what my brother Tom is trying to do, at the expense of a great deal of effort and anxiety, in a good cause in which I do my best to support and help him. And you see fit to amuse yourself at his expense?'

Charlotte thought she might faint with mortification. 'I beg your pardon – I have offended you. Please forgive me.'

'Offended me?' he said dismissively, one eyebrow raised. 'No, you have not offended me. It is I who is at fault. I should not have expected any more from a girl with so little experience and understanding. Excuse me.' With that, he turned on his heel and left her standing there alone.

She couldn't move. She thought that if she tried, she might just shatter into a thousand humiliated pieces. For the first time since her adventure in Sanditon had begun, she wished most fervently that she could go home to Willingden.

Chapter Seven

Early the morning after the ball, Charlotte slipped out of the house before breakfast. She had decided that a solitary bathe in the sea might dispel some of the horror of the night's events, which had played over and over in her mind as she tossed and turned in her bed. The water was so cold and invigorating that it did wipe her mind blank for a time but, as she made her way back to Trafalgar House afterwards, she found her thoughts straying back to Sidney Parker and what he had said.

So vivid was the terrible memory that when she looked up and saw the man himself, crossing the road in front of her, it seemed as though the power of her disordered thoughts had conjured him up. To her profound relief, he didn't see her. Indeed, he seemed quite as lost in his own thoughts as she had been in hers, his head down and his brow furrowed.

The Parker household, when she got there, was in much higher spirits than she could summon herself; the children creating an uproar as they chased each other down the stairs and through the hall. In the breakfast room, Mrs Parker looked up as she entered.

'Charlotte! Did you sleep well?' She gestured for her to sit down. 'How did you enjoy the ball last night?'

Charlotte suppressed a sigh. 'Very much, except . . .'

'Except what? What's troubling you?'

Charlotte took a deep breath. 'I am afraid I offended Mr Sidney Parker very gravely.'

Mrs Parker's face cleared. 'Oh, conversations at balls are always unsatisfactory.'

'No, I think he was very displeased with me. He seemed to think I was disparaging you all, and I was not, indeed I was not! I think Mr Parker's schemes for Sanditon are quite splendid! I wish I had something to do to take my mind off it.' She felt as though she might cry. She reached for the teapot to distract herself.

'You shouldn't let Sidney upset you. He can be rather volatile, and he is inclined not to think very highly of our sex.' She paused. 'He has had some bruising experiences in the past.'

Charlotte stopped what she was doing, the teapot suspended in the air. 'Oh?'

Mrs Parker nodded. 'And now I think he finds his guardianship of Miss Lambe a troubling responsibility.'

'*Miss Lambe*?' She couldn't imagine Sidney Parker being anyone's guardian, let alone that of a young heiress. It boggled the mind.

Mrs Parker gave her a weary look. 'It was a surprise to Mr Parker and myself too. Sidney was involved in . . .' – she hesitated – '. . . in the sugar trade for a time, and it seems he was a good friend of Miss Lambe's family in Antigua. So he feels an obligation.'

'Antigua,' Charlotte said wonderingly. 'That seems so far away. A different world.'

'I understand it is,' replied Mrs Parker, her expression thoughtful, even grave.

The children rushed in and Mrs Parker's countenance instantly lightened. 'Now,' she cried, getting to her feet and clapping her hands, 'we must get you all smartened up for church!'

Within the half hour, Charlotte, Mr and Mrs Parker and the older children had set off for church. The wind was by now blowing hard enough to tear the hats from their heads and Charlotte was holding fast to the ribbons of her bonnet so she didn't lose it. Only Mr Parker seemed to be enjoying rather than enduring the exercise.

'A fine bracing day,' he shouted back at them so that the wind didn't snatch the words clean away. 'I think Sanditon has the healthiest breezes of any seaside town in England! What do you say, Charlotte?'

'I think if we were anywhere else we could call it a gale, sir!'

'Exactly, exactly,' he said, before taking in a good lungful of it. 'But we have no gales here!'

'Gales are not permitted to blow in Sanditon, are they?'

Mr Parker gave her an approving smile. 'Well said!' He turned to his wife. 'You see I have made a convert, my dear. Ah, there's Mrs Griffiths with her charges. They made a charming debut at the ball last night. Good morning, good morning!'

Up ahead, Charlotte caught sight of Miss Lambe and the others filing into the church. By the time she and the Parkers stepped in out of the keening wind, a different sort of noise had set up – this time provided by the congregation who were already seated, most of them villagers who had not until now laid eyes on Miss Lambe. It was only the entrance of Lady Denham, who at that moment swept in empress-like, that stopped them staring, as they curtsied and bowed good morning to her.

Sir Edward and his sister Esther were close behind her. On spotting Charlotte, Sir Edward sidled over without delay.

'Miss Heywood. Looking very well, if I may say so.'

Recalling Clara's words the evening before, she gave him as cool a look as she could muster, wished him good morning without a smile and then walked on.

Esther, on witnessing this unsuccessful exchange, couldn't resist smirking at her brother as he turned back to her. 'You seem to have gone backwards in Miss Heywood's estimation, Edward.'

He didn't reply; he was too busy frowning in the direction of Clara Brereton as she followed Lady Denham towards the front of the church.

'Someone has been spreading false reports about me, I fear,' he said, just as Clara, almost as if she had heard him, turned and threw him a triumphant look.

Such was the level of interest in the newcomers, particularly Miss Lambe, that it took some time for the congregation to notice that the vicar, Mr Hankins, had climbed the stairs to the pulpit and was waiting to start his sermon. When they finally quieted, he began, though not before taking a moment to admire the young ladies he had not yet had the pleasure of meeting. Mr Hankins was a great appreciator of the fairer sex.

'*Consider the lilies of the field; they toil not, neither do they spin – and yet I say unto you, not even Solomon in all his glory was arrayed like one of these. Consider the lilies, dearly beloved.*'

He paused, cast a benevolent glance towards the Misses Beaufort, who made much of dropping their eyes modestly, and cleared his throat.

'A young lady, I often think, is like a flower: when we speak of a young lady, we do not think of what she does, but what she *is*. We do not need her to do anything but be lovely, like a flower, in the eyes of the Lord. And as I look around me this morning, I see many lovely young ladies: as it were, lilies of the fields of Sanditon – some of them lovely English roses, pink and white, and today,' he inclined his head in the direction of Miss Lambe, 'I see among us one or two more exotic blooms. And yes, my friends, there is room for them too in the garden of the Lord.'

If Miss Lambe was grateful for his words, she did not show it. He hurried on. 'And I say unto all you young ladies: there is no need for you to strive to do this or do that. You fulfil Jesus's will by simply blossoming. Simply *blossoming*. And readying yourselves for the day when you shall be plucked. Shall be plucked. Yes . . .' Such was the power of his own vivid metaphor that he seemed to fall into a reverie, only rushing on when his audience began to fidget. 'And now to God the Father, God the Son, and God the Holy Ghost. Amen.'

As everyone began to file out, Mrs Griffiths bustled up to shake his hand, her charges following in her wake.

'Thank you, Mr Hankins,' she cried. 'What a charming sermon!'

He ran his hungry eye over the young ladies. 'Mrs Griffiths, you and your precious flock, or should I say bouquet of blossoms, are very welcome!'

The Beaufort girls simpered prettily at this but Miss Lambe remained entirely unmoved.

Still well pleased with his sermon's delicate message, Mr Hankins could not resist continuing. 'Should your young charges need any nurturing, any spiritual guidance – young ladies are such delicate plants – please do not hesitate.'

'You are very kind, Vicar,' said Mrs Griffiths. 'Indeed sometimes I feel in need of a little nurturing myself.' She looked up at him through her lashes.

Mr Hankins's chest swelled, giving him the appearance of an ecclesiastically-minded pigeon. 'That too would be a pleasure. Good day, good day . . .!'

On the walk back to Trafalgar House, Diana and Arthur having joined their small party, Mrs Parker took Charlotte's arm.

'What did you think of Mr Hankins's address, Charlotte?'

'I didn't care for it,' she declared, in her usual frank way. 'I would rather be a toiler and a spinner than a lily of the field.'

'Why should not young *gentlemen* be lilies of the field?' put in Arthur, overhearing. 'That would suit me very well. I think I could blossom and be admired with the best of 'em. What do you say, Miss Heywood?' He squared his shoulders and smoothed down his hair for the wind off the sea was still lively.

Charlotte laughed. 'Very well – I will toil and you can blossom. Each to his own!'

Arthur looked pleased. 'So long as there's plenty of port wine and buttered toast, you know.'

Back at Denham Place, Sir Edward had also returned from church and was now frowning over his accounts.

'More damned bills,' he said bleakly.

His sister Esther, who had been gazing moodily out the window for some time, didn't bother asking him to elaborate. 'This garden is becoming more and more of a wilderness,' she sighed. 'Meanwhile, the house quietly rots about us. It's like living in a particularly unpleasant fairy story by one of the Grimm brothers.' She turned. 'What did happen with Clara Brereton, Edward? Clearly something has gone wrong there.'

He closed the ledger he'd been looking at with a bang and ran his hands through his hair. 'I can hardly bring myself to speak of it.'

'But you will, Edward. Come, your task was to seduce her and disgrace her.'

He wouldn't meet her eye. 'She proved too much for me.'

'She resisted you. That is only to be expected. You should have pressed your point home.'

Finally he met her eye. 'She pre-empted me, Esther.'

Something like dread clutched her. 'How?'

He coloured. 'She . . . took me in hand, and . . . quite undid me.'

'Edward!' She had not anticipated this, least of all from that milksop Clara. But it was more than that. The thought of him with another woman in such a way . . . It made her nauseous.

'I was as shocked as you, sister,' Edward said, a bitter laugh escaping him. 'She was no novice, I can assure you of that. And when I looked over her shoulder . . .'

'What?' said Esther sharply.

'Charlotte Heywood was observing us.'

Her hand went to her mouth.

'I don't believe she understood what she saw,' Edward said hurriedly. 'But she was clearly disturbed. And Clara, I believe, denounced me to Miss Heywood as a villain. I tried to convince her I was only comforting Clara, but I fear I was not believed.'

Esther sat down heavily on a chair, almost overcome. 'Edward, what have you done? Do you realise you may have ruined our prospects?'

'I should like to know what I *should* have done in the circumstances!'

She shook her head in disgust. 'You were thoroughly outplayed.'

Then something occurred to her and when she met her brother's eye again, something of her old spirit had returned. 'But she can hardly blacken your character to Lady Denham without blackening her own. As for Charlotte Heywood, I will deal with her.'

Chapter Eight

The following day was to be a busy one at Sanditon House. Lady Denham had hit upon the idea of hosting a gathering and nothing was to stand in her way. Its purpose was ostensibly to welcome Miss Lambe to the resort but, in truth, she was eager to see how the girl withstood further scrutiny. The invitations had just gone out with a footman, leaving Lady Denham and Clara to investigate an intriguing package that had not long since arrived from London. The two of them watched as a maid unwound yet another layer of protective muslin.

'What is it, a bomb?' Clara was utterly perplexed.

Lady Denham rolled her eyes. 'Oh my poor child. Such ignorance born of poverty and deprivation quite brings a tear to my eye. No, my dear, this is a pineapple – a rare and exotic fruit cultivated expressly for me by an old friend at Chelsea Physic Garden. It will form the centrepiece at my luncheon party.'

'Luncheon party!' Lady Denham had not yet thought to mention her idea to her niece. 'What a delightful idea.' She gave her aunt a sidelong glance. 'But then you are always thinking of bringing pleasure to others.'

Lady Denham nodded, gratified, as she was intended to be. 'I know, my dear, though it is an extravagance. But I thought we might make an exception to welcome Miss Lambe to our little community.'

Clara was surprised again.

'A luncheon party for Miss Lambe?'

'I know what you are thinking: why a luncheon party for *her*?'

'That is not what I was thinking, Aunt . . .' Clara began but her aunt spoke over her.

'Yes, it was – don't have the effrontery to contradict me – but with a fortune of a hundred thousand, Miss Lambe will be the guest of honour wherever she goes, no matter where she is from.'

But half a mile away in Sanditon, Mrs Parker and Charlotte were admiring the invitation that had just arrived. It was now occupying pride of place on the mantel.

'Lady Denham requests your attendance at a luncheon party and pineapple tasting in honour of Miss Lambe,' read Charlotte. 'That sounds very grand indeed!'

'And quite uncharacteristic of Lady Denham,' said Mrs Parker who, having known the chatelaine of Sanditon House rather longer, was more sceptical. 'I wonder what she's up to.'

The answer to that question was that Lady Denham had left her niece and the pineapple behind and gone to Denham Place to call on her other relations. Neither Sir Edward nor Esther had been expecting her, which was usually the way with her visits. The three of them now sat awkwardly together in the drawing room. Sir Edward was still troubled by the spectre of Clara Brereton and his accumulating debts, but he was doing his best to flatter his rich aunt, who seemed suddenly quite determined to marry him off without delay.

'This is very good of you, Aunt,' he was saying, though he hardly knew what he thought.

'It is intended as an investment, Edward. An investment in your future. Miss Lambe is a prize well worth the winning.'

Esther was doing her best not to betray any emotion. First, Miss Brereton and now Miss Lambe; it was really too much. Her hands curled into fists.

'You will be seated next to her, and you must present yourself as a serious and eligible suitor,' Lady Denham continued, while Sir Edward nodded obediently. 'You are an English baronet of impeccable family, with the further advantages of a handsome countenance and bearing, and a personable manner.'

'You're very kind, Aunt,' said Sir Edward mechanically.

But she had not finished.

'I am well aware that you have so far frittered away these advantages and used them in the pursuit of petty conquests and the sowing of wild oats.'

His face fell. 'No, no really, you misjudge me.'

In that moment, Esther, who had been listening in silence, almost despised him.

'I do not,' retorted Lady Denham. 'I trust that you do understand the difference between the arts of courtship and seduction?'

'I . . . well, I hope I do.'

'You'd better. And if you don't win her hand, I shall be very disappointed in you.' She gave him a steely smile. 'And you don't want to fall out of favour with me, do you?'

'No, Aunt,' he said meekly.

'There. You have your work cut out for you. No need to look so glum. Once you have secured her hand in marriage, you can tomcat around to your heart's content.'

Esther did her best to ignore the last. 'Do you have any instructions for me, ma'am?'

Lady Denham looked over at her in such surprise that Esther suspected her presence had been altogether forgotten.

'Just try to keep a civil tongue in your head, and put a curb on your smart remarks,' she said curtly.

Esther bowed her head so that Lady Denham wouldn't see the resentment simmering in her eyes. 'I will do my best.'

Mr Parker clutched the hair at his temples. Both he and his study were in even more of a disordered state than usual. Piles of bills and correspondence teetered on his desk, while books on design and architecture lay splayed open on the floor. 'Where *is* the confounded thing?' he shouted, frustration overpowering him. A movement at the door made him look up. 'Ah, there you are, Charlotte!'

She took in the confusion of the room. Its elegance and rich furnishings were quite obscured by the mess. 'I came to see if I could be of any assistance.'

He was already riffling through the papers again and hardly seemed to hear her. 'No, no, I'll have it in a moment. What an infernal muddle! Bills, invoices, plans and memoranda . . .'

Charlotte came forward and laid her hand on one of the tallest piles. 'Let me sort them for you.'

He finally looked at her properly. 'Would you? I'd be eternally grateful. I keep meaning to engage an assistant.'

'Perhaps I could be that assistant in return for your hospitality.' She smiled and, without waiting for a response, began sifting through documents. 'You see, if we could separate these papers into piles: income, expenses, rental payments, bills and so on . . .'

Mr Parker stepped back as she became immediately absorbed in her task, her small hands moving deftly.

'You have an eye for this sort of work, I can see!' The knot of anxiety that seemed to have lodged in his chest lately loosened, just a little, but enough to allow him a deep, restorative breath.

As Charlotte lifted a great mess of papers to see what was underneath, she caught sight of something intriguing hidden underneath. It was a scale model of a street, exquisitely rendered.

'Oh, that's beautiful!'

Mr Parker's eyes shone with pride. 'That will be the new terrace. You approve?'

'Most heartily. Who is the architect?'

'Myself! That is to say, I use Hargreave's catalogue of plans. Look here!'

He opened up a huge volume filled with meticulous ground plans and elevations to show her, and felt his usual enthusiasm swell inside him once more. How glad he was that Charlotte Heywood had come to stay!

'At first I'd take the designs straight out of the book,' he said modestly, 'but now I have more confidence I adapt them to my taste, choose a little of this, a little of that, talk it over with my foreman, and off we go!' A pleasing idea struck him. 'Would you like to see it taking shape?'

Charlotte was touched by the boy-like shyness of the question. 'Very much!'

'Excellent! I need to have a word with Young Stringer anyway.'

It took them but a few minutes to reach Waterloo Terrace. The scene was frantic with activity: surveyors taking measurements and labourers unloading a new delivery of bricks. Dust tainted the air and the hem of Charlotte's dress was already muddy, but she was quite thrilled to see it. The work looked as though it had already progressed in the time she had been at Sanditon, the new buildings now cheek-by-jowl to old Sanditon, which looked forlorn and rather shabby in comparison, as though it knew it was outshone by the clean, confident lines of Mr Parker's grand terrace.

He was already deep in conversation with his second-in-command, a local man known to all as Young Stringer in deference to his father, who was working on the terrace as a stonemason of many years' experience. Charlotte watched the two men as they pored over the plans spread out over a trestle so they might see them better. It surprised her to see that Young Stringer was hardly older than herself.

'Yes, yes, just here,' Mr Parker was saying. 'Very good, just as I said! What do you think, Miss Heywood?'

She stepped forward. 'I think it is a splendid enterprise, sir.'

'And only the best materials, of course,' he said, gesturing around them. 'No timber except red pine and oak!'

'With Welsh slate and Cornish stone for the roofs and frontages?' she hazarded, noting with pleasure the admiring look this won her from the young foreman. There was such pleasure to be had in surprising people, she thought; particularly men.

Mr Parker was naturally delighted. 'Oh ho! Do you hear that, Young Stringer? We have a lady architect amongst us!'

'I have been trying to persuade my father to refurbish his tenants' cottages along modern lines,' she said. 'Am I right in thinking there will have to be different roof levels?'

Young Stringer nodded eagerly. 'Aye, miss. Different roof levels.'

'And these will . . .' she began.

'. . . Draw the eye down the hill towards the vista of the sea,' he finished. 'Exactly, miss!'

The two of them smiled warmly at each other. What a pleasant person to be acquainted with, she thought, and a great part of the pleasure of it was knowing he thought the same.

Mr Parker cleared his throat, aware that he had been briefly forgotten. 'Yes, that was my idea, you know. Was it not?'

Young Stringer hesitated, for in fact it had been *his* notion, but then remembering his place, he gave a nod. 'Indeed it was, sir.'

But Mr Parker's attention had already been diverted. 'Ah,' he cried, 'here's my brother and his friends!'

Charlotte spun round, hoping it would be Arthur rather than Sidney. But of course it was the latter, flanked as he had been at the ball by Lord Babington and Mr Crowe. Immediately, and to her great annoyance, all the morning's ease and amiability melted away, so that she no longer knew how to stand or arrange her face.

'I just came to have a last look before we leave for London, Tom,' said Sidney. He gave her a cool glance. 'Miss Heywood.'

Mr Parker's mood instantly plummeted. 'But we counted on your staying at least until the end of the week. Lady Denham's luncheon party . . .'

'. . . has no need of my presence,' finished Sidney.

'I need you here,' said his brother in a pleading tone. 'And your friends have not seen nearly enough to appreciate the town's delights.'

Sidney sighed and Charlotte couldn't tell whether he was guilty or simply disobliging. 'We have made plans, Tom.

And Sanditon's delights don't quite measure up to London's, do they, gentlemen?'

Behind him, Mr Crowe chuckled.

Mr Parker took his brother by the arm and led him a little way out of earshot. 'You were to persuade your friends to take houses for the season!'

Sidney shrugged.

'And what about your young ward?'

'She will soon settle. I have a life, Tom, with many obligations you know nothing of. You cannot expect me to be always at your disposal.'

Mr Parker looked suddenly desperate. 'A couple of days, man . . .'

Sidney considered and then let out a long sigh. 'Very well. A couple of days. I'll talk them round.'

His elder brother, all smiles again, clapped him on the shoulder. Relief had flooded his face.

'Mr Parker?' Young Stringer needed his attention for the plans again.

Lord Babington and Mr Crowe having wandered off to see the building work at closer quarters, Charlotte found herself alone with Sidney. She took a determined breath.

'Mr Parker, may I have a word?'

His face remained closed and hostile, but she forced herself to press on.

'Our conversation at the party – I expressed myself badly, and I fear you misunderstood me. I didn't mean to disparage your brother, or to offend you. Indeed, I have the greatest admiration for what you and he are doing here in Sanditon.' She swallowed and tried to slow her words, which were rushing out of her. 'You were right to rebuke me, and indeed I am sorry. I hope you won't think too badly of me.'

Sidney looked down at her, and his mouth curled into its sardonic sneer again. It made her quail. 'Think badly of you? I don't think of you at all, Miss Heywood. I am not interested in your approval or disapproval. Quite simply, I do not care what you think, or how you feel. I am sorry if that disappoints you, but there it is. Have I made myself clear?'

For a moment, it was as though she was back in the Assembly Rooms, and she feared she would burst into humiliating tears. Fortunately, anger came to her rescue, allowing her to hold her emotion in check.

'Well?' said Sidney. 'I sense that you have more to say.'

'Only . . .' She lifted her chin and looked him square in the eye. 'Only that if you really don't care, I wonder that you take the trouble to be quite so offensive and hurtful. Good day.'

And with that, she turned and walked away, the emotion she had managed to contain now threatening to overcome her. She hoped fervently that he would not see how much she trembled.

In fact, though he could not see her quiver from the distance she had put between them, he could certainly see from the rigid set of her narrow shoulders that he had wounded her. To his confusion, he found himself flooded with shame. He hesitated, torn between going after her and dismissing the idea of the vexing Miss Heywood altogether, when Mr Crowe called him over, making the decision for him.

Chapter Nine

Sir Edward and his sister were idling away the afternoon in Denham Place's gloomy, gothic-like drawing room, where the candles had already been lit, though it was not past two. Esther was déshabillé, her long hair loose while her brother sat behind her, combing it out.

'I don't see why *I'm* the one to be put out to market,' Edward was saying bitterly. 'I'm sure she's perfectly hateful.'

Esther couldn't resist the sarcasm that she always reverted to in moments of jealousy. 'You've never been reluctant to charm the ladies, Edward. More's the pity.'

Edward took no notice. Something outside had caught his eye and he stood to see better. 'I say!'

'What?'

'Someone's coming. It's one of those fellows Sidney Parker brought from London.'

Esther stood. 'Oh yes,' she said wearily, recognising the dark-haired gentleman who had paid her so much attention at the ball. 'Babington. I thought he might come sniffing around.'

Some minutes later, Esther now dressed respectably, she joined Sir Edward and Babington in Denham Place's unkempt garden.

'I was just passing, you know, and I thought I might call upon you,' Babington began as she sat down. Without his companions and a good quantity of wine, he seemed less sure of himself than he had the previous night.

'Did you?' she replied, flatly.

'You're looking uncommonly well, if I may say so.'

She inclined her head as though it was a great effort. 'You may.'

Sir Edward, who had taken up a book as though he meant to have no part in the conversation, smirked to himself.

Babington didn't notice. He was too intrigued and indeed stimulated by Esther's implacable aloofness. Manfully, he tried again. 'Your hair – if I might be so bold – has such a glossy sheen on it.'

Esther stretched like a bored cat and threw her brother a glance. 'There, you see, Edward – your efforts were not in vain.'

Babington leant forward in his chair, stirred anew. 'Your brother attends to your hair?'

'Stepbrother. His father married my mother when we were young.' A small smile curled her lip. 'And yes, he does.'

Babington had flushed. 'That is a commission I should happily undertake.'

Esther laughed. 'Not a chance, Lord Babington.'

He was not accustomed to women treating him with such disdain. It was thrilling.

'Shall I have the pleasure of seeing you at Lady Denham's luncheon party?'

'I suppose so.'

She stifled a yawn and Babington realised his small stock of conversation was exhausted.

'Well, ah . . . till tomorrow, then.' He got to his feet, and ran his eye hungrily over her until she met his gaze. 'I shan't be put off, you know,' he said.

When he'd taken his leave, Esther, despite her performance of indifference, felt rather gratified. She turned triumphantly to her brother.

'Oh. Has he gone?' Edward looked about him.

Esther scowled. 'How I hate your sex.'

In a lodging house across town, Mrs Griffiths was having an excessively trying morning. Her heiress charge had locked herself in her bedroom and refused to come out, despite all appeals to reason. She was quite the most rebellious girl Mrs Griffiths had ever had the misfortune to take responsibility for. Eventually, she had been forced to send the maid to fetch Miss Lambe's guardian to see if he could persuade her out. Rather shockingly, he had been found in the bar of the Crown Hotel, where he'd been in the middle of a boxing match against a local champion by the name of Joey. This didn't seem at all gentlemanly to Mrs Griffiths and she thought it might be a topic she could discuss at length with Mr Hankins one day soon.

Still, she was grateful that Mr Parker had at least managed to gain admission to Miss Lambe's room, where he was at that moment remonstrating with her. Mrs Griffiths, for whom discretion was an overrated virtue, hovered in the doorway.

'I am not your slave!' Miss Lambe declared, jaw set stubbornly. Her maid Crockett, who was supposedly dressing her hair, was listening quite as avidly as Mrs Griffiths, her eyes as round as saucers.

'Nobody said you were,' said Sidney as gently as he could. 'Georgiana, you have to attend. You are Lady Denham's guest of honour.'

Miss Lambe's eyes flashed; she was caught between tears and anger. 'To be gawped at and served up for the general amusement! To be sneered at and laughed at. A public spectacle. Here we have a pineapple and here we have the negress. Feast your eyes!' She slammed her hand down on the dressing table.

'Georgiana.' He waited till she looked back at him. 'You know you are worth more than Lady Denham and all her circle put together.'

'Oh yes. The heiress from the West Indies, rich and black as treacle! Hold her upside down and shake her, hear the sovereigns jingle, a hundred thousand of them!'

Sidney massaged his brow. He was running out of patience, something he never had much of in the best circumstances. 'Stop talking nonsense,' he said sharply. 'This is what your father wanted – for you to take your place in polite society.'

'What about what I want?'

'I am afraid that what you want is neither here nor there.'

She turned to stare angrily out the window, where heavy clouds had turned the sky sullen and overcast. 'If you only knew how much I hate this miserable chilly island.'

'I can do nothing about the climate. But for the rest: trust me, Georgiana. All this is for your good.' He stood to leave her.

'So you say,' she said defiantly, though in truth her fit of temper had burnt itself out, leaving behind something much bleaker.

Chapter Ten

The respectable folk of Sanditon were making their various ways to Lady Denham's house, summoned as they had been for her surprise luncheon party. It had not even occurred to most of them to refuse, for unpopularity was no match for wealth and power.

Arthur and Diana Parker had set off in good time, mindful as ever of their delicate health. Still, no amount of preparation made the steep incline out of the town towards Sanditon House any less perilous. They clung to each other in order to offer the other support, both literally and inwardly, but the going was still proving intolerably hard.

'How much further can it be?' puffed Arthur, stopping to mop his brow with an already sopping handkerchief. 'Really, sister, my constitution isn't up to this. I hope there is a physician standing by at Sanditon House to revive me.'

Diana, paler but more stoic than her sibling, turned back to him. 'Courage, Arthur. Think of the pineapple. If I can manage, so can you!'

With a groan, Arthur moved off again. 'Do you know the fellows with the sedan chairs refused to carry me? They said I was over the weight limit. Infernal insolence. As you know, I'm practically wasting away – good God, who's this?'

A rattling din behind them was growing louder. As they turned to stare, a cloud of dirt approaching at speed revealed itself to be two light curricles. With no thought of vulnerable pedestrians, their drivers appeared to be racing each other.

'I say, I say!' cried Arthur, as he recognised Babington at the helm of one and his brother Sidney at the other. 'Could you . . .?'

'Sorry, Arthur!' shouted Sidney as the carriages flew past them in a great confusion of noise and dust. 'Can't stop!'

'Well!' said Arthur, all hopes of a ride vanishing as swiftly as the speeding curricles. 'Not very brotherly!'

Ahead of them, already through the park and in sight of Lady Denham's front door, was Arthur's other brother, Mr Tom Parker, accompanied by his wife and Charlotte. The latter felt her nerves worsening with every step. Her last social outing among Sanditon's finest had made her considerably warier of company.

'I swear the house has grown in size since I was last here,' she said quietly, as they crossed the threshold and once more entered the lofty hallway.

They had not been there upwards of a minute when Clara Brereton came to stand next to Charlotte, pale hair glinting against the decadent backdrop of Lady Denham's drawing room.

'I'm so glad to see you, Charlotte,' she said conspiratorially, leaning in so that one of her curls brushed Charlotte's cheek. 'I beg you, stay close. We shan't let him come near us.'

Charlotte was baffled. 'Who?'

Clara widened her china-blue eyes. 'That beast, of course. Sir Edward Denham.'

*

On the other side of the room, Mr Parker was exclaiming in jocular tones: 'Excellent! Excellent!' though his wife could see that behind the smile his face was rather tired and strained. 'This is very good of you, Lady Denham. Very generous and hospitable to be sure!'

'Hmp.' She was far too irritated to acknowledge him properly. 'Here we all are, waiting for the guest of honour to deign to make an appearance.'

'I'm sure it's no fault of hers, Lady Denham,' said Mrs Parker. 'You're looking uncommonly well today.'

She received nothing more than a scornfully raised eyebrow for this pleasantry. 'No need to butter me up.'

'And Miss Brereton too,' continued Mrs Parker doggedly. 'What a pretty dress.'

Clara missed this; she was too busy watching Sir Edward as he smiled and bowed a path through the assembled guests. 'There he is,' she murmured to Charlotte. 'The sight of him repels me.' She shuddered ostentatiously.

'Take heart,' said Charlotte. 'You are among friends. Nothing bad can happen to you today.'

'If you had experienced what I did you would understand, Charlotte,' she said tremulously. 'I feel violated by his very presence.'

It was at this moment that his sister Esther chose to join them.

'Miss Heywood. I do hope Miss Brereton is keeping you entertained.'

Clara, eyes narrowing, opened her mouth to retort but Lady Denham was beckoning her over. When she'd left them, Esther moved a little closer to Charlotte.

'I would take no heed of her words, Miss Heywood. Her imagination quite outstrips the truth.'

Charlotte was at a loss; she had never known such complicated, confounding people.

Babington had arrived and now came over to greet them. 'Miss Heywood. Miss Denham. Both of you looking uncommonly well, if I may say so.'

'Thank you, sir,' said Charlotte cordially.

Esther ignored him, speaking only to Charlotte. 'These events are so wearisome, aren't they?'

Charlotte stifled a laugh at the sight of Babington's face. 'I don't think so at all. But then we see so little society in Willingden.'

The next guests to enter were not walking but staggering, as exhausted as if their journey had taken not minutes but days.

'Mr Arthur Parker and Miss Diana Parker,' announced the footman.

'Wine,' moaned Arthur. 'Wine!' He was blotched and scarlet in the face as Sidney helped him to a seat, but seemed to rally almost immediately as a full glass of claret was pressed into his hand. Diana collapsed into another chair and drew out her fan.

'I really thought I was about to expire,' she said. 'And poor Arthur – he has such a delicate constitution, you know. But when duty calls . . .'

'You'd think they'd walked from Inverness.' Lady Denham's strident tones rang through the room.

'Ah, better,' said Arthur, once his wine was drained. 'I think another tiny glass?' A new one was handed to him and also swiftly dispatched. 'Thank you, thank you,' he said, wiping his mouth and letting his head loll back. 'I think I shall pull through.'

Lady Denham eyed him with contempt. 'What a buffoon that young man is.'

Mr and Mrs Parker exchanged an anxious glance; Lady D. was growing ever more irritable. Fortunately, the footman appeared once again, and finally announced the arrival of the guest of honour and her companions.

'Mrs Griffiths, the Misses Beaufort, and Miss Lambe.'

In they came, and it was hard to tell who was more a-flutter: Mrs Griffiths or the Beaufort sisters. Miss Lambe, by contrast, looked to be in high dudgeon still, her mouth a sulky moue.

'Edward!' hissed Lady Denham in the direction of her nephew. 'There's your quarry. Hunt her down!'

When he didn't immediately act, she prodded him hard, sending him scurrying towards Miss Lambe.

'Good day, good day!' Mrs Griffiths twittered, coming forward to greet her hostess. 'So sorry to be late, Lady Denham, but better late than never!' Her smile died away as she absorbed her hostess' expression.

'Slightly better,' Lady Denham said repressively. 'Miss Lambe, finally. Shall we go through to the dining room? Lord Babington?' She offered him her arm and, though he had hoped to escort Esther, it was not a request.

Sir Edward bowed to Miss Lambe. 'May I have the pleasure?' She took his arm with bad grace and they followed Lady Denham into the dining room.

Behind them, Esther fell into step with Clara. 'You can stop playing the injured innocent,' she said, the words sharp as needles. 'My brother told me exactly what happened the other day. Lady Denham would be surprised to hear about your little whore's tricks. Where did you learn them, I wonder?'

Clara turned to her with a brittle little smile. 'From a man even more depraved than your brother, when I was too young to know a prick from a pencil. You and I should not be enemies, Miss Denham.'

Esther snorted to cover her shock. 'How can we be otherwise, when we are competing for the same thing?'

'Money?'

'What else?' But her gaze had fallen on Edward, just ahead of her, his head inclined towards Miss Lambe's. She wouldn't have admitted it to anyone, least of all the nemesis at her side, but this battle had never been entirely about money, not for her.

The company, now gathered in Lady Denham's dining room, waited with great anticipation. In the middle of the polished table, which ran the length of the enormous room, a magnificent object had been displayed to full advantage.

'Oh, a pineapple!' cried someone. 'How splendid!'

Charlotte had never seen such a thing before and wondered how they might eat it given that it seemed to be nothing but scales and spikes. When the exclamations of delight had died down, Lady Denham turned to her reluctant guest of honour.

'I thought it might remind you of home, Miss Lambe. Antigua, was it not, or some such place?'

There was a pause while Miss Lambe eyed the fruit. 'That ain't no Antigua Black,' she said, not in her usual voice but a broad patois. 'I think you been sold a pup, Lady Denham. Someone done took you for a fool.'

Everyone in the room, which had fallen profoundly silent, turned as one to look at Lady Denham. Charlotte watched in horrified fascination as the old lady's face turned puce, her eyes even more protuberant than usual. A full-blown apoplexy was surely next.

'Of course I know this particular fruit was not grown in Antigua,' she said eventually, having narrowly mastered herself. 'It was cultivated specially under glass, here in England. And it is here, in your honour, as a mark of respect for your heritage. Do you understand that?'

'Georgiana . . .' said Sidney in a warning tone.

'Of course I do,' replied Miss Lambe, but then she reverted to the patois again. 'I was just pullin' your leg. But it ain't no Antigua Black, all the same.'

'That's enough, Georgiana,' said Sidney. 'You've made your point.'

But from the other side of the room, laughter could be heard. It was Arthur Parker, who seemed quite immune to the glares issuing in his direction from both his brothers and their hostess.

'Haha! Jolly good!' He shook his head in amused admiration. 'Well done, Miss Lambe!'

'Please take your seats,' said Lady Denham, her face set with fury. 'Sir Edward?'

He went forward to pull out Miss Lambe's chair.

'Thank you,' said she, demure once more, and took her place.

'What a very great pleasure it is to be placed next to you, Miss Lambe,' began Sir Edward, mindful of his aunt's instruction to charm her.

'Is it?' she said coolly. 'Why?'

'Well, you know – your beauty, your fascinating background . . .'

'And my money? I imagine that's what you're after.'

'No, no,' he stammered, rather at a loss in the face of such plain speaking. 'No, indeed. Ah . . . How do you like Sanditon?'

Miss Lambe rolled her eyes. 'Oh, for God's sake! Is that the best you can do?'

He swallowed, and found that his mind had gone completely blank. 'Erm . . .'

Miss Lambe waited, brown eyes mocking.

'Erm . . . who is your favourite poet?' He blushed for himself and as she turned away in disgust, he saw the same look reflected in the face of his aunt. Only Esther regarded him with anything less than total contempt.

A few places along, Charlotte had found herself unhappily seated next to Sidney Parker.

'So, Miss Heywood,' he said. 'Any observations on the assembled company?'

'As you have no interest in my opinion, I shan't trouble you with it, Mr Parker,' she said with dignity.

'But I'm sure you have one. Come, share it with me.'

She put her glass down. 'Not for the world. I've endured two tongue lashings from you, and I won't court a third. Save your unpleasantness for someone else. Or, better still, why not try to be civil?'

To her astonishment, he looked almost chastened.

'Well said. Perhaps I shall.'

But she wasn't going to give in that easily. 'But not with me, pray,' she said, and promptly turned to Mr Crowe, who was on her other side.

'Mr Crowe, how do you rate Sanditon's chances of succeeding?'

He raised his eyebrows. 'Pretty slim at present, ma'am. Can't hold a candle to Brighton, or Bath. There's not enough here to tempt a man – or a lady' – at this he gave her a flirtatious smile, which she ignored, '– of fashion.'

'But it has the capability of becoming as popular as those, has it not?'

'Are you telling me there's some pleasure to be had that I've been overlooking, though it's right under my nose?

Now I'm interested.' He leant in so close that Charlotte was obliged to move her chair towards Sidney.

'Mr Crowe. You deliberately misunderstand me.'

He gave her a wink. 'Rest easy, Miss Heywood. I'm only teasing you.'

At the top of the table, Mr Parker was trying to elevate the spirits of his hostess and business partner after the unfortunate exchange with the wayward Miss Lambe.

'I hope we will have a physician for you very soon, Lady Denham,' he said. His wife sighed inwardly, knowing that such a topic would only vex her more.

'So you keep saying,' Lady Denham said impatiently. 'And what, pray, should we do with a doctor? It would only be encouraging our servants and the poor to fancy themselves ill if there was a doctor to hand.'

Her shawl slipped to the floor but was almost instantly caught up by Clara Brereton, who placed it carefully around her aunt's shoulders with a sweet smile, though it turned rather astringent when she caught Esther Denham's revolted expression.

'Thank you, my dear,' said Lady Denham. She was still thinking about the physician. 'We get on very well as we are. There is the sea and the downs and the milk from my asses. We want the *right kind* of guests, Mr Parker. I hope you have not forgotten.'

'Well, Arthur and I wouldn't be able to consider staying long in any place unless we were under a reputable physician,' offered Diana Parker gravely.

Arthur nodded as he speared an enormous piece of meat with his fork and regarded it with pleasure. 'First class medical care is what will distinguish the fashionable resort of the future from the second-rate.'

'I rather agree with Lady Denham,' put in Sir Edward, who had had no further luck with Miss Lambe.

'You would agree with anyone, Sir Edward, so long as it furthered your ambitions,' said Lady Denham, casting him down again. 'If only your actions matched your words.' She raised her voice. 'Miss Lambe! What are your views on matrimony? An heiress with a hundred thousand must be in want of a husband, I think?'

But Miss Lambe was not cowed. 'I don't care to be any man's property, Lady Denham.'

'Oh!' The old lady's colour was rising again. 'Hoity-toity! I should have thought someone like you would be quite used to being a man's property. Was not your mother a slave?'

Sidney briefly closed his eyes.

'She was,' said Miss Lambe, without faltering. 'But being used to a thing and liking it are not the same thing, my lady.'

'I am beginning to think you are very opinionated, Miss Lambe! What do you think, Miss Heywood?'

Charlotte spoke up bravely. 'I know that young ladies are not expected to have opinions, Lady Denham, but I think Miss Lambe is quite right to value her independence, just as you do yours. Don't you agree, Mr Parker?'

Sidney threw up his hands and shook his head, clearly unwilling to join the fray.

'No answer from Mr Sidney!' cried Lady Denham. 'And you, miss,' – she trained her gimlet eye back on Charlotte – 'are you keeping up your pretence that you're not in Sanditon in search of a wealthy man to marry and keep you?'

'Indeed I am not, ma'am. I have no thoughts of marriage at all. And if I were to choose a husband, wealth would not come into it.'

'Poppycock!'

'Should not a good marriage be based on mutual love and affection? Without affection, marriage can become a kind of slavery, I believe.'

Lady Denham scoffed. 'Or an escape from it. Miss Lambe's mother would be a case in point, eh? A pretty negress catches the eye, and casts her spell on him. That's the way the world works!'

All other conversation had by this point halted. The shocked silence made Lady Denham's words seem to ring off the crystal, though she herself didn't notice.

'Ain't it, Miss Lambe?' she continued. 'And now here you are, with your hundred thousand – a rich prize for any young fellow with a title and a leaky roof. So what do you say to Sir Edward? Would not you and he make a pretty match?'

Sir Edward was mortified. 'Really, Aunt . . .'

'Well, you seem incapable of furthering your interests yourself. What about it, Miss Lambe?'

'We ain't suited, Lady Denham.'

'Good for you!' said Arthur loudly, between mouthfuls, picking his moment once more. 'Well said, Miss Lambe! "We ain't suited." Very good!' He stood and reached for the pineapple. 'May I cut you a slice?'

Miss Lambe inclined her head. 'If you like.'

'Mr Parker,' Lady Denham thundered at the same time. 'The pineapple is not yours to cut!'

But it was too late: he had already sliced it down the middle. He grimaced as he pulled it apart.

'What's the matter?' she demanded.

He held the two halves up to her. 'It's rotten, Lady Denham. Rotten to the core!'

*

The mood of the room quite as spoiled as the pineapple, it was not long after that the guests began to take their leave. Clara stood next to Lady Denham on the threshold as, one by one, the company made off in the direction of Sanditon.

'Well, at least *you* did not disgrace yourself,' Lady Denham said. 'Go inside – there's a good girl.' She caught sight of the eldest Parker brother and hailed him.

'Mr Parker! I want a word with you.'

All three brothers turned.

'No, not you, Mr *Tom* Parker! The rest of you can clear off!'

He turned with trepidation and followed her back inside the house.

She started in on him immediately. 'I am affronted, Mr Parker. *Affronted*. Did you mark that insolent girl?'

Mr Parker spread his hands diplomatically. 'You were pressing her rather hard. I think she may have felt offended by some of your remarks.'

'Am I not permitted to speak my own mind in my own house? And that other girl, Miss Heywood, *your* guest, Mr Parker – altogether too outspoken! And as for that boorish brother of yours, stirring them up, encouraging them – and then he had the effrontery to handle my pineapple!'

'I'm afraid I can't be responsible for my brother's behaviour, Lady Denham.' He smiled apologetically. 'Arthur's his own man – he is what he is.'

Lady Denham drew herself up. 'Well, think on this: I am my own woman, and I have a good mind to withdraw my investment from the Sanditon venture! The terrace, the new Assembly Room – everything! What do you say to that?'

Mr Parker paled, which was precisely the effect she had intended. 'I beg you not to consider that,' he said imploringly. 'Without your contribution we would be in dire straits.'

'Well, I am very displeased, very displeased indeed.' And with that, she left him alone in the hall to see himself out.

His walk back down to Trafalgar House passed in an anxious blur. Once inside, he hovered despondently in the hall until Mrs Parker led him into the drawing room where Charlotte was already sitting and entreated him to join her. He shook his head, too fretful to rest.

'She knows Sanditon is a good investment, Tom,' Mrs Parker tried next. 'She wouldn't withdraw her money out of spite. She's too canny for that.'

'Ah, you don't know her, my dear. She hates to be crossed.' He paced to the window.

Charlotte, increasingly worried, now stood. 'I feel it is my fault, at least in part. I felt I had to defend Miss Lambe and no one else was ready to speak for her, except your brother Arthur.'

'Lady D. is very angry with him as well,' said Mr Parker. 'Not so much for anything he said, but for the . . .' His mouth twisted and for a terrible moment Charlotte thought he would weep, but then he burst out in hysterical laughter. 'For the disrespectful manner in which he handled her pine-apple!' he managed to say before collapsing into mirth again.

Charlotte and Mrs Parker looked at each other, quite astonished, and then as his hilarity infected them, began to laugh themselves.

When Mr Parker had recovered himself, he shook his head and finally sat down, heavily. He looked more tired than ever. 'She is an appalling old woman. But she holds the fate of Sanditon in her hands. That's the problem.'

Charlotte made a decision. 'I couldn't forgive myself if I've put your great project in danger. I will go and beg her pardon.'

'Really, Charlotte,' said Mr Parker, 'there's no need.'

Mrs Parker got up and took her hands. 'My dear Charlotte, there's nothing . . .'

'I don't mind,' she interrupted, quite determined. 'And in any case I should have learnt by now that when certain people ask my opinion, I should tell them what they want to hear or say nothing at all. I will go tomorrow morning. It will be a useful exercise in humility for me.'

And the next morning she did go, and humbly begged Lady Denham's pardon.

'Hmp,' the old lady said grudgingly. 'Mr Tom Parker made you come, no doubt.'

'No indeed, ma'am. I came of my own free will.'

'Really? You expect me to believe you?'

Charlotte took a calming breath. 'Whether you do or not, it is the truth, ma'am.'

'Ha, you can't help it, can you?'

'Help what?'

'Speaking your mind! Standing up for yourself! Even when you're trying to be ever so humble and penitent. What's to be done with you?'

'I am truly very sorry if I offend you, Lady Denham.'

'Ha!' But her eyes were sparkling now. 'You don't offend me. You amuse me! I like to tease and provoke. I expect you think I was too hard on that young woman yesterday. But she gave as good as she got, did she not? Come on, Miss Heywood, answer me!'

'I do think you were very impolite to Miss Lambe.'

Lady Denham tutted extravagantly. 'But I gave a luncheon in her honour!'

'You made a spectacle of her,' said Charlotte quietly, but with admirable firmness. 'You didn't consider what her feelings might be – far from home, amongst strangers. It was unkind of you.'

'She has a hundred thousand to comfort her. I only speak the simple truth!' She stopped, caught the reproof in Charlotte's expression. 'What?'

'You insisted on hearing my honest opinion, ma'am.'

Lady Denham relented. 'So I did. And if I don't like it, that's no one's fault but my own, you imply. All right, off you go. You got what you came for: you can tell Mr Parker that he has nothing to fear from me – for now.'

Charlotte smiled and dipped a quick curtsey before hurrying from the room, fearful that if she did not, Lady Denham would change her mind again.

Chapter Eleven

Outside the coach house in Sanditon, a line of passengers had just clambered up into the carriage that waited there, the horses already hitched and impatient to be underway. The last person to board was clutching a small travelling bag tightly. It was Miss Lambe, and she had already drawn more than a few curious looks from the people round and about.

'If you please,' she asked the coachman hopefully, 'is this coach for London?'

He cast his eye over her. 'It is, miss.'

'Then may I board it now?'

'Indeed you may, miss, for six shillings.' He stuck his head into the carriage interior. 'No one here got any objections?'

An old lady poked her head out and gave Miss Lambe an appraising look. 'She looks clean and tidy enough, let her come.'

The coachman turned back to her. 'Six shillings then, miss.'

But Miss Lambe's face had fallen. 'I – I have no money on my person. I'm not in the habit of carrying it.'

The coachman sniffed. 'Then you won't be getting on the coach, miss. Did you hear that?' he said to the other passengers who, sensing some potential unpleasantness, had begun to lean towards the open door. 'Not in the habit!'

'What's the fuss about?' said someone.

'Her there,' came the indignant reply from the coachman. 'She wants a ride but she won't pay the fare!'

'Go on,' he addressed Miss Lambe. He was enjoying himself now. 'Off you trot, miss!'

'Please!' she cried. She was beginning to feel rather faint. 'My banker in London will make sure you are paid.'

'Oho, a banker in London, is it? Now I've heard everything!'

'Do you not know who I am?' She regretted the words as soon as they were out.

He had been amused; now he regarded her coldly. 'No, I don't. Who are you?'

She soldiered on. 'I am Miss Lambe. I am an heiress. I have a hundred thousand pounds!'

He smiled nastily. 'Six shillings will do, miss.'

'Don't you understand? I have to get to London. Let me pass!'

Suddenly desperate, she tried to board but he moved to block her path, close enough that she could smell the sourness of old tobacco and spirits on his breath.

'Now, now!' he cried. 'None of that! Go on! Be off with you.'

'Look at her!' Someone else was suddenly behind her and jostling her, even as another person reached out a hand to touch her hair. Dizzy with fear and humiliation, she pushed through them and broke into a run.

Just across the road, oblivious to Miss Lambe's predicament, in a snug corner of the Crown Hotel's rather disreputable bar, her guardian and his friends were contentedly drinking away the afternoon.

'How is your pursuit of Miss Denham progressing, Babington?' said Mr Crowe as he lifted the jug and poured himself another glass, spilling a little as he did.

'Very well,' he replied. 'She professes she wants nothing to do with me. She is deliciously disdainful.'

Crowe grinned and slapped his hand against the table. 'Saucy bitch! And you a peer of the realm.'

Babington shook his head admiringly. 'I love it.'

'So, how long before you bring her to heel?'

'Bring her to heel? She's not a dog, Crowe. She's a *young lady.*'

'But she needs to be mastered. Mind you, I like a bit of spirit in a girl.' He licked his lips. 'That little Miss Heywood now – she's got a bit of spunk about her.'

Sidney snorted.

'Or Miss Lambe, then. The way she stood up to that old witch yesterday – you could tell she'd be a lively handful in bed.'

Sidney's countenance darkened. 'Don't even think about it, Crowe.'

'No need to take that tone. I was only saying.'

'She's off limits.'

'All *right*, man. Understood.'

'I mean it.'

Crowe raised his hands in mock surrender. 'But if a fellow might ask without getting his head bit off, what is your history with her?'

'I am simply her guardian. Not a job I wanted, and I'm finding it damned irksome. The girl misses her homeland, hates the climate here, and doesn't care for being treated as a curiosity.'

'And she doesn't care for you?' asked Babington.

'Pretty much takes exception to everything I say or do. She's safer here than in London though. Anything can happen there.'

'Anything can happen anywhere,' said Crowe philosophically.

Sidney sighed. 'True.' He looked down at the table, apparently exhausted at the thought.

'Let's have another bottle,' said Crowe, and snapped his fingers at one of the landlord's comely daughters.

At Denham Place, Esther was still stewing over the previous day's luncheon party. She had been unable to settle at anything all day.

'It's all right, Esther,' Edward tried, in a placating voice. 'I never would have gone through with Miss Lambe, even if she liked me. A fellow has to draw the line somewhere.'

But Esther was not thinking about the heiress; her brother could be remarkably dull-witted sometimes.

'We have to dislodge that little interloper, Miss Brereton,' she said as she paced to the window. 'She will insist on getting in the way. That business with the shawl yesterday. I wanted to bite her.'

Edward smiled lasciviously. 'That is something I should like to see.'

'Two women fighting over you?' She shook her head in frustration. 'I just wish this would end. I preferred it when there was only us.' The last words almost choked her.

Edward went to her then, and cupped her face in his hands. 'Believe me, so did I. And I promise, as soon as we have the money, it will be.'

She gave him a long, questioning look, and then seemed to relent, allowing him to embrace her.

After her visit to beg forgiveness from the odious Lady Denham, Charlotte had returned to Trafalgar House quite worn out and a little despondent. She decided that writing a letter to her sister might comfort her. She had particularly missed the easy comfort of her family since the ball.

My dearest Alison,

I wish you were here so that we could compare impressions. I love the place itself, but the people here are so strange and contrary. Mr and Mrs Parker, whom you met of course, are delightful and very kind. Mr Tom is a wild enthusiast for his Sanditon, and seems full of confidence, but when no one is there I have seen him frown and bite his lip, and I fear all is not well with his schemes. His brother Sidney is a complete conundrum – nothing I say seems to strike him right. Oh Alison, yesterday was all made up of mistakes and upsets. I feel that every time I open my mouth I say the wrong thing. I have made a resolution to listen more and say less in future – but in truth I do feel far from home.

She broke off. Writing the letter had made her feel a touch easier but perhaps a little exercise would dispel the rest of her bad mood. She would take a walk on the cliffs.

The wind had strengthened by the time she got up above the town, nothing around her but the coarse grass that flanked the path with the sea below, and she had the pleasant sensation of her worries, like cobwebs, being blown clean away from her. She was so satisfied with this notion that she almost missed the small figure hovering at the cliff edge. With a start, she realised it was Miss Lambe and cried out in fright as a gust of wind blew hard at the other girl's skirts, threatening to carry her right over the edge.

'Miss Lambe?' she shouted into the wind as she approached. 'Do you remember me? Charlotte Heywood? We met at Lady Denham's.'

Miss Lambe turned but her face was blank and distraught. She was shivering violently.

'Oh, what is it?' said Charlotte, reaching out for her, just as Miss Lambe staggered and collapsed into her arms. 'What *is* the matter?'

After some minutes, Miss Lambe was able to stand with Charlotte's help. She led the girl away from the edge to safety. Eventually, Miss Lambe was composed enough to speak.

'I think I was half out of my wits,' she said tremulously. 'It was as if something was pulling me towards the edge. I thought of stepping off, dashing myself to pieces on the rocks below . . .'

Charlotte gasped in horror.

Miss Lambe didn't appear to hear her. 'I suppose no one would care if I did.'

'Don't say that.' She hesitated and then laid her hand on Miss Lambe's. 'I think it must be very difficult for you. I feel something of it myself – I'm a stranger here too.'

'But people don't look at you the way they look at me.'

'No. But people do wish you well. Mr Arthur Parker—'

'He's a funny man.'

Charlotte smiled. 'But very good-hearted, I think. And his brother Sidney is your guardian, isn't he?'

Miss Lambe sighed. 'He doesn't relish that role, and nor do I. I'm sure he regards me as an infernal nuisance.'

'If it's any consolation, I find him very impolite and cold too.'

After a pause, Miss Lambe met her eye properly for the first time. 'Do you think me very spoilt and sulky?'

Charlotte smiled again. 'Not at all. After what you had to endure at Lady Denham's . . .'

'She's a horrid old woman.'

'She can be – but I think she means no real harm.'

'I wanted to stuff her rotten pineapple down her throat.'

They looked at each other and then burst out laughing.

'We can survive this, Miss Lambe,' said Charlotte, and patted her hand once again.

'Please, call me Georgiana.'

'Charlotte.'

They smiled and then continued on their way, both of them feeling rather less lonely than they had only minutes before.

Back in the hotel bar, at least two of the three gentlemen were now very much in their cups. Babington was drinking with great concentration while Crowe had begun singing, addressing his song towards the landlord's simpering daughters.

> *When the heart of a man is oppressed with cares,*
> *The mist is dispell'd when a woman appears.*

With a smile, Babington and Sidney joined in for the second verse.

> *Like the notes of a fiddle, she sweetly, sweetly*
> *Raises the spirits, and charms our ears—*

Mr Tom Parker chose this moment to enter the bar. Sidney and Crowe, on seeing him, stopped singing.

'Ah, the great projector himself,' announced Crowe, his voice slurring.

Babington, noticing nothing, continued singing.

'*Like the notes of a fiddle, she sweetly, sweetly* – ah, Mr Parker!'

Tom nodded at them. 'If I might have a word with you, Sidney?'

'Of course – join us. Have a drink.'

His brother gave him a look. 'In private?'

Sidney sighed. 'If you must.'

'We'll join the young ladies over there!' declared Crowe, getting to his feet and pulling Babington to his.

When the brothers were alone, Sidney irritably turned to Tom. 'Well, what is it?'

'I am anxious to know what progress you have made. You know I depend on you. And when I see you doing nothing but carouse—'

Sidney put a heavy hand on his arm. 'Easy, brother. Men like Babington and Crowe can't be bullied into staying. They have to be jollied into it.'

Mr Parker ran an unsteady hand through his hair. 'Sidney, I am beset with worries. The workmen need paying, Lady Denham is threatening to withdraw her investment. I am at my wit's end! She has it in her power to ruin me. While you—'

'All right! Enough!' Sidney picked up his glass and drained it. 'I wonder why it is always my responsibility to pull you out of the fire.'

'I've done the same for you. As you know.'

Sidney paused, laid his glass down with great delibera-tion, as though if he didn't he might just throw it across the room.

'You'll have to trust me, Tom.' He spoke with no less care. 'The promotion of Sanditon is a delicate business, and I'm not sure you understand it. I am truly doing my best for you.'

'That's all I ask.' Tom stood. 'I'm sorry to have inter-rupted your pleasure.'

'Work,' said Sidney icily. 'Work. This is how I *work*.'

'Well, if you say so. Good afternoon.'

When he'd gone, Sidney stood up wearily and went over to join the others at the bar.

Crowe turned to him with a leering smile. 'We have decided to take a little siesta in our rooms upstairs, and Molly and Virginia here—'

'Aptly named,' guffawed Babington.

'. . . have consented to keep us company. Join us?'

'Ah, no,' said Sidney. 'If you'll excuse me, I think I need fresh air and bracing exercise. Enjoy your rest.' He turned to go.

'One can exercise indoors, you know!' Crowe called after him, to appreciative laughter from Babington. Sidney didn't have the wherewithal to turn, and simply raised his hand as he headed out into the blustery afternoon. If his brother couldn't comprehend that this was work, then he was an ungrateful fool.

Not yet ready to return home, Charlotte and Miss Lambe descended the path to the beach, their hair and ribbons flying as they laughed together. Ahead of them, Charlotte spied her friend Young Stringer. The sight of him, as well as the presence of Georgiana behind her, made the last of her earlier loneliness dissipate into the breeze.

'Good afternoon, Miss Heywood,' he called when he was close enough.

'It is, Mr Stringer! It is.'

They smiled at each other as they passed and, though she was too modest to look, she was certain he had turned so he might watch her until she was out of sight. If only Mr Sidney Parker could be so obliging.

When they reached the water's edge, Charlotte kicked off her shoes.

'I'm going to paddle. Will you join me?'

Miss Lambe frowned. 'I'd freeze.'

'No, you won't.' She pulled off her stockings and let them fall to the sand. 'Come on, I dare you.'

Miss Lambe watched as Charlotte gathered up her skirts and walked bravely into the water until her ankles were submerged.

'Come on!' she cried over her shoulder. 'It's fine.'

Her companion hesitated and then, in a great rush, tore off her own shoes and stockings and strode into the water, whereupon she screamed.

'You beast! It's freezing!' She kicked out with her foot and sent an arc of icy water towards Charlotte, who did the same before running off along the beach, laughing and shrieking. They were so intent on their fun that they didn't notice Mrs Griffiths approach until she was almost upon them. Bringing up the rear were the ogling Beaufort sisters.

'Miss Lambe! Miss Lambe! Come here at once!'

'Oh,' said Miss Lambe, her smile vanishing. 'My keeper.'

'Where have you been? This is most irresponsible of you!'

Charlotte went forward to meet the older woman, who was quite red in the face. 'Mrs Griffiths, forgive me – paddling in the sea was all my idea. Don't blame Georgiana.'

Mrs Griffiths scarcely acknowledged her; too exasperated with her wayward charge.

'Come back to the house at once, Georgiana. I am surprised at you! Anyone could have seen you, barelegged with your skirts up!'

Behind her, the Beaufort sisters giggled until Miss Lambe glared at them.

'At least I was enjoying myself,' she said. 'For the first time since I came here!'

As she followed the outraged Mrs Griffiths up the beach, Miss Lambe looked back and waved at Charlotte who smiled back.

Glad to have made a friend but still reluctant to return to Trafalgar House, she continued on down the beach. She had neglected to put her shoes and stockings back on and the damp sand underfoot felt wonderfully cool and smooth. She wandered idly, enjoying the sensation not only of the elements but the lack of worrying thoughts in her head. Mr Tom was right: the air at Sanditon *was* healing. Her eyes searched the sand for shells, the prettiest of which she put in her skirt's pocket.

Before long she came to a small outcrop of rock. She had never walked this far before but she wanted to see the little cove on the other side. It wasn't accessible when the tide was high. Lifting her skirts and still clutching her shoes and stockings, she picked her way carefully over the rocks. Jumping down onto the sand, she looked around her, ready to admire the secret spot where she could spend a solitary moment, and saw instead a pile of clothes. She had barely absorbed what this might signify when a movement to her right made her startle. There, emerging from the water, was a man: a naked man. It took her another moment to realise that this man, lean and strong and entirely without clothes, was in fact Sidney Parker.

'Oh!' She turned her back, cheeks aflame.

'Miss Heywood!' he said from behind her, with admirable calmness. 'Am I never to get away from you?'

'Mr Parker, I assure you, you are the last person I wished to see.' Her voice was strangled.

'I beg your pardon. I spoke in haste. Forgive me.'

She couldn't think what to say and, apparently, from the silence behind her, neither could he. Both of them stood, not looking at each other, for what felt like an age. Finally Charlotte gathered her wits along with her skirts.

'Of course,' she said, cursing the quaver in her voice. 'Excuse me.' Scarlet-cheeked, she hurried away as fast as her bare feet would let her, almost slipping on the rocks in her haste to leave him and a scene so excessively steeped in mortification.

Chapter Twelve

Though it was early enough that Sanditon's cliffs were still cloaked in the dawn's haze, the labourers of Mr Parker's new terrace had already been at their work an hour. Close to the building site of Waterloo Terrace, the air was rent with the sounds of stone being hammered and chiseled into shape. Among the workers was Old Stringer, who winced as he lifted a full hod and moved it onto his shoulder, his old knees creaking and the topmost bricks teetering dangerously as he gripped the ladder and began to climb. Watching this with concern was his son. He'd taken up the need for more paid men with Mr Parker a couple of times now, but it was no good; the man was too distracted to properly listen.

Not far away, the relentless din of the hammers had found its way through the open window of the Crown Hotel bar, where Sidney Parker was lying sprawled across a table in yesterday's clothes. Around him lay the sordid detritus of the previous night's excesses: guttered candles, empty bottles and claret-stained playing cards. He groaned as he came to, the rhythmic crashing finally penetrating his dreams, and clutched his head.

'Show some mercy,' he muttered. 'It's rudely early.'

The door banged open, adding to the general racket, and Babington and Crowe burst in. They grinned when they caught sight of him.

'For shame,' said Crowe, delighted. 'Look at the state of him, Babbers!'

Babington righted a glass which had rolled to the edge of the table. 'A wretched sight indeed!'

Crowe leant in close to Sidney. 'Is that not what Miss Heywood said when she ran into you by the coves last night?'

Both he and Babington laughed uproariously.

Sidney rubbed his temples. 'I should never have mentioned it. Had you not forced that fifth bottle on me . . .'

'Never mind that now, old friend,' interrupted Babington. 'You need to have a shave and get some devilled kidneys down you. We're leaving.'

At almost that precise moment, Charlotte Heywood had descended the stairs of Trafalgar House only to come to a halt below the portrait of a Sidney Parker in much finer fettle than the man himself. Observing again that his dark eyes seemed to peer right into her soul, she blushed, recollecting yet again the shaming encounter at the beach. A brief image of him emerging from the water stole into her head: the way the waves had lapped against his strong thighs, the sight of his . . .

'Good morning, Charlotte!'

Charlotte gasped and spun round to find Mrs Parker regarding her with amusement.

'Oh! Good morning.'

'Did you enjoy your walk yesterday? I didn't hear you come in.'

'Yes. No. I – I went down to the beach to gather shells and time . . . ran away with me.'

'Anything impressive catch your eye?'

Charlotte started and, as she felt herself colour again, fought the urge to simply run back up the stairs. 'What?' she stammered.

Mrs Parker raised a quizzical eyebrow. 'Shell-wise?'

'Oh. No. I – came back empty-handed.'

'How disappointing.'

After Mrs Parker went off in the direction of the servants' stairs, Charlotte found her gaze returning to the portrait. Much exasperated with her own foolish behaviour, she straightened her tucker and took herself off to Mr Parker's study, determined to think of his brother no more.

Though her thoughts still strayed where they shouldn't, she had restored some order to her host's untidy paperwork when she heard raised voices in the hallway.

'Damn it, Sidney.' She recognised Tom Parker's voice. 'Did my words mean nothing to you?'

'I cannot force them to stay!' Now it was Sidney. 'The fact of the matter is that there is simply not enough to tempt them here. They need more entertainment. I am sorry, Tom. We leave this morning.'

She froze as their footsteps grew louder, her eyes darting around the room for somewhere she might hide herself. In desperation, she ducked behind the desk just as the brothers strode in.

'How am I to fill these empty houses, Sidney?' said Tom. 'I confess I was relying on . . .' He paused and she knew she was spotted. 'Charlotte?'

She rose, a piece of paper clutched in her hand.

'*There* it is!' she said, inwardly cringing at the falseness of her tone.

Sidney was taken aback. 'Miss Heywood. Always popping up when least expected.'

She couldn't meet his eye, though she knew his was on her. 'I – I will leave you to it, gentlemen.' With that, she rushed past them with her head down. It was only on the stairs that she recalled what Sidney had said to Tom about leaving, and wondered how long it might be until she saw him again.

When, an hour later, Mrs Parker suggested Charlotte accompany her and the children to the beach, she was heartily glad of the distraction. It was a pleasant day – blue-skied, with the only clouds high and white and scudding fast overhead.

'Tom used to have all the time in the world for the children,' said Mrs Parker when Alicia, Jenny and Henry had taken off across the sand. Charlotte, still caught up in her own disturbing thoughts, was struck with guilt – for here was her hostess lacking her usual cheer, her problems so much larger than Charlotte's.

She took the older lady's arm in a gesture of comfort.

'I'm sure he will again, once things have settled a little.'

Mrs Parker gave her a rueful look. 'And when will that be, I wonder? Once the terrace is finished? Once every last house is let? Sometimes I fear he'll just keep adding and obsessing until the day he drops down dead, the plans still clutched in his hand!'

Charlotte felt quite useless. 'I wish there was more I could do to help.'

Mrs Parker patted her hand. 'I am afraid my husband, like most men, is reluctant to accept help from anyone. At the least, you must never let him catch you in the act.'

Though she was still not quite herself by the time they returned to Trafalgar House, the outing did seem to have raised Mrs Parker's spirits a little. Sadly, this was to be short-lived. As they climbed the steps to the front door it was flung open by Mr Parker.

'Wickens!' he was calling over his shoulder to the footman. 'I will need our coach and my hat right away!'

He opened his arms in greeting when he saw his wife and Charlotte on the steps.

'Where are you going?' exclaimed Mrs Parker.

'You shall see soon enough, my dear!'

'But how long will you be gone?' A note of exasperation had crept into her voice but her husband didn't appear to notice.

'For as long as it takes! If my plan succeeds, I may just have hit upon the perfect means to draw people to Sanditon!'

With that, he kissed her and the children and hurried down the steps. Charlotte caught Mrs Parker's eye, conveying her sympathy well enough without words. She remembered what Mary – for she was now Mary, as Mr Parker had become Tom – had said when she first arrived: that Sanditon was a second wife to Tom. Today it seemed that Sanditon was not just a rival to Mary; she was the wife her husband preferred.

On the sand that Charlotte had not long left herself, a trio of lady artists had set up easels. A closer look showed them to be Miss Lambe and the Beaufort sisters, Phillida and Julia. They were accompanied by Mrs Griffiths, who watched them hawk-like from under her parasol, and Mr Hankins the vicar, who was reading out improving passages of Genesis while they painted.

'. . . *But of the tree of the knowledge of good and evil, thou shalt not eat of it.* And why was that, do we suppose?'

'Because of sin, Mr Hankins,' intoned Phillida.

He bestowed on her an oily smile.

'Quite right! Although since you are under the aegis of Mrs Griffiths,' – another ingratiating smile – 'I am sure the very idea of sin is foreign to you! *And the Lord God said, "It is not good that man should be alone; I will make him an help-meet."* And who was that help-meet?'

'Eve, Mr Hankins.' It was Julia who spoke up this time. Miss Lambe resisted flicking her paintbrush at the girl's upright back.

'Eve! Very good, miss,' beamed Mr Hankins. 'The Mother of us all. And who else was there? The Serpent. And what did the Serpent do? He tempted Eve, didn't he? He tempted her to do something she was forbidden to do. And she couldn't resist, could she? Young women, sadly, often find it very hard to resist temptation.' He allowed himself to look over each young lady in turn: their smooth skin, their narrow waists . . . He swallowed noisily. 'So what did the Serpent tempt Eve to do?'

'Eat the apple, Mr Hankins.'

'That's right!'

Miss Lambe put down her brush with a clatter. 'And what's so bad about eating an apple?'

Mr Hankins adopted a grave expression. 'Because this apple was a special apple from the Tree of Knowledge. And because God had forbidden Adam and Eve to eat the apples from that tree.'

'Why?'

He was taken aback. 'Why? Because he's God. We don't question God, do we, Mrs Griffiths?'

'Certainly not, Mr Hankins!' said she piously, directing the words at Miss Lambe. 'Perhaps it is time you showed us your work, ladies?'

All three girls turned around their easels. The Beauforts' efforts were clumsy but anodyne: daubings of unnatural blue sea and with some vague attempt to capture the crests of waves in white. Mr Hankins and Mrs Griffiths were nodding and smiling encouragingly but then caught sight of Miss Lambe's infinitely saucier painting.

Mrs Griffiths covered her mouth with her hand. 'Why, Miss Lambe! I have never . . .'

'I thought the sea was a bit dreary, so I used my imagination.' She swallowed the laugh that was threatening to burst out of her.

'Girls, turn away at once, until Mr Hankins has removed this . . . this . . .' – her voice rose to a shriek – '*obscenity!*'

Mr Hankins darted forward as instructed, though it was noted by all that he took rather longer than was necessary to turn the offending item around, all thoughts of Genesis apparently having left his head.

Chapter Thirteen

Charlotte, who was on her way out of the house, was just closing the front door when someone arrived at the bottom of the steps.

'Oh, Mr Stringer!' she said, glad to see him.

He smiled shyly up at her. 'Morning, miss. I have just come to see Mr Parker.'

'You've missed him, I'm afraid. And I cannot even tell you when he'll be back, or indeed where he's gone.'

His face fell. Charlotte wasn't sure whether he was more disappointed or frustrated.

'Aye, that sounds like Mr Parker,' he said heavily, and she understood that it was the latter.

'Might I be able to help?' she tried.

'Thank you, miss, but I really do need to speak to Mr Parker himself. I will try again later.'

She was about to tell him that there was little point; that Mr Parker was not likely to return for a day or two at least, but Stringer had already turned and hurried away, so distracted that he hadn't even told her goodbye.

She was still thinking about this when, a little way along the street, she heard her name called. It was Miss Brereton, her pale hair bright in the sunshine. Charlotte smiled as she approached, though in truth it was impossible to feel easy in her presence after the peculiar episode in Sanditon House's grounds.

'Clara. Good morning.'

'I trust you have recovered from Lady Denham's luncheon?' she said eagerly, her mouth forming its habitual pretty moue. 'I fear she was less than kind to you.'

'I think we've made our peace. She seemed to accept my apology – in her own way.'

They continued along, Clara falling into step with her. Up ahead, just outside the hotel, a small group of gentlemen were standing about while their respective curricles were prepared, reins adjusted and various items of luggage stowed.

With a sinking heart, Charlotte realised that one of their number was Sidney Parker, yet again, accompanied by his cronies Lord Babington and Mr Crowe. Taking Clara's arm so firmly that she let out a cry, Charlotte half-dragged her across the road, and began to witter in earnest about the freshness of the buns in the baker's window.

Despite these desperate efforts, Sidney had not yet seen her. He was too engrossed in the note he'd just received.

'Apparently my ward grows more feral by the hour,' he said to his companions when he'd finished. 'You'll have to go ahead.'

'For God's sake, man!' said Crowe in disgust. 'It's as bad as having a bastard, though less fun to come by, I should think!'

Babington, who was facing the other way, nudged Sidney with his foot. 'Be alert, man. See who has approached!'

He looked over to see that Charlotte Heywood was on the other side of the road, looking intently into the baker's window. Lady Denham's niece, who was with her, was regarding the gentlemen with a knowing smirk.

'One would think she was trying to avoid you, Sidney,' said Babington, enjoying this development enormously.

'I cannot think why that would be!' said Crowe, who was no less amused.

Babington gave Sidney a wink. 'You must have made quite an impression on the poor girl.'

Sidney risked a glance towards Charlotte again, unsure whether he wanted her to turn and acknowledge him or not. It was a strange thing but whenever they encountered each other – which was so often it bordered on the absurd – he seemed incapable of behaving naturally. He wasn't sure he'd ever felt so awkward in the presence of a mere woman: half of him vexed, the other half intrigued, perhaps even stirred. With a scowl for his friends, he turned on his heel and went back inside the hotel.

Unnoticed as yet by anyone else, Sir Edward and Esther Denham were also out for a healthful stroll.

'Look at Clara,' hissed Esther at the sight of her enemy and Charlotte Heywood in furtive conversation outside the baker's shop. 'Dripping poison wherever she goes.'

'Patience, Esther,' said Edward easily. 'It takes a fair few traps to catch a mouse.'

'Or a cat.'

Edward gave her a little squeeze around her waist, making her suck in her breath. 'Better sharpen those claws then.'

She turned to him, mollified by his attentions. 'Miaow.'

But Edward had spotted someone approaching them. It was Babington, a determined look in his eye.

'Oh, here comes your wealthy admirer.'

'Not wealthy enough to make him bearable,' said Esther, without dropping her voice.

'What's the matter with him?'

'Nothing,' she said sulkily. 'It's just that only one man in the world holds any interest for me of that kind.

Unfortunately.' She sighed as Babington came forward to shake her brother's hand.

'Sir Edward, Miss Denham.'

'I'll leave you together,' said Edward, earning himself a scathing look from his sister as he sauntered off towards the square where a queue was beginning to form for the next coach to London.

Babington leant in close enough that Esther could smell his cologne; expensive but rather too liberally applied. 'I came to say I'm leaving Sanditon today, much to my regret.'

She looked into the middle distance. 'I shall try to bear your absence with equanimity.'

'Might I be permitted to write to you?'

'If you wish to waste your time.'

He smiled as though he'd scored an important point. 'Then I shall.'

She turned to him then, suddenly roused. 'Babington, why do you persist, when you are treated with so little civility? Are you addicted to pain?'

'Certainly not.'

'What, then?'

He let out a long breath, apparently mulling over the question. Then he looked directly at her, his eyes smouldering. 'Perhaps it's the fascination of what's difficult. All I know is that the more I see you, and the more nonchalantly you reject my advances, the more intense my desire for you grows.'

She laughed shortly. 'Well spoken, but to no avail.' And with that, she flounced away without so much as a backward glance.

Babington watched her take her brother's arm and laugh at something he said, her face transfigured. He returned to Crowe, chastened but no less aroused.

'No joy there, Babbers,' said Crowe, shaking his head. 'You may as well howl at the moon.'

On the other side of the road, Clara poked Charlotte in the arm.

'You can stop staring at the buns now. The coast is clear. What a dark horse you are, Charlotte Heywood! I would never have guessed it of you.'

Ignoring her, Charlotte looked over herself. Mr Crowe and Lord Babington were climbing up into their respective curricles but there was no sign of Sidney. Relief and disappointment enveloped her in equal measure.

While Babington and Crowe began their journey back towards the superior entertainments of London, Sidney Parker found himself back at Mrs Griffiths' lodging house, engaged in battle with his ward once again.

'Wilful, rude and obstreperous,' he was saying, counting them off on his fingers. 'What do you have to say?'

Miss Lambe stuck out her lip in a show of careless stubbornness, but there were tears of frustration glistening in her eyes. 'Just that this place is driving me to distraction. It's like a prison!'

'Do you think I enjoy this, Georgiana?' he cried, thoroughly exasperated. 'I have many demands on my time and would be glad to free myself of this one. Like it or not, I am your guardian until you turn twenty-one, and since that is still two years away . . .' He stopped, his headache so abruptly returned that he winced.

'Is something ailing you?'

'Yes!' he exclaimed, glaring at her. '*You* are.'

She was about to retort when Mrs Griffiths rapped on the door. 'Miss Lambe, you have another visitor.' Without waiting, she ushered in Charlotte.

Miss Lambe, most pleased to see her new friend, went forward to greet her, but Charlotte had spied Sidney, her smile fading fast.

He had looked up and seen it was her at the same time. 'Miss Heywood. It seems I cannot escape you.'

An awkward silence descended, neither of them able to meet the other's eye, while Miss Lambe looked on wryly.

'Well, I was just leaving,' Sidney eventually muttered, and immediately did so, without another word.

Miss Lambe's eyes were like saucers as she spun Charlotte round to face her.

'What did he mean – he cannot escape you? Have you been pursuing him?'

Charlotte's eyes blazed like her face. 'Good Lord, no!'

Miss Lambe narrowed her eyes at Charlotte; she couldn't tell if she was lying or not.

'He thinks you are a bad influence, you know,' she said, a gleeful smile spreading across her face. 'As if there could be any greater incentive for us to be friends!' She paused, thoughtful again. 'What is your opinion of him?'

Charlotte's colour was still high. 'I – I hardly know what to think of Mr Parker. I have never met anyone quite so . . . confounding.'

Not wishing to betray any sign of emotion, she looked down at her feet. Though Sidney had been gone some minutes, her heart was still thudding hard in her chest.

Chapter Fourteen

Mr Tom Parker returned the following day and went without delay to Sanditon House. He was shown into Lady Denham's drawing room but was so fit to burst with news of his success that not only was he unable to sit, but he did not notice her obvious displeasure as she received him.

'I called on Trafalgar House three times yesterday to be told they no idea of your whereabouts,' she began, eyeing him beadily as he paced up and down the length of the room. 'I was starting to think you'd jumped ship.'

He stopped pacing at that. 'Gracious no, my lady! Quite the opposite. I have returned from my mission with the most exciting news imaginable!'

'I am breathless with anticipation,' she returned with devastating sarcasm, though it was wasted on an irrepressible Mr Parker.

'I have secured the services of one of the finest physicians in the country,' he cried, unable to contain himself for another second.

Lady Denham rolled her eyes. 'Oh, not this again! We agreed that Sanditon has no use for a doctor!'

Mr Parker's smile faltered a little. 'We are a spa town, ma'am. If we are to attract visitors . . .'

'They have the sea! The air! The milk from my asses!'

He approached her, a pleading look in his eye. 'My lady,

I would beg that you save your opinion until you have at least met Dr Fuchs.'

'I do not need to *meet* a person to form an opinion. Often a name is more than enough. And I do not care for the name "*Fuchs*" one whit!'

Mr Parker gathered his courage by taking a fortifying glance out of the window towards the sapphire-coloured sea.

'The doctor has kindly agreed to demonstrate some of his treatments for you, free and gratis,' he said. 'Allow him an hour of your time and I promise that he will assuage every last doubt you possess.'

Though Lady Denham appeared less than convinced, Mr Parker left her with his high spirits intact. They rose once more at the sight of Trafalgar House, and again when he told his dear Mary and Charlotte about Dr Fuchs. Within the half-hour, all the household had heard about the famous doctor, and were watching at the window for the first glimpse of his carriage.

'What if, in spite of his demonstration, Lady Denham still doesn't approve?' Mary Parker said carefully. She looked anxious, as though she was trying to catch some of her husband's enthusiasm and failing in the task.

'I have heard her speak of physicians in the most disparaging terms,' said Charlotte, also rather worried.

'Ah, but Dr Fuchs is no ordinary physician!' said Mr Parker from the window. 'Once she sees him in action, she will undergo nothing short of a Damascene conversion. Ah, here he is now!'

Charlotte went to the window in time to see the fabled doctor step nimbly from his carriage. He was a jolly-looking fellow, with impressive side-whiskers and bright eyes.

'*Herr* Parker!' he said when Mr Parker greeted him from the steps. The men looked delighted to see each other.

'Dr Fuchs! Welcome.'

The doctor looked about him with happy approval. 'Sea air!' He took in a great lungful of it. 'Most refreshing. And what a charming little house! It reminds me of the Duke of Norfolk's hunting lodge.' He caught sight of the Parker children gathered around their father's legs. '*Ah, die Susen kinder*! Such healthy complexions! And who is this delightful creature?'

Mr Parker turned and gestured at Mary, smiling proudly. 'Doctor, may I present my wife.'

'*Gnädige Frau* Parker! It is my honour to make your acquaintance.'

He took her hand in his large one and kissed it at such length that Mary was quite abashed. 'Dr Maximilian Fuchs.' He bowed low. 'At your service.'

Chapter Fifteen

Charlotte carried a large pile of papers into her host's study. She had expected it to be empty but Mr Parker was there, silent and hidden behind his newspaper, his feet up on the desk.

'Mr Parker!' she said, pleased that she could show him how competently she had arranged his invoices and notes. But as the newspaper was lowered at the sound of her voice, she saw it was quite another Parker brother. 'Oh! I thought to find—'

Sidney Parker, for it was he, gave her an arch look. 'The ubiquitous Miss Heywood. Can't I even read the news in peace?'

Her ire was immediately aroused; it was she who had business in here, not him. 'If you don't wish to be disturbed,' she retorted, 'you might choose somewhere more secluded.'

'I tried that,' he said, dark eyes boring into hers. 'It wasn't entirely successful.'

She suddenly remembered the cove. Was that what he meant? She didn't know; she could never quite interpret his meaning. They stood staring at each other, the look only broken by Tom's arrival.

'Charlotte! Sidney!' He was glad to find both in one place. 'Come, it is time to leave. You don't want to miss Dr Fuchs' demonstration.'

Sidney raised an eyebrow and picked up his paper again. 'Actually, I'm pretty sure I can live without it. I shall stay and catch up on some paperwork.'

'Really, Sidney? Is it now too much for me to ask for an hour of my brother's time?'

With great deliberation, jaw set with irritation, Sidney put down the paper. Charlotte was still piqued and when he glanced her way, she took some satisfaction in silently conveying her disapproval.

A small procession of the Parker family and Charlotte were soon on their way to Sanditon House, Mr Tom having declared that the exercise would be beneficial. Sidney was still glowering at the imposition of the outing and Charlotte, ever mindful of his presence, was taking care to keep well behind him, walking instead with Diana and Arthur. Their excitement at meeting the great Dr Fuchs was palpable.

'The first thing we must tell the doctor, Arthur,' said Diana, 'is that we are both a hostage to our nerves.'

Arthur nodded gravely. ''Tis true, alas. Bedevilled by 'em, we are, Miss Heywood.'

Charlotte nodded as sympathetically as her amusement would allow.

Diana continued seriously. 'Then I should go on to catalogue my gout, my sciatica, my delirium, goiters, cankers, and assorted agues, rashes and exanthema. Oh,' she nudged her brother, 'and this past Tuesday you were struck by a most thunderous bellyache, you must mention that.'

'True,' he said. 'And it can't have been hunger, 'cause I'd only just polished off an eight-bird roast.'

Diana frowned. 'Perhaps I should set it all down for him. I'd hate to leave anything out.'

As she continued in this anxious vein, Charlotte found her attention drifting – not to the magnificent sea below, but the back of Sidney's head. She had never in her life met anyone who inspired in her such a strange combination of feelings. She couldn't even decide if she liked him. It was most unsettling.

Lady Denham's sitting room, like the rest of the house, was quite arresting under normal circumstances. Now it had been transformed into Dr Fuchs' temporary clinic, it had become something rather sinister. Long tables had been brought in and laid with a collection of mysterious implements and bottles. Various items too large for the tables stood covered by tarpaulin. These were the doctor's machines. Diana and Arthur looked about them, wide-eyed and utterly thrilled.

Lady Denham was already ensconced in a high-backed chair which had been positioned in the middle of the room, her face a picture of bad-tempered scepticism. She reminded Charlotte of a queen looking for the excuse to order some-one's head cut off. Next to her was Clara Brereton, looking studiedly demure. Sir Edward and Esther had also come for the demonstration, and were regarding with wry amusement the sight of Diana Parker reeling off her impressive array of ailments to the doctor, Arthur nodding eagerly at her side.

She had listed but half of them when Dr Fuchs held up a hand. 'Fear not, *Fräulein*. Sir. There will be time enough for the details anon. For now, perhaps you would like to sample *ein bischen etwas* I have just prepared, *ja*?'

Diana flushed with pleasure. She was never so easy in her mind as when she was in the presence of a doctor. 'Oh, *ja*,' she cried. 'I mean yes. Thank you, Doctor.'

He produced a pot of dubious-looking paste. 'My own little preparation: a light fard!'

With a flourish, he began to smear it on Diana's cheeks. Arthur, not to be excluded, offered up his own large phizog.

'What do you suppose the purpose of a fard is?' murmured Sir Edward to Esther.

'I think it is meant to extract impurities from the skin,' she replied, also *sotto voce*. 'And money from the gullible.'

She went over and picked up a small container. 'What is in here, Doctor?'

'Ah, now. Be careful with that, *Fräulein*. They are parasitic worms. Excellent for the circulation of the blood, and for relieving the tension!'

'D'you hear that, Edward? "Parasitic worms."' She dropped her voice. 'We could call this one Clara.'

They made their way over to Lady Denham, Sir Edward smiling obsequiously. 'This is surely the only time we shall ever see a doctor in your house, Aunt, given what radiant health you are in.'

Lady Denham rolled her eyes. 'How the words trip off his tongue, Clara! We could have done with more of your eloquence at Miss Lambe's luncheon party. You made a sorry showing there, didn't he, Clara? A hundred thousand there for the taking, and you muffed it!'

Clara smiled, eyes cast prettily down. Esther, observing this, thought how much she despised the little strumpet.

'Miss Brereton, I am minded to take a turn about the room,' said Sir Edward. 'Would you care to join me?'

She looked to Lady Denham for permission, who gave it with a wave of her hand. 'Go on, then. But no lingering!'

Esther swiftly took Clara's seat. 'I shall sit beside you, Aunt. There is nothing I enjoy more than hearing you pass judgement . . .' She glanced pointedly in the direction of Dr Fuchs and the adoring Parker siblings, '. . . especially when you are given so much to work with.'

Mr Parker could not keep still, so anxious was he for the demonstration to go well.

'What do you think, Charlotte?' he said, gesturing towards the doctor. 'Is he not remarkable?'

Charlotte, scrupulously honest but also mindful of Mr Parker's agitation, gave him a tactful smile. 'I have never seen anything like it.'

He sent her a grateful look. 'We must hope her ladyship agrees.'

Mary Parker, on his other side, was doing her best not to show her doubts.

Dr Fuchs, encouraged by the young Parkers, turned to Lady Denham and proffered a pot of white ointment.

'Now for you, Lady Denham,' he cried. 'I think perhaps *ein bischen* of Fuchs' vital essence?'

'Certainly not!' she harrumphed. 'I have no need of such stuff.'

He sidled closer. 'No, your ladyship has the complexion of a young girl! But surely if you could keep it forever, hmm? What would you say to that?'

'I'd say you were a fabulist of the most dangerous kind!'

Fuchs chuckled appreciatively. 'Such spirit! Such *lebens-freude*!' Before she could stop him, he took up her hand and began massaging the cream into it. 'And such soft skin! It is not easy of course to improve upon perfection – but one cannot resist trying!'

For a moment, Lady Denham was almost disarmed. Beside Charlotte, Mr Parker held his breath. But then she wrenched her hand away. 'That is quite enough of that!' she cried. 'Bother someone else.'

Fuchs gave a small bow and moved aside, allowing Lady Denham to catch sight of Charlotte.

'Ah, Miss Heywood,' she threw out. 'Still imposing on the Parkers' hospitality, I see.'

Charlotte bridled. 'I hope Mr and Mrs Parker would say if they felt I was imposing.'

Lady Denham snorted. 'They're the kind of people who'd sooner suffer than be thought of as rude. Not a mistake you'll catch me making!'

Charlotte was unable to think of anything polite to say. 'Lady Denham,' she managed eventually, and took her leave.

Esther, who had been listening with interest to this exchange, turned to her aunt.

'I am curious you should think Miss Heywood outstays her welcome. How long is it that Clara's been your guest now?'

'That is hardly the same,' retorted Lady Denham. 'Clara is a relation.'

'Albeit a very poor one.' Mischief danced in Esther's eyes. 'It is to your credit that you have kept her so far beyond the original terms of her stay. Everyone says it is *most* charitable of you.'

Lady Denham's eyes narrowed. 'I abhor charity. It helps no one.' She didn't notice Esther's small smile of satisfaction.

Charlotte, doing her best to be neither incensed nor wounded by Lady Denham's words, had wandered blindly across the room, eyes cast down. She looked up to see Sidney right in front of her.

'Mr Parker,' she stammered.

She waited for him to say something, but he seemed quite stuck for words. Apparently conscious of this, he scowled at her. 'Would you excuse me? You are standing in the way of the coffee.'

Flustered and annoyed in equal measure, she moved aside.

He poured himself a cup of coffee but instead of moving away, they stood next to each other in a silence so awkward Charlotte didn't know whether to laugh or run away.

'*Bloom de ninon!*' Fuchs was exclaiming from across the room. 'Incomparable for removing the freckles, the morphemes and the worms!'

'I have seen enough,' muttered Sidney. He put down his cup and walked away. Charlotte watched him go, irritated with herself for doing so even as she did.

In the hallway, Sir Edward and Clara were alone.

'I do not much care for our aunt's taste in furnishings,' said Sir Edward idly. 'I have a more modern scheme in mind.'

'That is assuming you inherit the house?' said Clara.

'My dear Clara, you have made a valiant effort, but you must know your claim is futile. And however much you play the innocent, our aunt is bound to find you out soon enough. Why not leave now, while you are still in her favour?'

She widened her china-blue eyes at him. 'How can I leave, when there is so much left for me to resolve?' She checked that no one was nearby and leant in so close that the words were hot in his ear. He hated how it stirred him. 'I know you think of me often,' she breathed.

He managed to step away. 'You flatter yourself. I feel nothing for you besides contempt and pity.' But they both heard it: the thickness in his voice that belied him.

Back in the drawing room, Dr Fuchs had lit his burner and set a copper pan on top. A strange smell was beginning to permeate the air and the small audience gathered closer, fascinated by the concoction that had begun to bubble and splutter.

'. . . And so,' the doctor was saying. 'We must boil the calf's foot in four quarts of river water until it reduces by half . . .'

Clara sidled past the table to rejoin her aunt.

'*There* you are, child,' said Lady Denham crossly. 'How long does it take to walk around a room!'

'I am sorry, Aunt, I . . .'

'I will not be taken for granted, you know? I feel it is time we discussed the terms of your stay.'

For once, Clara was without words. Esther, catching her eye, smiled.

'. . . Once distilled, this will soften and lubricate the skin,' the doctor was saying in his heavy accent. 'This is the same treatment I administered to the Princess Charlotte Augusta, and she was *ekstatisch* with its effect.'

Lady Denham harrumphed again. 'Then she was a credulous dolt!' She gestured to Mr Parker. 'I have seen and heard more than enough. It is abundantly clear this so-called "doctor" is little more than a travelling mountebank!'

Dr Fuchs' already ruddy complexion darkened. 'I can assure you I am nothing of the sort, madam! If you require further proof, then perhaps I could persuade you to sample my latest innovation . . .' He moved to one of the tarpaulins but Lady Denham shook her head.

'I detest modern contraptions and concoctions.'

'*Ja, ja,*' he said placatingly. 'Of course. But sometimes you know, nature needs a little help! I will make you a suggestion. You observe while I demonstrate. But please, I will need a volunteer.'

He whipped off the tarpaulin to reveal a clawfoot bath attached to something that appeared to be a boiler, with a great number of pipes and tubes attached. A curtain for modesty's sake hung from an encircling rail.

'I present to you the Fuchs Hydrotherapeutic Shower-bath!' he said, to general exclamations of wonder. 'Who would like to sample its effects? One at a time, please. Do not crowd around!'

An expectant hush descended. Charlotte had begun to squirm with embarrassment for the doctor and Mr Parker alike when Clara spoke up.

'I should like to try it, Dr Fuchs.'

Lady Denham turned to her in astonishment. 'Clara? What are you doing?'

Mr Parker took in a nervous breath.

Soon enough, the strange shower-bath was ready for its patient. It had been half-filled with steaming water, a servant operating a set of bellows to further build pressure in the system. Arthur and Diana, their faces blotchy after removing the doctor's fard, were stock-still with anticipation.

Clara was changing out of her clothes behind a screen. In front of her was a large mirror which afforded her a glimpse of Sir Edward. She saw the moment he noticed her, his face heating. She dropped her chemise and watched with satisfaction as he shifted uncomfortably, his sister frowning at him.

'Now, once you are inside the bath,' Fuchs was saying, 'you must hold the nozzle in your hand and direct the spray *verever you vish – votever* is most pleasing, if you follow me. I will draw the curtain to afford you total privacy.'

He helped her into the bath and drew the curtains. She immersed herself and began to experiment with the nozzle, first cautiously and then with enthusiasm. It imparted a quite heavenly sensation.

'Everything is satisfactory?' said Fuchs from the other side of the curtain.

'Quite satisfactory, so far.'

She regarded the gleaming boiler, piled high with red-hot coals and then, biting her lip with determination, pressed her arm against the metal. After a couple of seconds, she examined the burn and then opened her mouth to let out blood-curdling scream.

To his sister's disgust, Sir Edward rushed forward, tore back the curtain and lifted a swooning Clara out of the water, her scalded arm dangling in such a way that no one could miss the injury.

'This shouldn't happen!' spluttered Fuchs in horror.

Even Lady Denham had risen in the commotion. 'My poor child – what has he done to you? Have that man and his *equipment* removed from my house at once!'

As Sir Edward carried the dripping Clara out of the room, her aunt pointed an accusing finger at Mr Parker. '*This* is what will come of contradicting me!'

With that, she swept disdainfully out of the room.

Within ten minutes, the footmen had packed up Fuchs' contraptions and taken them out of the house. A devastated Diana and Arthur were looking on.

'Oh, Arthur. That we should find hope at last, only to see it snatched away again.'

Arthur watched the men shove the boiler into the cart and sighed. 'Given the miracles he worked on our faces, think what he could have achieved on the rest of us!'

Fuchs was also watching the sorry procession.

'I do not understand it, *Herr* Parker,' he said, with a mournful shake of his head. 'In all my years as a physician, I have never experienced such a – such a *funktionsstörung*.' He sniffed. 'I shall return to Worthing, where at least I shall be treated with respect.'

'I am sorry, Doctor,' said Mr Parker. His face was drawn with worry again. 'This is far from the outcome I was hoping for.'

He watched as the doctor took his leave. Mary placed a reassuring hand on his shoulder but he didn't feel it. His anxiety over Sanditon's future was threatening to overcome him.

Chapter Sixteen

After she had returned from Sanditon House, Charlotte – restless from the strange events of the afternoon – decided to go and call on Miss Lambe.

'How I wish I'd been there!' said the heiress now, who had been quite agog while Charlotte gave her account of Clara's terrible experience. 'It sounds far more entertaining than being trapped in here with Gorgon Griffiths and those idiot Beaufort sisters.'

'I would hardly call it entertaining!'

'But it doesn't sound as if Miss Brereton was badly hurt. And at least you've not been bored out of your mind.'

Charlotte considered this. 'Well, I think I would rather be bored than endure one more strangled non-conversation with your guardian.' She stopped talking; she had not meant to mention Sidney.

'He is not *still* in Sanditon?' said Miss Lambe, frowning. 'When is he going to leave? Before long, I hope.'

'You and me both,' replied Charlotte, with rather too much emphasis.

At the heart of new Sanditon, Mr Parker's terrace was beginning to take shape. Charlotte, who had to pass it on her way back to Trafalgar House, stopped to observe it for a moment. The walls of the houses were more or less complete by now, and most of the activity was going on high above her head. Pulleys were being used to haul up baskets of stone and tiles for the upper floors and roofs.

'Miss Heywood!' Her friend Young Stringer had spotted her and was making his way over. 'What can I do for you?'

She smiled a greeting and handed him an envelope.

'Mr Parker asked me to give you this.'

He read it, a frown marring his brow as he did. 'Right,' he said, suddenly grim-faced. 'All right. Thank you, Miss Heywood.'

'Something wrong, Mr Stringer?'

'No, no. I was hoping to speak to Mr Parker in person, that's all.'

'Oh, I'm sure he would have come down himself.' She thought back to Tom's chastened expression on the walk back from Sanditon House. 'But he has rather a lot to contend with today.'

'No doubt, miss.'

Though neither of them knew it, Young Stringer wasn't much less gloomy than his superior, though for different reasons. Earlier that day he had tried to stop his father heaving a load of bricks up the scaffolding.

'Here, Dad,' he'd said, trying to take the hod away from him. 'Let me.'

The old man had shook his head stubbornly. 'You're foreman. Not your job.'

It wasn't his father's job either but the fact was, there was no one else to do it.

'You shouldn't have to double as a labourer,' he tried again. 'You're a first-class stonemason.'

'Tell that to Mr Parker,' said his father, and pulled himself up the ladder, his face creased in pain.

Remembering Miss Heywood standing next to him, he judiciously changed the subject.

'So, how are you enjoying your stay in Sanditon, miss?'

'A great deal, on the whole,' she replied thoughtfully, looking about her. 'I love all this work going on – the idea that we're building something that wasn't here before. It seems almost a kind of miracle, doesn't it?'

He smiled for the first time that day. 'I agree, miss. As a matter of fact, I plan to design and build a town of my own one day.'

'As an architect?'

'God willing . . .' He looked for his father. He was on the ladder again, and clearly feeling the strain of it. 'Although my father doesn't approve of such talk.'

'That's your father?'

'He's a stonemason. Third generation. He thinks I've ideas above my station.'

'Surely ambition is a quality to be admired?'

He thought again how much he liked her.

'What is it?' she said, suddenly self-conscious as he gazed at her.

'Just – I never met anyone like you before.'

She had opened her mouth to reply when a shout rang out from on high. It was one of the labourers.

'Look out!'

They turned in time to see Old Stringer lose his footing on the ladder. There was a moment when it seemed as though time was suspended, as though he might stay borne up on thin air, but then, with a terrible inevitability, began to fall backwards, his load of tiles and bricks coming down with him. As he landed with an awful thud, a great cloud of grit and rubble rose. When it cleared, he was almost entirely buried by fallen debris. What could be seen of him was deathly pale with masonry dust.

Charlotte and Young Stringer rushed over and, along with some of the labourers, began pulling everything they could lift off him with their bare hands. Charlotte was just beginning to despair when, suddenly, Sidney appeared next to her, pulling off his coat and falling to his knees to help.

'Here, let me,' he said and heaved off one of the larger pieces of stone.

'Pray God it hasn't killed him,' said Young Stringer, voice weighted with dread.

Finally, Old Stringer's face was unearthed. To general relief he was alive, though only just: his eyelids fluttering weakly and his breathing shallow. He groaned in agony as another piece of stone was moved off him and blood ran down his cheek from a large cut to his scalp. Charlotte pressed her handkerchief to it.

'All right, Mr Stringer?' she said gently. 'How do you feel?'

'Don't mean . . . to cause any fuss, miss. I'll be right enough in a—'

He licked his dry lips, unable to continue talking through his pain.

By now, Sidney had removed enough debris to reveal a badly broken leg, the bone protruding grotesquely through the gore.

'There is a doctor in town,' he said to Young Stringer. 'Best he were fetched straight away.'

'I'm not about to leave my father.'

One of the labourers stepped forward and said he would go instead.

'Try the hotel,' said Sidney. The man broke into a run.

'It's a bad wound,' said Charlotte in an undertone. 'We need to stop the bleeding.'

An idea formed in her mind. She stood and hitched up her dress, revealing her petticoat. Taking hold of the hem, she tried to tear off a strip but the fabric wouldn't give.

'Could one of you . . . ?'

Sidney stooped and ripped off a broad band of the cotton, handing it to Charlotte. Their eyes met.

Pushing a loose strand of hair back with her hand, she knelt and tied it in a tight tourniquet, Sidney and Young Stringer looking on with admiration.

'That should do, for now,' she said. 'Just keep as still as you can.'

Young Stringer pressed his father's hand. 'Help's on its way.'

'Just don't let 'em take my leg,' the old man muttered through his agony, his eyes rolling back.

Sidney stood, concern etched in his face. 'We'd better take him to Trafalgar House.'

Chapter Seventeen

Tom and Mary Parker were horrified when the labourers carried in a half-conscious Old Stringer, absorbing both his groans of pain and the bandages around his head and leg that were already stained red with his blood.

'How could this have happened?' exclaimed Mr Parker.

'We need clean sheets, as many as you can gather,' said Charlotte firmly, taking charge once again. 'And boiling water. And I expect the doctor will want a table.'

Mrs Parker nodded grimly. 'Of course. Whatever you need.'

At that moment, Dr Fuchs made his entrance.

'*Fürchte dich nicht alle!*' he said, his capable demeanour offering immediate reassurance. 'The doctor has arrived! Now, where is the patient?'

The servants had cleared the table in the drawing room and covered it with a sheet. Old Stringer had been laid gently down.

'How long ago was this unfortunate accident?' said Dr Fuchs as he made his first inspection.

'Not more than twenty minutes.'

'Good. The muscles will have contracted, but not too much.'

'Tell me you can save his leg,' said Young Stringer, quite distraught, his voice cracking.

'*Villeicht.*'

'What – what does that mean?'

'It means you should trust that the doctor knows *vot* he is doing!'

Sidney touched the young foreman's arm and regarded him sympathetically. 'Perhaps you should wait outside. No one should see their own father in this much pain.'

'I can't just leave him.'

'Would it not be better? For his sake as much as yours.'

Young Stringer hesitated, torn between loyalty and good sense.

Sidney pressed his shoulder. 'He will be fine. I give you my word.'

Young Stringer finally nodded and, after a last look at his father, left the room.

Dr Fuchs glanced at Charlotte. 'Now this will not be pretty, *Fräulein*, so you might want to turn your head away.'

'I am not afraid of a little blood.'

'*Sehr gut*, then you can assist me.' He took out a flask of cognac and took a fortifying mouthful before handing it to Charlotte.

'He must drink as much as he can. This will hurt a lot worse than a little *schmerzen*.'

As carefully as she could, she lifted Old Stringer's head so that a little of the liquid could be directed into his mouth.

'Take his hand,' said Fuchs to Sidney, who after a slight hesitation, did as he was bidden.

'Now keep a good pressure on the wound. And you, sir, hold him still. First we must set the leg.'

Fuchs began his work. Old Stringer, determined not to cry out, could not help himself as his leg was manipulated back into position. While Sidney winced at the man's obvious pain, Charlotte remained calm and steady and he couldn't help glancing at her with admiration again. As for the doctor, he was in his element, singing softly as he worked with deftness and skill.

Some time later, Charlotte emerged from the front door of Trafalgar House, where Young Stringer was pacing. She smiled encouragingly.

'All is well. The leg is saved.'

In his relief, he rushed up the steps and embraced her, only remembering himself when Sidney appeared.

'Forgive me, miss. I . . .'

Charlotte was a little pink in the cheeks but waved away his concern. 'It's quite all right.'

'Your father will be glad to see you, Mr Stringer,' said Sidney.

The younger man shook his hand. 'Thank you, sir.'

When they were alone, Sidney turned to Charlotte.

'I must admit, Miss Heywood, you have given a good account of yourself today. I should never have guessed you were so . . . capable.'

'Because I am a young woman, or because until now you had dismissed me as frivolous?'

He gave her a wry look. 'I daresay a little of both. Forgive me.'

'How can I not, since I am equally guilty of dismissing you.'

That took him aback. 'Oh? As what?'

Charlotte wished she hadn't spoken but he pressed her.

'Go on, Miss Heywood. It is always instructive to learn how one is perceived.'

She looked at him consideringly. 'Well, if I am honest, I had come to the opinion that you were more or less devoid of empathy.'

He laughed. 'And what had I done to deserve such condemnation?'

'It is just that, well, for one thing, you always seem so reluctant to help Tom.'

'That is hardly fair. I have done all that I can for my brother.'

'Have you?' She wondered whether she should go on and decided that she would. Though frankness had hardly served her well before, she was a little less afraid of Sidney Parker than she had been. 'And if I may, you have hardly proven yourself a sympathetic guardian to Miss Lambe.'

'A guardian doesn't need to be sympathetic. My task is to see that she is taught to behave like a lady . . .'

But, Charlotte, who had warmed to her theme, wouldn't have this.

'That is the least of it!' she retorted. 'Georgiana is miles from home and you are the closest thing she has to . . .' She stopped and took a breath. 'And now you will tell me that I am speaking out of turn again and you do not care a fig what I have to say.'

His expression was still wry as he held up a hand.

'I invited your opinion. And actually – for once – there may be some small value in what you say.'

Charlotte was astonished by this admission. 'Coming from you, I shall own that as the greatest compliment imaginable.'

A silence fell as both pretended sudden interest in the street around them. It was Sidney who eventually spoke.

'Miss Heywood, I – I have been meaning to say: our meeting at the cove. I hope you were not too embarrassed.'

Charlotte hoped that her colour was already high from the drama of the operation.

'Why should *I* be embarrassed?' she said, with careful nonchalance. 'I was fully clothed.'

'Yes, good point,' he conceded. 'That was hardly fair of you, was it? To ambush me like that.'

She didn't know if he was teasing her or not. 'I can assure you it wasn't deliberate on my part,' she replied, annoyed when the words rang out so primly.

'Nor mine.'

'Well, then.'

'Well, then,' Sidney echoed. He was smiling now and she found she was doing the same.

Esther Denham was on the approach to Sanditon House. She was in high dudgeon after a very unsatisfactory exchange with her brother on the subject of that scheming hussy, Clara Brereton. Esther had taken him to task over Clara's performance in Dr Fuchs' bath earlier that day.

'I could scarcely believe how eagerly you raced to the mouse's aid,' she'd said, her tone veering between contempt and the searing jealousy she really felt.

'How would it have looked had I not?' Edward had replied rather wearily.

'As if you had not been hoodwinked by her pitiful attempt to gain our aunt's sympathy,' she returned.

He'd turned to her in astonishment then. 'You're not seriously suggesting that she deliberately . . . *wounded* herself?'

Remembering it now, as she waited for Lady Denham's butler to admit her, her fury was stirred again. How could he believe Clara's burn was accidental? Sometimes she believed the man she loved was little more than a fool.

'Why can't you see it?' she'd said. 'Are you completely under her spell?'

He had not liked that. 'There is nothing the least bewitching about her!'

Esther felt he rather protested too much.

'It is no good, Edward,' she said. 'If you are not prepared to confront her, then *I* will. We cannot allow her to get away with this!'

And that was how she now found herself being shown into the drawing room, where the hateful Clara was lying prone on the chaise longue, propped up by half a dozen silk pillows. With disgust, Esther realised that she was moaning softly.

'How are you feeling now, Clara?' said Lady Denham solicitously, apparently quite taken in.

'It is difficult to say,' came the tremulous reply. 'I am willing myself to be stoic, but it is so hard.'

'You poor child.'

Esther seethed at her aunt's credulity. The old woman was usually as sharp as a rapier.

'I still can't understand how it happened,' Esther said, eyeing her enemy coldly as she approached. 'Were it anyone else, one might almost suspect she had burnt herself on purpose.'

'Oh, Aunt, I am in agony!' cried Clara, writhing slightly.

'Of course you are!' Lady Denham shot Esther a reproving look. 'I fear sympathy is beyond my niece's abilities.'

With no little effort, Esther mastered herself. Her ability to change tack had always been her strongest suit. 'On the contrary,' she said. 'My heart bleeds for poor Clara.' She stood over her. 'Would it be a comfort if I were to sit and read to you awhile?'

Clara smiled angelically, though her blue eyes – should Lady Denham have been observing closely enough – were steely. 'I should like nothing better.'

After Lady Denham had left the room and some minutes of toneless reading had passed, Clara cut Esther off.

'You can stop now. She is out of earshot.'

Esther closed the book with a slap.

'I know very well you did this to yourself.'

'Do you?' said Clara mockingly. 'Then prove it. Lady Denham won't believe you. You and your brother can do what you like – you won't get rid of me.'

'I wouldn't be too sure of that.'

Clara put her head on one side. 'Your brother's trouble is that he is so, so easily led. He wants to resist me, but he can't.'

'You little bitch!' Esther's self-control was exhausted. She seized Clara by her injured arm and tightened her grip. 'How do you like that?' she hissed.

But Clara's delicate looks concealed a formidable opponent. 'Oh, Esther,' she said calmly, as if the pressure being applied to her arm was nothing at all. 'Did you imagine that any suffering you could inflict would bother me more than a fly crawling on me? You have no idea what I endured before I came here. And you have no idea what I am prepared to do to ensure I stay here. So you would do well to crawl away, and take your poor silly brother with you, if you don't want me to ruin him.'

Esther let her go, shocked to her core. She had badly underestimated the little viper.

'You may have got away with this,' she said shakily. 'But you will trip yourself up soon enough. And when you do, I will be waiting.'

She swept out of the room, hoping she appeared more unruffled than she felt.

After some searching, she found her brother up on the cliff, the sea breeze in his hair. The sight of him undid something deep inside her, as it always did. She wished it wasn't the case, but there seemed to be nothing to be done about it. He was her only weakness.

'Well?' he said when he caught sight of her. 'Did you vanquish the mouse?'

The unease that her walk from Sanditon House had done nothing to alleviate rose in pitch again.

'Clara Brereton is no mouse,' she said. 'She is a rat. She will chew off her own tail if it means surviving.'

Chapter Eighteen

At Trafalgar House, the operation was finished and Old Stringer was now out of danger, all thanks to the skill of Dr Fuchs. The patient, ready to be removed to his own bed, was being loaded with great care into the back of a handcart.

'There we are now,' said Mr Parker, much relieved. 'No permanent harm done, I'm glad to say!'

But Young Stringer, who was standing next to him, could no longer keep quiet. He turned to his superior.

'Time and time again I have tried to tell you we need more men, sir, but you wouldn't listen. And this is the consequence!' He gestured to the cart. 'Had the doctor not been close at hand . . .'

But his feelings overcame him and the sentence was left unfinished. He put on his hat and went to his father's side.

'Well now,' blustered Mr Parker, chastened and embarrassed by this unusual outburst from his young foreman. 'It's only to be expected that emotions are running a little high. Young Stringer's been through quite the ordeal. Still, on we go! No use dwelling on it!'

Neither Mary nor Charlotte could meet his eye. Fortunately, Dr Fuchs emerged from the house at that moment, bag in hand.

'*Ach so*, *Herr* Parker. The time has come for me to say *auf wiedersehen* once again.'

Mr Parker shook his head. Young Stringer's words still echoed in his head. 'No, Doctor,' he said firmly. 'No! You just saved that man's leg, nay – his very life! How can I possibly let you leave now?'

Once Dr Fuchs had been persuaded to stay, Mr Parker knew he must visit Lady Denham soon or incur her wrath when she found out from someone else what he had done. But if he had hoped to find her in an accommodating mood, he was mistaken.

'So he fixed a broken leg!' she said when he related Old Stringer's accident. 'That is the least I expect of a doctor.'

'He saved the man's life! If you had seen the state of Mr Stringer . . .'

Lady Denham fixed him with a gimlet eye.

'I have seen the state of Clara's arm. I was witness to her *immolation*!'

'That was unfortunate indeed. But Dr Fuchs assured me it was a freak occurrence.'

'It was certainly that!'

'My lady, Dr Fuchs has a reputation which spans the length and breadth of these Isles! My own sister and brother . . .'

Lady Denham snorted with derision. 'I would hardly consider *them* a barometer of sound judgement.'

'That is beside the point. They are prepared to spend money . . .'

Her eyes narrowed, a satisfied smile twitching at the corners of her mouth 'Ah, now we come to the quick of it.'

He turned his palms upwards. 'We need visitors, Lady Denham.'

'And you really think this man is going to reverse our fortunes? That a plague of hypochondriacs will suddenly descend upon us?'

'I believe that, as of this moment, he is our greatest hope.'

'Your only hope, you mean.' She was on the verge of dismissing him altogether.

He gathered his courage. 'I do not like to contradict you, ma'am . . .'

'Then don't!'

He persevered. '. . . But the fact of the matter is that you cannot have a seaside resort without a doctor. And there is no one more qualified than Dr Fuchs. I must insist that he stays.'

'Then you shall live with the consequences,' she said coldly, and quit the room without so much as a goodbye.

Mr Parker was so deep in thought as he walked back home from Sanditon House that he remained blind to the vistas that never usually failed to raise his spirits. The sea went unnoticed; the progress of the town unseen. There was some miserable relief in being alone, for at least he didn't have to maintain the exhausting cheerfulness he felt obliged to perform in front of his wife and children.

He was almost at the house when Young Stringer appeared on the street before him. As he had only just been thinking about him and his injured father, for a strange moment Mr Parker thought his strained mind had conjured up an apparition.

'Excuse me, Mr Parker, sir.' Like Mary, his foreman couldn't quite look him in the eye. 'I wanted to – that is to say – I owe you an apology. I spoke out of turn . . .'

'No, no,' Mr Parker interrupted, eager to articulate what he had just that moment decided. 'Think nothing of it. As a matter of fact, your father's accident has made me aware of – of certain improvements we could make to your working conditions. It strikes me that you could use more men, better equipment. I will see that you get them as soon as possible.'

Young Stringer's face cleared.

'Thank you, Mr Parker. I will let the other men know. They will be grateful indeed. As am I.'

Mr Parker waved Young Stringer's thanks away, embarrassed again. He knew this was overdue. 'Say no more about it. It is the least I can do.'

Pulling the door behind him, Mary appeared at the drawing room door.

'All is well?'

He pulled his face into a broad smile. 'Yes, yes. It was all a fuss of nothing! Easily remedied!'

She came forward and took his hands in hers, searching his face. 'My dear Tom, if there is something troubling you, I wish you would share it.'

For a brief moment, he considered what it would be to unburden himself, but knew he could not.

'Why should there be? You are far too inclined to worry, my dear!' He patted her hand and hurried off towards his study, afraid that if he didn't he would tell her of the anxiety that grew in him daily, like a tumour.

Charlotte was out walking, enjoying the golden patina with which the early evening light had gilded the town. Soon, she found herself at the river, whose waters burbled crystal-clear towards the sea, and walked idly along it, going over what had turned out to be a remarkably eventful day, from Dr Fuchs' doomed demonstration to Old Stringer's terrible fall.

The sound of voices up ahead brought her back to the present. Three children were gathered at the riverbank with their toy sailboats and, drawing closer, she saw that it was the Parker children: Henry, Alicia and Jenny. She was about to call out a greeting when she noticed who they were with, the realisation stopping her short. Kneeling there, sleeves rolled up and looking at least a decade younger as he smiled round at the children, was Sidney.

As if sensing her there, he turned, and she observed with dismay his demeanour immediately changing, as though he'd donned a mask once again. Little Alicia, following her uncle's gaze and quite oblivious to his change in mood, shouted in delight when she saw who had joined them.

'Charlotte! Come and play with us!'

'Oh, I . . .'

But the children's pleas were irresistible and she found herself being led down to the bank.

'We are having a sea battle with Uncle Sidney!' said Jenny.

Alicia pulled on Charlotte's hand. 'You have to be on our side.'

Sidney got to his feet and made much of brushing himself off so he wouldn't have to meet her eye, or so she suspected.

'Miss Heywood,' he said. 'You arrive at a rather critical juncture.'

'The British navy are about to rout the French!' cried Alicia.

'You can take charge of the French fleet,' said Jenny, regarding their small fleet with great seriousness.

Alicia was dancing with excitement. 'We shall call you *Admiral 'Eywood!*'

Charlotte laughed. 'I am not so sure I want to be routed!'

'Come on, Admiral,' said Sidney, thawing slightly. 'Don't be unsporting.'

Charlotte and the girls were in charge of the red boat, while Sidney and little Henry captained the blue.

'Come on then,' said Charlotte. 'We mustn't let those dreadful boys win.'

She and Sidney took up position next to each other, a boat each.

'I am afraid we have to win!' said Sidney. 'It is a matter of historical record, isn't it, Henry?'

Charlotte gave him a sidelong glance. 'Can we not rewrite our history, if we find it disagreeable?'

Sidney laughed and leant out over the water to place his boat on it just at the same moment Charlotte did. For an instant, their hands touched. They sprang apart, Charlotte rubbing her hand as though she'd been singed.

'Ready? Go!' shouted Henry.

The boats were released and Charlotte stood to watch their progress as they bobbed prettily downriver. The sight of it – the sparkling water, the sails bright against it, lit a spark in her mind.

'What is it?' Sidney said. He had been looking at her and seen her face change.

She smiled up at him. 'Something's just occurred to me. An idea . . .'

They were soon back at Trafalgar House, eager to speak to Tom. They found him in his study and, in the moment before he saw them, he looked as though he was carrying a heavy load, eyes shadowed and shoulders hunched.

'Sidney? Charlotte?' he said on noticing them, rousing himself effortfully. 'What is it?'

Sidney propelled Charlotte forward. 'Miss Heywood's had an idea. Not a bad one as it happens.'

'Has she?' He blinked wearily at her. 'Have you, Charlotte?'

'Well, it is just a thought. I hope you won't think I am trying to interfere.'

Sidney touched her arm. 'Go on, tell Tom. Just as you told it to me.'

'Well, I . . . I have been thinking about how you want to attract more visitors and I realised that what Sanditon needs is an event. Something exciting to draw people here. And once they arrive, of course they will fall in love with the place, just as I have.' She smiled, suddenly shy. 'Anyway, we were playing with the children, sailing their boats down by the river, when it suddenly occurred to me . . .'

She went on to explain and by the time she had finished, Tom looked like a new man, a genuine smile illuminating his tired face. Rushing to the door, he called into the hallway.

'Mary! I have had the most glorious idea! A regatta! To be held here in Sanditon.'

Mary came bustling in. 'A regatta!'

'Can you not just picture it, my dear? The river alive with a flotilla of boats – all shapes and sizes. The banks teeming with spectators – the ladies attired in the finest white dresses, and the gentlemen in straw hats! What do you say to it, Mary? Is it not a brilliant notion?'

She clasped his hands, relief and happiness mingling in her expression. 'Positively inspired, my dear!'

'It must be said that Miss Heywood deserves some credit,' said Sidney drily.

But Charlotte did not mind. She beamed back at him. After what Lady Denham had inferred about her outstaying her welcome, it was a great comfort to feel useful to her hosts. 'Oh, I merely provided the kernel of the idea,' she said modestly. 'It is Mr Tom who has brought it to life!'

Tom smiled at her fondly. 'No, no, Sidney is right. We must give credit where it is due, my dear. It was you who prompted me to have the idea. You are fast becoming quite invaluable, Charlotte. Whatever would we do without you?'

Sidney and his brother had retired to Tom's study after dinner, for a final conversation before Sidney finally left for London. The lamps had been lit, and the evening was beginning to press in through the undrawn curtains. Tom had lost something of his earlier enthusiasm, as though it was leaching away with the day.

'At least this time I leave knowing you are in good heart,' Sidney said encouragingly. 'A new physician; a regatta to plan. All is well with Tom Parker.'

'So it would seem.' Tom smiled, but something of his previous distraction was back in his face. As Sidney got up to take his leave, his brother spoke again, his tone carefully casual, 'Oh, I say, I just wonder if . . . while you are in London you could stop by the bank for me, see if they might consider extending me a little more credit . . .'

Sidney turned back to him, unable to keep the irritation out of his voice. 'For goodness sake, Tom. It's not as if I don't have my own affairs to—' He happened to glance out of the window, and saw Charlotte and his nieces enjoying the last of the day. The sight of them made him relent with a sigh. 'How much did you have in mind?'

He watched his brother's agitated hands run over the nearest stack of papers and wondered how many of them were unpaid bills.

'A couple of thousand ought to do it,' said Tom. 'Three at the most. It's just that with Fuchs and the regatta, I need to step things up if we're to be finished in time for the influx of visitors.'

'Very well, I will have an answer for you on my return.'

He watched his brother's face clear for the second time that day as he leapt up and called for his wife.

'Gather up the children,' he told Mary when she appeared with an enquiring look. 'We are going to the beach!'

'Right this minute? But it will be dark soon.'

'Then we'd better hurry!'

He turned to his brother with a grateful smile but Sidney, concerned now by how deep his brother was in this scheme, struggled to return it.

The beach was almost deserted when they got there. It looked quite magnificent with the tide out, the orange sun lowered almost to the horizon and casting rippling shadows across the sand.

'How glad I am to have my husband back,' said Mary happily as she took Tom's arm. 'I have missed that smile.'

'I'm sorry, my dear. I know I've been rather preoccupied of late. You do know it has no bearing on how much I dote upon you all?'

'Of course.' She gave him an impish look that reminded him of how she had been when they first met. 'But I never tire of hearing it spoken.'

Behind them, Sidney and Charlotte had fallen into step together.

'Miss Heywood, I wonder if I might presume to ask a favour?'

'Of *me*?'

'Extraordinary as it might sound.' He gave her one of his droll looks. 'But I believe you are better positioned than almost anyone else. Would you keep an eye on Georgiana for me? See that she is kept out of mischief?'

Charlotte couldn't help smiling at the irony. 'I thought you considered me to be a bad influence?'

'Is it conceivable that we have had each other wrong, Admiral Heywood?'

She gave him a sidelong smile. What a strange day it had been and, now, perhaps the strangest part of it was her realisation that not only did she no longer despise Sidney Parker, it was possible that she was beginning to like him rather well indeed. She glanced up at him again. It was excessively confusing.

After the walk on the beach, Sidney made his way to Mrs Griffiths' lodgings to say goodbye to Miss Lambe. She was in her room, sitting at the desk next to the window. The last of the sun's rays slanted across the blotter, turning it pale red.

'How long will you be absent?' she said when he told her.

'A week at least. I have pressing business matters.'

He watched her consider this. Then, with a determined nod, she raised her head.

'I am sorry my behaviour has been so wanting,' she said. 'I will strive to do better.'

He felt himself lighten, just as he had at the river with Charlotte.

'As will I,' he said.

Miss Lambe waited until she heard the front door close behind him, two floors down. She lifted the blotter and pulled out a half-written letter. Dipping her pen, she resumed writing, her hand moving fast over the page, as though it could never keep up with her thoughts. Breaking off, she reached into her dress at the bosom and pulled out something small and oval. It was a miniature of a man, handsome and black-skinned, his bearing proud and upright. She brought it to her lips and kissed it before tucking it out of sight once again.

Chapter Nineteen

A week later, Miss Lambe, blind to the fine morning outside her window, was pacing the floor of her room, ear cocked for the sound of her maid Crockett's tread on the stair. On eventually hearing it, she rushed to the door and snatched the letter she'd been praying for out of the maid's hand. Tearing it open, she scanned the lines and, as she comprehended their meaning, began to smile.

'It is good news!' she said to Crockett. 'Better than I'd dared hope for.'

A noise on the stairs made her startle. She stuffed the letter under her pillow.

'Not a word of it to anyone,' she hissed at the maid.

In the newer part of Sanditon, Charlotte had opened her own letter over breakfast. As glad as she was for the adventure of a new place, it filled her heart to see her sister's hand, which was almost as familiar as her own.

'Alison says our Harry's grown a whole two inches. I am certain she exaggerates. I have not been here three weeks!'

'Is that all?' said Mary. 'You are so much part of our family now that is seems far longer.' She looked at Mr Parker. 'Does it not, my dear?'

'Hmm?' He had clearly heard nothing of what they'd said.

Mary raised an eyebrow at Charlotte. 'I am sorry Mr Parker couldn't join us for breakfast. Apparently his mind has a prior engagement.'

That got his attention at last.

'Forgive me, my dear. It is only that . . . well, I had rather hoped the post might bring word from Sidney at last.'

'At last? He has been gone but a week!'

'Yes, I suppose that is not so long in Sidney terms.'

Charlotte gave an encouraging nod. 'I am sure you've no cause to doubt him. He seemed quite galvanised at the thought of our regatta and set off with great purpose.'

'Quite right, my dear!' he declared, in such an altered tone that it didn't ring quite true. 'He'll doubtless return with good news at any moment!'

The two women exchanged a glance and then, picking up the teapot, Mary gently steered the conversation into more benign waters.

'I am glad to hear you speak well of my brother-in-law, Charlotte. You were not always so convinced of his virtues.'

Charlotte felt herself colour slightly. It was vexing how he invariably had that effect. 'No, I admit I may have been a bit overhasty in forming an opinion. I fear I rather misjudged him.'

'Ha!' Tom slapped the table. 'You need feel no shame on that account. My brother's merits are often slow to advertise themselves.'

Charlotte smirked. 'Perhaps he is an acquired taste then, sir. Like anchovy paste?'

Tom was amused. 'Well said, Charlotte! That's it exactly. Far too peppery for me. But altogether habit-forming once you get the hang of it!'

Charlotte felt her cheeks redden again. Sensing Mary eyeing her beadily, she bent her head as if her boiled egg was an object of great fascination.

Another recipient of the morning's post was Lady Denham though, unlike Charlotte, she had not deigned to walk to meet the mail coach on Sanditon's high road, instead receiving her letters on a silver salver brought in by the butler. She sliced open the last of her small pile of correspondence and began to read but almost immediately flung the letter down on the table.

'Not bad news, I hope, Aunt?' said Clara.

Lady Denham was outraged. 'The Earl of Sussex is engaged! How dreadfully inconsiderate of him.'

She reached for the mysterious list which was now always about her person, and scored out one of the lines.

'I had no idea you were minded to marry again, Aunt,' said Clara idly.

Lady Denham threw her a look of utter contempt. 'I am not thinking of myself, you ninny! I already own a title and wealth. What possible reason could I have to marry a second time?' She swept her hand over her papers and letters. 'No, all this exertion is for the benefit of my ungrateful nephew and niece.' She tapped a be-ringed finger on the gilt arm of her chair and then reached for a clean card.

'That is typically generous of you, Aunt,' said Clara, lowering her eyes meekly. She had perfected the pose after weeks in Lady Denham's company.

'I know!' said Lady Denham as she wrote, somewhat mollified. 'My largesse shall be my downfall. As for your prospects, Clara, I fear they are beyond remedy.'

'I should be content to remain here as your ward forever, Aunt.'

'Hmp, well, nothing lasts forever.'

Clara found herself digging her fingernails into her palms. She watched as Lady Denham sanded and blotted her note.

'Here, you can deliver this to Denham Place for me.'

Clara read the names of her enemies written on its front. 'Oh, I would, Aunt. It is only that, with my injured arm—'

'For heaven's sake, child!' Lady Denham expostulated. 'It was barely a singe. You've had more than your measure of sympathy. A walk and some fresh air will do you good. Go on, run along now!'

With as much bad grace as she ever dared show, which was very little in her precarious position, Clara took the letter and hurried from the room.

After breakfast, Charlotte set off for a part of Sanditon she had not yet visited, beyond the building work and on through the old part of the town that seemed almost to cower at the feet of Mr Parker's ambition. There was hardly any wind out on the promenade, the sea below like a sheet of blue glass. The sun warmed the back of her neck most pleasantly.

The cottage where Mr Stringer and his son lived was perhaps a little ramshackle but no more than she had been used to in Willingden. To Charlotte, such a place was not cramped but homely-looking. She was looking forward to seeing her friend, and rapped smartly on the door.

Young Stringer was abashed when he opened it and saw who waited there.

'Please forgive the humble state of our dwelling, miss. It is hardly Trafalgar House, I am afraid.'

She was about to demur when a large shaggy dog raced out of the cottage to greet her enthusiastically.

'Down, Hercules!' cried Young Stringer, but Charlotte was already petting the scruffy animal.

'Oh, this is far more comfortable!' she said, looking up at him with a smile. 'In fact it much reminds me of my home.'

He led her into the cottage, which was gloomy after the bright sun. Old Stringer was sitting staring into the fire, his injured leg raised on a chair and a pair of rudimentary crutches propped next to him.

'Miss Heywood has come to see how you are recovering, Father.'

He nodded politely in her direction but didn't smile. 'Kind of you, miss, but 'tis a fuss over nothing. I have known far worse. You can tell young 'un here that I'm more than ready to resume my labours.'

Young Stringer sighed under his breath and Charlotte wondered how many times father and son had been over it. 'I am afraid my father is much mistaken,' he said. 'The doctor was clear . . .'

Old Stringer turned in his chair. 'Pah! He made a good enough job of my leg, but what does he know about masonry?'

Charlotte's eye had been caught by an intricate architectural drawing which was spread across the table and she wandered over to look at it more closely.

'A pagoda!' she cried. 'One of Mr Nash's designs?' She turned to Young Stringer who was shyly delighted.

'Inspired by him, I will admit. Mr Parker asked me to prepare it a few weeks ago.'

'Young 'un was up half the night with it. Wasted three candles!'

Charlotte frowned. 'Hardly wasted, sir. It is a work of art.'

'Beg your pardon, miss, but that is by the by. My son is a foreman. It is not his place to be drawing up plans.' Bitterness hardened his voice.

'But might a man not elevate his position, Mr Stringer, if he is blessed with talent and prepared to work hard?'

Old Stringer shook his head. 'I beg to differ, miss. You make the best of the hand you're dealt and it's a fool says otherwise.'

There was an awkward pause. Charlotte straightened the hem of her spencer.

'Well,' she said, with false cheer. 'I am glad to find you in such good heart, Mr Stringer, but I have kept you long enough.'

After she'd gone, her neat little figure disappeared out of sight, Young Stringer turned to his father.

'You had no need to be so rude.'

The old man shrugged, his gaze back on the fire. 'I was respectful enough. She is a lady. A guest of Mr Parker. She weren't here to seek out our friendship. Ain't my place to be familiar.' He lifted his eyes. 'Nor yours neither.'

'Meaning what?'

'You are the son of a mason. No use aiming for grouse when you should be shooting pigeons. Else you shall end up hungry.'

Young Stringer went over to the drawing on the table, brushed it with his fingertips and then rolled it up carefully.

Charlotte, feeling somewhat dispirited, and as though she might have blundered once again, was glad to coincide with Diana and Arthur Parker on the high street. They were walking arm-in-arm at their usual cautious pace.

'Good morning, Mr Parker, Miss Parker,' she called.

Arthur doffed his hat. 'And what a splendid morning it is, Miss Heywood!'

But his sister was fanning her face with a trembling hand. 'It is by no means splendid,' she said querulously. 'It is quite unbearable! If we are not blinded by the sun, we shall be incinerated by the heat!'

'Can't stop, I am afraid,' said Arthur to Charlotte. 'Dr Fuchs expects us for our daily repairs!'

Charlotte watched them go, cheered by the quirky pair. They might have been three score years and ten, not below thirty. What a curious assortment the four Parker siblings made. Before her mind could linger on a particular one of them, she set off towards Trafalgar House at a brisk pace, only stopping when she heard her name being called.

It was Miss Lambe's maid Crockett, who was quite breathless from chasing her. On learning that she was needed by Georgiana, she agreed to accompany Crockett back to Mrs Griffiths' lodgings.

'I came as fast as I could,' she said, after being shown up to Miss Lambe's bedroom. She took in the heiress's radiant smile and was confused. 'I was told it was an emergency?'

'Indeed it is! It is a glorious day and I am trapped inside with the Gorgon and those prattling Beaufort sisters. You must rescue me at once before I lose my mind.'

Charlotte was still perplexed. 'Rescue you? How do you propose I do that?'

Georgiana smiled mischievously and began to lay out her plan to convince her landlady to let her out that afternoon.

In the rather airless sitting room a few minutes later, Mrs Griffiths regarded Charlotte doubtfully. 'A picnic?'

'I thought since it is such a fine day . . .' she said lamely, wondering why she had been tasked with persuading her when it was Georgiana's idea.

'I am afraid is it out of the question!' said Mrs Griffiths with a pious shake of her head. 'Picnics are the preserve of farmhands and savages! It would quite undo all my efforts to improve Georgiana.'

Charlotte tried again. 'Forgive me, Mrs Griffiths, but I cannot entirely see the danger in eating out of doors.'

'It is an invitation to licentiousness! For a lady to be seated on the ground while eating in full view of anyone who cares to pass! That is not just undignified, Miss Heywood, it is ungodly!'

'But Mrs Griffiths,' said a determined Georgiana, 'what of Reverend Hankins' sermon about the loaves and the fishes. Could we not think of *that* as a picnic?'

Mrs Griffiths visibly deflated but then, catching sight of the Bible at her side, rallied.

'Well, whilst I am glad to hear the good Reverend's words struck such a chord, Georgiana, I must remind you that we are not in Galilee now!'

Miss Lambe paused, apparently deep in thought. Then she brightened. 'I wonder if it might reassure you to know that we shan't be alone? Mr and Mrs Parker will be joining us.'

Charlotte opened her mouth to demur but Georgiana gave her a sharp look.

'Mr and Mrs Parker?' exclaimed Mrs Griffiths. 'Well, why did you not say so?'

Mrs Griffiths reassured, the proposal was swiftly agreed, and there was no longer anything to detain the two young ladies. Clutching a basket in one hand, Miss Lambe used the other to pull Charlotte towards Sanditon's small selection of market stalls so they might purchase some items for their picnic. Her excitement now that her plan was underway lent her a hysterical edge. It was only as they made their way down towards the river that she noticed Charlotte's expression.

'What is it?'

Charlotte paused. 'It's just that I'm not sure I have ever seen anyone lie with such virtuosity.'

Georgiana dismissed this peremptorily. 'The fault is entirely hers. Were she not so pious, we'd have had no cause to lie. And it worked, did it not? Here we both are – at our liberty!'

Charlotte wasn't sure what to say and so said nothing. She was taken aback not only by Georgiana's guile but her determination when it came to getting her own way. They were by now walking along the riverbank. It was not the open glade where she'd sailed the toy boats with Sidney and the children, but a much more secluded spot. The sun was diffused by the branches overhead, dappling the damp ground underfoot with bright pennies of light.

'I have never been down this way before,' she said. 'It's rather removed, is it not?'

'That's what makes it so perfect!' returned Georgiana with a smile that made her look suddenly older.

They turned a corner and up ahead of them, half obscured by the trees, was a small stone temple. As they approached it, a most unexpected person stepped out from the dim recess of the doorway. Handsome, black-skinned and immaculately dressed, the sight of him stopped Charlotte dead.

'Oh!' was all she could think to utter.

She watched in astonishment as Georgiana threw herself at him. Instinctively, she took a step backwards, and it was then that he caught sight of her.

'Georgiana?' he said, suddenly fierce. 'Who is this?'

Charlotte, startled out of her surprise by his hostility, drew herself up. 'My name is Charlotte Heywood. And who, sir, might you be?'

The occupants of Denham Place had risen late. Esther was ensconced in the drawing room in a state of undress, wearing nothing but her chemise, through which it was possible to see the outline of her naked body. She ran a brush idly through her hair.

Sir Edward bustled in, clutching a letter.

'Look what the morning post has brought! Yet another billet-doux from your unflagging suitor.'

'Urgh,' she groaned, stretching like a cat for Edward's benefit. 'If you love me, you will burn it along with the others.'

'And deny us our morning's entertainment? Not a chance!'

He threw himself down, forcing her to move up, and tore open the letter from Babington. She watched him scan the lines, his smile mocking.

'*Others might find your silence disheartening,*' he began to read in a mocking tone, '*but I have always believed that a prize too easily won has no real worth.*'

Esther was growing annoyed. 'Edward, stop! You are making me bilious.' She stood and let her hairbrush drop to the floor. She knew that the light slanting softly through the dark nets at the window cast her in an ethereal light. 'If you wish to be useful, come here and lace me up.' She held up her corset with a teasing smile and was finally gratified when he came over and took hold of the stays. They met each other's gaze in the foxed mirror.

'Be sure to pull them good and tight. Unless you want me to look like a boy.' She pouted and saw the lust slacken his face.

'No one wants that,' he muttered into her neck and then pulled the laces tight, watching as her bosom was pushed up.

'I can't believe you aren't at least a *little* amused by the letters,' he continued, and Esther's pout was genuine this time.

'Is the notion that a man might be in love with me really so laughable?'

'Oh, *that* part I can entirely understand . . .'

She sought his eyes in the mirror. 'Harder, Edward!'

He pulled them hard, causing her to gasp.

'. . . it is the very idea that you could ever favour him that I find so . . . deliciously preposterous.'

She tilted her head to one side. 'But how can you be certain? Babington is passably handsome, outrageously rich, and a lord.' She let the words settle. 'For all you know, he wears down my resistance with every letter.'

He laughed, none of the jealousy she had hoped to inspire apparent in his expression. 'How many would-be suitors have I seen founder on the rocks of your disdain? It will take a bolder man than Babington to pierce your armour.'

A noise in the hallway made his head snap up.

'Who was that?' said Esther.

Edward shrugged. 'I don't know. Probably one of the servants.'

But Esther's lingering unease was well founded. In the gloom of the hallway, hurrying on silent feet back towards the front door she'd not long slipped through, was Clara Brereton. The excuse of Lady Denham's letter had offered her the perfect opportunity to confirm her suspicions about the Denham brother and sister. As she closed the door softly behind her, she was torn between shock and glee.

*

Charlotte, who had been put in a most awkward position on the riverbank, was no less torn than Clara Brereton, though for quite a different reason. She looked on as Georgiana clutched at the man who had been introduced as Mr Otis Molyneux.

'Has Otis not the most handsome face you've ever seen?' said Georgiana adoringly.

'Forgive her,' he remarked rather aloofly. 'She has far too high an opinion of my virtues. You may disregard almost everything she's told you of me.'

'As a matter of fact, she has told me nothing,' said Charlotte, looking pointedly at her friend. 'Until a moment ago, I did not even know of your existence.'

'I'm sorry, Charlotte. I couldn't risk anyone knowing of Otis's presence. The truth is we are forbidden from seeing each other.'

'By whom?'

'My wretched guardian, who else?'

Mr Molyneux turned back to Charlotte. 'Miss Heywood, I must thank you for delivering Georgiana to me. I am much in your debt, but we will not trouble you beyond this point.' Having summarily dismissed her, he turned back to Georgiana and began to lead her away. 'I have found the most perfect place for our picnic. Close your eyes.'

Both anxious and irritated that she now found herself cast in the role of disapproving chaperone, Charlotte could only go after them.

'I am sorry but I cannot simply abandon Georgiana.'

He turned and regarded her with weary condescension. 'She will hardly be *abandoned*. *I* will be keeping her company.'

'Forgive me, sir, but we have only just met. All I know is that you are forbidden from seeing each other. I gave my word I would keep an eye on Georgiana.'

'Your word? To whom?'

Charlotte looked down. 'Mr Sidney Parker.'

'You are his spy?' Georgiana's face fell in dismay and disappointment.

'No! I agreed to see that you were kept safe. That is all.'

But Georgiana's face had hardened. 'I thought you were my friend, not his,' she said, and, taking Mr Molyneux's arm, stalked away.

Miserably, Charlotte followed them. After some minutes, the path widened and a small wood carpeted in purple revealed itself as hundreds of bluebells, their clean, watery scent making them all stop and breathe deeply. Georgiana turned to her beloved with a delighted smile.

Charlotte couldn't remember ever feeling so trapped and put upon. Three was certainly a crowd, but as much as she wished she could simply walk away, she couldn't neglect her duty. If someone was to see Georgiana alone with a strange man, she would be ruined. Cross to be so cornered, she began to unpack her basket noisily, shaking out the blanket and rustling packets of food.

'I cannot imagine a lovelier spot,' Georgiana breathed, apparently oblivious.

'It would not be half so lovely without you in it,' Otis replied. He bent his head, intending to kiss her, but Charlotte was quicker.

'Tongue?' she cried.

They pulled apart and she held up the slices of meat to him, raising an eyebrow. 'Or a little pork pie perhaps?'

Mr Molyneux's nostrils flared in annoyance. 'Thank you. But I might take a drink first.' He poured himself a cup of beer and sat down next to Georgiana at the far end of the blanket.

'So tell me, Mr Molyneux,' said Charlotte. 'What is it that keeps you in London?'

'I am a merchant.'

'And what is it you trade?'

'Mind what you say, Otis. This will all be reported back to Sidney.'

'That is not fair.' When Georgiana said nothing, only looking petulant, Charlotte once more addressed Mr Molyneux. 'How is it that you and Miss Lambe became acquainted?'

Georgiana interrupted again. 'We met at a ball. Otis mistook me for a servant. He demanded that I fetch him a cup of wine.'

'I did not *demand*. I was quite polite about it.'

'The very request was offensive.'

'Only because you held yourself in such absurdly high esteem.'

'I found him to be rude and sanctimonious.'

'I found her to be spoilt and petulant.'

They gazed longingly into each other's eyes.

'I was uprooted,' said Georgiana with an adoring smile. 'Lost. In despair. Otis restored me to life. Those three months were the happiest I've known.'

Despite her inherent good sense, Charlotte found herself sighing dreamily.

'But then your friend Mr Parker took it upon himself to rip us apart and lock Georgiana away in this . . . backwater,' said Otis. He took his beloved's hand. The anguish in their faces was genuine but Charlotte couldn't forget the assurances she'd made to Sidney.

'However painful that might have been,' she said carefully, 'Mr Parker surely must have had Georgiana's best interests at heart.'

Mr Molyneux eyed her grimly. 'Then you clearly don't know Mr Parker as well as you think. Would you like some beer, Miss Heywood?'

Also out of doors in the clement weather were Diana and Arthur Parker. Though they wished heartily to be at home next to a good fire roaring in the grate, they were being led in a brisk walk across the beach by Dr Fuchs. This was not the kind of treatment they had sought from him. Solace was to be found in tinctures and unguents, not physical exertion.

'It's this dreadful hot weather, Doctor!' exclaimed Diana breathlessly, when she managed to catch up with him. 'It has swollen every one of my extremities!'

'You must stay calm, sister,' puffed Arthur at her other side. 'You will only exacerbate things.'

The doctor slowed a little to regard them with amused forbearance. 'I could see no evidence of swelling, *gnädiges Fräulein.*'

'Well, of course not!' cried Diana. 'It is as yet invisible to the naked eye, but if left unchecked, I dare not imagine the consequences. A friend of an acquaintance – a Miss Parsons – swelled to such a great size that to this day she is known as the Whale of Whitstable. So take out your needle and lance, Doctor! I implore you.'

Dr Fuchs stopped and smiled politely, only a little impatience creeping into his expression. 'It has been my honour to examine you twice each day this past week, and it seems clear to me, *gnädiges Fräulein*, that all of your symptoms derive from an acute case of hysteria. As for you, *Herr* Parker – your condition is entirely the result of a sedentary lifestyle. I believe you would both benefit from the same remedy.'

'And what, pray, is that?' said Diana tremulously, fearing the worst.

The doctor gestured triumphantly at a pair of donkeys standing nearby with their handlers. Their bridles clinked as they shifted on the sand. 'Regular and vigorous motion!' he cried.

Arthur shook his head in horror. 'Egad!'

Waterloo Terrace was beginning to resemble the completed street Mr Parker liked to imagine on the long dark nights when he couldn't sleep for thinking about the reams of unpaid bills on his desk; when the wind was keening in the chimneys and his worries seemed innumerable. At these times, he had always found it soothing to picture the terrace finished; every room taken for the season: his grand project realised.

And yet, now that the terrace was taking shape – tangible evidence that progress was being made; that the end was finally heaving into view – he didn't feel any relief. There was only more worry to add to the teetering burden he was already shouldering.

He was startled out of these black thoughts by his foreman, Young Stringer, who had approached clutching a large roll of paper.

'I have drawn up plans for the pagoda, sir,' he said eagerly. 'Just as you asked. Perhaps I could show them to you now?'

Mr Parker resisted the urge to close his eyes. 'Ah, yes, the pagoda!' he said with the false cheer that was becoming habitual. 'I'd quite forgotten about that. In fact, on consideration, I'm not so sure we need it. What purpose would it serve, after all?'

Young Stringer's face fell. He took a moment to reply and when he did, the gleam of enthusiasm in his eye had dimmed. 'We agreed it would provide a focal point for the seafront, sir . . .'

'Yes, well. Never mind. Why don't we concentrate on the job in hand?' Mr Parker gestured at the emerging terrace with a sweep of his hand, his guilt at dismissing Young Stringer's efforts making him impatient.

'I must say,' he continued, 'I had rather hoped the terrace would be further along by now.'

His foreman's jaw visibly tightened. 'So had I, sir. I'm afraid being a man down has slowed our progress . . .'

'Ah. Yes. Of course.' Mr Parker had the grace to look ashamed. 'I'm glad to hear your father is recovering well.'

Young Stringer ignored this, determined to make his point. 'Once the new labourers and equipment are in place, we shall soon pick up the pace. Have you any idea when that might be, Mr Parker?'

They met eyes for a moment, and each read the frustration in the others'. Mr Parker looked away first.

'Soon! Soon!' he said, too loudly. 'All in good time!'

But Young Stringer wouldn't be deterred. 'Sir, we were stretched enough when my father was working. You promised me a week ago—' His voice rose, causing a couple of the men to turn round.

Mr Parker's smile faded. He began to bluster.

'There are certain – arrangements I need to make first. That is all. Patience, Young Stringer!'

He turned on his heel and left without another word. Young Stringer watched him go. He was still holding the plans for the now-abandoned pagoda. If the other men hadn't been looking on, he'd have trodden them into the mud.

Instead, he decided to go home. He couldn't bear to be on the building site for another moment. It wasn't like him to feel so angry, so impotent. The thought of home – where the familiar gloom would be quite welcome compared to the mocking sun – was a balm.

He had forgotten that his father would be there.

'How goes our terrace?' he said before Young Stringer had even closed the door. 'I fear for the craftsmanship without me there.'

'Well, there is nothing to be done,' he replied, trying to quell the anger that was still simmering inside him. 'You're not likely to return any time soon. As for the men we were promised . . . I begin to wonder if Mr Parker's word has any worth at all.'

His father laughed bitterly. 'I told you it was a waste of time, young 'un. If you'd only listened to me.'

Young Stringer put down his plans with deliberate care. If he didn't, he feared he would throw them on the fire, or else bellow with fury.

'And what is it that makes you so wise, Father?' he said, trying to control his voice. 'Where have you been? What have you done?'

His father tutted and turned back to the fire. 'This life's been good to me. And it were enough for my father . . .'

'Aye, and his father before that.' Young Stringer's voice shook and he knew he would have to leave the room or they would descend into argument. 'But it's not enough for me,' he muttered under his breath, as he banged back out the door.

Close to the riverside, hidden among the deep carpet of bluebells, the afternoon was passing in a haze. Charlotte was persuaded to accept first one, then another cup of beer. Soon she was feeling a good deal more genial. Her companions had gone further still, and were now reclining on the rug with their shoes off.

'This is such a blessed relief from life in dull, dreary old Sanditon,' said Georgiana. 'How I wish we could escape it altogether.'

'Come, now,' said Charlotte, thinking of poor Tom's efforts. 'Sanditon is not as bad as all that. As a matter of fact, I am exceedingly fond of the place.'

'Fond of *what* exactly?' asked Mr Molyneux. 'I'm afraid its appeal is lost on me.'

She opened her mouth to reply but he had leapt up and was walking purposefully out of the woods and back towards the river.

'Otis, where are you going?' Georgiana called after him.

'You yearn to escape, and earlier I saw a boat just along the riverbank.'

Georgiana clapped her hands and jumped to her feet, scrambling after him excitedly. Charlotte stood to pursue the pair again, and found herself swaying slightly, her head thickened by the hot afternoon and the beer.

'You're not suggesting that we steal a stranger's boat?' she said when she caught up with them.

'Absolutely not, Miss Heywood. We are simply going to borrow it!'

Georgiana, who had begun dancing around with glee, tweaked Charlotte's skirt as she whirled past. 'Don't be such a stick-in-the-mud, Charlotte!'

'I am not a stick-in-the-mud. It is just that . . .'

'If you are worried about what Sidney will think then don't. He is in London. He need never know about any of this.'

Despite her earlier misgivings, the beer and lassitude of the last hours had done their work in softening her sense of propriety. With Georgiana's encouragement and the word *escape* echoing in her ears, she began to smile.

At the same moment, in the town above them, Sidney Parker was striding towards Trafalgar House, having just dismounted from his horse. He was quite evidently not in London.

Mary Parker was delighted to find him in her hall.

'Tom will be overjoyed to see you!' she exclaimed as she came forward to greet him. 'He has been so impatient for your return. I daresay you understand the source of his concern better than I?' She gave him an anxious smile.

Sidney paused but didn't seriously consider telling her the straits Tom was in. It was not his place.

'Tom asked for my help with the – the regatta,' he said evasively. 'That is all. Will I find him in his study?'

She looked embarrassed. 'I'm afraid I have no idea where he is.'

He turned to go and then stopped, shifting awkwardly. 'And what of your house guest?'

'Charlotte? She has gone to see Miss Lambe. They seem to have struck up quite a friendship.'

A small smile played at the corners of his mouth. 'Then she has been as good as her word. I am minded to visit Georgiana now. Perhaps I shall find Miss Heywood still with her.'

He gave his sister-in-law a nod and took his leave.

Diana and Arthur Parker, their unquestioning respect for a physician's instruction having overcome their extreme reluctance, were astonished to find themselves galloping across the sand. Or, at least, being led by two grooms in a stately walk on two of Sanditon's most peaceable donkeys.

'Going at quite a canter now, what?' said a much-roused Arthur to his sister. 'Is it not bracing?'

'That is hardly the word I would use,' she replied, knuckles white from her vice-like grip on the reins. 'I fear a fall at this speed would certainly prove fatal. And this bumping is playing havoc with my lumbago.'

'Well, I for one feel utterly invigorated! That Fuchs fellow is a German genius!'

Diana was dismayed. 'Oh, you poor soul. You have taken leave of your senses. All the jerking must have jangled your brain!'

'On the contrary. I feel as if I'm awakening for the first time. No more shall we confine ourselves to darkened rooms, sister!' He gestured at the glittering sea, the curve of the bay ahead. 'I am minded to follow this up with a ten-mile march!'

Diana was horrified; Arthur was her great ally in the battle against disease and bodily ruin — in truth, he was her only ally and comfort for much of the time. 'But Arthur, you and I are not built for such things,' she said plaintively. 'Our constitutions are altogether too delicate for physical activity.'

But the faraway gleam of the convert was in Arthur's eyes. '*Yours* may be, sister, but I'm starting to think I might be a sight hardier than I've been given credit for.'

'No, Arthur, please. You must listen to reason. Dr Fuchs doesn't know you like I do. No one does!'

She was about to entreat him further, as much for her own sake as his own, when she recognised the couple just up ahead.

'Mr Parker, Miss Parker,' Sir Edward called out as they drew closer. His sister merely nodded in greeting, as though that was quite imposition enough.

'I had no idea the two of you were so inclined to athleticism,' Sir Edward continued.

'Nor I, Sir Edward,' said Arthur good-naturedly, ignoring the other's mocking tone. 'Were it not for our marvellous new physician, I should never have discovered I have such a propensity for it. Tally Ho!'

And with that, he dug his heels in. The surprised donkey set off down the beach at a brisk trot.

'Arthur!' shrieked Diana, appalled. 'Wait! Do not leave me behind!'

She motioned for the groom to follow him.

The Denhams watched them go with supercilious amusement. 'What a preposterous pair!' said Edward with a laugh.

Esther eyed him suspiciously. 'You're in a peculiarly good mood.'

'Should I not be?'

'Our aunt has summoned us. That hardly bodes well.'

She was still thinking about the mysterious noise in the hallway just before the letter from their aunt appeared. She knew to her bones it hadn't been one of the servants.

'On the contrary,' said Edward blithely. 'She probably wants us to help Clara pack her bags!'

'You act as though this was nothing more than some schoolboy game.'

'It *is* a game! And soon enough, Miss Clara Brereton will be sent to the baths with a bloodied nose!'

Esther took hold of his chin and turned it so he had to look at her. 'And what then? What happens once this undignified contest is over?'

'Then? Then we shall have the life we deserve! No more mouldering walls and creaking floors. We shall assume our rightful place in one of the finest houses in the country. Think of the freedom our inheritance will buy! Have we not always dreamed of travelling?'

'A grand tour?' Esther grew thoughtful.

Edward took her hand. 'We shall enjoy a life that even poets would envy. We shall swim the Hellespont! Roam the canals of Venice! Whatever it is that your heart desires, my dear sister, you shall have it.'

She could not help smiling then, the unease that had been roiling inside her all day ebbing away. If Edward were right; if they could go to Europe, alone . . . For a moment, the possibility felt so close that she could almost taste it.

Chapter Twenty

Up on the shadeless cliff above Sanditon, the sun was beating down relentlessly. It was too hot for many to have ventured out and the path was deserted but for a handful of gulls eyeing the sea below. As a peculiar-looking creature heaved into view, a strange noise emanating from it, they lifted into the air in fright. The portly figure did not so much walk as stagger. As he came closer, the noise revealed itself as a Scottish air.

'*For a' that, an' a' that,*' puffed Arthur Parker, for it was he, but half a mile into his first ever ten-mile walk. After the success of the donkey ride, Diana had been quite unable to dissuade him from setting out on it immediately.

> *Our toils obscure an' a' that,*
> *The rank is but the guinea's stamp . . .*

He rounded a corner and was faced with an approaching party of ladies armed with parasols. Taking out his handkerchief, he mopped his forehead and attempted to regulate his breathing. His face was the precise colour of beetroot.

'Ladies,' he began, as he moved aside to let them pass. 'A . . . most . . . goodly day . . . for a . . . constitution . . . a const—' But the words had used up the last of his dwindling stock of breath. He stumbled forward, his knees going down on the stony path as the ladies gasped. With relief, and a last thought that Diana always knew best, he gave himself up to blessed unconsciousness.

He knew no more until he came round and saw Diana's dear face looming over his, framed by a celestial blue sky. For a moment he believed himself in heaven but then Diana turned to address someone and he saw it was Dr Fuchs.

'Be honest, Doctor,' she was saying, 'is there a chance he may yet live? Or must we accept what is to come?'

Shockingly, the doctor barked out a laugh. 'My dear *Fräulein* Parker, I have but rarely known a case of sunstroke to be fatal.'

'Sunstroke?'

'*Ja, ja.* That is why at this moment his epidermis has the appearance of a boiled ham!'

Diana clasped her hands together in profound gratitude.

'But if I may,' Fuchs continued, 'Rome was not built in one day. The next time you exercise, *Herr* Parker, I suggest that—'

'The next time?' said Diana in disbelief. 'We have surely proven beyond a doubt that such exertions have a pernicious effect on my brother!' She turned to Arthur and dabbed at his forehead with her handkerchief. 'I am sorry, but I can never allow you to exercise again. From now on, you are to move only when it is essential.'

Arthur closed his eyes. 'Very well, sister. If it will put your mind at rest, I shall henceforth restrict myself to a recumbent position.'

Diana patted his hand and gave him an affectionate smile. 'Dear Arthur.'

A borrowed fishing skiff cut through the green water of the river. Its three occupants were in a state of quiet bliss, the breeze cool on their faces. While Georgiana and Mr Molyneux clasped hands, Charlotte's fingers were trailing in the water. She was halfway to sleep.

'I wish we could carry on forever,' said Georgiana softly. 'Follow the current to the sea and just keep on. Then no one could keep us apart.'

'There is a way we can be together forever,' he said meaningfully.

She gave him an anguished look.

'Not again, Otis. It is not fair.'

Without warning, he stood up in the boat, which made it rock. Charlotte grabbed the sides in fright.

'Georgiana Lambe,' he said, hand on his chest. 'I cannot live another day without you at my side. I must beg that you do me the honour of becoming my wife.'

Charlotte gaped at him in disbelief but he had not finished.

'And I swear that if you refuse me this one last time, I shall be forced to throw myself overboard.'

Georgiana was near tears. 'I cannot marry without Sidney's consent. You know that. If my life were my own, how different the answer would be.'

Mr Molyneux nodded, his expression grave. Charlotte felt quite bereft herself.

'Well,' he said, in tones of heavy sorrow. 'Never let it be said that I am not a man of my word.'

Without ado, he jumped overboard, disappearing beneath the surface as though he'd never been there. Charlotte and Georgiana leant over the side as one, the boat rocking dangerously once more, and stared horrified at the water, their fears multiplying as it remained undisturbed. Just when Charlotte was certain he was lost, he surfaced, water beading in his tightly curled hair, his face split by an enormous smile.

'You fool,' exclaimed Georgiana, laughing even as her tears fell. 'You stupid fool.'

He swam to the boat and pulled himself over the side, tumbling into Georgiana's arms and saturating her dress. Their joy was so tangible that Charlotte couldn't stop herself first from smiling and then bursting into wild laughter. She had never met anyone like them, so in love, so unconstrained. It only brought Sidney's determination to keep them apart into sharper relief. She had at various times regarded him as disobliging, insufferably arrogant and rude, but she had never had to admit the notion that he might be cruel.

Esther and Edward Denham had been shown into Lady Denham's drawing room. The late afternoon sun without, richly enhanced by lit candelabra within, served to make the room an even more opulent setting than usual. Clara was already seated, her creamy skin and pale hair glowing in the flattering light. A satisfied smile rather spoiled the angelic effect.

'For too long, the pair of you have idled about in the vague hope of some future inheritance,' Lady Denham began in on the Denhams, without preamble. 'Well, it will not do! You may have squandered your chance with Miss Lambe, Nephew, but there is plenty of more low-hanging fruit to be found, if you know where to look.'

She reached into her reticule and, with a stern look that didn't auger well, pulled out a piece of paper.

'You have drawn up a list?' Sir Edward was aghast.

'In descending order of eligibility. Naturally the primary requirement is wealth, followed by title . . .'

'And what about beauty, charm . . .?'

She silenced him with another look. 'Don't be pedantic!' Adjusting the pince-nez on her nose, she consulted her list. 'A gentleman in Norfolk named Marston has eighty thousand and six daughters. The eldest is married but he has struggled in vain to find a taker for the second. I cannot think why – I'm told you barely notice the squint from side-on.'

'Aunt, please,' said Sir Edward despairingly.

Esther, looking up, realised that Clara was smiling fixedly at her. It was disquieting. She glared at her, which only seemed to amuse Clara more.

'For heaven's sake,' Lady Denham was saying, 'he still has four other daughters. I can't believe one of them won't be to your liking. I shall arrange a visit.'

'That is kind of you, Aunt, but . . .'

She ignored him and turned to Esther, who straightened her shoulders for the assault.

'As for you, if you can keep that scowl off your face for long enough, there is no reason we shouldn't find you a husband by Michaelmas.'

'I wouldn't count on it,' said Sir Edward, determined to battle on, even in the face of a superior foe. 'Given how skilled Esther is at deterring suitors. Even Babington is bound to give up sooner or later.'

Lady Denham went quite still. '*Lord* Babington?'

Missing his sister's repressive look, he nodded eagerly at his aunt. 'Oh, he is quite besotted.'

Lady Denham threw down her list and fixed Esther with a beady eye. 'And? I trust you have been fanning the flames of his ardour?'

'Certainly not. I have been ignoring him.' She noticed Clara, who was now smirking into her lap, unsettling Esther again.

'You foolish, ungrateful child!' exclaimed Lady Denham. 'Lord Babington could hardly be a better prospect if he were advanced in years and in poor health! He would be a perfect husband!'

'For someone else perhaps.'

'And why not for you? What is it that you want?'

Esther felt suddenly too hot.

'Could it be that no one else will ever measure up to Edward?' Clara said sweetly.

'It is a fair question, I grant you!' said Sir Edward. 'I am more or less peerless.'

Never had Esther wanted to slap him so much as she did then.

'I have rarely seen two people enjoy such intimacy,' went on Clara in a musing tone. 'If you could,' – a tinkling little laugh – 'I suspect you would marry each other!'

Thankfully, their aunt seemed baffled by this. 'Really child, what nonsense you talk! Why would anyone wish to marry their own brother? I have never heard anything so preposterous.'

Lady Denham wanted music then, and Clara obediently took her place at the pianoforte. While Sir Edward was apparently only a little chastened, Esther felt queasy with foreboding.

'This piece is to be played *allegretto*,' cooed Clara. 'I will need some help turning the pages. Esther! Would you be so kind?'

'Oh, I have no talent for reading music.'

Clara smiled beatifically. 'No talent is required, my dear. I shall simply nod when the moment arrives.'

Esther didn't move but Lady Denham would not be kept waiting.

'Well, you heard her!' She gestured to the instrument. 'Up you trot!'

Esther sat down as far away from Clara as the stool would allow.

'Do you care for Italian songs, Esther?' mused Clara as she began the piece.

'Not in the least.'

'Shame. Perhaps your tastes run closer to home?'

Esther regarded her with as much disdain as she could muster in her anxious state. 'I find silence is much undervalued.'

But Clara would not be deterred. 'If I were an aria, I believe my tempo would be *semplice*. Do you know Italian, my dear?'

Esther turned the page with a trembling hand at Clara's nod. 'Well enough.'

'It means "simple". As for you . . . I think – this evening at least – you would be *agitato*.'

'You are confusing agitation with boredom.'

'And what of Edward? What kind of tempo should we give to him?'

A bead of perspiration inched down Esther's spine. It was she who was the mouse now.

'I do not see the point of this exercise.'

'We are amusing ourselves, that is all! How would you describe him? *Giocoso*? He is undeniably playful. But perhaps that does not go far enough. You would know better than I. How about *lusingando*? *Forza*?' She broke off from playing to look Esther right in the eye. '*Appassionato*?'

Esther could bear it no longer. She jumped up from the piano stool.

'Esther?' exclaimed Lady Denham. 'Whatever is the matter?'

'This mawkish music is insufferable,' she managed to say as she fled towards the door to the garden. Sir Edward stood, concerned, but Clara was already on her feet.

'Do not trouble yourself. I will see to her.'

*

In the stultifying sitting room of Mrs Griffiths' lodging house, she and Mr Hankins were trying to listen to the Beaufort girls reading a scene from *Twelfth Night*. The sisters' astonishing lack of expression was in danger of sending their small audience to sleep.

'*The honourable lady of the house, which is she?*' intoned Phillida.

'*Speak to me,*' said Julia, reading over her sister's shoulder. '*I shall answer for her. Your will?*'

'*Most radiant, exquisite and unmatchable beauty, I pray you, tell me if . . .*'

But Mrs Griffiths could bear it no longer. 'Really, girls,' she said, interrupting. 'You might put a little feeling into it. It is supposed to be poetry, after all.'

'Not too much feeling though,' put in Mr Hankins. 'Unrestrained passion in a young lady is a very dangerous thing.'

Mrs Griffiths sighed happily. 'How wise you are, Mr Hankins. Are you fond of Shakespeare yourself?'

'More of the comedies than the tragedies, madam. Indeed, as a younger man, I once played in *A Midsummer Night's Dream* and, if I may, I received a great deal of praise for my Bottom.'

Mrs Griffiths clasped her hands together. 'How I wish I could have seen it!'

As the Beaufort girls dissolved into helpless giggles, Sidney Parker was shown in.

A surprised and slightly hot-faced Mrs Griffiths rose to her feet.

'Mr Parker! I had no idea you were back in Sanditon.'

'I am sorry to interrupt, Mrs Griffiths. I came to see Georgiana.'

'Alas, she is not here. She and Miss Heywood are guests at your brother and Mrs Parker's picnic.'

Sidney frowned. 'You must be mistaken. I have just now come from Mrs Parker. I saw no sign of a picnic, nor of my ward.'

'But she said . . .' Mrs Griffiths stopped and, as everyone in the room understood the deception, put a trembling hand to her forehead.

Back on the river, the illicit boat trip was coming to its end. Mr Molyneux steered them deftly towards the bank and leapt out to pull the small vessel out of the water.

'Otis was more or less raised on the water,' said Georgiana admiringly, when they were all on dry land again. 'He is half man and half porpoise.'

'Was your father a mariner then, sir?' said Charlotte.

He paused. 'No. But the man who gave me my freedom was.'

'Your freedom?' Charlotte was confused.

'I was born in Africa but taken from my mother and sold as a child. But then providence placed me in the path of a gentleman. He gave me freedom, an education. That is why I spend my days fighting for the liberty of others.'

'Otis belongs to the Sons of Africa,' said Georgiana. 'They are devoted to ending enslavement for good.'

'But surely slavery is now mercifully consigned to history?' said Charlotte.

'Would that were so, Miss Heywood. I'm afraid there are thousands who yet remain in bondage. And its legacy is all around us.'

'I'm not sure what you mean.' She knew well how young and naive she sounded and was embarrassed for it.

'It's in the sugar in your tea.' He gestured towards her. 'It's in the cotton of your dress. It's in the grand houses of half the nobility of this country, built with fortunes wrung from the blood and toil of my brothers and sisters.'

Georgiana leant towards her. 'Perhaps you should ask your friend Sidney Parker how he came by his fortune.'

Charlotte felt herself sway. She couldn't tell if it was from the sudden absence of the water's movement or shock at this revelation. She remained deep in thought as they walked back to the bluebell woods to collect their belongings. Georgiana was by now growing distressed, having realised that Otis's departure would soon be upon them.

'You cannot leave yet,' she said tearfully. 'It is too soon! You have only just arrived.'

'It shall not be long before I return. There is not a thing on God's earth that can keep us apart.' He kissed her and it seemed to calm her.

'I will walk you to your coach,' she said.

Otis shook his head. 'We cannot risk being seen together.'

'I know of a back route,' said Charlotte. 'There is far less chance of our being discovered.'

Otis stopped and turned to her. 'Forgive me, Miss Heywood. I fear I was rude when first we met.'

'I was hardly charitable towards you either.' She paused. There was something she wanted to know. 'I must ask – for the life of me, I cannot think what Sidney's objection to you could be?'

He hesitated, suddenly uncomfortable.

'Is it not obvious?' Georgiana said quietly. 'Look at him.'

Charlotte was rendered speechless again and they continued back towards Sanditon in pensive silence. Soon they were passing along a quiet backstreet, eliciting curious looks from the mercifully few people they passed, not least because Mr Molyneux's fine clothes were dripping wet.

At the end of the road, Charlotte peeped around the corner. 'The London coach stands ready,' she said, turning back to her companions. 'Mrs Griffiths will never know you were here.'

'Can you imagine what she would say if she knew?' said Georgiana, managing to raise a smile. 'I fear she would actually burst into flames.'

Charlotte, happy leave the difficult earlier conversation behind, put on a dour expression that was not unlike Mrs Griffiths.

'Really, Miss Lambe. Look at the state of you! This licentious behaviour will not do. I shall be asking the Reverend Hankins to pray for your soul!'

It was a passable impression and Georgiana laughed.

'He can pray all he likes,' she said, when she had recovered herself. 'I don't think his God is the same as mine.'

Charlotte tried another impersonation, this time taking on a proud stance, her brow furrowed exaggeratedly.

'You see, Georgiana, this is exactly why I locked you away in Mrs Griffiths' dungeon!'

'Oh, now that *is* uncanny,' said Georgiana, impressed.

Charlotte struck another pose. *'To keep you out of mischief while I, Sidney Parker, gallivant around London with my high society dandy friends!'*

'Stop.' There was a warning note in Mr Molyneux's voice.

'No, do go on,' said a deep voice from behind Charlotte. 'I am intrigued to know what I might say next.'

She spun round, heart beating wildly. She had not known Sidney had approached but he must have heard every word of her mockery. Mrs Griffiths and Mr Hankins stood close behind him. Sidney was not looking at her now, however. His attention had been drawn by someone else.

'Mr Molyneux,' he said with terrifying coldness. 'You are the very last person I'd hoped to find in Sanditon.'

But Mr Molyneux was not cowed. 'Forgive me, sir, I would have notified you of my visit, but I could not be certain of the welcome I would receive.'

'You could be entirely certain. My position has not changed. Nor will it. The London coach departs in ten minutes. Allow me to assist with your passage.'

He reached for his pocket book but Mr Molyneux was shaking his head, a look of disdain on his face.

'Thank you, sir, but I wouldn't dream of accepting *your* money.'

Sidney turned to Georgiana.

'We have plainly allowed you far too much liberty. Mrs Griffiths, see to it that Miss Lambe is not afforded any chance to see this man again.'

The toadying Mrs Griffiths almost bobbed a curtsey. 'Very good, Mr Parker.'

Sidney turned back to Otis. 'And if I ever find you within a mile of my ward again, I shall not be responsible for my actions. Am I understood?'

Mr Molyneux's eyes blazed. 'Perfectly.'

'Kindly take Miss Lambe back to her lodgings,' said Sidney, addressing Mrs Griffiths once more.

Otis gave Georgiana a long, meaningful look and then walked away, in the direction of the coach house. She, overcome, looked as though she might faint away. Mrs Griffiths rushed forward to catch her.

'Come, my dear. We don't want to make a spectacle of ourselves, do we?'

Charlotte, quite distraught for her friends, found herself stepping forward. 'Wait! You could at least allow them a proper parting.'

Sidney turned to her with a thunderous expression. 'Thank you, Miss Heywood. This is not your concern.'

Mrs Griffiths began to lead a boneless Georgiana away, half-carrying her. 'This is what will come of your picnicking, Georgiana!' she muttered. 'You cannot say you were not warned.'

Sidney and Charlotte were left alone.

'Did we not agree you would look out for Georgiana?' he said tightly. 'I should have known you were not to be trusted.'

Charlotte was wounded but determined. 'And I should have known that despite your professed concern, you care nothing for her happiness.'

He ran a hand through his hair and groaned in pure frustration. 'I'd ask you to refrain from judging a situation you don't understand.'

'I understand perfectly well.'

He shook his head at her. 'Of course you do! Even though you have known Georgiana but a handful of weeks and him a matter of hours.'

'That was time enough to learn that Mr Molyneux is as respectable a gentleman as I have ever had cause to meet.'

Sidney sneered. 'Given that you have spent your entire life in Willinghurst that is hardly saying much.'

'Willing*den*. And I do not see any need for your conde-scension, sir.'

'You seem to find it impossible to distinguish between the truth and your own opinion!'

Charlotte lost her temper. 'The truth! You wish to speak of the truth, Mr Parker? The truth is that you are so blinded by prejudice that you would judge a man by the colour of his skin alone . . .'

His countenance darkened. 'You speak out of turn.'

But she couldn't stop now. 'Why should I expect any better from a man whose fortune is so tainted with the stain of slavery?'

'That is *enough*!' he shouted, so loudly that several people turned. Young Stringer, who had just spotted Charlotte and was making his way over, stopped dead.

Sidney opened his mouth and Charlotte thought that he would refute what she'd said but he just shook his head, face rigid with anger. The sight of it made her quail.

'I have no need to justify myself to the likes of you,' he said eventually, and she could think of no response. 'Mr Stringer!' he went on, beckoning the younger man over. 'Be good enough to see Miss Heywood back to Trafalgar House.'

'Thank you,' she threw out to Young Stringer, 'but I am in no mood to go home. I think I shall take a walk!'

With that, she marched off in the direction of the cliffs, Young Stringer hurrying after her. It wasn't until they were high above the sea, the wind in their hair, that she was calm enough to speak.

'Forgive me, Mr Stringer. I fear I am very poor company.'

'On the contrary, miss, after the day I've had, a walk in companionable silence is just what is needed.'

Charlotte felt rather foolish now her anger had left her. 'I am rather ashamed of myself, for losing my temper like that.'

Young Stringer smiled. 'If it helps, I've lost my temper twice today, and it took all my powers of restraint not to lose it a third time. I'm sure you wouldn't lose your temper unless you had good reason.'

'Oh, I did! Indeed, I did. But still, it is hardly seemly for a young lady to disagree with a gentleman like that.'

'Perhaps a gentleman shouldn't give a lady cause to disagree with him in the first place.'

She gave him a smile. 'Certain people are inherently disagreeable. You can try to convince yourself otherwise, but the more you get to know them, the more you realise just how disagreeable they really are.'

Young Stringer regarded her with something like awe. He had never in his life met a woman to match her. 'Upon my word, miss,' he said, with an admiring shake of his head. 'You are not afraid to speak your mind!'

'Perhaps I should be. Perhaps I would do better to merely simper or . . . or say nothing. Is that not what young ladies are supposed to do?'

'Please don't,' he said firmly. 'I wouldn't wish you to change for anything.'

Charlotte turned to him, her fury briefly forgotten, and gave him a smile.

'I fear you may be alone in that opinion.'

'And what does it matter what young ladies are supposed to do,' he continued, warming to his theme now he had Charlotte's approval. 'We can't let others dictate who we should be. We have to be true to ourselves, don't you think?'

'I could not agree more.' She smiled again. 'Thank you, Mr Stringer. 'Would that all men could be like you.'

Distracted as she was, she didn't notice the delight suffusing his face, the mooncalf glow in his eye. 'And would that all ladies could be like you, Miss Heywood,' he murmured.

Chapter Twenty-One

In a secluded corner of Lady Denham's garden, where the shadows were thickest as the day came to its end, Clara found her quarry. Esther whirled round when she heard her step.

'One of your servants must have left the door unlocked,' said Clara in a tone that was softly dangerous. 'I wanted to be certain that you received the invitation.'

Esther drew herself up but there was fear in her eyes, visible even in the failing light. 'A person with the least breeding would not have presumed to enter,' she managed to say.

'I thought at first the house was unoccupied but then I heard your voices – I didn't like to disturb you. I must say, it is kind of Edward to help you dress in the morning. I wonder . . . does he also undress you at the day's end?'

Esther realised she was backing away and stopped herself. 'One cannot lace one's own petticoat and I didn't have a servant to hand. That is all.'

'I see. So why did you leap up from the piano with such a start?'

'I couldn't bear to hear you torture it for a moment longer. My ears were affronted.'

Clara took a step forward. 'I'm sorry you don't like me, Esther. I'd always hoped we might even find a sort of kinship.'

'Then you will hope in vain.'

Clara smiled. 'Men can be so artful in their persuasion, can they not? And it is so much harder to resist when you are sleeping under the same roof. For me, it was an uncle.'

'You are not suggesting that I'm the victim of some . . . unnatural coercion?' Esther heard herself splutter.

'He is your brother. What could be more unnatural than that?'

'By marriage alone! We share no blood! Were it not for the fact that we bear the same name, we would be . . .' She stopped. She was breathing hard.

'You would be what?'

Esther racked her brains but no answer came.

'Oh, no.' Clara's smile was wider now; triumphant. 'No. It cannot be. You are not – in love with him?'

'What? I – That is the most ludicrous thing I have ever heard!' The words sounded hollow.

'Of course you are. It is so obvious now that I think of it. My poor, dear Esther. You have my pity.'

'I have no need of your pity.'

'Oh, but you do. I've seen enough of Sir Edward Denham to know how this story ends.'

'Do not presume to know the first thing about my brother.'

'May I give you some advice, my dear? Listen to our aunt. Find yourself a wealthy husband now, while you still can. Because whatever this happy future is that you imagine for the pair of you, it is quite impossible. But you must know that.'

Then she turned and walked back towards the house, leaving Esther in the gloom, all dreams of her and Edward's grand tour dissolving into the twilight.

*

In the privacy of the coach returning them to Denham Place, Sanditon House and Clara Brereton thankfully retreating behind them, Edward turned to Esther.

'I do wish you would tell me what the matter is. You have scarcely uttered a word since we left. And whatever kept you and Clara so long in the garden?'

She looked straight ahead. 'Idle gossip. Nothing of any consequence.'

'I didn't think her playing up to much. A bit mechanical. There was no feeling in it.'

'She is a wretched woman,' exclaimed Esther. 'I am sick of her. I am sick of it all. The entire stupid . . . game.' Her voice cracked on the last.

'Then it's a good thing it's almost won,' said Edward, sitting back with satisfaction. He didn't seem to have noticed the depth of her distress. There was very little he seemed to notice at all.

'Is it?' she cried. 'I don't see how we shall ever be rid of Clara. Our aunt won't give us another shilling while she lives, and there's every chance she'll live another twenty years!'

Edward laughed. 'We'd have to be extremely unlucky.'

'And what are we to do in the meantime? How long are we to continue with this . . . this *half-life*?'

He looked astonished at this outburst. 'What is the alternative?'

'You said it yourself. We could escape all of this.' She clasped his hand. 'Swim the Hellespont. Cruise the canals of Venice. Why wait for our life to begin when it could begin this very moment?'

Edward pulled away. 'In case you have forgotten, we are dirt poor. We could scarcely afford the most basic apartment. And what if Clara were to seize the advantage in our absence?'

'What if she does?' Esther flung herself back in her seat with frustration. 'It is only money! We will have each other. Is that not enough?'

Edward was still looking at her curiously. She took a deep breath. There were times to leave things unsaid. Perhaps this should not be one of them.

'There is no one alive I love so much as you,' she said, voice trembling with emotion. 'Tell me you do not feel the same?'

'Of course.'

She let herself loosen. But he had not finished.

'You are my sister. You are all the family I have. But I do not see the merit in running away. That money is our birthright. We must be practical, Esther. Our aunt was right. Sooner or later, I must find a wife. You, a husband. Else what kind of future can we look forward to? We will find ourselves twenty years from now still living in some miserable little cottage! Can you imagine?'

She felt herself die a little inside. There was nothing he had said that she didn't already know – she was sharper than he and always had been – but it still smote her to hear the words spoken aloud. The carriage clattered on towards Denham Place as she turned her face to the window. She was grateful to the noise and the dark, which prevented him from witnessing her tears.

'Of course you are right, brother,' she said in a low, despairing tone she knew he wouldn't discern. 'For a moment there, I quite forgot myself.'

Chapter Twenty-Two

Sidney and Tom Parker were in the latter's study. Tom's appearance was rumpled, the shadows beneath his eyes the colour of ash.

'No, no, no,' he was saying. 'That's not possible. There must be some sort of mistake. Did you not explain about the regatta – that we're soon to be the most popular resort on the south coast?'

His brother sighed. 'I spoke to three different banks. None of them were willing to extend your credit any further.'

'Then what do you suggest I do now, Sidney? Hmm? What *exactly* do I do now?'

His agitation made him accusatory but Sidney knew Tom well enough to know that his cross words masked the fear beneath. Still, he felt he had already shown a great deal of sympathy and support for his idealistic brother's grand project. If this setback slowed his brother's profligacy, perhaps it was no bad thing.

'I'm sorry, Tom,' he said. 'I have done as much as I can. I am not your keeper. I will gladly own my mistakes but I cannot own yours.'

He stood and walked from the room. In the hallway, he encountered Charlotte. He was hardly surprised, so often did they seem to coincide.

'Miss Heywood.'

'Mr Parker.'

All their amiability after they had sailed the children's boats had gone, entirely undone by the episode with Otis Molyneux and the ugly conversation that followed it.

'I expect you will be wanting to apologise,' he said, looking down his nose at her.

She bridled at that. 'Then I must disappoint you.'

He watched her walk away, her narrow shoulders set with determination, and sighed.

After the door closed behind his brother, Tom allowed himself to put his head in his hands. Then he remembered something – a purchase he had made on a whim the previous day. He opened a desk drawer and fingered the small box that was hidden inside. A necklace for Mary. A necklace he could ill afford.

At that moment, as if she knew, he heard his wife's light step on the stairs. She came in beaming.

'You see?' she said triumphantly. 'I told you Sidney would return before long.'

He attempted a weak smile. 'Right as always, my dear.'

'And? Was his news as good as you had hoped?'

With an enormous effort, he straightened in his chair. Inside him, fear and dread formed impossible knots. He looked deep into Mary's eyes and knew himself to be a hair's breadth from telling her everything: the mounting debts, the slowing pace of the work, Lady Denham's threats. The trouble was, he loved her too much. He couldn't bear to see the light in her face gutter and go out.

'Better, even!' he said with his last ounce of willpower. 'Sidney has worked wonders!' With a trembling hand, he fumbled for the box. 'As a matter of fact, I have bought you a little something to celebrate.'

'Tom! You had no need to.' She was delighted with it.
'Think of it as a promise.'

She fastened the clasp and admired herself in the glass
over the mantel. When she looked back at him, her eyes
were merry. 'A promise of what?'

'Of things to come, my dear! Of things to come!'

When she turned back to the mirror, he allowed his
smile to fade. For a brief moment, had she looked round,
Mary would have comprehended the very depth and gravity
of her husband's predicament. But she did not, and Tom
remained alone in his terror.

Within an hour of her encounter with Sidney Parker,
Charlotte was at Mrs Griffiths'. She was shown into the
drawing room, where a wan-looking Georgiana was staring
glumly at the landlady's beloved Chinese wallpaper.

Charlotte knelt at her side and reached for her stricken
friend's hands.

'I am sorry I ever doubted you, Georgiana. I am no
longer under any illusions. Sidney Parker is self-important,
prejudiced and cruel. But he will not be allowed to ruin
your happiness.'

Mrs Griffiths, who was pretending to read the Bible
in the far corner of the room, raised her head. Charlotte
didn't notice.

'If he has made it his mission to keep you and Otis
apart,' she continued passionately, 'well – I shall make it
mine to defy him.'

Georgiana thought for a moment and then began to smile.

Not twenty minutes later, Charlotte had left and was
hurrying through the town so swiftly that she was almost
running. Stationed next to the portico of the hotel was the

mail coach, which was preparing to leave. She quickened her pace again and handed the letter to the coachman just as he was preparing to tie up the mail sack. She made sure he dropped it in and then stepped back, out of breath. As the coach moved off, she thought of the note that was now safely on its journey to London. She had accomplished two things in one: done her friend a favour while defying her wretched guardian at the same time. She couldn't help but smile.

Chapter Twenty-Three

Miss Georgiana Lambe was stationed at the window, frowning at the glorious weather the new day had brought for nothing, for what good was sunshine if one wasn't allowed out in it. At her back, she knew without turning, was her gaoler, Mrs Griffiths. The only time she could escape her now was in sleep. She let out a heartfelt sigh.

The door opened and Crockett's face appeared.

'Miss Charlotte Heywood,' she announced, and Georgiana's spirits lifted instantaneously.

Charlotte came in smiling, a book tucked under her arm.

'Georgiana. Mrs Griffiths.'

'Charlotte, what a lovely surprise,' cried Georgiana.

'I've brought you that book we were discussing.' Charlotte gave her a meaningful look.

'Oh, yes. *That* book. I shall devour it with interest.' She took it. Just visible inside its pages was the white corner of an envelope. A letter!

Georgiana turned with a bland smile. 'Mrs Griffiths, I'm sure you'd welcome some respite from watching my every move and I'm equally sure Miss Heywood would be more than happy to pick up the mantle and sit with me for a while. Charlotte?'

'I would be delighted. We can read together.'

'I would like that very much,' said Georgiana emphatically.

Mrs Griffiths hesitated, suspicious but not quite sure why. 'Well, I do have some errands to attend to.'

'She will be quite safe with me,' said Charlotte.

After more deliberation, Mrs Griffiths finally took her leave.

Georgiana waited until the front door had closed before she pulled out the letter.

'I thought you would never come!' she said, tearing it open. 'This morning has been interminable.'

Charlotte laughed. 'Georgiana, has no one ever told you that patience is a virtue?'

'Patience will be the death of me and virtue is of no interest.'

She fell silent as she read, her eyes scanning hungrily across the lines. When she had finished, she looked up, eyes alight, and pressed the precious missive to her lips.

'Mr Molyneux says he wants to see me. Nay, he *must* see me or he will die from the wanting.'

Charlotte rolled her eyes a little, though she was secretly quite enchanted to be party to such a romance. 'I'm sure talk of his demise is somewhat premature.'

'We cannot take that risk. Time is of the essence. We must think of a plan.'

'That is not going to be easy given you are practically under house arrest.'

Georgiana's dark eyes flashed in temper as she stood and began to pace the room. 'It's outrageous. I only want to see him for a brief hour. Or two. Why is that so wrong?'

'You're right, of course,' said Charlotte soothingly. 'No man should have the right to impose his will upon another. But that would appear to be the way of things. For the time being, at least.' She reached out for her friend's hand. 'We will think of something. Do not despair.'

*

Charlotte left a much brighter Georgiana in private possession of her letter and began the walk back to Trafalgar
House. Her route took her past the building site of Waterloo
Terrace, where the keen-eyed such as herself could see some
change occurring every day. She hadn't intended to linger
long but when she got there and spied Mr Tom Parker and
Young Stringer in close conversation she thought to say
hello. It was only as she drew closer, that she saw that whatever passed between them, as well as one of the labourers,
was not good-natured. Mr Parker was agitated, his hair
standing on end and two bright spots staining his cheeks.

'Patience, patience,' he was saying as she approached
them, still unobserved. 'All in good time! You will get every
penny you are due. You have my word.'

'With all due respect, Mr Parker,' said the labourer, whom
Charlotte now recognised as Fred Robinson, 'we've been
patient for weeks now. We've got mouths to feed. You're
a father – you must understand that.'

'Yes, Mr Robinson, I do,' said Mr Parker. 'I understand
only too well. All I ask is for a little more time.'

Young Stringer spoke up then. 'It might help matters if
you could give the man a date, Mr Parker. Then we'd all
know where we stand and could get on with the work.'

It was at this moment that Mr Parker noticed Charlotte.
Relief transformed his face; he was heartily glad of the
diversion she had brought.

'Ah, my dear. How splendid!' he cried.

She nodded at the men. 'Mr Parker, Mr Stringer, Mr
Robinson. I trust all is well.'

'Miss Heywood.' Young Stringer gave her one of his shy
smiles. She couldn't help notice how his face had also lit
up at the sight of her.

'Is there some problem?' she said. 'Perhaps I can assist?'

No, no, my dear,' said Mr Parker in a rush. 'No problem. None whatsoever. We were just discussing the day's activities.' He held out his arm. 'Come along, my dear. Mrs Parker will be wondering where we've got to. She sent me out to find you.'

Charlotte hesitated, searching Young Stringer's face, and felt somewhat frustrated when he kept smiling, as though nothing was amiss at all. Seeing no other choice, she took Mr Parker's arm.

'Of course,' she said, suspiciously. 'Good day.'

In the drawing room of Denham Hall, Sir Edward was watching his sister over the top of his newspaper. For the past couple of days he had been feeling curiously unsettled and, though he was loath to admit it even to himself, he knew Esther was the reason. At some moment he could not precisely identify, the tables had turned. Where before she watched him, he now found himself following her every movement.

'Good book?' he said now, with deliberate insouciance.

'Unbearably tedious,' she replied without bothering to look up.

'Excellent.'

She eyed him then, though only lazily. 'How is your paper?'

'Riveting. I can hardly tear my eyes away.'

Their gazes locked and he was about to say more when a servant entered.

'Lady Denham.'

Their aunt sailed in as they rushed to stand. The room seemed instantly smaller.

'I was passing and thought I'd do you the honour of taking tea with me,' she announced.

'How thoughtful of you,' said Esther with a brittle smile. 'We're delighted, aren't we, Edward?'

Lady Denham regarded her sceptically.

'Really, are you sure?'

Edward got to his feet and gestured for her to sit down. 'Of course. You're up and about early today, Aunt.'

'I'm not sleeping well. I'm hoping you two might bore me enough to send me off later.'

'I'm sure Edward will do his best,' said Esther before turning to the servant. 'Some tea please.'

'And cake,' added Lady Denham. 'The more ancient I become, the more sustenance I require for elevenses.'

'You're hardly ancient, Aunt,' said Edward gallantly. 'You're in your very prime.'

She eyed him beadily. 'What are you after?'

'Aunt, really! Can't I pay a simple compliment without everyone doubting my motives?'

'No one's doubting your motives, Edward. They're always crystal clear.' She smiled, pleased that she had bested him, and he returned it, though only thinly. The nephew put in his place, she turned to the niece.

'So Esther, have you heard any more from that nice Lord Babington?'

'No, Aunt. I'm sorry to disappoint.'

'Oh, I'm far from disappointed. On the contrary; I'm expecting a great deal more fruitful correspondence between the two of you from now on. In fact, I've told him so myself.'

Esther started in her seat. 'You? How?'

'I've written to him. On your behalf.' She gave Esther a triumphant look.

'To what end?'

'To inform him that you are delighted by his attentiveness and very much looking forward to seeing him when he arrives in Sanditon for the cricket match this Thursday.'

Esther was too appalled to respond but Edward, who held his own opinions on the matter, spoke up instead.

'Aunt, Esther has expressed no interest whatsoever to see that popinjay Babington. Ever.' He was surprised by how outraged he felt.

'More fool her,' said Lady Denham, unperturbed. 'That's why I have taken matters into my own hands. If I waited around for you two to do anything useful I'd be six feet under. And I've no intention of giving you that pleasure.'

'I wish you hadn't done that,' said Esther. 'Now I'll appear rude.'

'It's rather late to worry about appearances, Esther. Now, you will do as I instruct. You are to write to Lord Babington immediately – before he comes to his senses and changes his mind.'

Esther looked to her brother and a great deal of silent emotion flowed between them. Lady Denham waited impassively for the answer she knew would come.

'Very well,' Esther said eventually. 'If you insist.'

Of course, there was no need for her aunt to take so much trouble as to insist. Both Denhams knew that well enough.

'That woman is quite intolerable,' said Edward, when she'd finally left. 'You'll just have to grin and bear her ridiculous match-making. It will come to nothing but perhaps you could have some fun playing with Lord Popinjay along the way.'

There was a short silence while Esther regarded him.

'Why do you think it will come to nothing, Edward?' she said after a time.

'Because you cannot stand him. He's a buffoon.'

She held out her left hand and regarded it thoughtfully. 'I may have been unfair to him.'

'Unfair?' Edward's voice was slightly too loud for the room. 'He deserves all your contempt and more.'

'Does he? He has been extremely attentive. And persistent. I could do far worse. If I must marry, why not marry a lord?' She turned and finally met his gaze. 'You said yourself I should consider marriage, did you not?'

'Did I?' He was feeling peculiarly frustrated. Esther, by contrast, seemed as cool as marble.

'Yes, Edward,' she replied. 'You did. Perhaps our aunt has done us both a favour.'

She returned to her book and he to his paper, though he read not a word of it. He could think of nothing but Esther and Babington, his hands pawing her lily-white skin.

Charlotte and Tom arrived back at Trafalgar House to find a happy scene. Diana and Arthur were now in attendance and the children had managed to coerce a reluctant Arthur into joining a makeshift game of cricket.

'Ah, there you both you are,' said Mary, when she saw them. 'Come and see. This game is teetering on a knife-edge.'

The children rushed to greet their father, clutching at his legs and begging him to play. Diana turned to greet Charlotte, her expression caught between enjoyment and her customary agitation.

'The tension is quite unbearable!'

Arthur held out his bat to his elder brother. 'Well, I've borne enough,' he said. 'You're in, old chap.'

Mary smiled. 'It's good practice for Thursday, my dear.'

Tom, seemingly relieved to be at home and away from the troubles of the building site, took the bat and gamely took up his position, the children cheering as he did.

'The whole town is fit to burst about the match,' said Diana to Charlotte in a confiding tone.

She was confused. 'Match?'

'The annual cricket match, my dear,' put in Mary, joining them. 'Between the Parkers and the workers. It's a noble Sanditon tradition.'

'The refreshments are particularly noble,' said Arthur with a hungry look.

Charlotte smiled. 'How splendid.'

'The whole town will be there,' said Mary. 'It really is one of my favourite days of the year.'

'The whole town? Everyone?'

'Oh, yes. Everyone. No one would miss it, would they, Tom?'

'No, my dear,' he called as he waited to be bowled. 'The men could do with the day off and this is an excellent opportunity for us to come together. As one.'

He hit the ball with a satisfying thwack. The children, half delighted, half complaining, tore after it. But Charlotte was watching them without really absorbing anything. In her mind, a plan was forming. She stood.

'If you'll excuse me, I've just remembered there's something I really must attend to.'

With that, she was up and away. Mary called after her in surprise, asking if she would require lunch, but she had already gone.

No more than seven minutes elapsed before she was back at Mrs Griffiths' lodging house and being shown in by Crockett once more.

Mrs Griffiths looked up from her embroidery. 'Again? So soon?'

'Forgive me, Mrs Griffiths, but I had to leave rather unexpectedly when we were at a particularly exciting part of the book.'

She glanced at Georgiana.

'Miss Heywood promised me she would return as quickly as possible so we could continue,' the heiress said quickly. 'The suspense has been killing me.'

Mrs Griffiths frowned. 'I sincerely hope it's not too exciting. It's still early in the day.'

Charlotte sat down next to Georgiana on the chaise and made heavy work of finding the right page, while Mrs Griffiths gathered herself and reluctantly left the room.

'I have a plan,' said Charlotte as soon as they would not be overheard.

Georgiana's eyes shone. 'Pray tell.'

'There's to be a cricket match on Thursday. The whole of Sanditon will be there. If everyone is there, they won't be anywhere else. The town will be deserted, allowing you a few hours' grace to spend with your beloved.

'You must ask the Gorgon Griffiths to take you. I'm sure she will be more than happy to do so. It appears to be one of Sanditon's most anticipated events. When she and the rest of the crowd are distracted by the excitement of the match, we will sneak away.'

'We?'

Charlotte looked serious. She wanted to help but she would not be a friend if she allowed Georgiana's reputation to be in jeopardy.

'I must go, Georgiana. To keep watch, if nothing else.'

Georgiana relented, seeing the sense of it, and began to smile.

'Perfect,' she breathed.

She sprang up and went over to the little writing desk by the window. While she wrote, Charlotte read obligingly aloud from the book, in case Mrs Griffiths lurked outside the door.

Dear Mr Molyneux, Georgiana wrote.

I would be most delighted to meet with you. Shall we say four o'clock, this Thursday coming, outside the hotel?

Yours in anticipation,

Miss Georgiana Lambe

She sealed the letter with care, and then handed it to Charlotte, who tucked it into the pages of the book. They smiled at each other, the first part of their plan complete.

Chapter Twenty-Four

The day of the cricket match had dawned a peerless blue. Standing outside the Crown Hotel were three gentlemen, newly arrived from London. Only one of them looked glad to be there.

'This must be the least enticing hostelry I've ever had the misfortune to get blind drunk in,' said Crowe glumly, once they were inside. 'Your round, Parker.'

Sidney sighed. 'I should go and see Tom.'

Babington, who'd been looking about him with pleasure, slapped his friend on the back. 'We'll see you at the match.'

'How is it we always end up in this godforsaken place?' said Crowe when Sidney had gone. He drank down half of his first drink.

Come now, it's not that bad.' Babington's eyes were bright with anticipation. 'I have some rather agreeable business to attend to here. I intend to indulge in a spot of light flirtation.'

Crowe looked with surprise at their fellow patrons.

'What, in here?'

'Not here. *Here*. If you take my meaning.'

Crowe rolled his eyes. 'Oh, not Miss Denham, please. I'm becoming quite exhausted at the mention of her name. You're uncommonly smitten with that woman. Heaven knows why, though she is clever, I grant you. She knows it's the chase that keeps you dangling.'

Babington smiled serenely. 'You could not be more wrong, Crowe. Miss Denham does not waste time with petty games. She is entirely herself at every turn. She has finally answered my letters.' He patted the pocket of his tail coat. 'The response is short and lacking in any courtesy whatsoever. I have taken great heart from it.'

'How so?'

'If she had softened in her manner towards me, I would deduce that to be a bad sign.'

Crowe shook his head, as much amused as appalled. 'Good grief, man. You are lost.'

Babington's smile widened unrepentantly. 'And I am rather enjoying it.'

At Trafalgar House, Charlotte was standing at the window when movement on the street below caught her eye. It was Sidney Parker, walking in his usual determined manner towards the house. She drew back an instant before he looked up, her heart fluttering in her chest. Every encounter with that man filled her with confusion. It was almost like a physical affliction.

Downstairs, Tom Parker found his brother handing his hat and gloves to a servant. It was the first time they'd seen each other since their awkward exchange over Tom's debt. Still, his face lit up.

'Sidney! I knew you wouldn't let me down. Good news, I hope?'

Sidney shook his head. 'The situation is unchanged. I'm sorry.'

Tom's face fell but, with some effort, he restored his smile. 'Ah, well. At least I have your prowess on the cricket field to be grateful for.'

'In truth, you have Lord Babington to thank. I'm here at his behest, to give moral support in his hour of need. God knows he'll need it.'

'What a good friend you are, Sidney.' He paused, considering. 'I don't suppose you could try one more time to . . .'

Sidney's countenance darkened. 'Tom, stop. I cannot be drawn on this subject any longer. I have done my level best to help you and I can do no more. Is it any wonder I'm so reluctant to return?' Seeing Tom's crestfallen expression, he softened. 'Let's just enjoy ourselves, as brothers – and friends.'

At this moment Charlotte appeared at the top of the stairs.

'Mr Parker.'

'Miss Heywood.' He seemed to address a point just over her shoulder.

Tom, his mind already on other matters, did not notice the *froideur* between them. Picking up his hat, he gave Charlotte a distracted smile.

'I must get back to the terrace. If the men are to have the afternoon off, I should ensure they complete certain tasks beforehand. Mary will be delighted to see you, Sidney. Delighted.'

He let himself out, leaving Charlotte and Sidney alone.

'I assume you're here for the cricket, Mr Parker,' she said eventually, when the silence stretched out.

'You're never short of assumptions, Miss Heywood.'

'Well, I was not expecting you to return so soon.'

'Believe me, neither was I.'

Charlotte, already riled, was about to respond when Mary appeared.

'Sidney, what a lovely surprise! Have you seen Tom? He'll be so pleased you've come.'

'I met him on his way out. Now, if you'll both excuse me, I must pay a visit to Mrs Griffiths.' He nodded and then was gone, leaving Charlotte with two thoughts: the first that his presence would make her and Georgiana's plan much more difficult to carry out, and second that Sidney Parker was surely the most disobliging man she'd ever had the misfortune to meet.

The small relief Tom had felt to be away from his brother's sharp eyes drained away when he reached the terrace. Young Stringer approached him immediately, his face taut with worry.

'They're angry, Mr Parker – and with good reason,' he said.

Tom felt anxiety twist inside him, but pride stopped him admitting it. 'That's as may be,' he said instead. 'But I need you to do your job now, Mr Stringer, and pacify them.'

His foreman shook his head. 'It might be too late. They're talking about refusing to play in the match, Mr Parker – to show how unhappy they are.'

That penetrated. 'They can't!' he cried, horrified and unable to hide it. 'If they do that, the whole town will know.'

Young Stringer shrugged. 'That's what they're banking on.'

Tom let out a sigh so deep it seemed to come up from his boots. 'Very well. Tell them I'll pay them in a fortnight and no later.'

'You can't break any more promises, Mr Parker. They won't stand for it.'

'I won't. I'll find the money. I'll do my job, you do yours and tell them so from me. Two weeks and not a day more. They have my word.'

He walked away, knowing that if he turned, he would see the scepticism on Young Stringer's face. He couldn't blame him; he, Tom Parker, didn't know where the money would come from either.

*

Sidney Parker had been shown into Mrs Griffiths' parlour.

'Where is Georgiana?' he said by way of greeting. 'I hope she's not slipped your net again, Mrs Griffiths.'

She smiled nervously. 'No, no, Mr Parker, rest assured. I have been assiduous in my vigilance since that last unfortunate episode. She is upstairs with the Beaufort girls and quite safe.'

'I trust you will continue to be as watchful, Mrs Griffiths. The responsibility for Miss Lambe's welfare is now to fall entirely to you. Do you understand?'

'Oh, I see,' she said falteringly. 'Will you be travelling abroad again, Mr Parker?'

'In the first instance, I'll be at Lord Babington's country estate. Who knows after that. What I do know is I will not be returning to Sanditon for the rest of the summer. Accordingly I've settled Miss Lambe's accounts, in full, for the entire duration.'

The business settled, he made for the door, only for it to burst open. The Beaufort sisters and Georgiana rushed through it in a confusion of laughter, hair and satin. The sisters, upon seeing Sidney, looked delighted. Georgiana, in contrast, could not hide her dismay.

'What are you doing here?' she cried.

'Georgiana!' Mrs Griffiths gave her a reproving look.

'I do not have to explain myself to you,' said Sidney severely, 'but since you ask so politely, I'm here to play cricket.'

Julia Beaufort clasped her hands together. 'Oh, Mr Parker, that will make it even more exciting to watch.'

Mrs Griffiths looked apologetic. 'The young ladies have asked to attend, Mr Parker, but I must confess I do not see the appeal in sitting about on the sand, perspiring in the afternoon sun, watching grown men cavorting in their shirtsleeves.'

'Presumably you intend to forbid me from attending?' said Georgiana to Sidney.

'Why would you think that?'

She raised her chin proudly. 'Because you keep me locked up like a criminal, when my only crime is love.'

Sidney looked suddenly weary. 'Georgiana, as long as you do exactly as Mrs Griffiths instructs, you can do what you like.'

'Am I meant to thank you for that contradiction?'

'If Mrs Griffiths is happy to bring you to the cricket then so be it. The sea air might even restore your good humour.' He put his hat on. 'Good day.'

The venue of the annual cricket match was, somewhat unconventionally, the beach. Mr Parker had devised this plan himself, believing it a far more fitting celebration of his beloved resort to play on the sand which would surely soon welcome society's finest.

By mid-morning, a large crowd from the town had gathered, many of them bringing picnics and rugs on which to sit comfortably. There was a keen sense of anticipation in the fresh air and, happily, the sky continued cloudless and blue. To one side, trestle tables had been set up next to a small tent, and on these Mary Parker, Diana Parker and Charlotte were laying out the cricket tea. In truth, Charlotte was not proving much help, so distracted was she by the spectacle, as well as her plot with Georgiana.

'Charlotte, my dear . . . ?'

Mary's words brought her abruptly back to herself. She turned to see her hostess regarding her with amusement.

'Yes?'

'You've been guarding that plate for the past five minutes. You can put it down. The sandwiches will be quite safe!'

Charlotte laughed. 'Forgive me. It's just all so exciting!'

A presence at her arm made her start. It was Arthur, who was carrying a ball, a bat tucked casually under his arm. She was about to offer him a sandwich when she caught sight of Sidney striding towards them.

'Help yourself, Mr Parker,' she managed to say, shoving the plate towards Arthur's considerable stomach, before rushing off in the opposite direction. She had no wish to engage in yet another stilted conversation with his older brother.

Mrs Griffiths and her coterie of young ladies had arrived on the beach. She scanned the sand for somewhere suitable to settle, preferably as far away from the young men who would be playing as possible. Sidney Parker's severe expression was still foremost in her mind.

'We shall set ourselves up over here by the dunes,' she announced.

Phillida Beaufort groaned. 'But we won't be able to see anything!'

Mrs Griffiths smiled grimly. 'Precisely. Remember what happened to Lot's wife when she dared to look.'

Charlotte appeared, her cheeks flushed from hurrying over to greet them. 'Miss Lambe, Misses Beaufort, Mrs Griffiths.'

Georgiana pulled her aside and put her mouth to Charlotte's ear. 'My despicable guardian is here and is going to ruin everything.'

Charlotte shook her head. 'No, he's not. We do exactly what we agreed. Once the game starts, everyone will be distracted, especially your guardian. He'll be too busy trying to win. Listen for the church bells at a quarter to four and you and I will sneak off.'

'What's all the whispering about?' Mrs Griffiths was regarding them with suspicion.

'We were just discussing the next part of our book,' said Georgiana.

Mrs Griffiths frowned, missing the Beaufort sisters' stifled giggles. 'I really must read this book.'

'Dear ladies.' It was the Reverend Hankins, who was already perspiring. He tipped his hat and smiled round at them.

'Are you looking forward to the match, Reverend?' said Julia, mouth twitching.

He inclined his head, pleased by the attention. 'Oh yes, indeed. I have been charged with ensuring the match is played in a fair and sporting manner. I am to be the umpire.'

'How impressive, Reverend,' breathed Mrs Griffiths.

He was most gratified. 'Are you partial to a ball game, Mrs Griffiths?'

The Beaufort girls exploded into a new fit of giggles, much to the Reverend and Mrs Griffiths' bafflement.

Tom Parker was alone, close to the tent where the cricket tea would be held after the match. Everyone else seemed happily occupied but he could not enjoy himself. His ability to put his troubles aside – something he'd always been adept at doing – was becoming more difficult by the day.

His earlier exchange with Young Stringer was turning over in his mind, again and again. It had given him one of the headaches that seemed to be afflicting him more frequently lately. He could only liken the sensation to having his head in a clamp which was tightening slowly.

It was something of a relief to see his brothers approach, along with Sir Edward and some of the other players for their side. He stopped massaging his sore head and adopted the air of jollity that was expected of him.

'Splendid, you're all here!'

'We are but the opposition aren't,' said Sidney.

'Is it off then?' said Sir Edward with a yawn. 'Good.'

'No!' said Tom, too loudly. 'No, of course not.'

'That's a relief,' said Arthur affably. 'I wouldn't like to think I'd done all that exercise for nothing.'

In the distance, the church bell struck and then again.

'Two o'clock,' said Sidney. 'They're late.'

'They're probably just delayed at the site,' said Tom, but his head was pounding harder now.

Lord Babington and Mr Crowe arrived, the latter rather unsteady on his feet.

'All right, I'm here,' he said thickly. 'Willing and able. Where d'you want me?'

'Are you drunk?' Tom was horrified.

Crowe guffawed. 'No more than usual!'

He and Babington fell about laughing. Tom grimaced as another pain shot through his head. Usually, he couldn't think of anywhere he'd rather be than Sanditon, especially in fine weather. Today he wished he might be anywhere else. As if to taunt him, Lady Denham at that moment appeared on the sand, parting children and dogs before her like a general on inspection. Clara Brereton struggled in her wake, weighed down as she was by a large assortment of cushions, parasols and fans. Tom could see Lady Denham's dissatisfied expression from where he stood. Steeling himself, he set off to greet her.

'Here, you take this,' she was saying to Clara when he arrived. 'I really can't be expected to carry everything.'

'Lady Denham,' he said, as enthusiastically as he could manage. 'How splendid. Splendid.'

She ignored him.

'This is a particularly pleasant spot. You'll see everything from here.'

She wrinkled her nose as if something under it smelled bad. 'I'm glad it has something to recommend it.'

His duty done, Tom made for the tent again, only to be stopped by his wife.

'Why the delay, my dear?' she said brightly. 'If it goes on much longer, we'll run out of sandwiches.'

He lifted the corners of his mouth. 'Don't worry, my dear! We'll be up and running very shortly.' He left her standing there before she could ask any more of him.

A reluctant Esther had just joined Lady Denham and Clara when the former spotted a person she had particularly hoped to see.

'He's coming,' she hissed at Esther. 'Sit straight. Smile. No, don't smile, it'll confuse him.'

Esther shaded her eyes with her hand. Of course: Babington.

'Lord Babington,' Lady Denham beamed at him. 'Delighted I'm sure.'

'Likewise, Lady Denham, Miss Brereton,' he returned, but his gaze was already straying to Esther. 'Miss Denham, I had no idea you were such a cricket enthusiast.'

'I'm not,' she said baldly.

Lady Denham let out a tinkling laugh, even as she frowned at Esther. 'She jests, Lord Babington. Sadly, she lacks my wit.'

Babington was still looking at Esther. 'Thank you so much for your letter. I was delighted to finally hear from you.'

'Esther was delighted to oblige,' put in Lady Denham as Esther opened her mouth to retort. 'Weren't you, Esther?'

She briefly closed her eyes. 'Yes. Delighted.'

But Babington was not deterred. 'That makes all three of us, then!' He bowed and took his leave, joining Sidney and Crowe at the crease. Sir Edward, who was close enough to hear, watched him through narrowed eyes.

'What on earth do you see in her?' said Crowe. 'She's positively mirthless.'

Babington smiled, his eye already drawn back to her elegant figure. 'On the contrary, she is the wittiest woman I have ever met.'

Crowe shook his head in disgust. 'Then you are moving in the wrong circles.'

Neither of the men noticed Edward's jealous scowl.

Lady Denham was now settled on the sand, but the arrangement was not yet to her satisfaction. She snapped her fingers.

'Clara, my parasol.'

'Yes, Aunt, of course.' Clara was still slightly breathless, her usually porcelain complexion stained pink. 'Here it is.'

'My fan.'

Clara obediently handed it to her.

Lady Denham began to fan herself extravagantly. 'At least someone considers my welfare,' she remarked pointedly to Esther.

Over her shoulder, Esther caught Clara's sly smile but, with some effort, ignored it.

'A little charm goes a long way at this stage in the courtship,' Lady Denham went on. 'You'll have to make more of an effort.' She peered in Babington's direction across the sand. 'He's looking at you again: smile.'

Esther did so, weakly.

'Lord Babington!' put in Clara. She had finally sat down herself, and was now thoroughly enjoying Esther's discomfort. 'I imagined you to favour a rather different kind of man.'

'Perhaps you should be wary of where your imagination leads,' said Esther with as much asperity as she could muster. 'Excuse me.' She stood and walked away.

Clara watched her go, satisfied to have successfully goaded her once again.

'Clara, fetch me a cordial,' said Lady Denham sharply, cutting short her pleasure. 'I seem to be plagued by an unquenchable thirst today.'

Clara sighed, quietly. 'Yes, Aunt.'

On the crease that had been marked out in the sand, Tom was pacing restlessly. While their eleven had lined up ready to play, there was still no sign of the men who were to make up the opposition.

'It seems the other team have let you down, Tom,' said Sidney quietly.

'No point in wasting the entire afternoon,' said Crowe, planting his bat in the sand. 'I believe I will return to the bar.'

'From one gentleman's pursuit to another,' said Babington happily.

Tom was just about to object when a roar of approval went up from the crowd.

Visible at the far end of the beach, Young Stringer and his gang of labourers were marching purposefully towards them. Compared to Crowe and Babington, already in their cups, and his portly brother Arthur, who must already have eaten a dozen sandwiches, the working men looked like Roman gods, the sun burnishing their muscled arms. Superior players they might have looked but Tom's overwhelming emotion was relief. The humiliation of them not coming at all would have been a thousand times worse than being roundly beaten might be.

'I knew they'd be here,' he said, though he hadn't known but a moment before.

'I don't wish to alarm,' said Arthur, 'but they look rather good. Then again, appearances can be deceptive.' He straightened his shoulders.

Crowe snorted from behind him. 'Not in this case, I'd wager.'

Also watching the men's approach with interest was Charlotte, who had just been joined at the trestles by Clara.

'Their Captain is agreeably handsome, is he not?' she said in her insinuating way.

Charlotte was perplexed. The captain was surely her friend Young Stringer.

'Is he?' she said, and looked again. The sunlight glanced off his fair hair, and she could plainly see the outline of his broad shoulders through the thin stuff of his shirt. He caught her eye as he drew close and she nodded at him, feeling unaccountably flustered.

'But then so is Mr Sidney Parker,' mused Clara.

Charlotte turned her gaze that way and found that, to her confusion, Sidney was already looking at her. She looked away hurriedly, and thought how hot the day had suddenly grown.

The spectators were now on their feet, their cheers even louder. Young Stringer went towards Tom and shook his hand.

'Good luck, Captain Parker.'

Tom was suffused with gratitude for his foreman, whom he suspected had got the men there singlehanded. 'And to you, Captain Stringer.'

Fred Robinson stepped forward. His smile didn't reach his eyes.

'Is there a prize for the winners, Mr Parker?' he said.

'Glory!' Tom declared after a moment's awkward hesitation.

'Not money then?' said Robinson. 'Didn't think so.' He smiled so that the words might be taken for a joke, though it was clear to everyone present that there was no mirth in his expression. Still, Tom pushed out a hearty laugh.

Everyone was relieved when Reverend Hankins stepped forward to perform the coin toss.

'Heads,' said Young Stringer.

'Tails,' called Tom.

But Young Stringer and the men had it.

Arthur groaned. 'We can't even win the toss.'

'We'll bat first,' said Young Stringer.

He led his team off the crease, passing Charlotte as he went.

'Good luck, Mr Stringer,' she called. 'Not that you'll need it.'

'Thank you, Miss Heywood.' He smiled broadly at her.

She smiled back. 'You seem to have gathered several admirers already.' She nodded towards the Beaufort sisters, who had temporarily escaped Mrs Griffiths' guard and were whispering and simpering openly about the men, and particularly Young Stringer.

He gave them a cursory glance and turned back to Charlotte.

'I do hope you're among them.'

She blushed; unsure what to think of this newly masterful Stringer. 'Ask me again, once I've seen you play.'

He went off, well pleased, and suddenly Sidney was passing her.

'Good luck to you too, Mr Parker,' she said, without warmth. 'Although I don't imagine you think you need it.'

He didn't smile. 'Yet more assumptions, Miss Heywood.'

The other fielders took their positions: Babington as close to Esther on the sidelines as he could get away with.

'The opposition have come prepared,' she remarked.

'At least one team has.' He grinned at her and she had to stop herself smiling back. She didn't notice her brother Edward take up a position where he could closely observe both her and Babington.

The match was finally underway. First up to bat was Young Stringer, who would face Sidney's skilful bowling. Nevertheless, Young Stringer made excellent contact with the first ball, the loud thwack of leather on willow causing the crowd to roar. Charlotte was amongst them – something both batsman and bowler noted.

Arthur, who had been keeping a close eye on the food, was alarmed to find himself in the path of the ball and ducked. It was Crowe who scrabbled to scoop it up and throw it to Tom. But it was too late and Young Stringer safely made the run. Charlotte stood and clapped enthusiastically.

'You've picked a good place to stand,' remarked Esther to Babington, who was still hovering close by as, some distance away, Sidney bowled again. 'You've hardly touched the ball.'

'Anyone would think I chose it for a reason,' said Babington, his eye back on her rather than the game.

'Did you?'

'You know I did.'

'Don't get too carried away,' she said. 'This is entirely my aunt's idea, not mine.'

But he only smiled, quite undeterred. 'She does appear to be taking a great interest in our activities.' He raised a hand at Lady Denham, who was watching them intently from the other side of the crease.

'She takes a great deal of interest in everyone's activities,' said Esther wearily.

At that moment, Crowe shouted over. 'Babington, are you playing or not?'

'Your friend Mr Crowe doesn't care much for me,' said Esther.

'He doesn't care for anyone. Does his opinion matter to you?'

'Certainly not. He's a strutting peacock. You're two of a kind.'

He turned at that, all the good humour gone from his face. 'Is that really all you think of me?'

'You've done nothing to convince me otherwise.'

'Then perhaps I could invite you on a short walk later, to give me the opportunity to prove you wrong.'

She hesitated, half-intrigued. A glance towards Edward and her aunt told her that both were watching keenly. At that moment, by chance, the ball rolled their way.

'Yours, I believe, Lord Babington.'

He gave her a speaking look and ran to retrieve it.

Lady Denham was growing hotter by the minute, the sun beating down relentlessly. It was becoming intolerable. She fanned herself harder, though it didn't seem to make any appreciable difference.

'Is everything all right?' said Clara.

'It most certainly is not. I cannot get cool and my throat is parched.'

'I'll fetch another cordial.'

Lady Denham cast around for a sharp retort but her thoughts were oddly disordered; as sluggish as if her head had been filled with molasses. The noise of the people around her had dulled to a strange hum. She had such a famously formidable constitution that the sensation was initially unfamiliar, but then the realisation struck her: she was not well at all.

She only dimly heard Reverend Hankins call out the labourers' score. 'All out for eighty-six!' The numbers meant nothing to her; she could not think what they signified. She could scarcely think at all. It was as much as she could do to stay sitting up.

Among the dunes, it was relatively quiet, the sound of the game and crowd muffled by the grass-strewn hillocks of sand. The Beaufort sisters were sulking, furious to be so far from the action, while Georgiana was lying back, counting gulls as they passed high overhead. Her thoughts were not on birds, though, let alone cricket. They were fixed instead on Mr Molyneux. Every time she thought of him, which was often, she was rewarded with an inner thrill she could barely contain. He would be close now, surely. Perhaps he had already arrived. She wondered how it was possible that Mrs Griffiths couldn't read her thoughts, so loud did they seem to clamour in her head.

Seeing Charlotte hurry towards them, she sat up eagerly. Perhaps her friend would offer her a chance to escape.

'This really is one of the most exciting cricket matches I have ever seen!' announced Charlotte with genuine enthusiasm as she reached them.

'I sincerely doubt it,' said Mrs Griffiths, who had her back to the play, though she couldn't resist a quick glance over her shoulder.

'Did you see that?' cried Charlotte, shading her eyes from the sun. 'Young Mr Stringer really is the most accomplished bowler. He has taken a great many wickets already. I pity anyone who has to face him.'

Georgiana realised with a start what Charlotte was trying to do. She stood up. 'I know! I can hardly bear to look!'

Mrs Griffiths frowned as she struggled with her natural inquisitiveness. But then her head snapped round of its own volition; she could resist no longer. Standing, she peered towards the distant game.

'Why don't you move a little closer?' said Charlotte.

'Oh, please can we?' cried Julia Beaufort. 'Please?'

'No,' Mrs Griffiths shook her head. 'We're perfectly fine here.' She peered harder. 'I will just say though, that Reverend Hankins is one of the most impressive umpires I have ever seen.' She moved a little closer.

In the thick of the game, Young Stringer was still accumulating wickets. Now there was only one man left to bat: Tom. He looked pale as he strode as manfully as he could towards the stumps.

'Good luck, old chap!' said Crowe sardonically. 'Watch he doesn't take your head off.'

Seeing Mary and the children smiling and waving, Tom lifted his bat though it was a rather half-hearted gesture. He would have given a great deal in that moment to be lying prone in a darkened room. He wondered how obvious it was to the crowd, and to Mary, how coldly the men eyed him as he took up his position. Immediately behind him on the wicket was Fred Robinson. He could almost feel the hot breath of the man on his neck, and pulled at his collar to loosen it.

Sweat ran down his face. He blinked it out of his eyes as Young Stringer took a long run-up. The ball was high and fast and whistled past his head as he ducked. He had barely recovered himself before Young Stringer was coming at him again, thundering down the wicket at speed. This ball was a spinner. So quickly it didn't seem possible, the ball had bounced off his leg and was rolling away. Fred Robinson caught it up, face triumphant.

'Leg before wicket!' called Young Stringer.

Tom turned to him. 'I'm sorry but I don't think it was.'

'Out!' bellowed Fred.

'Now, look here,' Tom began. He'd intended his tone to be good-natured but it rang out querulously. 'I really don't think I am.'

Young Stringer looked towards the Reverend. 'Umpire?'

Mr Hankins hesitated. In truth, the intricacies of the LBW rule had always eluded him.

'His leg hit the ball,' protested Young Stringer. 'It's against the rules.'

Hankins, grateful for some clear guidance, nodded. 'OUT!'

The crowd erupted with a combination of cheers and boos. Robinson and the other labourers surged towards their bowler to clap him on the back. Catching Tom's eye, Robinson insolently gestured for him to head towards the tent. But there was a stubborn look on the master's face. Even as a boy, Tom had never been able to abide what he felt was unjust.

'Now come along,' he said, a definite edge to his voice now. 'Be reasonable. Fair's fair. My leg was nowhere near it.'

Robinson rounded on him, as though he'd been waiting for the chance, which perhaps he had.

'I might have known you'd try to cheat,' he spat. 'Your sort always do.'

Sidney strode across the crease towards him.

'How dare you speak to my brother like that.'

But Young Stringer stood between them, looking uncharacteristically belligerent. 'Why not? It's the truth. We haven't been paid a penny in weeks.'

Sidney, shocked, had no reply.

Young Stringer looked at Tom. 'I warned you it would come to this.'

The noise of the crowd dropped as though a curtain had fallen. Even the tide seemed to pause while Tom stood there, humiliated, his eyes darting round the crowd, knowing what everyone had heard. He saw Mary but as she looked away, he caught the gleam of tears in her eyes.

Suddenly too distraught and ashamed to remain there another moment, Tom dropped his bat and walked away.

Sidney called after him but he didn't turn, his head down.

In the lull that followed, Mr Hankins cleared his throat. 'I'm sorry but I must confess that . . . Well, I must say that, in all honesty, in the heat of the moment, I made a mistake. *Not* out!'

A shout of laughter went up from Crowe. 'Bit late now.'

Sidney ran to catch up with his stricken brother.

'Tom, come back,' he called. 'Finish the game.'

He didn't stop. 'It's finished, Sidney,' was all he would say.

'You can't go like this. Where are you going?'

'What do you care?'

Sidney, knowing there was nothing he could say, let him go and then turned back to the match.

'You haven't got anyone left to take his place,' said Young Stringer. 'We win.'

Charlotte, without thinking, stepped forward. 'I'll play.'

Both men looked at her in astonishment.

'Isn't this a gentleman's pursuit?' mused the Reverend piously.

'Woman play cricket in Willingden,' she returned.

'Willingden sounds infinitely livelier than Sanditon,' said Crowe drolly. 'Reverend Hankins, is there anything in the rule book that prohibits a woman playing cricket?'

Mr Hankins took out his battered rule book and began to thumb through it. 'I'm afraid there's no guidance in this book,' he said eventually.

Sidney picked up Tom's discarded bat and held it out to Charlotte. He didn't smile as she took it.

'You heard the umpire,' he said to the collected players. 'His mistake. My brother wasn't out. We play on.'

The crowd cheered.

Charlotte tucked a loose tendril of hair behind her ear and adjusted her grip on the bat. In front of her, Young Stringer was preparing to bowl.

'Keep your eye on the ball,' called Sidney from the other wicket.

Charlotte gritted her teeth. 'Thank you, I know what I'm doing.'

'If you can't get the run, stay put.'

She straightened up and threw him an exasperated look.

'Yes, thank you! I know exactly what I'm doing. Now, please, I'm concentrating and you're putting me off.'

Young Stringer, torn between his admiration for Charlotte and his team, made his approach and bowled her an easy ball. She took revenge for his condescension by hitting it hard and true. It sailed towards the makeshift boundary.

'Run!' shouted Sidney, but she had already hitched up her skirts and set off. The crowd was transfixed.

As she ran back down the crease, Charlotte locked eyes with Sidney. He could not hide his surprise and her traitorous heart swelled at the sight of it.

Babington, whose poor play had released him, returned eagerly to Miss Denham's side. He bowed.

'Out for a duck, Mr Babington,' said Esther archly.

'I know. How embarrassing.'

'You don't seem remotely embarrassed.'

'Given that my services are no longer required on the field of battle, I wondered if you might take that walk with me now?'

Esther hesitated, casting a look towards Edward. He was still watching her. Quite decided by this, she stood up.

'Come on then, if you're coming. I can't abide a man who dawdles.'

Babington smiled triumphantly and hurried after her, Edward watching them go.

As they walked away, the game progressed: Charlotte and Sidney accumulating runs with every ball, to the unalloyed delight of the crowd. Their gazes met every time they passed each other.

'Was that a smile I detected, Mr Parker?' Charlotte said, on one pass.

'I doubt it, Miss Heywood. I'm not given to outward displays of happiness. I am merely making the best of a bad job.'

But she could see he was enjoying himself as much as her.

Young Stringer was openly admiring, grinning at her as she faced him again.

'Let's see if you can hit a six this time!' he called.

'Steady on, lad,' said Robinson disapprovingly. 'She's on the other side.'

But Young Stringer didn't hear him. He was too intent on the neat figure holding the cricket bat, her dark curls lifted by the breeze.

Clara Brereton, running yet another errand for Lady Denham, was intrigued to see that Sir Edward was utterly lost in thought as she approached him, his expression much more serious than usual.

'All by yourself, Edward?' she murmured close to his ear, making him start. 'I would offer myself as company but your aunt sent me to tell you that she is retiring for the day.'

He barely looked round at her. 'What's that to me?'

'Shall I tell her that?'

When he didn't reply, she followed his gaze. Esther and Lord Babington were further up the beach in conversation, though every so often, Esther glanced back to where her brother – and now Clara too – were. Seeing this, Clara leant in towards Edward again, so close this time that he could feel her breath on his cheek.

'Your aunt seemed delighted by the prospect of Esther's growing liaison with Lord Babington,' she said softly. 'With clever Esther safely married off and in the lap of luxury, that just leaves you and me. And your aunt's money. I wonder which of us will triumph.' She smiled. 'Actually, I don't.'

With that, she was gone, leaving him alone again. Clara's words echoing dully in his head, he found himself seeking out the figure of his sister again. She and Babington were further away now, the two of them apparently quite comfortable in each other's company as the lowering sun threw their shadows long across the sand.

*

Once the game had safely resumed, Mary Parker hastened home. She knew Tom would be there. Her natural sympathy for him, usually so abundant, was fast depleting, replaced by a growing anger.

Inside the silent house, she saw him an instant before he saw her, and the sight shocked her. He was slumped in his usual chair like a man much older – and not just older but sadder; someone almost broken.

'Why didn't you tell me?' she began.

'Tell you what?' For a moment, she thought he would paint on his usual smile, but this time it was seemingly beyond him.

'That you couldn't afford to pay the men.' Her voice shook.

'Because it was only a temporary situation. The men know that. The regatta will sort it out. You make too much of it, Mary. It's hot out there. Tempers got frayed, that's all.' He waved his hand dismissively but she would not be placated this time.

'Stop lying to yourself, and stop lying to me,' she said. 'You couldn't find the money to pay your men and yet you can give me this.' She reached round and unfastened her necklace, putting it on the table. 'How, Tom? How? I'm ashamed.'

She was almost weeping. He dropped his head in shame.

'I could bear anything. Anything, if you had confided in me.'

'Mary, no . . .' He got up and reached for her but she recoiled.

'Mary, you are my life,' he said desperately. 'I will repair this. You have my solemn word. I'll go straight to London now. I will make amends if it's the last thing I do.'

She lifted her face to his but there was little warmth in her eyes, only bald disappointment.

'No more promises, Tom,' she said softly, devastatingly. 'All you ever do is break them.'

She walked from the room and he didn't attempt to go after her. He felt as though he might never move again.

Like Tom Parker and Sir Edward, Mrs Griffiths was experiencing her own difficulties that afternoon. Some time earlier, after admiring the Reverend Hankins in his position of authority on the cricket pitch, she had returned to where she had left Georgiana to find her vanished. Since then, she had been circling the beach for her charge, growing more anxious by the minute.

Spotting a pair of familiar faces, she hurried over.

'Miss Parker, Mr Parker. Have you seen anything of my charge, Miss Lambe? I've been looking everywhere for her.'

'No, Mrs Griffiths, I can't say I have,' said Diana. 'Arthur?'

'Nor me. But then I have been out there,' he gestured towards the cricket, 'upholding my family honour.'

'Oh, that girl!' cried Mrs Griffiths, irritation and anxiety mingling uncomfortably inside her. 'She is the very definition of tiresome. If you see her, can you send her to me at once?'

Diana nodded earnestly. 'Of course.'

Mrs Griffiths hardly heard her. Her eyes were fruitlessly roving the sand for Miss Lambe again. She *did* see Sidney Parker, but thankfully he did not yet seem to have noticed the girl's absence. She hurried away, hoping fervently that she would find his ward before she had to admit her negligence to him yet again.

*

Esther and Babington were on horseback, the cricket and crowds left far behind them as they took the path that would take them to the river. The sun was sinking slowly towards the horizon and, in a couple of hours, the sky would be set ablaze, turning the sand a spectacular rose-gold. But for now it was still hot and Esther was glad when they reached the shade of the tree-lined riverbank. It was quite deserted, the whole of Sanditon on the beach, the only sound the silvery rush of a waterfall and the horses' clinking bridles as they dismounted.

'It's very beautiful here,' said Babington, though he seemed quite oblivious to the scenery and rather more intent on her.

'I thought your heart lay in London, Lord Babington. Are you suggesting a change of affection?'

'I think that is exactly what I am suggesting. And, believe me, there is no one more surprised than I.'

She looked at him, her curiosity piqued by his evident sincerity. This was a side to Babington she had not much seen before, nor believed existed.

'What are your feelings, Miss Denham?'

'About what, the sky? The water? The company?'

'Yes, all of that.'

A small smile softened her face. 'It's growing on me. But I wouldn't want to be in agreement with you too much, too soon.'

He laughed. 'Whatever you do, you must guard against that. The humiliation! You have your reputation to consider.'

'And you yours. Though I'm sure yours is already beyond redemption.'

'I cannot imagine what leads you to think that.'

She cast him a sidelong glance. 'Wild speculation.'

He smiled. 'I think you would be surprised. I am not such a good-for-nothing as I would like.'

That made her laugh this time, and not in her usual sardonic way. 'Are you suggesting you are a fraud, Lord Babington?'

'I am starting to believe my life has been something of a pretence.'

Esther looked thoughtfully across the water. The reflections of the trees had transformed the river into a skein of rippling green. 'I doubt there are many among us who can honestly say they live a life free from pretence,' she said softly.

He paused. 'Then, surely,' he said carefully, as though afraid of saying something clumsy, 'if we are to lead a better life, we are honour-bound to free ourselves from such a burden?'

She turned to him and bestowed on him her first truly warm smile.

'Why, Lord Babington, you amaze me. I'm beginning to find you slightly better company.'

That made him laugh uproariously. 'I have never met anyone else who can give a compliment in such a way that it might also be an insult. You are extraordinary, Miss Denham. Quite extraordinary. All pretence aside, I have never met any woman who has conjured up such feelings in me. I am all at sea.'

She looked down, suddenly shy. Something between them had altered in that quiet place, away from prying eyes. 'We should go back, Lord Babington.'

'I cannot go back. I am compelled to go forward.'

To her profound shock, he fell to one knee in the damp earth.

'Miss Denham, will you do me the honour of becoming my wife?'

A laugh bubbled out of her, though her heart was beating fast. 'This is ridiculous!'

'I'm serious.'

She didn't know what to say. They stared at one another.

'I wasn't expecting this,' she said finally.

He shook his head ruefully. 'Believe me, neither was I.'

He was sincere, she knew it. She would have mocked him yesterday for such a declaration. Now she could not.

The match was almost at its end. The Parker-led team, though now led by Sidney, were one run short of the opposition side's tally.

As Young Stringer was preparing to bowl, Fred Robinson lent in for a word.

'Once this is over, you should tell that young lady how you feel,' he said, grinning. 'But for now, don't go soft on her.'

'You don't need to tell me,' said Stringer, but as he took his run-up, he knew he couldn't do it to her, standing there with her determined face, her eyes so bright. She was so lovely, so sincere; how he admired her. The ball, when he let it go, was an easy one. Charlotte hit it with all her might and began to run. The match was won for the Parker side.

The crowd rose to their feet, stamping and cheering. Fred Robinson shook his head, half amused, half despairing.

Charlotte, triumphant, caught Sidney's eye. He'd begun, instinctively, to run towards her but now stopped. They held each other's gaze.

'Is that a smile I detect?' she said, beginning to smile herself.

'I doubt it,' he replied, but he couldn't help grinning back at her. Neither moved for a long moment but then she turned to Young Stringer.

'I'm sorry you lost, Mr Stringer, but thank you for going easy on me. It was very chivalrous of you.'

He smiled. 'You won fair and square. Perhaps we might play on the same side next time?'

She nodded. 'I'd like that very much.'

He watched her as she walked away, unable to do otherwise. He jumped when Fred nudged him with an elbow. 'If you don't tell her, how will she ever know?'

Sidney was also watching Charlotte when someone pulled on his sleeve. Mrs Griffiths had finally given in to her fears and could no longer put off telling him of Miss Lambe's disappearance.

'Mr Parker!' she cried, wringing her hands and, after her fevered circuits of the beach, quite crimson in the face.

Sidney looked questioningly at her, his mind still on other things.

'It's Miss Lambe,' she said breathlessly. 'I've lost her. I can't find her anywhere.'

In the distance, the church bell began to toll again. It rang four, five times, and Charlotte – who had been entirely distracted by her victory – remembered the plan she was accomplice to. She alone knew that Georgiana had intended to meet with Mr Otis Molyneux an hour before.

She dropped the cricket bat and began to run.

Chapter Twenty-Five

Evening had stolen over the Denham drawing room but no candles had yet been lit. It was so dim that Esther didn't initially notice her brother sitting there. It was the smell of his cigar smoke that betrayed him. When he saw her, he didn't greet her; only drained the rest of his glass of port and poured another.

'Who won?' said Esther.

'Does it matter?'

'I thought winning was everything to you, Edward.'

'It depends on the prize.' He looked up at her. It was too dark to tell but it seemed as if he looked right through her. The thought made her feel cold. She lit a lamp and sat down on the chaise.

'You looked flushed,' said Edward from the armchair. His eyes were hooded and difficult to read. 'Where have you been?'

'By the river.'

'With him?'

'You know I was.' She was suddenly impatient. 'Why are you pretending? It's tedious.'

'Because I wanted to hear it from your own lips.'

She took in a breath. 'He asked for my hand.'

'And are you going to accept?'

'Isn't that what you wanted?'

He stood. 'No, Esther. It is not what I wanted.' He came closer. 'Not now, not ever.'

'But you said . . .'

'You know I didn't mean it – I could never mean it.'

He sat down next to her, so close she could smell his cologne as well as tobacco and the unidentifiable scent that was indefinably Edward to her.

'If you accept him, you will be lost, Esther,' he said in a thick voice she had never heard before. 'Not just to me, but to yourself. Yes, you will be rich but you can never be free with him. Not as you are here, with me. As time goes on, he will demand your silence, because that is what those men do.'

He moved closer still. She couldn't meet his eye.

'He makes me laugh,' she said softly. 'I have forgotten how that feels.'

'I can do so much more than make you laugh.' He reached up and brushed the back of her neck, just at the sensitive point where her hair met her smooth white skin. As he leant in to kiss her, she sighed, all thoughts of Babington dissolving into the gloom.

Charlotte was out of breath by the time she got to Mrs Griffiths' lodging house. She had looked everywhere for Georgiana but to no avail. She had even gone down to the cove, and the riverside where they had picnicked when Mr Molyneux had visited before. It was as she knocked on the door that the awful thought occurred to her. She hadn't allowed it admittance before. If Georgiana wasn't in Sanditon, then what else could she have done but eloped?

Crockett announced her. Sidney was already in the parlour, clutching a letter, and when he looked up and saw her, his face was stricken.

'Mr Parker . . .' she breathed.

'Georgiana has disappeared off the face of the earth,' he spoke over her. 'No one has seen her anywhere. Where can she be? Where would she go?'

'Mr Parker, there's . . .'

But she was interrupted again, this time by the arrival of Mrs Griffiths and Young Stringer. The former's face was pale and tear-streaked.

'Mr Stringer has some news of Miss Lambe, Mr Parker,' she said tremulously.

Sidney got to his feet. 'What is it?'

'One of the men saw her waiting outside the hotel,' said Young Stringer.

'Waiting? When? What time?'

'Four o'clock.'

Charlotte's heart clutched.

'The next thing was a carriage drove up. A man got out.'

'A man? She was meeting a man?'

Charlotte knew she must speak. 'Was this man black?'

'Why would you ask that?' said Sidney sharply.

'Was he?' Charlotte asked again.

Young Stringer shrugged. 'All he said, was that there were two of them. The other was in the carriage. She was bundled in, and then they took off.'

Charlotte covered her mouth. 'Bundled!'

'Thank you, Mr Stringer,' said Sidney. 'I'm grateful to you.'

'I hope you find her. It must be a worry.'

Mrs Griffiths burst into renewed tears.

Sidney touched her arm. 'Show Mr Stringer out, Mrs Griffiths.'

When they were alone, Sidney turned to Charlotte. 'You know something. Tell me what it is.'

She quailed at the thought of his fury but then she thought of her friend, out there in the unknown.

'I've been acting as a go-between for Georgiana and Mr Otis Molyneux these past few weeks,' she said, trying to keep her voice steady. 'Since you forbade them from seeing each other. Her heart was broken, Mr Parker, and I could not bear to see it. I sent Mr Molyneux a letter on her behalf, this past Monday, arranging for them to meet today, during the cricket match.'

'You did what?' His tone was icy.

'I was to accompany her,' she rushed on. 'I would never have let them meet alone, but I was caught up in the excitement of the match and forgot.'

'You forgot?' he shouted, his fear heating to anger. 'You forgot!'

'Yes! Yes, and I'm sorry. She must have sneaked off. She was desperate to see him. She would not be stopped.'

He regarded her with cold fury. 'If anything has happened to her, this will be on your head.'

He picked up his hat and strode from the room, leaving Charlotte alone, trembling and painfully ashamed of herself. She had clashed swords with Sidney more than a few times; she had even thought him cruel in his treatment of Georgiana. Never before had she known so clearly that right was on his side, and not her own.

Esther waited outside Denham Place in the fading light, listening to the plaintive cooing of a wood pigeon. She saw Babington approach before he spied her in the long shadows of early evening. She felt herself closed to him again now, despite what had passed by the riverside.

'Miss Denham.' He studied her closely, the hope in his eyes dying as he did.

'Lord Babington.'

'You sent for me.'

'I did.' They stood there in silence for a long moment.

'I see I am not to be invited in.'

'No.'

He stilled and squared his shoulders for what was surely coming.

'Lord Babington, you must see it would be an unmitigated disaster,' she began, not quite looking him in the eye. 'The whole notion is ridiculous. The sea air has addled your brain. I could never contemplate a proposal from someone as shallow as you.' She glanced at him but looked away quickly when she saw how her words wounded him.

'You still believe me shallow?'

'You proposed on a whim. That is hardly a sign of depth.'

He reached out before dropping his hand, apparently resisting the urge to touch her. 'Is this your honest answer, without a shred of pretence?'

He searched her face but she still would not look at him.

'It is,' she said, in a clipped little voice.

He left her then, striding away without looking back. She thought of what Edward had said, the way he had touched her, but it didn't comfort her as it once would have. Babington was almost out of sight now, his figure merging with the shadowy trees lining the drive. She understood then that what she was feeling was probably regret: that things couldn't be more simple; that she had already given her heart to Edward long ago.

In Trafalgar House, Charlotte had related to Mary the bad tidings about Georgiana.

'Where will all this end?' she said, visibly distressed, her poor face terribly strained.

Charlotte was pacing up and down, quite appalled with herself. 'How can I have been so wrong? This is all my fault. Mary, I must do something.'

'There is nothing you can do now. You must leave it to Sidney.'

Charlotte kneeled at her feet. 'Please let me take the carriage. I will go to London and look for her and Otis myself. I know where he lives because I've been writing to him. I will start there.'

Mary was shocked. 'No, Charlotte! You would be alone. It's too dangerous. I will not countenance it.'

'Then I will go to Tom as soon as I arrive. Please, Mary.'

'You cannot rely on Tom,' she said in a bitter tone quite unlike her. 'No, Charlotte, this is my final word.'

With that, she left a desperate Charlotte alone in the drawing room. Whatever Mary said, and however saddened she was at the thought of disappointing her, she simply could not do nothing. She would lose her wits if she tried. Quite decided, she went to Tom's study and wrote a short note and then ran upstairs to pack some essential belongings. Leaving the note on the table in the hall, she slipped out of the front door quietly enough that she wouldn't alert any of the servants, let alone the exhausted Mary.

It took but a few minutes to reach the hotel and the coach waiting outside it. With a last look around and a deep breath to fortify herself, she stepped aboard. Soon, she would be on her way to London, where she would do her best to make amends.

Though it was the last thing she wanted to do, Esther went straight to her aunt's house after seeing Babington, without a word to Edward. She knew how angry the old lady would be and didn't want to put off the inevitable for the next day.

In fact, Lady Denham was even more furious than she could have foreseen.

'He is a lord,' she repeated for the third time, as though speaking to someone unforgivably dull-witted. 'He has a fortune. Why did you refuse him?'

'Because I don't love him,' Esther said stubbornly.

Lady Denham's face turned an even darker shade of puce as she gripped the arms of her chair. 'Love? Love! What does love have to do with anything? Marriage is a business arrangement; nothing more. Do you think I married for love?' She stopped to catch her breath, which was growing shallower and more stertorous with every sentence. It was loud in the cavernous room.

'Aunt . . .'

'You have the Denham name but a name will not see you through without a dowry. You would be a decent catch if there was one. But there is not – not a single penny.'

Esther stared. 'You would not do that.'

Lady Denham's head had gone down and the whole of her shook. 'Oh, I would,' she muttered. 'Go. I am done.'

Esther moved towards the door but a sound made her turn. It was her own name but so strangulated she could barely make it out. Her aunt had slumped forward in her chair.

'Esther . . .' she managed to say again, though not above a whisper. 'I feel quite unwell.'

Esther ran and knelt by her, taking up her hand, which was clammy and cold. Lady Denham's face, which had been so livid, was now quite drained of colour.

She stood, still clasping her aunt's limp hand.

'Help!' she cried. 'Help me!'

Chapter Twenty-Six

It was deep night by the time the coach shuddered to its final stop. Charlotte had been suspended between sleep and wakefulness for what seemed like weeks. Even now that they had stopped, her head still seemed to move with the rocking of the coach.

She turned to the stranger whose rough shawl had been brushing her cheek for hours.

'Are we here? Is this London?'

But the woman was already getting to her feet, her hip bones clicking in protest. Charlotte followed her, and stepped down into a scene reminiscent of a nightmare.

'Excuse me?' she called up to the coachman, who was readying the horses to leave. She fumbled for the note in her bag. 'Do you know where I might find Honey Lane?'

But if he heard her, he affected not to, and she could only watch as the carriage moved off into the night, leaving her quite friendless.

Though the sun had long set, the street was alive with people, noise and smell. Street hawkers shouted, stray dogs so thin you could count their ribs fought over scraps, and beggars crowded the shadows, their backs up against dripping walls, their hands out. Everyone else seemed to want to leave the scene as quickly as possible, an impulse very understandable to Charlotte, especially when a speeding carriage sent up an arc of filthy water and soaked her to the skin.

Indeed, her every sense was so assailed that her first inclination was to find another coach that might take her straight back to the clean civility of Sanditon. Then she remembered Georgiana's plight.

'Courage, Charlotte,' she murmured under her breath, and it did help, a little.

She consulted the small scrap of paper once again. 'Mr Otis Molyneux,' it read. 'Seven Stars, Honey Lane, London.'

Though she had little idea where she was in the great city, and even less where the Seven Stars inn might be, she did eventually find it – though the journey through endless streets took almost two hours, and left her perilously close to exhaustion. If she'd hoped for a respectable sort of public house, those hopes were quickly dashed. The door was blocked by a couple pressed up against each other: a pock-faced, half-dressed woman and a sailor who must have come from the Far East. Peering inside through one of the smut-streaked windows, she could see that the dimly lit, smoke-filled interior was no more salubrious. Some of the patrons were singing bawdily, others were gaming, others still were sprawled unconscious across tables. From the look of them, they had washed up at the Seven Stars from every corner of the globe: some from China like the sailor, others from Spain or perhaps Greece – Charlotte couldn't be sure – others so ebony-skinned they were surely from Africa.

She was steeling herself to push past the couple by the door, when it banged back, causing the pair of them to dive out of the way, and Charlotte to jump. An older black man, grey at the temples but his arms still roped with thick muscle, held a slighter man by his filthy collar.

'I shan't warn you again, Mulligan. This ain't that kind of establishment.' With that, he half-threw the man to the gutter. It was then he caught sight of Charlotte, as out of place as the sun at midnight.

'And what are you gawping at, Duchess?'

Charlotte swallowed. 'I—'

'If it's a drink you're after, you can come inside. This ain't no pleasure garden.'

He turned to go in.

'No, wait. I'm not here for . . . I need to speak with Mr Otis Molyneux. This *is* where he resides?'

'Ain't no one who resides here but me, Sam Sidaway. Oh, and Mrs S. on the rare occasion she ain't taken agin me.'

'But I have been sending letters to this address and he has been answering them!'

'Ah, well. Now and then he might come by to fetch his post. Take a drop or two.'

'*Now and then?*' Alarm was beginning to course through Charlotte. 'So when do you expect to see him next?'

The publican shrugged. 'No way of telling. Ain't seen him in a week or more. Even sent some other cove to fetch his post last week. Gone to ground, you might say.'

'But I *must* see him. It is a matter of great urgency. I have travelled a good many miles to get here.'

'Then you've had a wasted journey, ain't you, Duchess?'

He went back inside and the door slammed shut in Charlotte's face. Alone once more, she tried to gather her scattered wits but the thought of wandering back through the hostile city until daybreak made her want to weep. Someone emerging from the shadows jostled her and she almost dropped her precious bag, but at least the surprise of it set her in motion once more.

She walked on for a time but then, faced with a fork in the road that she didn't recognise, hesitated. Taking the better lit way, she was dismayed when it narrowed, the air noticeably colder as the walls closed in. She had just decided to turn back when a figure stepped out of the darkness ahead. As a sliver of moonlight caught his face, she saw his awful smile, the dark, toothless maw of his mouth. A flash at his side revealed itself to be a knife.

She gasped and turned to run but he was too quick for her, pulling her close and clapping a huge hand over her mouth. She felt herself half-lifted, half-dragged back towards the darkness and began to kick, her screams muffled. *I am lost*, she thought quite clearly, but the next moment was all confusion. There was a rush of movement, a billowing great-coat, the hard crack of a fist meeting bone and the answering howl of pain. She found herself suddenly, miraculously released and upright, the arms that had been crushing her gone. She looked down in astonishment to see her attacker sprawled in the muck, clutching his jaw.

She spun round, her mouth open and round with surprise. 'Mr Parker?'

She couldn't believe her eyes. For a moment she thought it was the shock but when she blinked and opened them again, he was still there, not a figment of her imagination after all. It really was Sidney Parker standing there before her, as large as life and evidently displeased to see her. Before she could speak, he took her arm and led her back to the road.

'As if this situation were not insufferable enough, I now have the added burden of protecting you.'

Worn to a ravelling though she was, Charlotte still had her pride.

'I have no need of your protection, thank you,' she managed to say.

'You just came within a hair's breadth of being knocked down in the street!' cried Sidney as he marched her towards his carriage, which was waiting outside the Seven Stars. 'And Cheapside is no place for a young lady, let alone unchaperoned, let alone at night! What possessed Mary to let you come?'

'She doesn't know I am here. In fact, she expressly forbade it.'

'But you stole away on the London coach regardless?'

'I left a note, explaining that I had come to help . . .'

'Help? How exactly did you think your presence here would help?'

'Well, for one thing, I did not think you would have Mr Molyneux's address.'

He gestured at the public house before them. 'As you see, it has hardly taken me long to find it.'

'It is no use to us anyway,' said Charlotte heavily. 'He has not been seen here in over a week. Apparently he has all but vanished.'

'Of course he has: with Georgiana.'

'We don't know that he is to blame.'

'How much more proof do you need?' He held open the carriage door for her. 'Thank God Tom is at our London house. He will see that you are kept out of harm's way.'

Charlotte gave him a pleading look. 'I didn't come all this way to sit uselessly by. I am in large part to blame for what has happened. You have to allow me the chance to help put it right. Please.'

His face, framed in the lamplight coming through the carriage window, seemed to soften slightly as he took in her words, but then he shook his head. 'You have done enough.'

They had been driving in silence for some time when Sidney spoke again.

'Of all places, I thought she would be at least safe in Sanditon.'

He was addressing himself rather than Charlotte but, suffused with guilt as she was, it felt as though he blamed her alone.

'If you had been honest with me,' she said. 'If you had only told me that you feared for her safety, then I would have thought twice before—'

'I could not have made my feelings for Mr Molyneux any clearer,' he interrupted.

'You spoke only in the vaguest terms. You gave no reason for your antipathy. No explanations . . .'

'So you supplied your own? You baselessly accused me of prejudice—'

'Hardly baseless, given how you made you fortune . . .'

He rounded on her. 'For God's sake, I despise slavery! I long since renounced the sugar trade for that very reason. The man's race plays no part in it!'

Charlotte raised her chin obstinately. 'I can think of no other reason for you enmity.'

'And what do you know of Mr Molyneux?' His voice was harsh. 'You spent a single afternoon with him! Did it never occur to you that I might have been trying to protect her?'

'All I could see was that they were very much in love, and that for some reason you were hellbent—'

'Love? This had nothing to do with love! The only thing that man ever cared about is her fortune.'

'That you should think so speaks more of you than it does of him.'

He had been looking out at the passing city streets but now he rounded on her.

'Are you really so naive? Why do you think he is so desperate to marry her? Because the moment they are wed, everything she owns will become his!'

But Charlotte didn't want to dwell on this possibility. If it was true then she was even more of a fool.

'Are we not wasting time?' she said, preferring to concentrate on the matter in hand. 'Instead of taking me back to Tom, we could be searching for Georgiana.'

'And where do you suggest we look?' Fear and frustration made his voice harsh. 'This is a city of a million people! That is supposing they are even still within its walls.'

But Charlotte had had a flash of inspiration. 'The Sons of Africa,' she said.

'What?'

'It is the movement he belongs to. If we can find out where they meet . . .'

She didn't need to finish her sentence. Sidney was already banging with a gloved fist on the ceiling of the carriage.

Some miles across town, another Parker was also beset by worries. Tom Parker was at his desk, attempting to write his wife a letter.

My dearest Mary, he had begun. *I can scarcely express the guilt I have felt since that humiliating episode at the cricket. You have every right to be angry, but you must trust that I am well on my way toward remedying . . .*

No, that would not do. He crossed the last out and tried again.

That I will do whatever I can to put this right . . .

But that was no good either: too weak. He made another attempt.

   . . . to restore our fortunes. I beg you not to lose faith in me.

He put the pen down. The open bottle of madeira at his elbow had been his only company that evening. As he poured himself another glass, he reflected that it was probably the only company he was fit for.

Tom had grown somewhat used to living with fear – fear of failure in business, and in his ambitions for Sanditon – but never before had he had to contemplate the fear of Mary's loss. Despite the heaped fire in the grate, the notion turned him cold.

Chapter Twenty-Seven

Much to the displeasure of its mistress, Sanditon House had once more been invaded by a doctor of medicine. After her collapse, Lady Denham had been put to bed, and was now eyeing Dr Fuchs with as much suspicion as her weakened condition would allow.

'I can no longer stand idle, *mein* lady,' the accursed man was saying. 'You must allow me to treat you. I implore you.'

She tried and failed to sit up. Clara rushed forward to settle her comfortably on her pillows.

'Begone with you!' she managed to cry from her prone position, though it made her nauseous to exert herself so. 'The last thing I need is your ludicrous nostrums and panaceas. They will only sicken me further!' She closed her eyes.

The doctor regarded her with great concern. 'Your fever is *gefährlich* high.'

'More seawater!' Lady Denham said querulously. 'That is all I need. And some warm ass's milk. See to it, Clara! And get rid of this perfidious quack while you are about it!'

Roused by her own speech, she threw back the covers and tried to stand. But she had not the strength for it, and her legs went from under her, sending her tumbling to the floor before Clara could catch her.

'Aunt!' she cried, as she knelt beside her. Lady Denham's eyelids flickered as she swooned. With the doctor's assistance, she was with some difficulty helped to her feet and returned to bed.

'What is to be done, Doctor?' murmured Clara when the old lady was safely tucked in again.

Dr Fuchs shook his head. 'My dear *Fräulein*, I fear it may already be too late.'

In an unprepossessing back room in London, the air thick with the stink of sweat and tallow, Mr Otis Molyneux commanded the attention of a motley audience: black and white; young and old. All were enthralled by his impassioned words.

'. . . Now is not the time to be disheartened,' he was saying, eyes roving around the room and fixing on each of his fellow Sons of Africa in turn. 'We don't seek bloodshed like our brothers and sisters across the water. We ask only that every soul be considered equal . . .'

He stopped as the door banged open and Sidney Parker strode in, Charlotte hard on his heels.

'What have you done with her?' the former shouted without preamble, rushing towards Otis as if he meant to throttle him. Instead, he instructed the audience to leave immediately, which they did without demur. There was no mistaking the murderous glint in the stranger's eye. When the last one had filed out, Sidney gestured for Otis to sit down opposite him and Charlotte. He did so, and immediately began to protest his ignorance again.

'I haven't the least idea where she is,' he insisted. 'Why would I abduct her?'

Sidney slammed his hand down on the arm of his chair. 'Because she is mistress to a fortune and you are a servant to debt!'

'I played no part in it, I swear!' He put a hand on his heart. 'I would sooner die than dishonour her.'

Charlotte raised an eyebrow at Sidney. She had felt sure Mr Molyneux truly loved Georgiana and, to her, this seemed confirmation of the fact.

'And what of Miss Heywood's letter?' said Sidney, who was not convinced. 'In which she proposed a tryst for you and Miss Lambe at the exact time and place from whence she was taken? Mere coincidence, I suppose.'

'I never received such a letter.'

'Do not insult me.' Sidney leaned threateningly towards the other man.

'Sam Sidaway said you'd sent someone else to fetch your mail,' broke in Charlotte.

Otis shook his head, dawning fear clouding his expression. 'No, I did not.'

'Then – why would anyone wish to steal your post?' said Charlotte.

He cast his eyes to the floor. 'There is a particular gentleman to whom I owe a certain debt. Lately his men have been shadowing me at all hours. I could not put it past him . . .'

'Which gentleman?'

'Mr Beecroft.' His voice was thick with shame.

Sidney put his face in his hands.

'What is it?' cried Charlotte. 'Who is Mr Beecroft?'

'He owns a gambling house,' said Sidney heavily.

In an instant, Charlotte saw it all – the deception, the debt, the danger Georgiana was surely now in.

Sidney stood, his jaw set. Charlotte knew him well enough by now to know behind the scowl lurked fear, and that made her afraid too.

*

It was in the very deepest part of night that Sidney and Otis were admitted to Mr Beecroft's notorious gambling house. Inside, the place gave the initial impression of a reputable business, but Sidney knew better.

'Sure you won't take a little coffee, Mr Parker?' said Mr Beecroft. He was sitting behind a polished mahogany desk and Sidney wondered how many men had lost everything to pay for it. Undeterred by Sidney and Otis's hostile expressions, Beecroft poured himself a coffee. 'Or something stronger?'

'Thank you, Mr Beecroft,' said Sidney tightly. 'We shan't be staying long.'

'Where is she?' said Otis from between gritted teeth. He could no longer remain quiet.

'Watch your tone, young man,' said Beecroft, making a great show of being affronted, though in raising his voice something of his low-born roots came through in his accent. 'A little decorum if you don't mind. I thought you kept better company, Mr Parker.'

'This man is no friend. We are compelled here by the disappearance of my ward, Miss Lambe.'

Beecroft steepled his hands and smiled. 'Ah yes, the famous Miss Lambe. Mr Molyneux speaks of little else. Miss Lambe this, Miss Lambe that. I was minded to ban the subject from my tables before it became altogether tedious.'

'That is a lie! If I mentioned her, it was only in passing . . .'

Beecroft turned on Otis again. 'I am not the liar here! You told me a wedding was imminent. That her fortune was as good as yours. I'd never have let you run up such a debt otherwise.'

'All I wanted was to buy some time. If I had thought even for a moment . . .' Otis addressed this last to Sidney.

'Whatever this man has told you, he and my ward are barely acquainted,' Sidney interrupted. 'He had no right to invoke her name.'

'An impertinence indeed, sir!' said Beecroft obsequiously.

'So I would ask that you share her whereabouts with me at once. Whatever debts Mr Molyneux might owe – they are not her concern.'

Beecroft smiled nastily. 'Oh, there is no longer any debt. It has all been paid in full, with interest.'

'By whom?'

'I am told she is a pretty little thing. Just as you described her, Mr Molyneux.'

As both men took in his words, the same expression of horror and revulsion covered their faces.

Outside, Charlotte – no longer able to wait in the carriage – had just reached the door when Sidney flung it back. Otis stumbled out after him.

'He has sold her,' he cried desperately. 'The villain has sold her.'

'What?' Terror clutched at her.

'In return for a promise to buy his debt, she's been handed to some dissolute named Howard who can usually be found on Drury Lane,' said Sidney. 'Even now he'll be dragging her to some altar.'

'An altar?' Charlotte's heart was in her mouth. 'But that cannot be allowed. Without your permission . . .'

'There are no such laws across the border. There they will marry you with impunity.'

'No,' cried Otis, wild-eyed at the thought. 'No! We have to find them. Stop them . . .'

'How?' Sidney's voice was cold. 'They will be halfway to Scotland by now. You should have thought of the consequences before you sacrificed her to your greed.'

'This is Beecroft's doing. Not mine! Had you but allowed *us* to marry . . .'

Sidney seized him by his collar before he could finish his sentence. He was breathing hard.

'You would blame me?' he hissed. 'It is *you* who has ruined her. You gambled with her life and you lost. I should avenge her honour right here and now . . .'

Charlotte, certain Sidney was capable of murder in that moment, rushed forward. 'Stop! What good will that do?'

She wasn't sure that he had heard her but then, abruptly, Sidney loosened his hold. Otis staggered backwards and almost fell.

'Get out of my sight,' Sidney said in a dangerous undertone. 'Go!'

Otis looked as if he wanted to say something more but then, suddenly defeated, turned and walked away. Without a word to each other, Charlotte and Sidney climbed back into the carriage. Both were lost in their own agony of guilt and self-recrimination.

'We cannot give up,' Charlotte said eventually. 'I cannot accept that she is lost. How am I to live with myself if . . .'

'And what do you suggest we do, Miss Heywood? We have no chance of catching them up now.'

A thought occurred to her. 'But how can we know for sure they've even left? You said Mr Beecroft had only received a *promise* of payment. Not the payment itself. He doesn't sound like the kind of man who would give her up unless he was already in receipt of the money.'

Sidney looked up at that.

Encouraged, a small spark of hope lighting inside her, she hurried on. 'So . . . Could there not be a chance that he is still holding her? Somewhere in London, even?'

He met her eye and she saw in his the same small ember of hope.

If they had only known that Georgiana was indeed still in London, and not very far from where they sat in their chilly carriage. She was in Mrs Harries' parlour, which on first glance appeared to be a well-appointed if rather gaudily dressed room. A closer inspection revealed how tawdry it would look by day: the stained upholstery of the chairs and the chipped gilt of the candlesticks. Despite the blowsy flowers displayed in one corner, the air was slightly foetid. Someone more jaded than Georgiana Lambe might have guessed what it really was, which was the principle receiving room of a house of ill repute.

Mrs Harries herself was not unlike her parlour: over-dressed and over-stuffed; her liberally-applied rouge along with her comfortable, even motherly expression masking a steely determination.

'Come now,' she said with exaggerated patience, pushing a bowl of stew towards Georgiana. 'Eat up, before it gets cold.'

But Georgiana, terrified and furious in equal measure, could not contain her emotion a moment longer. She picked up the bowl and flung it at the wall, where it smashed, the contents running down the satin wallpaper, looking for all the world like old blood.

'Well now, wherever did you learn such coarse manners?' exclaimed Mrs Harries, her composure gone. 'We are not in Africa now!'

'I am from *Antigua*,' Georgiana said angrily. 'And if you had any idea of my position, you would not dare to speak to me so.'

'Oh, I know fine and well who you are, *Georgiana*. And what you are worth.'

She turned to one of the girls who occupied the dim corners of the room, who had been regarding Georgiana with a combination of pity and fascination since she arrived.

'Clarissa, fetch her ladyship a fresh bowl!' she said with a mirthless laugh. She turned back to her prisoner. 'We need to fatten you up for the morning. Can't have you looking less than your best on your wedding day!'

Georgiana blanched at the word, the last of her temper draining away. So that was what they had planned for her.

As Sidney and Charlotte's carriage jolted and rocked through London in the direction of Drury Lane, the first grey fingers of dawn were lightening the sky. Sidney was oblivious to it.

'I curse the day she met that man,' he said. Exhaustion had aged him during the night. His dark hair stood on end where he had pulled at it.

'And yet I cannot entirely condemn him,' said Charlotte sadly.

'In spite of everything?'

'As I see it, he is a good man who made one terrible mistake.'

Sidney looked scornful. 'He is an inveterate gambler.'

'You seemed quite familiar with Mr Beecroft yourself,' she retorted.

He gave her a black look. 'I have never played a hand I couldn't honour. I've never staked anyone else's life.'

'Otis never meant to place Georgiana in harm's way – any more than I did!'

'And yet you both did.'

'All I ever cared about was Georgiana's happiness.' Charlotte was so tired and anxious she felt she might weep.

'What do you think *I* care about?' said Sidney.

'That is anyone's guess.'

'I have done the best I can by Georgiana.'

She felt anger stir inside her again, and it briefly pushed aside the fear. 'No,' she said, with so much emotion that her voice shook. 'At every turn you have abdicated responsibility. You exiled her to Sanditon, entrusted her to the care of Mrs Griffiths, and to me. If you were so concerned for her welfare, why did you not watch over her yourself?'

'It is a role I neither sought nor asked for.' His words were bitter.

'Of course not! Because you are determined to remain an outlier. God forbid you give something of yourself . . .'

'Please don't presume to know my mind.'

'How could anyone know *your* mind? You take pains to be unknowable. All I know is that you cannot bear the thought of two people in love.'

'And what do you know of love, Miss Heywood, besides what you have read?' His voice had taken on a low, dangerous quality once again.

'I would sooner be naive than insensible of feeling!'

That seemed to strike him hard. To her great surprise, she saw she had wounded him.

'Is that what you think of me?' he said quietly. 'I am sorry you should think so. How much easier my life would be if I were.'

He turned to look out of the carriage window while Charlotte continued to watch him. He had confounded her again; she was beginning to lose count of the times he had done that.

*

At Mrs Harries', the guest they been waiting for had arrived and was now seated at the parlour table. Mr Howard was an excessively unattractive man to look at: in his fifties, his complexion was sallow, his jowls loose and his body prone to fits of sweating, his shirt straining over a distended stomach. Still, seated between Miss Lambe and Mrs Harries at the table as the latter poured tea, the scene made for a peculiarly genteel tableau – the illusion only ruined by Mr Howard's burly manservant, who was stationed at the door and wearing a look of menace.

'I confess I'd given no thought to how you might look,' Mr Howard said to Georgiana. 'It seemed beside the point. But I am pleasantly surprised. You have a youthful, exotic charm about you.'

She fixed him with a look of pure disgust. 'And you are a corpulent, loathsome swine.'

'Upon my word!' His fawning expression had soured instantly.

Mrs Harries clucked her disapproval. 'I am afraid she is somewhat spirited, Mr Howard. She will require a firm hand.'

'No matter,' he said, running his eye over Georgiana dispassionately. 'I have broken enough horses before now. I suspect a wife is not so different.'

He laughed but it was a sound entirely devoid of warmth and feeling. Georgiana felt the fine hairs on the back of her neck rise. She had thought him a buffoon, but he was far worse than that. He was cruel.

The manservant stepped forward and, at Mr Howard's signal, handed over a small pile of letters. Georgiana recognised the handwriting immediately. She forced a sweet smile and clenched her fists for courage.

'There is a gentleman named Otis Molyneux. Remember his name because when he hears of this, he will find you and kill you.'

Mr Howard smirked. 'I hardly think so. Given it was Molyneux who offered you up to pay his debts. Feckless gambler by the sounds of it. You're lucky to be rid of him.'

'You're lying.'

'Oh, bless your heart,' said Mrs Harries. 'They all think it's love till they wake up with nothing. Ask any girl in here, they'll sing the same song.'

Georgiana gripped the edge of the table so she didn't simply slide off her chair to the floor. She could not believe it of Otis. She wouldn't. And yet . . .

'Well, no matter,' said Mr Howard. 'You are mine now, so you can forget all about him.' He got to his feet and gestured to Georgiana that she should get to hers. Panic swelled in her breast. 'Come,' he said, 'we have a long road ahead of us.'

Chapter Twenty-Eight

In the relative calm of Sanditon, Young Stringer had steeled himself to call at Trafalgar House. When Mrs Parker came down to receive him, he was grieved to see how tired and drawn she looked; not her normal bright self at all.

He hung his head when she looked at him questioningly. 'I want to apologise for the way my men behaved at the cricket, ma'am. I hope you were not too embarrassed.'

But to his surprise, she shook her head. 'You have no need to apologise, Mr Stringer. Your men work hard. The least they should expect is to be paid on time. It is my husband who should apologise.'

'Thank you, ma'am,' he stammered, uncomfortable that Mrs Parker would speak so frankly. 'Like I told the men, I know Mr Parker will make things right.'

'I hope so, Mr Stringer.'

He forced himself to go on. 'Oh, and Mrs Parker,' – his carefully casual tone made him cringe – 'I – I just wondered if you'd had any word from Miss Heywood?'

'Not since the note she left. Silly girl! I expressly told her not to go to London. The thought of her alone in that big city . . .'

'I'm sure you've no need to worry yourself, ma'am. I've never met a woman as . . . spirited as she is.' He couldn't help but smile at the thought of her.

'Yes, we have all grown very fond of Charlotte. I will be glad for her safe return.'

'Aye, ma'am,' he said longingly. 'As will I.'

At Sanditon House, Lady Denham remained in her sickbed, surrounded by her family. She was still pale and weak, and looked quite diminished in the enormous bed, but her infamously sharp tongue was apparently unaffected.

'Look at you, clustered around my bed like bloodhounds,' she said, eyeing them beadily, a triumphant smile on her cracked lips. 'Ears cocked for my death rattle!'

'Good Lord, Aunt, not in the least!' said Sir Edward.

'Well, you shall be waiting in vain. I wouldn't give you the satisfaction!'

But the effort of speaking was too much for her and she collapsed back against the pillows, a coughing fit snatching away her breath. Clara rushed over and lifted her forward to rub her back.

'Do not fuss, child!' Lady Denham cried, as soon as she had sufficient strength. 'I am perfectly well. It is a hard cold, that is all. More seawater!'

Clara lifted the cup of salt water to her lips, which Lady Denham swallowed with a grimace. 'There. I feel my strength returning already . . .'

Esther stepped forward. 'I do not doubt your resolve, Aunt, but Dr Fuchs believes you are gravely ill.'

'Well, he would! It is entirely in his interest to say so.'

Sir Edward, with a glance at his sister, patted his aunt's arm. 'We have every faith that you will make a full recovery but, just for peace of mind, will you allow us to fetch a priest, or a – a solicitor?' He had the grace to colour at the last word.

'I have no use for either,' she replied, thumping the coverlet. 'I have as much faith in religion as I do in medicine, which is to say none! And my solicitor has been instructed. He knows where the will is kept. Not that it will be needed for . . . decades . . . to come.'

But she had gone, faded back into unconsciousness.

'You have exhausted her!' hissed Clara at the Denhams. 'Let her rest now.'

Sir Edward nodded and turned to go, gesturing for his sister to follow him. His mind was already busy, going over his aunt's words; which is to say he was wondering where in her gargantuan house she might have secreted her will.

He wasted no time. As soon as Clara closed the door after him and Esther, he went straight to the drawing room and began searching.

'Edward?' Esther was watching him suspiciously. 'What are you doing?'

'You heard her. Her solicitor knows where the will is kept. And so should we.'

'What is the rush?'

He stopped and turned to her. 'She is likely dying, Esther! And we have no idea how we stand.'

'If the will is written, then surely there's nothing to be done?'

'Of course there is. While she breathes, there is time enough to alter it, if I have to place the pen in her hand myself.'

'Our aunt is grievously ill, and all you can think about is her fortune?' Though neither of them had ever pretended much love for their aunt, at least to each other, she was shocked by his callousness.

'We are *so* close, Esther,' he said, as if she'd spoken her unease aloud. 'I need to know our future happiness is assured. We haven't come this far to see it slip from our grasp now.'

She nodded. 'Very well. You look through these shelves. I'll make a start over there.'

'There is no point in us both looking. People will want to know about our aunt's condition. You go and spread the word. I shall follow close behind, just as soon as I've found the wretched document.'

She left him there, tearing through their aunt's belongings like a man possessed.

In London, Charlotte was absorbing her first glimpse of the city by day. To her mind, it was no more attractive for it. As Sidney's carriage drew to a halt at their Drury Lane destination, she couldn't help stare at the confusion, chaos and sheer mess of the place. Hogarth's depictions of the place had not exaggerated.

Sidney jumped down and turned back to her, his face strained.

'Under no circumstances are you to set foot outside the carriage,' he said firmly.

Mrs Harries herself answered his heavy knock at the front door.

'Why, Mr Sidney!' she cried, evidently surprised. 'Ain't seen you in a fair while. I've some new ladies who'll be delighted to make your acquaintance.'

He reddened. 'No. Thank you, Mrs Harries. I am not here for . . .'

'And who is this young lady?'

He spun round. Of course Charlotte had ignored his instructions. He should not have expected otherwise.

'I told you to wait.'

She lifted her small chin. 'I decided against it.'

Mrs Harries was watching this exchange with amusement. 'Not made an honest man of Mr Sidney, have you?'

'Gracious, no,' said Charlotte. 'I am a friend of Miss Georgiana Lambe's. We believe she might be staying with you?'

'No, I don't believe I am acquainted with anyone of that name,' she said, her friendly manner quite gone. 'Good day.'

She went to close the door but Sidney's foot was in the way.

'Wait, please,' he said. 'Miss Lambe is my ward.'

'Mercy, someone entrusted their daughter to *you*!'

He ignored the barb. 'She is only nineteen and about to be forced into marriage against her will, her life destroyed . . .'

'No. Don't sound the least familiar.'

But she could not meet his eye. For all her years in Drury Lane, Mrs Harries was not a good liar. Charlotte, seeing her chance, ducked under her arm and ran towards the stairs.

'Georgiana! Georgiana!' she called.

She blundered into the nearest room and stopped short. Three hollow-eyed girls, their thin faces heavily rouged, their breasts half-exposed, looked impassively back at her. A couple of gentlemen, if they deserved the epithet, turned to see who disturbed them, and ran their practised eyes over Charlotte as though she might be for sale. The penny dropped, loudly, and she felt herself colour. So it was *that* kind of establishment.

Mrs Harries had followed her in, Sidney at her heels. 'You missed them by half an hour,' she said, all pretence gone. 'They will be well on their way by now. I'm sure she'll make a bonny bride. She's the envy of my other girls.'

Having extracted what little additional information Mrs Harries had, Sidney and Charlotte had no reason or inclination to stay. As they returned to the waiting carriage,

Charlotte's cheeks were still hot. Glancing over at Sidney, she didn't think he was much less embarrassed.

'A boarding house, you said,' she couldn't resist saying.

'I told you to wait in the carriage,' he replied shortly.

'Is that your idea of love?' Something to be paid for?'

'I make no claims to be infallible. I am subject to the same weaknesses as any other man.'

But her ire was up now. It took little when it came to Sidney Parker, it seemed. 'You, who stood in judgement of Otis and everyone else!' she cried. 'When you are all too familiar with the gambling house and the – the *bagnio*! Is that why you are so threatened by Otis? Because you recognise yourself in him?'

'That will do!' He looked at her thunderously. 'If we are to stand a chance of catching them up, we will have to make haste. It is best if I drive.'

He climbed up beside the driver, took the reins and looked down at where she still stood on the pavement.

'I don't suppose there's any point in telling you to stay behind?'

By way of reply, she clambered into the carriage and slammed the door.

After Young Stringer's visit, Mary was hoping she might be left in peace for the remainder of the day. This wish was not to be granted: just before eleven, she heard more visitors being shown in. It was Tom's younger brother and sister, Arthur and Diana.

'As if Miss Lambe's disappearance were not enough,' Diana began once they were seated in the drawing room, 'now Miss Heywood has absconded too! Our nerves are in tatters just thinking about it.'

'Indeed,' said Arthur with a distracted manner. 'I am sorely in need of some sherry. And a reassuring slice of seedcake, if you have any?' He got up and left the room, apparently in search of the necessary sustenance.

'I doubt we shall hear of Miss Lambe again,' said Diana conspiratorially, once the two women were alone. 'She has been captured by bandits, I shouldn't wonder. I expect she is even now tied to the mast of a pirate ship bound for the Americas.'

'Hmm?' Mary was only half-listening. She had folded the handkerchief in her lap so many times that it was quite crushed.

She looked up to find Diana regarding her with great concern.

'My dear Mary,' she said. 'Forgive me. Prattling on when I came to listen.'

'Listen to what?'

'To whatever it is you wish to say. We were all present at the cricket. I am a devoted sister, but I am not blind to Tom's shortcomings. No one's patience is inexhaustible, not even yours, my dear.'

These kind words, especially from her husband's fragile sister, almost undid Mary. Her burden lifted, just a little. In silent thanks, she reached out and clasped Diana's hand.

Chapter Twenty-Nine

On a lonely stretch of road somewhere north of London, Georgiana was queasy with fear and the speed of Mr Howard's carriage. The air was stale inside it. She could smell her captor's sweat and stale breath, and the unwashed breeches of his manservant.

Mr Howard, who was seated opposite, abruptly leant forward, forcing her to press herself back into the seat.

'I know we didn't meet in the most auspicious of circumstances,' he said with a sickly smile, 'but in time I trust you will come to regard me with affection.'

'I would sooner cut my own throat,' she spat.

The smile faded, leaving behind a sneer that made her shiver. 'That would be a shame. It is a rather pretty throat. At least wait until after we are married.'

A disturbance beyond the confines of the carriage diverted his attention. He peered out of the window. Another carriage was gaining on them, fast. He pushed the glass down and leant out, just as the other carriage overtook them. To his surprise, it was a gentleman spurring his horses on so hard that the driver beside him could do little more than hang on for dear life.

Inside that other carriage, Charlotte gripped the seat under her so as not to be thrown to the floor. She caught only a brief glimpse of the pallid-faced man peering out of the window as they drew level.

The two carriages rattled alongside each other, the rutted ground rushing past below. Sidney indicated for his driver to take over and bring the two racing carriages even closer together. When there was but a few feet between them, he leapt across the breach and boarded the other carriage. Charlotte gasped in relief as he landed safely. Overmastering the other driver with little ado, Sidney took up the reins and brought Mr Howard's carriage to a halt, Sidney's driver following suit.

Mr Howard's head poked out just as Sidney jumped down to the road and pulled open the door.

Mr Howard was outraged. 'What do you want? We have nothing worth stealing!'

'I beg to differ,' said Sidney.

'Sidney?' Georgiana hardly dared believe her eyes but then her guardian held out his hand to her. She went to take it when Mr Howard grabbed her arm.

'Oh no, you don't,' he said, stiff and red-faced with fury.

But Georgiana was too quick for him. She elbowed him as hard as she could in his ribs, hearing with satisfaction his groan of pain. She scrambled out of the carriage and ran towards Sidney's, where Charlotte – her dear friend! – was holding open the door for her.

'Come back!' cried the livid Mr Howard, but seeing it was to no avail, he addressed Sidney. 'What is the meaning of this? Who are you?'

'I am her legal guardian. That is all you need to know.'

'I made a deal with Beecroft in good faith. She is my property!'

'I am no man's property,' shouted Georgiana as Charlotte pulled her inside the carriage. 'Least of all yours!'

Mr Howard, now trembling with rage, gestured at his manservant. 'Don't just stand there!'

The man, who was taller and considerably wider than Sidney, began to advance on him, but Sidney stood his ground.

'Last I heard, the penalty for kidnapping was hanging. Is that a price you are willing to pay?'

The manservant stopped and looked to Mr Howard who, for his part, had begun to look more resigned than outraged.

'You owe me eighteen hundred pounds!' was all he could say as Sidney strode towards his own carriage.

'You can go to hell,' he called over his shoulder before getting inside.

The carriage moved off and, for a moment, no one said a word. Georgiana sat very upright, as though the last of her dignity depended on it.

Charlotte, as relieved as she was exhausted, found herself close to tears. She took Georgiana's hand, which trembled in hers.

'Oh, Georgiana, thank God! I am so sorry.'

But the girl only shook her head, her gaze fixed on the passing road outside. 'The fault is not yours to own.'

Charlotte exchanged concerned glances with Sidney but did not press her further. She knew that Georgiana's pride was all that kept her from complete breakdown after such a terrible ordeal.

In Sanditon House, Sir Edward was surrounded by chaos. Papers littered the floor and were strewn over every surface. He had not taken care in his fevered search for Lady Denham's will.

'Looking for this?'

He turned. Clara was standing in the doorway, an infuriating little smile on her lips. She was holding up a roll of paper and he knew instantly it was what he'd been looking for.

He snatched it from her and began to read, his expression changing from avidity to disgust as he did.

'"The entirety of my fortune to be left for the development of Sanditon town and the foundation of a donkey stud in my name,"' he read aloud. He turned it over but there was nothing more. He gave Clara a look of stupefaction. 'That cannot be the end of it?'

'I assure you it is. Even in death, she has found ways to torment us. It is better for us both if this were never found.'

Edward stilled. 'What are you suggesting? That we hide it?'

'Gracious no. We need to be a great deal more thorough than that. We cannot risk it falling into her solicitor's hands.'

She turned her china-blue eyes on the fire that was blazing in the grate. Edward visibly jolted when he understood.

'Yes,' he said in a low voice. 'She has left us with no alternative. I'm damned if I'm to be pauperised by a drove of donkeys!'

He strode determinedly towards the fire, but Clara reached out and snatched back the document.

'Wait. We haven't agreed our terms.'

'What terms? If she is intestate, her fortune will revert to the holder of the Denham title. I am sorry but that is simply how it is.'

Clara stared him down. Esther had been wrong when she dismissed Miss Brereton as a milksop.

'There is nothing simple about it,' she said. 'I need to know what my silence is worth.'

'Your word against mine.'

Clara's tight little smile did not slip. 'I could go to Lady Denham right now and confess to everything, with four or five servants and a doctor to witness it.'

'You wouldn't dare.'

'What have I to lose?' She walked to the door.

'Wait! A thousand pounds.'

'And leave you with the rest? I would sooner let the asses have it.'

'A tenth.' He despised himself for the desperation in his voice.

'Half.'

'A fifth and no more.'

She walked back towards the fire and dropped it in. Both of them watched as the paper began to catch, the first words consumed by the flames. He went to stand next to her.

'What will I say to Esther?'

'I see no need to involve her.' She moved a little closer to him. 'Her claim is weak after all. And you wouldn't wish to dilute your share further . . .'

'Be that as it may, she is still my sister.'

'You know better than I how biddable she is.'

Edward allowed himself to look at Clara. Her pale hair had been burnished to copper in the fire, her blue eyes to gleaming pewter. She met his gaze and the room around them faded to nothing.

'I have always suspected that, unlike us, dear Esther is burdened with a conscience,' she went on, her voice soft now, persuasive. 'It would be a shame to let her hold you back, now that you are so close to getting what you have always wanted.'

She gestured at the fire, where the last corner of the will was succumbing to the flames. It was done.

'Look at that,' she murmured. 'You have just become shockingly wealthy.'

He didn't consciously reach for her but suddenly they were upon each other, their mouths bruising as they kissed, their hands tearing at each other's clothes. As Clara pulled him down to the floor, Edward had the thought that nothing, not even his sister at the door, could have stopped him. He wanted Clara even more than he despised her.

Tom Parker was still in the sitting room of his London house. How long he'd been staring into the fire he couldn't tell. It was only the sound of the front door opening that startled him out of his reverie.

'Who's there?' he said, squinting into the dimly lit hallway.

As his eyes adjusted, he realised it was his brother and two ladies. Was it – yes! Miss Lambe and Charlotte. Though still exhausted in body and mind, he painted on his usual smile and called out jovially to them.

'Sidney! Miss Lambe! And Miss Heywood! To what do I owe such a delightful surprise? Might I assume you've all come to help raise interest in the regatta?'

But Miss Lambe was already heading for the stairs, her face shuttered.

'I need a scalding hot bath at once,' she addressed a maid who been summoned by the noise of their arrival. 'And you will take this dress away and burn it.'

'What on earth . . .?' Tom was more befuddled than ever.

In an upstairs bedroom, waiting for her bath to be ready, Georgiana sat in front of the mirror, wiping off the last of Mrs Harries' powder with a damp handkerchief. Charlotte, who had followed with Sidney, watched Georgiana's reflection, unsure what to say. Sidney, no less awkward, still hovered by the door.

'What will become of him now?' Georgiana said eventually. 'The debtor's prison? Worse?'

She was speaking not of Mr Howard but Otis.

'He is no longer your concern,' said Sidney.

'Whatever he has done, I cannot just cauterise my heart. I am not you.'

Charlotte saw the spasm of hurt cross his face.

'At this moment, your world feels undone,' he said, quite gently. 'I know that. But you must put him from your mind or you will go mad.'

Georgiana's bath ready, Sidney went wearily downstairs. He found Tom in his study. His London desk was in quite as much confusion as the Sanditon one had been before Charlotte's intervention. Sidney sat down opposite his brother. Exhaustion had turned his face grey.

'Never was a person less suited to the role of guardian than I.'

'You have done your best.'

'No, Miss Heywood was right. I have done my utmost to abdicate responsibility. For God's sake, her father saved my life! He pulled me from the depths when I was a lost and miserable wretch. And how have I repaid him? By failing to honour the one thing he asked of me.'

Tom let out a humourless laugh. 'You wish to talk of failure? My labourers have gone unpaid for months and everyone knows it. I promised poor Mary that I'd come to London and put things right, but I've knocked on a hundred doors and no one cares a damn about Sanditon or its stupid regatta. I begin to fear it is over for me, Sidney.'

'It is far from over. You haven't been knocking on the right doors, that is all.' He rubbed his eyes. 'I will talk to Babington – he will know where to go. As for your labourers, what if I lent you the money the banks would not?'

Tom looked up. 'No. I could not ask . . .'

'Three thousand. That was what you needed, wasn't it?'

'It is too much.'

'I am your brother. There was a time when you did the same for me. And if I cannot do right by Georgiana's father, at least – for once – let me do right by you.'

'My dear Sidney . . .' Tom's voice was thick with emotion but Sidney interrupted him.

'More pressing than any of this is Mary. I have always envied your marriage. You found a woman who accepts you for the man you are. Sanditon failing is one thing. But I will never forgive you if you fail your wife.'

It was rare that Sidney spoke so freely, so sincerely. It made the words all the more powerful. Tom sat back in his seat and let out a long sigh.

There was a tap at the door and a maid entered with a letter on a tray. She hesitated, apparently unsure who to give it to.

'Thank you, Maud.' Tom took it, read the name on the front and then handed it to Sidney.

'I expect you'll want to open this.'

Written in a slightly wild hand, it was addressed to Sidney's troublesome ward.

Mary welcomed yet another visitor into her drawing room, wondering if there was to be no end to the stream of callers that day. This time it was Esther Denham, who had already been preceded by Mrs Griffiths, the Beaufort sisters and the Reverend Hankins. With Diana and Arthur showing no signs of leaving, the room was quite full. Mary's head ached. Really, she wanted nothing more than to lie down in her bedroom with the curtains pulled.

'Miss Denham,' she said, with some attempt at civility. 'No doubt you have also come to show your concern for

Miss Heywood and Miss Lambe.'

Esther looked a little shamefaced. 'Oh. No. I assumed, if anything dreadful happened, word would reach me soon enough. Actually, I come with news of my aunt.'

'And how is Lady Denham? I trust she has recovered from her episode?'

A silence descended as all present awaited the answer.

Esther adopted a serious expression. 'Quite the opposite, I am afraid. She is gravely ill. Dr Fuchs begins to fear the worst.'

'Mercy!' exclaimed Mrs Griffiths.

Mr Hankins patted her arm. 'We must pray for her soul.'

Arthur swallowed whatever it was he had been chewing. 'Whoever would have guessed that she was mortal?' he mused.

'But what will this mean for Sanditon?' said Diana. 'For us?'

Mary, whose precise thoughts her sister-in-law had just voiced, could not bring herself to answer.

In Sanditon House's splendid drawing room, their lust now spent, Edward and Clara were straightening the clothes they had so recently shed. As Edward fumbled to fasten the buttons of his breeches, Clara walked over to the fire. A single fragment of the will had escaped the flames. She picked up the poker and nudged it to the hottest part of the fire.

'There is no turning back now,' she said. 'I hope I can trust you to honour our deal. A quarter of all you inherit.'

'We agreed on a fifth.'

Her sly little smile was becoming quite familiar to Edward. 'It is a lady's prerogative to change her mind.'

'You have just proven quite conclusively that you are no lady.'

Her eyes narrowed. 'What about Esther?' she said in a knowing tone. Too knowing. 'Is she a lady?'

Edward started.

'Don't fear. I haven't breathed a word to anyone. I know how judgemental people would be if they knew how close you really are.'

'I have no idea what you mean,' he blustered.

'Yes, you do. It would break her heart into tiny little pieces if she were to learn of this, would it not?'

Foreboding filled Edward like ice-water.

Clara gave him a triumphant smile. 'A quarter share will suffice.'

Charlotte warmed her fingers against the cup of hot tea that had been poured for her. Though it was not cold in Tom's London sitting room, the fire burning brightly, recent events had shaken her so that she felt chilled to the bone.

'I do hope Mary will forgive me for stealing away,' she said anxiously, having just remembered it. She had quite forgotten in the desperate hunt for Georgiana.

Tom smiled distractedly. 'Oh, Mary is the most forgiving person I know. She will just be glad to know you are safe and sound.' He peered at her more closely. 'My dear Charlotte, you are trembling.'

'It has all been rather overwhelming. I hardly know what to think anymore.'

'About what, my dear?'

'About anything! I have always felt certain of my own judgement, but I see now that I have been blinded by naivety and sentimentality. How could I have had it all so wrong? No wonder your brother has such a low opinion of me.' She stared despondently into her cup.

'I am certain that is not the case,' said Tom gently. 'Sidney can be rather hard to read that is all. He is a conundrum.'

'But a conundrum can be solved. He seems determined to keep the whole world at arm's length.'

'That hasn't always been the case. In his younger days, he was a very different man.'

She paused, oddly reluctant to hear more, even as she was intrigued. 'Mary has spoken of a broken engagement.'

He nodded gravely. 'Yes. Eliza. They were very much in love, but at the last moment she passed him over in favour of an older, wealthier man. Sidney set out on a rather self-destructive path. We were all greatly concerned. In the end, I paid his debts and he sailed for Antigua in a bid to forget her. It made him a wealthy man, but the man I knew has never quite returned.'

Charlotte's mind was filled with images: a younger Sidney setting sail for the tropics, his heart frozen and closed; not even the heat of Antigua able to thaw it. She tried to picture the face of this Eliza who had so bewitched him, but she couldn't; all she could see was a slender figure turning away.

The sound of the front door closing brought her back to the present. Sidney walked in followed by another man.

'Mr Molyneux!' she exclaimed. He was the last person she had expected to see again.

'I thought they at least deserved a proper parting,' said Sidney.

This gesture was so uncharacteristic of the man she'd just been thinking of that she could do little more than gape at him. Before she could look any more foolish, she hurried from the room to fetch Georgiana.

Miss Lambe, however, was not in the mood for leniency.

Even after Charlotte had persuaded her downstairs, she sat rigidly on her chair, unable or unwilling to even look at the wretched Otis, who for his own part remained standing with an agonised countenance, nervous fingers turning his hat over and over.

'I didn't come to ask forgiveness,' he began. 'I have no right to ask for that. I came because I need you to hear the truth – whether you believe it or not. I have gambled, that is true. But whatever they tell you, I never gambled with your name. I never boasted of your wealth. I boasted of you. Of your wit! Of your beauty! Because I couldn't believe a man of my birth could win the heart of a woman like you. It was pride, that was all. And God knows I have paid for it.'

'We have both paid for it,' she said shortly, her eyes still lowered to her clasped hands.

'I will never forgive myself for putting you in harm's way,' pleaded Otis. 'But before I take my leave for this last time, please know this: I never cared a damn for your fortune. I fell in love with your soul. Tell me you believe me.'

'What difference does it make now?'

Her voice was cold, but she was battling hard to keep her emotions in check. A single tear escaped, rolling down her cheek. Otis closed his eyes at the sight of it and, obviously close to weeping himself, took his leave.

Charlotte could not bear it. She rushed out after him.

'Otis! Will you not say goodbye?'

He stopped. 'Miss Heywood. I had hardly thought you would want to speak to me.'

'What will you do now? How will you settle your debts?'

He spread his hands and smiled sadly. 'My debts have all been paid. I have been shown a grace I don't deserve.'

'By whom?'

She followed Otis's gaze to one of the upstairs windows. There, framed in the glass and watching them with a thoughtful expression, was Sidney.

Some hours after a miserable Otis had taken his leave, Babington called with some welcome news – this time for Tom.

'I have asked around and, as luck would have it, Mrs Maudsley is hosting a rout for three-hundred particular friends this very evening in Grosvenor Square!' he announced, holding up an impressively thick square of embossed card. 'Here is your invitation.'

Tom's eyes lit up.

'My dear Lord Babington, you are a wonder! It sounds as if London's entire *beau monde* will be there – all of them eager to hear about our regatta!'

'Oh, and of course you must come as well, Miss Heywood.' Babington smiled at Charlotte, but she shook her head.

'Thank you, but I should keep watch over Georgiana.'

'Our servants can do that!' cried Mr Parker, quite brimming with his old *joie de vivre* again. 'You must come.'

Charlotte was still reluctant. 'I am afraid I have nothing to wear that would befit such an occasion.'

'You needn't worry on that score,' said Babington. 'My sister Augusta is about your size and she owns acres of silk and organza. She never wears the same thing twice.'

But Charlotte had already stood. 'Thank you, Lord Babington, but I am really not in a mood to be sociable.'

With that, she rushed from the room, Sidney watching her go with a concerned expression.

She hadn't been in her room long when there was a soft knock at the door. Sidney put his head round it.

'Tom has sent me up in the hope that you might reconsider.'

She sighed. 'How can I attend a ball while Georgiana lies devastated? What right do I have to enjoy myself?'

Sidney smiled mischievously. 'Oh, I do not expect to enjoy myself. But for Tom's sake . . .'

Charlotte's confusion and guilt spilled over as frustration. 'Why would he even want me there? I am a liability.'

'Tom doesn't seem to think so.'

'Well, he is inclined to see the best in everyone.'

'Unlike his brother?'

She regarded him curiously. 'Why did you pay off Otis's debt?'

Now it was his turn to sigh. 'I am not entirely sure.'

'You must have a reason.'

He looked away, embarrassed. 'Perhaps I came to the realisation that a good man shouldn't be condemned for one terrible mistake.'

'And what did you ask in return?'

Sidney shook his head. 'He has lost the woman he loved. That is punishment enough.'

'Loved?'

When he looked up again, his dark eyes were soft and melancholy. She hadn't seen him look so vulnerable before, and she found herself unable to look away.

'Otis wrote Georgiana a letter,' he said. 'I took the liberty of reading it. It would seem that he did love her, a great deal. You were right all along.'

*

At Denham Place, Esther lay in wait for her errant brother on the chaise longue. She had expected him to return from Sanditon House some time ago. Finally, she heard his footstep in the hall.

'You were gone a long while,' she said, trying to read his expression when he came in. The word that sprang to her mind was *furtive*. 'How fares our aunt?'

'Sicker by the hour,' he said bluntly. 'She's even acquiesced to Fuchs' treatment.'

'Dear God, things must be even worse than we thought.'

He gave her a strange smile she didn't understand.

'And the will?' she pressed. 'It must have been carefully hidden given how long you took to find it.'

He paused. 'As a matter of fact, it was nowhere to be found. I – I turned the entire house upside down. I have concluded it doesn't exist.'

'Then why did she say . . .?'

'Her fever has plainly left her confused,' he interrupted. He had still not met her eye. 'She barely knows her own mind.'

'We are her nearest living relatives,' said Esther, brightening. 'If there is no will, does that not work in our favour?'

'You would think so.' He went over to stand by the fireplace.

She covered her eyes with a limp hand. 'Thank God it is almost done. I shall be glad if I never hear another word about that wretched will or Clara Brereton as long as I live.'

Edward continued to stare pensively into the fire, where he half-expected to see a fragment of the wretched will holding out against the flames; proof of his guilt and betrayal.

'As will I,' he said heavily. 'As will I.'

Chapter Thirty

Evening had drawn over London like a rose-coloured veil. In a grand part of the city, the ballroom at Mrs Maudsley's house was already admitting its first guests. Charlotte, for her part, was still in Cheapside. She stood at the glass in her room, inspecting herself in her borrowed gown. Vanity was not one of her faults but she could not tear her eyes away. The dress made her look like another sort of person altogether: older, more sophisticated; someone almost worldly. A woman. Though she was still nervous, her altered appearance helped: it was almost as though she would be impersonating someone else for the night. Her mask would make the illusion complete.

She was acutely aware of Sidney's eyes on her as she descended the stairs. When she dared to meet them, she saw that he believed her transformed too. Suddenly, she doubted she could carry off such a sophisticated look.

'Does it not suit me?' she said worriedly. 'Will it not do?'

He looked up at her in such a way that she could only look down at her slippered feet, her cheeks beginning to burn.

'It will do very well,' he said, his eyes still on her.

The ball was well under way by the time they were announced. Mrs Maudsley's house was barely recognisable as a house; Charlotte thought it was like something from a dream, with hundreds of lit candles, the glitter of jewels around the ladies' necks and dripping from their ears, and everyone's faces obscured by every description of mask. Her nerves, which had sweetened to excitement in the carriage as it swept through a darkening London, returned with interest.

Tom, seeing the ball as nothing more than a God-given business opportunity, looked about him with delight. 'Upon my word, there can hardly be a person worth a fig left in London who is not here. You don't need to see their faces to know these are people of influence!'

They had been spotted by Babington and Crowe, who pushed through the throng to greet them.

'The brothers Parker!' cried Crowe. He caught sight of Charlotte. 'And who is this spellbinding creature? I demand you introduce us at once, Sidney.'

'This is Miss Heywood, you buffoon,' said Babington, elbowing his friend in the ribs. 'You have met on several occasions.'

'Miss Heywood, I would not have known you.' He bowed and kissed her hand. 'A mask becomes you!'

'Thank you, Mr Crowe,' she said with a wry look in Sidney's direction, who smiled back, 'if that was indeed a compliment.'

Tom leant in conspiratorially. 'Now, we must all remember why we are here. To spread the word of the Sanditon regatta! Like Nelson, I expect every man to do his duty. Aye, and woman!'

Crowe rolled his eyes. 'I did not come here to work. I came here to imbibe, carouse and generally make an ass of myself.' With that, he made off towards the dance floor, Tom and Babington in his wake. She and Sidney were left alone.

'Well, Miss Heywood,' he said. 'Aren't you glad you came, after all?'

'I cannot say that I am,' she began, although this was not entirely true. 'I feel dreadful for leaving Georgiana. At least I am glad of this mask. I am certain I don't belong in this company.'

'You've as much right to be here as anyone else. I'm not sure I belong here either.'

'But this is your natural habitat, is it not?'

'Perhaps I don't truly belong anywhere. As you have observed, I am an outlier.'

She looked sharply up at him. He always seemed to remember everything she said.

'Come, Miss Heywood,' he continued, offering her his arm. 'I regret that we are obliged to mingle.'

In a side room for playing cards, Charlotte was growing hot. There were people everywhere; more people than she had ever seen in one place. She had hoped the air would be cooler away from the dancers and the dozens of candelabrum but if anything it was more fiercely hot in the smaller room. She jumped as one of the more inebriated gamesters slammed his cards down on the table. She was glad of Sidney beside her, apparently unaffected by the heat and quite as enigmatic as ever.

On the other side of the room, she watched Tom trying to engage strangers in conversation about Sanditon. Snatches of speech found her over the general racket.

'. . . The most refreshing sea breezes, a coastline of unequalled beauty, and grand apartments that are the envy of the Continent! To which we now add a grand regatta!'

Charlotte's heart ached for him as the grande dame he was talking to moved away without even responding.

'I cannot see how conversation is even possible when the room is so loud and everyone is on the move,' she said to Sidney.

'No one here is to make conversation. They are here to be seen. Once their presence has been acknowledged, they will leave for the next gathering.'

'I think I would like to leave now too, with your permission?'

'Since when have you required my permission to do anything?'

She was suddenly shy again. 'Mr Parker, I must apologise for my earlier behaviour towards you.'

'I do not accept your apology.'

'Why not?' she cried, already bristling and readying herself for one of their arguments. Then she saw his sincere expression.

'Because it is I who should apologise,' he said. 'I have done you a great discourtesy, Miss Heywood. I have under-estimated you.'

The room grew yet hotter and, though it was hard to tear her eyes away from Sidney's, Charlotte feared she would faint if she did not.

She was glad when Babington suddenly appeared at Sidney's side.

'I hate to admit defeat, but the word "regatta" seems to be falling on deaf ears.'

Tom, still on the other side of the room but looking a little discouraged by now, beckoned Sidney over. He was evidently in need of some assistance.

'Excuse me.'

She watched him go, reflecting that the profound confusion he stirred in her was utterly exhausting.

She turned to Babington, determined to think of something else.

'I noticed you and Miss Denham were enjoying each other's company at the cricket match.'

Babington looked surprisingly downcast. 'I had thought so too, Miss Heywood. Alas, I fear I made rather a fool of myself.'

'I am sure you judge yourself too harshly.'

'With all due respect, I will never understand the inconstancy of your sex. You are a woman, Miss Heywood, so tell me this: is it possible for your affections for a man to alter entirely within the space of a day?'

She realised her gaze had been drawn like a magnet back to Sidney.

'Forgive me, Lord Babington, this room is rather too crowded. I find I can hardly breathe.'

'My dear Miss Heywood. Of course, you must . . .'

But she had already hurried away, leaving Babington more confused on the subject of women than ever.

Charlotte pushed through the crowd, which seemed to clot and thicken as she grew more breathless. The masked guests took on a nightmarish quality as they turned to look at her, quite expressionless. She stopped to catch her breath at the doorway to another room and caught sight of an enormous bewigged man lying with his head in a lady's lap while another poured wine directly into his mouth. She threw back her head and laughed as it ran down his face and soaked into her fine dress.

Charlotte stumbled away and found herself at the bottom of a wide curving staircase hewn out of white marble. It was blessedly free of people; the landing just visible above also tantalisingly empty. She ran up without another thought. Entering a dimly lit room she collapsed onto a chair and let out a sigh of relief.

'My sentiments exactly.'

Charlotte's head flew up. In the opposite corner of what appeared to be a library sat a woman who was regarding her with amusement. She was older than Charlotte, perhaps in her early forties, but with her smooth dark hair and fine eyes full of laughter and intelligence, she was quite the most striking woman she had ever seen.

'I am sorry. I thought I was—'

'That's quite all right. I cannot blame you for seeking a safe harbour. It's an unspeakably tedious gathering.'

Charlotte saw that the lady was holding a book. She went over to see the name on the cover. It was a writer she knew. 'So you have taken refuge with Mrs Wollstonecraft?' she said shyly.

Her new friend seemed pleased by this. 'I don't know why Mrs Maudsley even keeps a library. To the best of my knowledge, she is barely literate. It is the height of affectation. And now you are going to tell me she is your mother and I have just committed a terrible solecism.'

Charlotte smiled. 'No. I do not know her in the slightest. Indeed I barely know a soul in London. But from what I have seen of the place, that is no great hardship.'

The lady suppressed another smile. 'If you dislike London so much then why are you here?'

'My friend Georgiana was abducted and I was in large part to blame so I stole away to London in the hope of finding her.' She was talking too fast.

'Gracious! And did you find her?'

'Yes, eventually. She is an heiress, you see, and her suitor Mr Molyneux had accrued certain gambling debts he couldn't pay so she was sold into a forced marriage to this dreadful man named Howard.'

'How simply shocking!' But her companion was clearly entertained by this lurid account.

'It was,' said Charlotte. 'Anyway, thank goodness we found her in time and now she is safe, but Mr Tom insisted we come here this evening to spread word of the Sanditon regatta, but as you see I am singularly failing at that task.'

'Sanditon?'

'Oh, it is the resort Mr Parker is building by the sea. It is the most beautiful place but he has been struggling to attract visitors.' She dropped the book she'd picked up absently. 'So I had the idea of a regatta . . . Forgive me, I am inclined to talk too much, Mrs . . .?'

'Susan.' She put her lovely head on one side. 'And who might you be?'

'Charlotte Heywood.'

'Forgive me for saying so, Charlotte, but you seem somewhat befuddled.'

'Do I? Yes, I do believe I am. It has been as troubling a day as I have ever known and I just had a conversation that . . . well, I hardly know what to make of it.'

Susan leant forward, eyes sparkling once again. 'How so?'

Charlotte hesitated but then realised it would be a relief to let out some of her troublesome thoughts. Perhaps it would bring back some of her usual equanimity. She took a deep breath.

'There is a certain gentleman, Mr Sidney Parker – Mr Tom Parker's brother. He inspires an anger in me that I didn't know I possessed and yet I find that his good opinion means more to me than anyone else's. How can that be?'

Susan smiled kindly. 'It sounds to me as if you are in love with him.'

'What? No! I assure you, nothing could be further from the truth. If I should ever fall in love, it should not be with a man like him.'

'My dear girl, you cannot determine who you fall in love with! It is an affliction, like the measles.'

Charlotte opened her mouth to protest and then shut it again. Susan's words had the unmistakable ring of truth about them.

'It cannot be,' she murmured, her thoughts entirely disordered.

A knock at the door made her startle. Sidney, of all people, walked in.

'There you are!' he cried. 'I was beginning to fear you had made your escape.'

'Oh!' She dropped the book she had only just retrieved from the floor.

Susan smiled mischievously at him. 'Might I presume you are Mr Sidney Parker? We were just discussing you.'

Charlotte froze while Sidney frowned in confusion.

'I see. Well. I wondered if Miss Heywood might like to dance. Unless I am interrupting?'

'Not in the least. I expect Charlotte would like to dance with you very much indeed.'

Unable to think of anything to say, or a reason to refuse, an embarrassed Charlotte allowed him to lead her out and down the stairs. She knew she was trembling and hoped Sidney could not tell.

'You did not have to ask me, you know,' she said, feeling she had to say something. 'Out of politeness.'

Sidney gave her a sidelong look. 'Is this not what people do at dances? Dance? Unless you would rather be reading?'

'No.' She shook her head in confusion. 'It – it is just that there are so many other ladies here you could ask.'

His eyes, when she met them, had taken on that softness again. 'I don't want to dance with them.'

As the music struck up and the dancers moved into position, Charlotte felt sure she would trip over her feet, stamp on Sidney's or simply fall down with sheer mortification. But the rhythm and sway of those around her came to her rescue and soon she was moving unthinkingly, the room around her and Sidney blurring and quietening until there was nothing but the two of them. What she had only dimly sensed before – mere hints of a connection between them – now seemed undeniable.

But then she felt Sidney stiffen. He had seen something, over her shoulder. The softness left his eyes and something else stole into its place. Something darker, wilder. At that moment, the dance came to its end, and he bowed mechanically.

'Thank you, Miss Heywood.' But he was distracted now.

'Thank *you*, Mr Parker,' she said, the first small whispers of doubt in her voice.

Tom suddenly appeared at Sidney's shoulder. 'Might I have the pleasure of the next dance, Charlotte? Or has Sidney worn you out?'

She glanced up at Sidney but he was still looking at someone behind her. She tried to look round but Tom was waiting for a reply.

'Not at all,' she said. 'It would be my pleasure.'

As he whirled her away, she couldn't help thinking that she and Sidney had simply fitted together, as though they had been made to be dance partners. The doubts that had crowded in dissipated as she danced with an ebullient Tom. She forgot what it was that Sidney had been looking at.

He, though, was searching the crowd for the woman he had caught only the merest glimpse of. Perhaps he had imagined her. For a time, after she had severed all contact with him, he had seen her everywhere. He'd even seen her face in the white crests of the waves during the voyage to

Antigua and, after he'd arrived, in the sordid places he had drunk himself into a stupor – though it was impossible that she should be anywhere like that.

He had almost given her up as a figment of an imagination, stirred by the transformation of Charlotte Heywood that evening, when the crowd seemed to part with the express purpose of revealing her. He rushed forward and, sensing his approach, she turned. Her mask was on, and he still couldn't be entirely sure.

'Mrs Campion?' he said, hearing the desperate note in his voice.

She lowered the mask. It was her, as he had known in his soul it would be: a decade older but her hair still golden, the bones of her face sculpted even finer. He thought she was only more beautiful for the passing of the years.

'Sidney,' she said in her melodious tones. His heart contracted. He had heard that voice in his dreams.

Another dance had finished. Tom and Charlotte bowed exaggeratedly to each other, both of them laughing.

'How happy I am to see the light return to your eyes, Charlotte,' exclaimed Tom.

'There is nothing like dancing to restore one's spirits!'

'Quite so, my dear. Quite so! It seems to have had a similar effect on Sidney.'

Something inside her turned over. 'Do you think so?'

'Oh, it is undeniable. He is positively revivified! Ah, but perhaps that is not so much due to the dancing as to the presence of a certain young lady.'

Charlotte blushed. Did he mean her? She hardly dared think so, and yet. . . 'Which young lady do you have in mind, sir?' she said, as carelessly as she could.

But Tom was looking away, over to the other side of the dance floor. 'He is talking to her now. Mrs Campion. It is unmistakably her. I knew she had been widowed but had no idea she was in London. How strange that you and I should have been discussing her just this afternoon. Fate must have overheard us!'

Charlotte followed his gaze, heart thudding painfully. Sidney was deep in conversation with a woman more elegant and sophisticated than she could ever hope to be, however many dances she attended, and dresses she borrowed.

'Look at them,' went on Tom, obliviously. 'It is as if the past decade just vanished!'

Charlotte felt suddenly heavy, as lowered in spirits as if she had been turned to lead, but still she couldn't stop herself saying. 'Forgive me, I – I don't recall discussing a Mrs Campion.'

'Ah! I daresay I referred to her by her Christian name, Eliza. Perhaps they will get their chance of happiness after all!'

Charlotte swayed on her feet. Though she wanted more than anything to run, she couldn't tear her gaze from the couple across the room, whose good looks had begun to draw every other eye to them, too.

Chapter Thirty-One

Charlotte had hoped that her return to Sanditon from London would raise her spirits. Though it was doubtless unfashionable and parochial to admit it, she had not formed a good opinion of the place. If pressed, she might have attributed this to Georgiana's ill-treatment, and perhaps the squalor of the poorer districts glimpsed from the carriage window, but in truth it was how London made her feel: a person of no consequence, whose daydreams of herself and Sidney Parker were shown in their true light to be nothing more than ridiculous fancy. It seemed humiliatingly obvious to her now that they were two very different people, destined for very different futures.

'Charlotte?'

Mary's enquiry startled her out of her despondent idlings.

'Is something troubling you, my dear? Ever since you returned from London, you have seemed a little . . . discountenanced.'

With some effort, Charlotte raised a smile. 'Not at all. Although I am certainly in no hurry to return. It struck me as a rather monstrous place.'

Tom burst into the room before she could say more. 'Well, my dears,' he began. He wore the overexcited expression that Charlotte, like Mary of old, had come to recognise with trepidation. 'The day of the regatta is almost upon us! Do we stand prepared, Charlotte?'

In reply, she indicated the long list of tasks she had been working methodically through, when her mind wasn't drifting back to what had happened in London.

'I believe so,' she said. 'The spectator stand is built, Mrs Ennis is baking enough to feed an army, the hotel is laying in an extra twenty-three barrels and here I have drawn up the final programme. All we need now are some visitors.'

'Oh, they will come!' he cried, his eyes darting feverishly between Charlotte and his wife, and rather belying his words. 'I have not the smallest shred of doubt. By this time tomorrow we shall be thronged with visitors! Thronged, I tell you! Our very future depends on it, does it not Mary?'

Mary smiled, and laid a calming hand on his arm. She had forgiven him after reading his letter. She could not help herself; she loved Tom too much to be angry with him in his hour of need. Even now, his narrow frame was fairly trembling with nervous anticipation. She was about to impart some soothing words when Diana and Arthur bustled in.

'Sit yourselves down, my dears,' said Diana with great solemnity. 'We are the bearers of dreadful news. Poor Lady Denham is . . . no, I cannot say it!' She slumped into a chair, hand pressed to her brow.

'Dead,' finished Arthur, indelicately. 'Well, all but.'

'I have had no use of Dr Fuchs for almost a week,' said Diana. 'He has not left her bedside. By all accounts she will likely be gone by morning.'

Silence descended upon the room as each of them considered a Sanditon without Lady Denham. Then Tom stood, apparently decided, the fevered light back in his eyes. It was impossible to conceive of what he would do if she died, so therefore she would not die. Bald denial had served Tom Parker very well in the past and would do so again now.

'My dear, Diana,' he said with every appearance of unshakeable confidence. 'I am afraid you must be deceived. The very idea of Lady Denham dying is impossible! I should be left without a principal investor. At the very least, we would have to cancel the regatta! No, no, no: it cannot be. She has an iron constitution. She will outlive us all!'

The words rang out loudly and Charlotte wondered if she was the only one for whom they sounded as hollow as a cracked bell – but then she caught Mary's anxious expression and knew that she was not.

At Sanditon House, Tom and Mary Parker had joined Sir Edward, Esther and Clara to pay their last respects. Now that Mr Parker had seen the old lady with his own eyes, his conviction in her certain recovery had faded. When he had come from her bedroom where she lay so still and uncharacteristically silent, he looked as though he had aged ten years.

Dr Fuchs gathered them together in the drawing room. Without Lady Denham's inimitable presence, its cold grandeur made it seem even more like a mausoleum than ever. Reverend Hankins had also been summoned and now stood at the doctor's shoulder, his expression veering between sorrow and self-importance.

'I regret to say I have reached the limit of my abilities as a physician,' Fuchs said. 'I fear she will not see out the night.' He bowed his head.

'Oh, our poor dear aunt,' said Clara, dabbing at her eyes with her handkerchief.

'Come now, Doctor,' said Tom desperately. 'You cannot admit defeat so readily.'

But Fuchs only shook his head.

Hankins saw his chance and stepped forward, hands fumbling on his Bible. 'Rest assured, I shall be on hand. She is going to a far better place, where our Lord shall welcome her into his loving arms.'

'What a comfort that is,' muttered Esther.

'Well, I had better pay my last respects while I still can,' said Sir Edward, with rather too much nonchalance for the occasion. As he passed Clara, he met her eye and something passed between them. Esther, who was almost always watching her brother, did not miss it.

Mary, understanding that they should leave Lady Denham's family alone, ushered her husband outside and back into their carriage. The sun was climbing towards its zenith and he regarded it anxiously. The next time it did so, the regatta would have begun.

As though she had read his mind, Mary turned to him. 'I suppose we shall have to postpone it, out of respect.'

'I see no need for that.' His gaze was still trained on the view beyond the carriage window. 'I said it earlier and I say it again now: Lady Denham will outlive us all!'

'She is gravely ill, Tom. Everyone else can accept it, why not you?'

He said nothing until she reached out to touch his arm. The gesture of affection seemed to unlock something inside him at last.

He turned and reached for her hands. 'Don't you see, Mary? She cannot die and leave me without a principal investor.'

Mary pulled her hands away. 'She is on her deathbed and your only concern is what it will mean for your town?' Her voice had hardened and Tom, hearing it, only grew more frantic.

'No, no. You misunderstand me. My concern is for you and the children. Without her investment, I should soon face bankruptcy. Our house, our security – everything would be at risk. I am simply speaking frankly, Mary, as we agreed I would.'

Inwardly, he begged her to relent, to reassure him and understand, as she always did. But her reply, when it came, was curt. 'I see,' she said, and then turned away.

Clara and Esther were sitting outside Lady Denham's bedroom, waiting for Edward. Esther was unable to shake off her disquiet. The look exchanged by Edward and Clara had been secretive, yes, and that was bad enough, but it was also knowing, and that worried her more.

It was Clara who finally broke the silence.

'Edward is taking his time. I cannot think what is keeping him, given conversation with our aunt has become somewhat one-sided.'

'He is showing due respect to a dying woman,' said Esther reprovingly. 'You might consider doing likewise.'

Clara turned to her with a sneer that quite spoilt her doll-like prettiness. 'What has she ever done to merit my respect?'

'And yet she took you in when no one else would. She fed you, housed you, clothed you. Despite you being the most obscure of relations.'

Clara laughed. 'I cannot be that obscure, else you and Edward would hardly have been so threatened by my claim.'

'Do not flatter yourself. You were never a threat. Merely an irritant. I take comfort in knowing that once our aunt is buried, we shall never think of you again.'

'I cannot entirely agree with you there, my dear. Although the two of you will hardly think of me in the same way.'

There were questions Esther was burning to ask, and answers Clara clearly wanted to give, but she managed to resist.

'I will not be goaded into another quarrel. The source of our enmity is finished. There never was a will. All that she has will be divided between us and this whole miserable business will be ended. Thank God.'

She stood but so did Clara, the latter smiling strangely. 'Oh, you poor dear thing,' she said, her mouth twisting so she didn't laugh. 'I felt certain Edward would have told you by now. I did not think the two of you kept secrets from each other . . .' She widened her blue eyes.

A cold hand clutched Esther's heart. 'What are you talking about?'

'Well, I suppose you have a right to know. Contrary to what you have heard, there was a will, but its contents were demonstrably absurd. None of us would have received a penny. It would not do, so Edward and I took the only sensible action available to us. We burnt it. We agreed a half share was a far more agreeable outcome.'

Esther took a step towards her. 'There is not a chance Edward would ever conspire with you. He regards you with absolute contempt . . .'

'And yet,' Clara spoke over her, 'there is no way to feign the kind of fondness he showed me that night.'

Blood began to thrum loudly in Esther's ears. 'You are lying,' she said, but the words were little more than a whisper.

Clara's lips curled into a triumphant smile. 'I *was* lying. With him – on the floor of her ladyship's drawing room, if you must know. I admit it was a fleeting encounter, but he was touchingly eager. Like a little boy. Has that been your experience too?'

Emotion took Esther over. She raised her hand and slapped Clara across the face as hard as she could. For an instant, she looked as shocked as Esther herself was, but then she began to smile. It was that knowing look again.

'Oh!' Clara didn't bother to hide her glee. 'Could it be that you have never given yourself to him? Small wonder he was so keen to take his pleasure elsewhere.'

Esther's fury spent, the truth of Clara's words only added to her sudden and terrible faintness. She gripped the arm of a chair to stop herself simply falling down. 'You are a worthless whore,' she managed to say.

'A whore?' said Clara consideringly. 'Possibly. But worthless? Quite the reverse.'

With that, she left Esther alone, as usual waiting for Edward.

It was not only Lady Denham who suffered in her bed chamber that morning. At Mrs Griffiths' lodging house, Miss Lambe could not leave hers, either – or rather, *would* not. She lay in the darkness, professing that she could not bear the bright light of day. Unlike Lady Denham, it was not a physical ailment that so afflicted her but a depression of spirits that seemed hopeless.

Her guardian climbed the stairs, as he had for the last two days without success.

'Still no improvement this morning, I am afraid,' murmured Mrs Griffiths, as she led the way. 'I begin to fear she is beyond salvation!'

'Georgiana!' She tapped on the door. 'Mr Parker is here to see you again.'

'Send him away!' came the inevitable reply, though Sidney was at least heartened by the strength of her voice.

Mrs Griffiths opened the door a few inches. The air of the room was hot and stale.

'I wish only to talk, Georgiana,' he said into the half-dark. 'I am concerned for you.'

'No, you are not.' Her voice was strangely expression-less. 'You have never seen me as anything other than an inconvenience, so why affect compassion now?'

He hovered in the doorway, not quite brave enough to enter and incur further wrath.

'Georgiana, I am all too aware that I have fallen short as your guardian, but please believe me that I am sincere in my desire to make amends.'

Her voice, when it came, remained flat and unmoved, as though all her liveliness of character had been siphoned away. 'Men like you cannot change,' she said. 'You may leave me now.'

As he descended the stairs, he reflected that he would rather she had been angry with him. He was almost at the door when Charlotte was admitted. He felt his heart lift at the sight of her.

'Miss Heywood,' he said warmly.

'Mr Parker. How did you find her?'

He shook his head. 'I daresay you will have more luck than I. If you don't mind, I will wait for you.'

'Of course.'

'I am at a loss,' he said when they were walking back towards Trafalgar House. 'She seems to think I'm an irredeemable monster.'

'And that strikes you as an unfair assessment?'

He looked sharply at her and then saw the sparkle in her eyes and laughed. They were not yet accustomed to the new form their acquaintance had taken. Where once they were adversaries, there was now something like friendship between them. He wasn't entirely sure how to navigate these mysterious new waters.

'You must be patient with her,' Charlotte went on. 'For a young woman in love, every minute spent apart is . . .' She stopped and coloured, turning her face away. 'Well, you know how sharp the agony of separation can be, and Georgiana has no hope of being reunited with her love.'

Sidney sighed. He hadn't noticed anything. 'I expect you are right, Miss Heywood. Although fate has a way of surprising even the most jaded of us.'

Though she suspected he was talking of his old love Eliza, Charlotte smiled bravely. 'You are not nearly as unfeeling as you pretend.'

'If that is the case, I will thank you to keep it to yourself. I have a reputation to uphold.'

Her heart fluttered as he smiled at her. It was more open than any he had yet given her. 'Your secret is safe with me,' she managed to say.

She did not think she was imagining this new intimacy between them, but she had not imagined how Sidney had looked at Mrs Campion at the ball in London either. She had not been able to forget the sight of their heads so close together in the ballroom, and the admiring whispers that had greeted the spectacle of such a handsome couple. Indeed, she had dreamt of it more than a couple of times since, waking with a beating heart and a rising gorge. Her great comfort was that Sidney had not uttered the widow's name since, at least not in her presence. Mrs Campion was a hundred or more miles away, and there Charlotte hoped she'd stay.

*

After Sidney had left her, Tom requested that Charlotte should join him in his study. She was disheartened to see him pacing the floor when she got there, his face as agitated as she had ever seen it. Since he had returned from Sanditon House, he had apparently not sat down, even for luncheon.

He turned to her, and gestured to the lists they had been compiling since the idea for the regatta had struck.

'So, we will start with the sandcastle competition at eleven, followed by the fishermen's boat race.'

Charlotte held up her pencil. 'Did we not say that the fishermen's race would be—?'

'Oh yes, that's it! Yes, quite right, my dear.' He pushed his hands through his hair. 'So, after a respectable break for luncheon, comes the fishermen's boat race.'

'And then we end the day with the men's amateur rowing.'

'Splendid! There is something for everyone to enjoy. All that we need now are some visitors.' He laughed but the sound was strangulated, his eyes on the empty street below the window. His fear that it would remain so tomorrow was palpable; Charlotte could almost smell it in the room.

A tumult in the hallway revealed itself to be the children as they ran in.

'Papa! Papa!' singsonged little Jenny.

'Uncle Sidney is here,' exclaimed Alicia, triumphant to have announced it first.

Not to be outdone, Jenny grasped her father's leg. 'And he's brought a pretty lady with him!'

Charlotte's heart plummeted. She followed Tom and the children into the drawing room, where Mary was already welcoming the new arrival. It was Sidney who drew her eye first, as he always did, but he did not turn to smile at her, as he had just an hour or two earlier, when they returned from seeing Georgiana. Now he was entirely occupied with looking at another.

'Tom,' he said, 'you remember Mrs Campion? Although of course you knew her as Miss Eliza Stirling.'

Mary, who'd greeted them already, widened her eyes at Tom. 'Sidney has invited Mrs Campion down for the regatta.' Her eyes strayed to Charlotte. 'Isn't that a wonderful surprise?'

Tom went forward to take the new arrival's hand. 'Absolutely wonderful. Welcome!'

'You are most kind,' said Mrs Campion. She had a low, thrilling voice, as though designed to encourage men to lean closer. 'I must say, the pair of you have barely altered since I last saw you.'

Though Charlotte could not help but inspect the interloper with grim fascination – from her fashionable hair and delicate features to the fine silk of her gown – Eliza Campion did not glance at Charlotte once. This snub, intended or not, made her feel like a girl in smock and ribbons by comparison; no kind of rival at all. Without anyone noticing, a miserable Charlotte slipped away.

At Sanditon House, Edward emerged from his aunt's bedchamber. He had paid no respects, last or otherwise, and was in fact smirking.

'I am no Dr Fuchs,' he said to the waiting Esther in some thick approximation of a Prussian accent, 'but I do not *zink* she is long for *zis vorld*.'

Esther did not dignify him with a response, only sweeping past him with a look of disgust.

Her aunt's room was almost in darkness, the heavy curtains closed and only a few candles lit. Esther could smell something, slightly rotten and sweet, and wondered if it was the scent of approaching death. She did not feel grief for the old woman; she had never liked her aunt and it would be disingenuous to pretend affection now, at the end. That would be make her no better than Clara Brereton and, well, no better than Edward, too. She hated to think ill of him – she had long ago trained herself to ignore his less attractive traits – but that was before. Only a fool could think kindly of him at this moment, and Esther would no longer be a fool, not for him.

She approached the bed, wherein her aunt seemed to have shrunk yet further, her form small and rather vulnerable, surrounded as it was by a mountain of pillows. Even in the low light, her skin was terribly pale and waxen.

'I – I know what I am supposed to say,' Esther said softly, watching for a flicker in the old lady's face. There was nothing and it emboldened her to go on.

'I am supposed to talk about the fondness I bear you, about your fine and noble qualities, how your passing shall leave me wretched with grief . . . Well, I cannot weep crocodile tears like everybody else. This house has heard too many lies. You deserve the truth. You should know there is not a person alive who holds you in the least affection. Not Clara. Not Edward. Not me. To my eternal regret, we cared only for your fortune. I have realised too late what a foul corrupting cancer your money is. It never brought you the least happiness. It turned you into a cruel, miserly old woman who will die unloved and unmourned. And it turned Edward . . . My Edward . . .' Her voice cracked.

She took a deep breath, sat down next to the bed and reached for her aunt's hand. The skin was as dry as paper, the bones under it as fragile as a bird's.

'The truth is, he has betrayed both of us. He betrayed us when he and Clara lay with each other on your drawing room floor. He betrayed us when he and Clara conspired to burn your will and share your fortune. My life lies in ruins and your money is the cause. I hope you will find happiness in heaven, because this earth has become a living hell.'

She bowed her head, and allowed a single tear of pity for both of them to fall upon the silk coverlet.

Once the appropriate greetings had been made at Trafalgar House, Sidney suggested that he show Mrs Campion Sanditon's beach. Her presence had affected him more strongly than he had anticipated; he wanted them to be alone together.

'I still can't quite believe you are here,' he said now, as they walked slowly in the direction of the beach. It did not occur to him that he was retracing the steps he'd taken with Charlotte just a few hours earlier.

'Oh, I'm quite real,' said Eliza teasingly. 'Flesh and blood, see?' She held out a narrow white hand for him, and he took it, briefly.

'The town looks just as I remember it,' she went on, looking about her with a keenly appraising eye.

Sidney paused. 'At first glance, perhaps, but, well it is only to be expected that things will have altered, after all this time. I hardly suppose either of us are entirely the same people that we were.'

She turned to him in surprise. 'Are we not? I believe I am still the same girl I ever was.'

He thought back to the exchanges he'd had that morning, first with his ward and then with Charlotte. He was not quite willing to relinquish the notion of himself as someone who might be capable of change; of evolving.

'But who is to say if I am still the same man?' he said, more seriously than he intended.

'You are,' Eliza replied easily. 'I knew it the moment I saw you in London.'

He did not know if he was reassured or frustrated by this. Then he looked at her again – the face he had loved for more than half his life, and realised it hardly mattered.

'I am so very glad you accepted my invitation. I wasn't entirely sure you would see the appeal of a provincial regatta.'

Under the pretence of moving aside for an old gentleman, she allowed the silk of her dress to brush his hip. 'Oh, I am not here for the regatta, Sidney,' she said softly. 'I am here for you.'

Chapter Thirty-Two

The morning of the regatta dawned and then, to Tom Parker's consternation, proceeded to wear on fast. At ten o'clock, the town remained stubbornly hushed. Bunting strung across the street lifted unadmired in the warm breeze and stallholders chatted amongst themselves, their untouched wares covered with cloths to keep off the flies. It was all anticipation, with none of the activity that should follow.

Tom, leading the Parker clan through the town, along with Babington and Crowe, was growing flustered. A large banner announcing 'The Grand Sanditon Regatta' seemed to mock him from above.

'I must say, I had hoped we would have more visitors by now,' he said.

'Perhaps some people have gone straight to the river,' said Mary.

'The men's race is not till four,' put in Charlotte. 'There is bound to be a good-sized crowd by then.' The words came out more irritably than she intended. She had hoped the regatta would prove a distraction but so far, she could think of nothing but Sidney and Mrs Campion.

'Yes, yes, I'm sure you are right,' said Tom. 'Although I do have concerns about the weather. Those clouds look rather ominous, don't you think?'

'No one minds a little rain,' said Mary, in her usual placatory tones. 'It's a regatta. Getting wet is to be expected.'

Babington, who was with Crowe at the head of the party, was no less preoccupied than Charlotte.

'I do wonder if we should have done at least a little preparation for the race,' he said idly, his mind elsewhere as his eyes roved around, in search of a particular head.

'Tsk,' said Crowe, as he took a generous swig from a hip flask. 'A gentleman does not practice. It is tantamount to cheating. Why do you keep looking around? Not keeping an eye out for that Esther Denham creature, I hope?'

'Heavens, no,' said Babington unconvincingly. 'I have called off that particular hunt. It was a futile pursuit.'

Crowe gave him a sceptical look and handed over the flask. 'Thank God. We have already lost Sidney to the siren's call. I'm damned if I'm going to lose you as well.'

Edward awoke with a start, quite disorientated. Bright sunlight streamed into a room far bigger than his bedroom. It was his aunt's drawing room, he suddenly realised, and then he startled again. Esther was standing watching him, just a few feet away.

'Is it over then?' he said blearily. '*La tante est morte?*'

'Not yet.' She regarded him strangely. He couldn't read her expression at all. It was disquieting.

'If I had known it was going to be this drawn out, I would have slept in my own bed,' he said. Feeling disapproved of always made him petulant.

At that moment, Dr Fuchs rushed in, followed by a dazed-looking Clara.

'Quite unexpectedly, a short while ago, your aunt's fever broke,' said Fuchs excitedly. 'She is now able to sit up and talk *ein bischen*! It is entirely possible that she might yet recover!'

Edward stood and briefly met Clara's eye. 'I . . . I am quite lost for words.'

Clara was quicker. 'You are a miracle worker, Doctor.'

Realising the doctor was expecting a response from him, and that Esther was also watching him beadily, Edward belatedly strode over and shook the man's hand.

They found Lady Denham sitting up in bed, propped up by the usual multitude of cushions and pillows. The canny gleam in her eye was back. It was clear that while her illness had ravaged her bodily, it had had little effect on her character.

'Words cannot express our relief, Aunt,' said Edward with an unconvincing smile.

'We have been praying for you,' said Clara, not to be outdone. 'We have kept up a constant vigil.'

Lady Denham pursed her lips. 'I am touched. But console yourselves. I found dying highly disagreeable. I have no intention of repeating the experience. Although it must be said there is nothing like an imminent demise to focus the mind.'

'How so, Aunt?'

The old lady paused, and looked hard at each of the three of them in turn.

'I have always found your ham-fisted attempts to grasp my fortune faintly endearing. But I had underestimated the fathomless depths of your venality.'

There was a pause. It was Edward who recovered quickest this time.

'Aunt, you need to rest awhile. Your fever has left you confused.'

'I am anything but! Like a phoenix, I am rising from the ashes! Unlike the remains of my last will and testament.'

Clara and Edward both visibly paled. Esther clapped her hand over her mouth in shock. She had been heard after all.

'Like your miserable hearts,' continued Lady Denham, 'they are blackened beyond redemption!'

'It – it was Clara,' cried Edward. 'I did all that I could to stop her, Aunt . . .'

'Liar!' Clara said with venom.

'Silence! Both of you. You pathetic vipers! You will neither of you ever set foot across my threshold again. Sir Edward Denham, from this moment you are disowned. As for you, Miss Clara Brereton, you will be on the next coach back to London. You should know that I have summoned my solicitor and from this day forth, the sole beneficiary of my will shall be Esther.'

'What?' Esther was stunned.

'Needless to say, I will also be laying a new floor in my drawing room. It seems the old one has been indelibly stained.'

Satisfied with her performance, Lady Denham folded her hands over each other and closed her eyes. They were dismissed – two of them, it seemed, permanently.

As the door was closed peremptorily behind them by a servant, Edward turned to Clara, real hatred burning in his eyes.

'Why would you tell her? What were you thinking?'

'It wasn't me. Why would I—'

'Then how did she know? How else could she possibly . . .?'

Esther interrupted him. 'It was me,' she said flatly. 'I told her every last detail. It was just as Clara described it to me. I thought she had a right to know.'

Edward was speechless, but Clara managed to raise a bitter smile.

'Bravo then, Esther. It looks like you won.'

But Esther was still looking at her brother as she began to walk away, her face twisted in pain.

'Nobody won.'

Edward caught up with her on the drive, grabbing her roughly by the arm.

'What on earth possessed you? To betray your own brother!'

She shook him off.

'You wish to talk of betrayal?'

'I had the situation in hand. If you could only have trusted me instead of taking the word of that scheming bitch . . .'

'You were scheming *with* her.'

'I did what I had to! It was all for our benefit. We would have been left with nothing.'

'"*We*"?'

'I would have seen to it that you were taken care of, of course I would. Just as you have no wish to see me flung out without a penny now.' He stopped; something had occurred to him. 'It is all right, Esther. It is not too late. You can still rectify this. Just tell Lady Denham that you had it all wrong. That you . . . you misconstrued the situation. It was all Clara's doing. I have been wronged just as you have . . .'

Esther shook her head in disbelief. 'Even now, that is all you care about? The wretched money?'

'Of course not. This is about us. Securing our future.'

'Don't you see?' Her voice wobbled on the last word but she swallowed down the tears that threatened. 'There is no us. There is no future. You have seen to that.'

With that, she walked away. She didn't look back.

*

It was nearly eleven o'clock and, though the town could not yet be called busy, the fine weather was beginning to draw some to the beach. The much-vaunted sandcastle competition was chiefly to thank for this, with dozens of children intent on their creations, watched over by doting mothers, fathers and nursemaids.

Sidney was walking with Eliza along the shoreline. Perhaps it was the new day, or the happy children in the vicinity, but a new ease and familiarity had sprung up between them. The years they had been apart seemed to have contracted to nothing.

'At the last regatta I attended, they raced Arab stallions,' Eliza said. 'The one before that featured eight clippers in full sail. For sheer exhilaration though, what could compare to a sandcastle competition?' She gave Sidney a mischievous smile.

'Ah, but these are no ordinary sandcastles,' he said, unwilling to join in any mockery of Sanditon, however gentle. 'Look at this one, for instance.'

Just ahead of them was a barefoot woman who, as they drew closer, revealed herself to be Charlotte. She was helping the Parker children with their own enormous castle, laughing easily as Henry put sandy hands on her dress. Sidney found himself smiling at the pretty picture they made, the child so appealing and Charlotte blooming with health. As fresh and pink as a rose, he thought idly.

'What a handsome construction,' he called. 'Might I assume you're the architect, Miss Heywood?'

She turned and he thought her happy expression faltered at the sight of him. But then she looked down at the sand and he told himself he'd imagined it.

'Oh no,' she said. 'That would be Jenny. I am merely a labourer.'

'Well, it is a fine piece of work. If it doesn't win, there is no justice.'

She met his eye then, and he felt obscurely guilty, though she smiled brightly enough.

'Well done, children!' said Eliza, rather late, and he tore his gaze from Charlotte's. Next to her wholesome charm, Eliza was an exotic bloom, elegant and rather formal. He shook the comparison away.

After wishing the children luck, they went on their way and, for the first time, Sidney was at a loss for what to say next.

'Who did you say that girl was?' Eliza said eventually.

'Miss Heywood. She is a guest of my brother and Mary's.'

'And she helps with the children?'

He frowned. 'Well. Amongst other things.'

'She is a rather sweet little thing,' Eliza said, her tone was somewhat dismissive. He sensed her turn to study him, and the odd unease he'd felt earlier returned.

Diana and Arthur were walking through the town in a state of disagreement over Arthur's fitness to row that afternoon when a grand carriage of the very first order rolled smoothly past them, leaving in its wake a hubbub of excitement and speculation as to whom it might contain. Those who were already in attendance looked to each other triumphantly: they had chosen right if Sanditon could attract such people.

The coach came to a halt not far from the curious Parker siblings, and they watched with great interest as two bewigged footmen jumped down and opened the door, putting up their arms to help out three arrestingly fashionable ladies. One in particular stood out, not only for her erect and elegant bearing, but her air of comfortable entitlement.

Diana, quite forgetting her argument with Arthur, had observed all this with great intensity and now let out a gasp. She poked her brother with a sharp elbow.

'Do you realise who that is?' she hissed.

He peered closer. 'I'm sure I don't know. When ladies are rigged out in their hats and parasols and lace wot-nots, they all look the same to me. Though that one does rather look like Lady Worcester.'

'That's because it *is* Lady Worcester!' said Diana reverently.

With great swiftness, given their usual perambulatory care, Diana and Arthur hurried to the beach, where Tom was awarding prizes for the sandcastle competition.

When Diana announced the new arrival, Tom started so violently he almost lost his footing in the soft sand. 'Lady Worcester? Are you quite sure?'

Diana raised an eyebrow. 'Had I the least doubt, the lavishness of her dress and carriage would have confirmed it!'

'But why did she not alert us to her arrival? We should have been there to welcome her!'

He rushed away, a determined smile already painted on, one hand twitching, ready to hail the guest who might be about to reverse his fortunes. 'Lady Worcester!' he could be heard muttering to himself as he went. 'We must leave nothing to chance! Her every whim must be indulged! If we can secure her patronage, we will be rendered fashionable at a stroke!'

Charlotte, amused and relieved for Tom in equal measure, turned to Diana.

'Who is this lady?'

'My dear, she is quite notorious! London society positively revolves around her. It is a well-known fact that she and the Prince Regent are . . .' She paused, searching for a delicate turn of phrase.

'*Simpatico?*' offered Arthur with a wink.

Diana tittered. 'To say the least!' Unwilling to miss anything, she turned and sped after Tom, Arthur and Charlotte following close behind. They caught up with him close to the hotel. The street outside it was now teeming with a class of people Sanditon did not generally see. Most of them were already holding champagne glasses.

Tom, spotting Lady Worcester in the melee, approached her almost at a canter, bowing as he did – a peculiar spectacle that successfully caught her attention.

'My lady, a thousand welcomes!' he cried. 'I beg your forgiveness for missing your arrival. Mr Tom Parker.' He bowed again. 'We are greatly honoured and you will not regret venturing to Sanditon. As you shall see, we have quite the finest situation on the south coast! The seawater and the breezes are—'

Lady Worcester waved him away. 'Oh hush, never mind all that.' She was already looking past him to someone else. 'If I gave a fig about the sea, I would have gone to Brighton. I am here to continue my conversation with Miss Heywood.'

She moved a couple of people aside with her fan. As they locked eyes, Charlotte was flooded with belated recognition. Here was her friend from Mrs Maudsley's library!

'Susan!' she exclaimed, before she could check herself.

'Charlotte, I have been so looking forward to renewing our acquaintance.' She came forward and took Charlotte's hands, her smile warm and genuine.

As she turned Charlotte round to display her to the grand entourage, who promptly burst into fawning applause, Tom could only stand gaping in astonishment.

*

One o'clock had come and gone and the crowds were beginning to drift towards the river. In close step behind the Parkers were Lady Worcester and Charlotte. The former's impressive retinue followed in their wake, a magnificent flock of silk and lace and self-assurance. Charlotte was slightly out of breath, having related to Lady Worcester all that had happened since they had last met, at the latter's insistence.

'So,' she said now, counting on her gloved fingers, 'the lady of the town is on her deathbed and the heartsick heiress has taken to her bed. How thrilling! But more important than any of this, does a certain person yet know that you are in love with him?'

Charlotte, colouring instantly, looked about them to check who might have overheard. Though she couldn't see Sidney, Mrs Campion herself was not far behind.

'I fear you are mistaken, my lady,' she said, mortified. 'I was not . . . am not . . .'

'Susan, please. I am never wrong when it comes to matters of the heart.'

'Even if it were true, he is now spoken for.'

Lady Worcester curled her lip. 'Oh, I know all about Mrs C. She must be the wealthiest widow in the country, not to mention the most elegant. I can see why you would find her a dispiriting rival.' She caught sight of Charlotte's despondent expression and leant in closer. 'But she will have a chink in her armour. We just need to find it!'

She stopped and turned. 'Mrs Campion!' she called. 'I have been longing to meet you. I have heard so much about you.'

Charlotte could bear no more. She hurried away down the hill, and was excessively relieved to see Young Stringer waiting for her, like a figure from a much simpler world. He was smiling eagerly.

'Miss Heywood, I wondered if I might persuade you to take a walk. Unless, of course, now is not a . . .'

She took his arm before he could finish and steered him down the hill. 'Now is the perfect time. I need to make sure everything stands ready at the starting line. Perhaps you could accompany me?'

When she glanced behind her, missing Young Stringer's smile of triumph, Lady Worcester and Mrs Campion were deep in conversation.

'It looks like the regatta is going to be a success,' Young Stringer was saying, oblivious to her agitation, 'and that is in large part down to you. You have put so much work into it.'

'In truth, I have been glad of the distraction.'

'Distraction from what?'

'My own thoughts, I suppose.'

'What kind of thoughts?'

'It is difficult to say.'

'Perhaps you will find me a more sympathetic listener than you might imagine. It could even be that you and I share the same thoughts.'

She missed another adoring look. 'I doubt it. You are far too sensible to form such a misguided and futile attachment.'

'Why should it be futile, Miss Heywood? For all you know, your feelings are repaid five times over.'

'I allowed myself to believe it for the briefest of moments, but I cannot deny the evidence of my own eyes. No matter, there is nothing to be done. You were right, Mr Stringer, you are a sympathetic listener indeed.' She patted his arm and moved away, blind to the disappointment in his face.

'Think nothing of it, miss,' he said quietly, too low for her to hear.

Meanwhile, the Parker brothers were in the middle of their own discussion of the opposite sex as they walked.

'What news of Miss Lambe, Sidney?' said Arthur. 'She is notable by her absence.'

'I fear she still refuses to leave her room. I do not know what is to be done.'

Tom was scarcely listening; intent as he was on his most important guest. 'I am as fond of Charlotte as anyone,' he said, almost to himself, 'but I cannot fathom Lady Worcester's fascination.'

Sidney allowed his gaze to rest on Charlotte, up ahead of them with Young Stringer. 'Most young women choose their opinions according to the fashion, so they become quite interchangeable. Miss Heywood not only has opinions of her own, she is unafraid to voice them.'

Just as he said this, she caught his eye and smiled.

But Tom was gesturing towards a quite different woman now.

'And what of Mrs Campion? I cannot believe you find *her* interchangeable?'

'Indeed, no. She is equally singular.'

'I should say so!' said Tom admiringly, though whether for her character or her fortune was not clear. 'She is a lady of many fine qualities. Not least of which is that, following the untimely departure of Mr Campion, she is once more at liberty to wed!'

'I think you are getting a little ahead of yourself, Tom.' Sidney found himself looking at Charlotte again.

'All I know is that since you last returned from London, you have seemed more alive than you have in years.'

Tom bent to pick up little Henry, who was pulling at his breeches, and Arthur turned confidingly to Sidney.

'It's funny. For years growing up, all I knew of my brother Sidney was that he had been driven to the West Indies by a broken heart. That a woman named Eliza had broken off your engagement to marry someone wealthy and you had been driven half mad . . .'

Sidney sighed. 'What is your point, Arthur?'

'I suppose what I am saying is . . . I admire your spirit of forgiveness. That is all. If it were me, I do not think I could bring myself to trust her again.'

'Well, I am not you, Arthur,' he replied, almost without thinking. Eliza, seeing the two men looking at her, threw Sidney a pretty smile.

As if Georgiana's suffering could not be worse, she had – on a day when everyone in Sanditon was out of doors enjoying themselves – been visited by Mr Hankins, who had taken it upon himself to read her educative passages from the Bible.

'. . . *Be not afraid, neither be thou dismayed: for the Lord thy God is with thee whithersoever thou goest . . .*' he intoned now. 'Shall I continue, my child?'

'I would sooner be crucified.'

'Now come, Miss Lambe,' he blustered. 'I do not doubt the depths of your suffering, but it hardly compares to the agonies of the cross!'

A knock at the door made them both look up. Arthur Parker showed himself in, his impressive bulk carried surprisingly lightly.

'Forgive the interruption, Mr Hankins,' he said brightly, 'but I urgently need Miss Lambe's assistance with a matter

pertaining to the regatta, that is to say a Regatta Matter!'
He laughed, pleased with his own joke.

'Of what nature?'

But Arthur's deception – for it was that – had not been
thoroughly planned. 'Er . . .' he stammered, 'with, er . . .
that is to say the . . . erm . . . duck race.'

Mr Hankins, as confused as Arthur himself, shook his
head. 'I am afraid you find us at an inopportune moment.
We have only just started with Joshua, so there are still
thirty-three books yet to go . . .'

Georgiana, however, had gone to the window. Beyond
the heavy net curtains of Mrs Griffiths' Chinese parlour she
could see that the sky was a peerless blue. Bereft as she was,
the choice between leaving the house and sitting with Mr
Hankins for another moment was no choice at all.

'May I let you into a secret, Miss Lambe?' Arthur said
when they were out on the street, a rather scandalised Mr
Hankins left to himself and his Bible. 'There is no duck
race. It was a ruse.' Arthur puffed up his chest proudly.

He could not match Miss Georgiana Lambe for pride,
though. Few could. She drew herself up.

'You can leave now,' she said loftily. 'I have no further
need of your company.'

'Come, Miss Lambe!' said Arthur, unperturbed. 'Now
that we have sprung you from your quarters, we might as
well enjoy the regatta. Do you suppose there will be a cake
stall? I do hope so!'

He offered his arm which she refused with a withering
scowl. She didn't turn back towards her lodging house,
though, but towards the hubbub of the regatta. As far as
Arthur was concerned, this was a victory of sorts. He bought
a bag of winkles in celebration.

They hadn't got too much further when she rounded on him again.

'I hate you for dragging me out here. Everyone is staring at me, judging me. The ruined woman.'

He swallowed a winkle. 'To be fair, Miss Lambe, people have always stared at you. I'd have thought you'd be used to it by now. You are beautiful and brown. Around these parts, that's rarer than a sheep with two heads! As for the judging, no one holds you accountable. You were deceived, that is all. And you are far from ruined. You have your whole life ahead of you!'

Sidney found Charlotte next to the starting line, where she was counting and checking the oars laid out on the grass of the riverbank.

'It is a little over an hour until the race, Mr Parker,' she said, when she saw him. To her frustration, her eyes were drawn – and now lingered – on his rolled-up sleeves, or rather the strong, bare arms they revealed. 'I am letting all the competitors know.'

She turned to go but he called after her. His eyes were soft when she met them.

'Well, what do you think?' he said. 'Do I look ready to you, Miss Heywood?'

'I am no expert.'

'Neither am I, regrettably. This is the first time I've picked up an oar in years.' He bent to choose a pair of oars and carried them over to the Parker boat.

'I am sure it will all come back to you,' she said.

Sidney looked thoughtfully at the water. 'I wonder. "A man cannot step into the same river twice." Have you ever heard that?' He jumped nimbly into the boat. Charlotte watched him from the riverbank.

'"For he is not the same man and it is not the same river." Heraclitus.'

He looked up at her admiringly. 'Of course you would know that. Here, I need a second person to balance the boat. Would you mind . . .?' He reached for her without waiting for an answer.

'I am not sure if – oh!' But he had already picked her up as though she weighed nothing.

'Careful,' he said gently. 'Just sit here.'

He put the oars in position and rowed a couple of strong strokes so that they moved away from the bank. When they were clear, he let them drift.

'Are you all right, Mr Parker?' she said when she had gathered her wits. 'You seem rather preoccupied.'

He paused and then looked directly at her. 'May I ask you something, Miss Heywood? Why, when I have a chance of happiness at last, will my restless mind not accept the fact?'

'With Mrs Campion, you mean?'

He looked out at the water. 'I had convinced myself that I was destined to remain alone; an outlier. I'd convinced myself I was ill-suited to matrimony. What if I was right?'

She felt uncomfortably torn. 'I don't believe that to be true,' she said eventually. 'Loneliness seems a terrible price to pay for caution, does it not?'

Instead of answering, he leant forward, his arm on hers. 'Could you perhaps take up your oars? Like this.' He moved her hands into the correct position. His skin was warm and it made her breath come shallow. She dared not look up at him but felt his eyes on her. Swallowing nervously, she began to row, feeling the boat respond and move with purpose through the water again.

'You should feel it here,' he said, gesturing to his abdomen.

'Yes,' she murmured, her blushes deepening. 'I – I feel it.'

A voice, tight with displeasure, called Sidney's name and broke the spell between them. It was Mrs Campion, standing on the riverbank watching them, her eyes narrowed with suspicion.

Chapter Thirty-Three

The riverside was by now alive with activity and anticipation. The tents that had been erected for the visitors were full to bursting. Tom watched proudly as the pop of another champagne cork was heard. The bright sun above gilded them all.

'Do you see, my dear?' he said. His face looked years younger since Lady Worcester's carriage had rolled into town. 'It is as if London has been emptied and the entire *beau monde* transported here!'

'Yes, I am pleased for you,' said Mary, stiffly. She had not forgiven him yet. 'I know how much it means to you.'

Charlotte had reunited with Lady Worcester, whose companions had taken up a prime position close to the finish line. She had not yet told Susan what had passed between her and Sidney in the boat, though her blood still thrummed from the encounter.

'Mr Mullan! Lord Grasmere!' cried Lady Worcester, beckoning some new arrivals over. 'How good of you to come.'

'Are *all* these people here at your invitation, ma'am?' said Charlotte wonderingly, after they'd been greeted.

'Not necessarily, but a social circle is like the cog of a clock. Once you set one in motion, the others are bound to follow.'

'How did you persuade them all to come?'

'Never underestimate the potency of the "new". Once Lady Harper learnt I was visiting a resort she had never heard of, she determined to follow. Then Mr Fowler followed her, Mrs Dowling followed him, and so forth. No one wants to be left behind. It is a fate worse than death for those who aspire to be *au courant*.'

'You have made the day a success,' said Charlotte. 'I hardly know how to thank you.'

Lady Worcester dismissed this with a shake of her elegant head. 'There is no need to thank me. I came here to enjoy your company.'

At that moment, their gaze was drawn towards Sidney and Mrs Campion, who were walking towards the rowers' tent. Lady Worcester smiled and bent towards Charlotte. 'And I think we can safely say we have found Mrs Campion's Achilles Heel.'

'Oh?' Charlotte looked questioningly at her.

'You!' she replied.

Mrs Campion arrived, Sidney just behind her. Charlotte did not know what to do with herself.

'May we join you? What is the topic of discussion?'

Lady Worcester raised an eyebrow at Charlotte. 'Miss Heywood and I were just discussing marriage.'

Charlotte looked at her feet.

'What is your opinion of marriage, Mr Parker?' Lady Worcester persisted.

Sidney shifted on his feet, as patently uncomfortable as Charlotte. 'I cannot speak of it with any authority.'

'What about you, Miss Heywood?' said Mrs Campion. Unlike Lady Worcester, she did not smile. 'You are of marriageable age. It must be much on your mind.'

Charlotte wished she might disappear. 'There seems little point in considering marriage until you've found someone you'd wish to marry.'

Mrs Campion let out a brittle laugh. 'Oh, come. There must be a boy in your village who has caught your eye?'

'And why should Charlotte be limited to her village?' said Lady Worcester.

'I always think it helps to share a common background, that's all. Miss Heywood is hardly likely to find a kindred spirit in this company.'

'And why not?'

'I just imagine she must find all our London talk unspeakably tedious. Wouldn't you agree, Sidney?'

For a moment, no one spoke. Then Sidney attempted a light-hearted smile. 'I've no doubt she'd rather be sitting quietly reading Heraclitus somewhere.' He tried to catch Charlotte's eye but Mrs Campion broke into peals of icy laughter.

'Heraclitus! You are wicked, Sidney. That is *certainly* not going to help her find a husband.'

Those who had overheard joined her in laughing, though Lady Worcester frowned. Charlotte looked around at them all – these fashionable people she didn't know or understand – and flushed to the roots of her hair.

'You are quite right, Mrs Campion,' she managed to say. 'I am a farmer's daughter who reads books. What could I possibly have in common with anyone here? Excuse me.'

She turned and walked away but had not got far when Sidney caught up with her. They were out of sight of the others now, obscured by one of the tents.

'Miss Heywood.'

'Would you excuse me? The race is about to start and I must . . .'

'Just for a moment.'

She stopped and the sight of him made her suddenly furious.

'Well?'

'I wanted to say that I – I hope you were not too offended by Mrs Campion. It was meant only in jest.'

She raised her chin. 'Is that all I am to you, a source of amusement?'

To her surprise, he looked quite distraught at the thought. 'No! You are . . . You are . . . Forgive me.'

She shook her head. 'There's nothing to forgive. On the contrary, you have done me a great service. I am no longer in any doubt as to how you regard me.'

'Miss Heywood . . .'

'What?' Her voice shook. She was quite desperate to be alone. 'What is it you want from me?'

'What do I want?' He stopped and considered, his face as troubled as she'd seen it. But she could bear no more.

'*Please*, be kind enough to leave me now.'

As Charlotte fled, Sir Edward Denham arrived. His usual insouciance had deserted him; he appeared to be unravelling. Dishevelled and flushed, he was apparently already half in his cups.

'Fetch me a drink,' he barked at a passing footman. 'No half-measures!'

Babington gave him a severe look. 'Sir Edward.'

'Oh God, Babington. I thought we'd seen the last of you.'

Tom Parker joined them, his countenance half-anxious, half-guilty. In the excitement over Lady Worcester's arrival, he'd almost forgotten his benefactress's plight.

'Tell me, how is your aunt, Lady Denham?' he said.

Sir Edward let out a mirthless laugh. 'Alive, if that's what you're asking. She has risen, Lazarus-like, from her deathbed.'

'But that is wonderful news!'

The footman reappeared with a glass of champagne for Edward, who snatched it, draining its contents in one.

'Is it not?' he said, as he clicked his fingers for another. 'Although sadly it seems that while she was ailing, my sister was all the while dripping poison in our aunt's ear, filling her mind with the most preposterous slurs about me. All in a cynical bid to steal my share of the inheritance.'

Those around them, whose inquisitiveness had been piqued first by Charlotte's novel opinions and now by Sir Edward's indiscreet tones, gathered closer.

'That hardly sounds like the Esther Denham I know,' said Babington.

'Then you have clearly never seen the real Esther. The truth is, she's always been subject to hysterical delusions, but this time she has gone too far. To think my own sister could so misuse me. I am heartbroken.'

Babington watched Sir Edward as he downed another glass of champagne as if it were water. He didn't look heartbroken to Babington; he looked furious; thwarted. If Esther had finally seen her brother for what he really was, his – Babington's – fortunes might be on the turn. He felt his heart lift.

Down on the water, in the shade of the trees by the bank, Sidney and his companions were readying themselves for the race. Both sides of the river were now thronged with spectators, the hum of their excited chatter amplified by the water. Despite the air of anticipation, Babington's mind was elsewhere. He was still thinking about Edward Denham.

'What could be the meaning of it?' he wondered aloud. '*Hysterical delusions*? Not one word of his account rang true.'

Crowe, overhearing, threw him a disgusted look. 'Who cares, man! Concentrate on the job in hand. I have five pounds on us taking first place.'

Charlotte, who had by now resumed her organisational duties, hurried past them. 'Fifteen minutes, gentlemen, fifteen minutes. Oh, and good luck!' Sidney brightened at the sound of her voice but when he looked up realised she was addressing Young Stringer.

Chapter Thirty-Four

The teams had assembled at the start line. One trio had even travelled from another resort: the Bridport Blades who, to a man, were moustachioed and serious. They would compete against the Parker brothers; Crowe and Babington; and Fred Robinson and Young Stringer, along with their coxes. The men took up their oars and boarded their boats. Charlotte, having counted them all in, made off gratefully towards the finish line.

Out on the water, the teams jostled for position until a ragged approximation of a starting line was formed. In truth, only the Bridport Blades looked poised and ready. The starting officer, having failed to light the rocket that was to begin the race, fumbled for his flag and finally they were off. The crowd assembled on the banks cheered that it was finally underway, and only a few minutes past four.

Crowe, who did not much care for honourable sports-manship, immediately steered his and Babington's boat into the Bridport Blades, ruining their start. This proved a great advantage to Young Stringer's boat, leaving them plenty of clear water to pull swiftly into. They gathered speed and took a narrow lead ahead of the Parker boat, which was hampered by Arthur's apparent inability to operate the rudder.

Behind them, the Bridport Blades disentangled them-selves from Crowe and Babington and began to find their stroke, the margin between them and the Parker boat beginning to narrow. As the starting rocket belatedly went off, tearing upwards with a screech, rowers and spectators started as one.

Through sheer will and determination, Young Stringer's boat kept the lead, the Parkers only just behind. The Bridport Blades, for all their dedication and willingness to travel, could not match them and had dropped behind. To everyone's surprise, not least the occupants, Babington and Crowe's boat was moving up from last place and gaining on them fast. For a joyful minute they were ahead, but then the Blades found their rhythm again.

'They're gaining on us,' cried Babington.

'Bugger that!' returned Crowe and steered once more into their path.

In order to avert a collision, the Blades sacrificed an oar, offending not only their sense of fair play, but Babington's.

'Easy, Crowe!' he exclaimed. His dismay only increased when he understood that their momentum was propelling them fast towards the riverbank, with no hope of avoiding the impact.

Up ahead, among the leaders, Arthur took over the stroke and began to justify his place in the Parker boat. 'Ten hard strokes!' he bellowed. 'That's it, Parkers!' It was now a race of two boats.

On the riverbank, close to the finish line, Charlotte and Mary – both rather breathless – joined Diana and Lady Worcester's crowd.

'It seems a curiously pointless exercise, does it not?' Lady Worcester was remarking as the boats heaved into view round a bend in the river. 'As if the virtue of a man were measured in how well he rows. Were that the case, I would find myself the nearest fisherman!' Her friends laughed and

Charlotte smiled. It faded when she noticed Mrs Campion had sidled up. Feeling dishevelled and hot next to her, she began to re-pin the strands of her hair that had worked loose.

'Miss Heywood.'

'Mrs Campion.'

'Is that not my brothers' boat in the lead?' Diana exclaimed over them. She was suffused with excitement. 'Oh, come on, Parkers!'

The revellers around them, heartened to have a view on proceedings now, also began to cheer.

Mrs Campion gave Charlotte a brittle smile. 'I do hope Sidney's boat comes in first. I have never seen the point of entering a race unless you win it.'

Charlotte did not reply; she knew only too well that Mrs Campion was not referring to rowing or any other sport, at least an organised one.

In the Parker boat, Sidney had discovered a peculiar kind of solace in the physical exertion of the race. It had stopped the constant tumbling of his thoughts. As he saw Young Stringer's boat closing the gap between them, inch by certain inch, their oars perilously close as they drew level, he grunted and pulled harder, the muscles in his chest burning.

But Young Stringer was determined, too. The image of Charlotte was fixed in his mind as surely as Sidney's was blessedly empty. He was certain she would be at the finish line, which they were now fast approaching. The thought of her watching spurred him to a greater burst of strength than any the Parkers could match and, as the line rushed towards them, it was the foreman's boat that surged ahead to cross it first, though only by a mere foot.

On the bank, Young Stringer's father, not generally given to outbursts of emotion, threw his hat in the air.

Diana pressed her hand to her heaving breast. 'Thank goodness that's over. My poor heart could not take another minute of it.'

Out on the water, the rowers were exhausted, the sweat running freely off them. Only the jubilant Young Stringer managed to stand. The spectators helped to pull the boats in and the men out of them. As they found their legs, the crowds parted and they trudged towards the tent where refreshment awaited them.

'Not a bad effort,' said Old Stringer to his son when he reached him. He was beaming, belying the gruff words. 'You proved yourself the equal of any man out there.'

Diana went forward to embrace and console her brothers, but Tom sought out Mary's eye. Seeing him so exhausted and bedraggled, she could not help but offer him a small smile. For now, he was forgiven. Sidney, for his part, found himself between Charlotte and Eliza. All the blank respite of the river left him as if it had never been.

Sir Edward Denham had missed the race entirely. Having been quietly removed from Lady Worcester's vicinity for his ungentleman-like behaviour, he had repaired to the less salubrious surrounds of the Crown Hotel bar, where he had endeavoured to get yet more drunk. Now, weaving along the street outside with no real purpose, he spied a familiar and most despised face. It was Clara Brereton in hat and spencer, carrying a small and rather threadbare carpet bag. She was clearly on her way to meet the London coach.

'The vanquished enemy retreats!' he slurred.

Still admirably composed, despite her misfortune, she shook her head. 'I was never your enemy, Edward. And you are hardly in a position to gloat.'

He staggered a little as he tried to hold her eye. 'I am still a gentleman. I have a title. All that you own is contained in that pathetic little bag.'

She put her head on one side, blue eyes laughing. 'You had one chance to secure your fortune and you threw it away. I had nothing to lose. It was a game.'

'A game you lost!'

'All right. I will concede the first round. But we live to fight another day, do we not?' She threw him another teasing look and then turned on her heel, leaving him swaying in her wake, aroused despite his inebriation, and despite his loathing for her. Their paths would cross again, he knew.

The race over, the prizes handed out, the regatta drew slowly and – for many – regrettably to its end. Tom was elated, floating on the soft cloud of unexpected success. He, Mary and Charlotte were saying farewell to the woman who had been such a gift: Lady Worcester.

'Well, Mr Parker,' she said, inclining her gracious head. 'I must thank you for a most invigorating day.'

He resisted embracing her. 'It is I who must thank you, ma'am. And if I might presume, I hope we might welcome you back to Sanditon again, perhaps for longer next time?'

'There is a distinct likelihood.' She smiled mischievously. 'I have one friend in particular who would be rather taken with the place.'

Tom blushed and blustered. 'He – he would be most welcome, of course. Or she. Whoever the gentleman is, I mean. Or – or lady.'

Lady Worcester stifled a laugh and turned to Charlotte, taking her aside. 'Goodbye, dear Charlotte. You mustn't lose heart. The race is not yet run.'

'Thank you, but I am more or less resigned to its outcome.'

'My dear, when it comes to love there is no such thing as foregone conclusion.' She gave Charlotte a last smile and turned to be handed up into her carriage.

'Did you hear that, my dear?' Tom said to Mary as the carriage moved off. '*One friend in particular*. She can only have one person in mind: the Prince Regent himself! Sanditon has arrived. My regatta was a triumph.'

'Indeed it was, my dear. Although is it entirely fair to call it "your" regatta? Given that it was Charlotte who persuaded Lady Worcester to attend, and that the regatta was her idea to begin with . . .'

'Of course. Of *course*.' He turned to Charlotte and took her hand. 'This is just as much your triumph as mine, dear girl. You are a quite remarkable young woman. I bless the day you came to Sanditon!' He turned back to his wife. 'Nor could it have happened without you, Mary, my dear. Why did I ever think to hide anything from you, when you are my strength, my inspiration. What a fool I have been!'

Mary smiled, and it was the first full and true smile he had received from her in some time. His heart rejoiced at the sight of it.

'I promise you this much,' he said, holding her in his arms, 'I shall never hide the smallest worry from you again.'

Miss Clara Brereton had been early for the coach, but after only fifteen minutes contemplating her new, friendless life, she was engaged in conversation by a gentleman. It was Mr Crowe who, released from his rowing duties, had decided to return immediately to the more disreputable entertainments of London. Seeing her little bag and trim figure, he had made his approach in time to overhear her asking when the carriage would depart.

'Excellent question, my dear,' he said in a conspiratorial tone, suddenly at her elbow. 'How soon can we escape this infernal backwater?'

She turned and gave him her most dazzling smile.

'Miss Brereton, is it not?' he said. 'This is a stroke of luck. I am heading to London myself. But, if I may, it would be quite unwise for an innocent like yourself to attempt such a journey alone.'

She lowered her eyes, knowing how well her long eyelashes would look fanned upon her cheek.

'Thank you for your concern, sir,' she said softly, with the hint of a lisp. 'I must confess to a degree of trepidation.'

'And tell me this, miss. Do you have any friends in the city?'

'None worth knowing, I'm afraid.'

A lupine smile spread across Crowe's face. 'Well, you do now.'

Sidney had been sitting alone in the tent where he had taken his time changing out of his wet rowing garb. His brothers and friends had long gone, back towards the town along with everyone else, but he had not yet been able to rouse himself to follow. It was remarkable how quickly his thoughts had crowded in again, now that the race was over. He stood and walked slowly out of the tent to find Eliza standing there.

'You had no need to wait for me.'

She looked at him intently. 'I have waited ten years. What is another quarter hour?'

He dredged up a smile but could not formulate a reply.

'The truth,' she went on hurriedly, filling the silence, 'is that now I have found you again, I can scarcely bring myself to let you out of my sight.' She couldn't hold his eye then, and instead began to twist one of her rings around her finger. He couldn't remember ever seeing her so unsure.

'Eliza . . .'

'I never lost hope that we would stand beside each other once more.' She stepped towards him, eyes blazing. 'Yet here we are! Fate has gifted us with a second chance. It is almost a miracle. I lost you once before; I am not going to make that mistake again.'

Evening had stolen over Denham Place. Edward long gone, who knew where, Esther was alone except for the servants, who had almost finished packing up the house's contents. The home she had shared with her brother looked like a tawdry sort of place now, with their personal effects and pictures stripped away. She thought the sight of it so denuded would break her heart.

A disturbance at the door made her breath catch. Could it be . . .? But it was not Edward. It was Babington.

'I told you to refuse all visitors!' she said to the maid who hovered at the door. 'You may show Lord Babington out.'

'Wait!' cried Babington. 'I ask only for a moment, that is all. Miss Denham, I have done all I can to forget about you, but it is quite impossible. I feel I could spend a thousand years in your company and still not fathom you out. And yet, when I heard your brother speak of you today in the most derogatory terms, I felt I began to understand at last . . .'

'You know nothing,' she said coldly.

'I think you have been his prisoner for too long. He alone has had the power to determine your self-worth and he has abused that power in ways I can barely guess at. Am I in any way close, Miss Denham?'

To her inward fury, she began to weep, the tears she could no longer hold in rolling down her cheeks in a steady stream.

Babington seemed to take in the disorder of the room for the first time. He moved towards her. 'Miss Denham, dear Miss Denham, I do not know what has transpired, but I only hope this means you are free at last of his pernicious influence. I know you do not hold me in much esteem, but I came here without exception and in the spirit of friendship to make you a promise. Your brother is not going to make a victim of you. I will not allow it.'

He hesitated and then brought out a clean handkerchief. For a long moment, she just looked at it. Then, just as he was about to give up and take his leave, she reached out for it. It was but a small gesture of acquiescence but one Babington drew some hope from.

Charlotte was alone in Tom's study. It was getting late and the house was quiet: the children in bed and Tom taking a bath to soothe his aching muscles. She was holding a pile of receipts and other sundry papers but could not think what to do with them. Indeed, her gaze had been fixed on the window for the last twenty minutes, though she could see nothing beyond the glass, the lamplight from the desk only throwing her own lonely reflection back at her. She wasn't aware of Sidney's presence in the room until he was almost upon her.

'Oh!' she started. 'If you are looking for your brother . . .'

He stepped towards her. His eyes were dark and liquid in the low light. 'I am not looking for my brother. I am looking for you.'

'I thought you and Mrs Campion were heading back to London.' She could not meet his eye.

'*She* has. I decided against joining her.'

She frowned in confusion.

'On reflection, I realised I would rather be here.' He turned to go and she found she couldn't speak, her thoughts too disordered. At the door, he paused. 'I am a good deal less than perfect. You have made me all too aware of that. But for whatever it is worth, I believe I am my best self, my truest self, when I am with you. That is all.'

With that, he walked out, leaving Charlotte entirely stunned, her heart lifting with unexpected joy even as her more cautious mind wondered exactly what his words might signify.

Chapter Thirty-Five

How strange was the passage of time, Charlotte thought. It seemed but a week or two since she had arrived in Sanditon, and yet it also seemed like years. The thought of Willingden was so distant that she could not believe she would soon be returning.

She had begun a letter to her sister that morning, in the hope that she could explain her thoughts about the season she had spent away from everything she had previously held dear, but her feelings were as yet too confused and contradictory to be clearly set down, and she had given it up. It was a shame because she was in great need of advice about a particular person. There was no one in Sanditon she could comfortably confide in.

Restless in her mind, she decided to leave the house, so that at least her physical body might be exhausted. She would call on Georgiana.

On the way, she was hailed by Arthur, who was arm in arm with his sister, the pair of them walking at such a sedate pace that some very ancient townsfolk were overtaking them with ease. He warned her to take care in the freezing wind, which made her smile. It was a perfectly clement day; the breeze little more than a warm breath on her face.

'I do like Arthur Parker,' Charlotte said to Georgiana, once they were seated in Mrs Griffiths' blue parlour. 'He is a very good fellow, despite the fuss he makes about his own and everyone else's health.'

Georgiana nodded. 'He is one of the few people I can bear the sight of in this horrid place. I saw you talking to Mr Sidney Parker after the regatta and felt very sorry for you. What a beast that man is.'

As Charlotte had been thinking directly opposing thoughts all morning, she could not help but protest.

'Georgiana, you don't really think that, do you? He cares for you. He did come to your rescue, after all.'

'I wish he had not.'

'Really, how can you wish that?'

'Otis would have rescued me without that man's interference.'

Charlotte frowned. 'You really think he would?'

Georgiana's lip trembled. 'Otis loved me, and I sent him away and told him I wouldn't see him again, and now I wish I had not. What if he *was* after my money? I have more than enough for us both. Who is Mr Parker to tell me how I should live my life? Hateful man.'

Charlotte could not reply truthfully without giving offence. It was not just that she wholeheartedly disagreed with Georgiana's retelling of what had occurred in London, but also what she thought of the man.

Georgiana gave her a sharp look. 'You're not going to tell me that you are fond of him now?'

'I – I do have feelings for him.' She could no longer keep it in.

Georgiana paused. 'And what about him?'

'I think he returns them.' She blushed and was glad of the relative dimness of the room.

Though she had expected an outburst of indignation and contempt, Georgiana merely looked thoughtful. 'Oh. I thought he was promised to that wealthy widow with all the jewels and high-falutin' ways.'

'He – he told me he wasn't returning to London with her. He is staying here in Sanditon – and he told me . . . he hoped very much that I would stay here too.'

She couldn't help it; her heart swelled as she spoke the words aloud. But Georgiana looked sceptical.

'And? Is that all?'

'He – he seemed very sincere.'

Georgiana harrumphed, sounding peculiarly like Lady Denham. 'Very sincere he'd like to keep you dangling after him. Do you know what I think? I think he's just playing with your feelings. I notice he hasn't made you any promises.'

'No, but . . .' Charlotte fell silent just as a knock on the front door was heard.

'Here we are!' said a jocular voice. The maid showed in Arthur and Diana. They were clutching books and a large paper bag from the baker's.

'Buns, buns, buns! Lovely sugary buns!' exclaimed Arthur, by way of explanation.

'And all the latest novels from the circulating library,' said Diana.

'Buns and books, all you need for perfect happiness!' Georgiana smiled. 'You are too good to me.'

'Not at all. It's a pleasure to share them with you.' Arthur gestured at the bag. 'Will you join us, Miss Heywood?'

'Now don't gobble them all, dear brother,' said Diana. 'You'll make us late for our treatments. Dr Fuchs is available again, now that Lady Denham is on the mend. I have at least ten treatments to catch up on, and so does Arthur!'

Lady Denham was indeed on the mend, to the degree that she had forced a miserable Esther to play cards with her.

'Fifteen two, fifteen four, twenty-five seven, and a pair's nine!' she declared. You shouldn't have put your noddy out so soon! You're playing like a nincompoop. What's the matter with you?'

Esther heaved a great sigh. 'I suppose it's a grave weakness but I cannot make myself excited about card games, Lady Denham.'

Her aunt tutted as she shuffled the cards. 'You are not a very stimulating companion, Esther. I hope you're not pining for that degenerate brother of yours.'

'No, but I confess I miss the man he might have been.'

'Don't get all metaphysical with me, young lady. Now, go over to the pianoforte and play something jolly.'

Esther briefly closed her eyes. 'Must I?'

'Something rousing, mind!' said Lady Denham in reply. 'And stop that pouting or I'll make you sing as well!'

Esther, heavy of limb and heart, dragged herself over to the instrument and began to play. She was glad to break off when a footman came in.

'My lady, Lord Babington is here.'

Lady Denham's small eyes lit up. 'Well, send him in, man!'

Babington entered wearing his usual affable smile and bowed to both of them.

'Lady Denham, Miss Denham.'

His eye lingered on Esther, his expression visibly softening. This did not go unnoticed by Lady Denham.

'Well now, I wonder you dare show your face here, after your shabby showing at the regatta,' she said joshingly. 'Beaten by the local yokels, I heard. For shame!'

Babington smiled easily. 'Indeed, we ran 'em pretty close, but they were too much for us.'

The niceties attended to, Lady Denham leant forward. 'So what brings you here?'

'I thought to tempt Miss Denham with a carriage ride.'

Esther lowered her eyes. 'No, thank you.'

Lady Denham shot her a dangerous look before turning back to Babington.

'But that's an excellent idea! She needs a good shaking about, to jolt her out of her despondency. Come along, miss! Up you get!'

'Really, I beg you, I would not . . .'

Babington spread his hands in appeal. 'In truth, there will be no shaking about, and as little jolting as possible. My carriage is well-sprung and hung, the air today is as mild and fresh as could be wished. Miss Denham, I appeal to you—'

Esther sighed. She drooped at the pianoforte stool like a broken flower. 'Must I?'

Lady Denham gave Babington a steely smile. 'She will do as she's told.'

Seeing no choice in the matter, and having little enough will to object further, Esther soon found herself being helped up into Babington's phaeton. Though she wouldn't have admitted it, there was some relief to be had in being outside under the sky, feeling the breeze on her skin and – most of all – leaving behind Sanditon House and its mistress.

With Babington at the reins, Esther beside him, they made swift progress through the park and down the hill into the town. They slowed on reaching the sea front but then, to Esther's surprise and secret delight, Babington steered the horses straight on to the beach. The compacted sand was wonderfully smooth under the wheels. It felt as though they were flying.

'Why do you do this?' she said to Babington, who was smiling happily beside her, hands loose on the reins.

'Indulge me, won't you?' he said. 'It simply makes me happy to have you here with me.'

'I cannot imagine why. I feel the exact opposite about you.'

He turned to her. 'Do you, truly?'

'Didn't I just say so?' Another layer of lassitude blew off her. There was no doubt that upbraiding a lord of the realm could be invigorating, even when one was in the depths of despair.

'I refuse to believe you,' he said.

'Babington, give up. I am a lost cause.'

'I know. I don't care. Do you like to go fast?' He shook the reins and the horses responded.

'I don't care if you drive us into the sea,' said Esther. She had a sudden urge to laugh.

'Good idea!' he cried. 'Giddy-up!'

'Babington, you are the world's worst carriage driver!'

'Care to take the reins?'

She hesitated and then reached out. 'Why not? Give them here.'

She shook them hard and the horses broke into a full gallop. Her bonnet, only loosely tied, was flung back and her bright hair came loose. Babington turned to watch her with frank adoration. To him, she was like Boudicca reborn: a warrior queen. As for her, for the first time in many days, Esther Denham felt alive.

When Charlotte returned from her visit to Georgiana, she found Trafalgar House in uproar. Tom, his spirits still dizzyingly raised after the success of the regatta, was wearing a tricorn hat and apparently leading his offspring in a victory against the French.

'Napoleon in full retreat!' he was bellowing happily as she crossed the hall, avoiding the various Parker children who assailed her as she did. 'Rule Britannia! Board that galleon, men!'

She found Mary in the drawing room, where she had retreated to its relative calm. Young Stringer was also there, standing somewhat awkwardly in a corner, patiently waiting for his employer to cease fighting.

'Charlotte!' said Mary. 'How did you find Miss Lambe this morning?'

'Oh, much more like herself. Full of strong opinions – and buns.'

'Buns?'

'Arthur has been feeding her up.'

Mary smiled. 'He is such a dear man.'

'Enemy on the port side! Strike the top-gallants!' cried Tom, as he was pushed into the room by his over-excited children.

'All right, all right! Enough, I surrender! Run up the white flag! Mary, do something with them!'

'Come along, children. Your father's busy.' She led them from the room.

'There you are, Charlotte,' said Tom, noticing her for the first time. 'What an absolutely splendid day! The whole world wants to come to Sanditon! I was telling Young Stringer about the correspondence. We're going to be full from now till the end of the season so it's all hands on deck to get the last apartments fitted out. We've let every last one!'

'That's wonderful!'

Young Stringer stepped forward, still awkward. 'But I was telling Mr Parker I doubt we'll get the work done on time.' He looked down, embarrassed, but didn't take back the words.

Tom was unconcerned. 'Tell the men they're on double time if they'll work around the clock. The future of Sanditon depends on them! Ah, morning, Sidney!'

The room felt immediately airless to Charlotte. She turned to see him for herself and their eyes met. They always seemed to find each other's gaze now. He smiled at her; an intimate sort of smile that made her feel like the only person in the room. No, the only person in Sanditon.

'What's the matter, Charlotte?' said Tom. 'Does something you had for breakfast disagree with you?'

She blushed and then caught Young Stringer's injured expression. Tom might be oblivious but he was not. But still; she could not temper her happiness.

'No, no. I am well,' she replied with another glance towards Sidney. 'I am very well indeed.'

Sidney cleared his throat. 'I just called to say I'm walking into town, if there's anything you need there?'

'Oh, I have a dress fitting for the ball,' cried Charlotte, the words tumbling out of her. 'Perhaps I could walk with you?'

'Of course. My pleasure.' He smiled at her again.

'Go on then,' said Mary indulgently. 'Off you go, the pair of you!'

It was a particularly pretty day, the sunlight gilding Tom's new buildings and the dark-blue sea with bright points of gold. As far as Sidney and Charlotte noticed, however, it might as well have been raining stair rods. Neither spoke as they walked, both of them remembering the previous evening's momentous exchange. Charlotte felt buoyant enough that she was in danger of simply floating away.

'A fine fresh day,' said Sidney eventually.

Charlotte smiled up at him. How profound he was. 'Yes, indeed.'

'Bodes well for the ball tonight.'

'Yes.'

'Though, being an indoor occasion, good weather is not so – not so much of a consideration.'

'No, quite.'

They smiled at each other again.

'Are you looking forward to the ball?' he tried again.

'Very much – I love to dance.'

A silence fell between them yet again and, happy as she was, the awkwardness of it began to tell on her.

'Are *you* looking forward to the ball?' she echoed weakly.

'Yes, very much. And ah . . . how are your family? Have you heard from them recently?'

'Yes, a letter from my sister came just this morning.' She pictured Willingden briefly and, again, had the sense that her home was as distant as the moon.

'And . . . any news?'

'You know that nothing ever happens in Willingden. Everyone is well, though, and very busy with the harvest.'

'Yes, of course, they must be. A farmer is always busy, and exceptionally so just now.'

Charlotte looked about her and realised that they had long passed Sanditon's shops. There was not road underfoot now but the sand and sparse grass of the cliff path.

'We seem not to be walking into town.'

Sidney glanced around, apparently as surprised as her.

'No. Oh, of course – your dress fitting! What a fool I am. Should we turn back?'

She laughed and any awkwardness between them vanished into the breeze.

'No, there's no urgency, none at all. A walk on the cliffs is much more to my taste.'

He gave her one of the looks that seemed to turn her legs to water. 'Good. My thoughts exactly. In fact, I was

346

hoping that we might find a moment when we could be alone together.'

'You were?' Her heart began to pound. They had come to a natural stop. Behind Sidney, the sea dazzled, lighting his edges with a bronze glow.

'I woke very early this morning,' he said, 'my head full of the conversation we had last night.'

'Yes?'

'Charlotte . . .'

'Yes?'

She tipped her chin up to him just as he bent towards her. The kiss was gentle at first, and then more passionate. There had been no decision; no hesitation. They had acted purely on instinct, the rightness of it confirmed as the rest of the world dropped away, leaving nothing but the two of them, and the heat between them.

Esther paused for a moment outside Lady Denham's drawing room to adopt her customary droop. She did not want to give the old lady satisfaction.

'Well, did you enjoy yourself?' she quizzed as soon as Esther walked in, suitably weary-looking.

'It was – tolerable. It passed the time.'

But Lady Denham's beady eyes were not deceived. 'Nonsense. I may be old, but I am not blind. I can see the brightness of your eyes, and the colour in your cheeks. You should marry that young man.'

'He's a fool.'

'He is no fool, Esther.'

'He is a fool if he cannot see that I am not worth having,' Esther returned. 'Perhaps I was once, but now I am good for nothing and no one.'

'It is infinitely better to be loved, than to love. Especially in a marriage. After all, to love someone is to be held captive.'

Esther head snapped up in surprise. She wondered how much her sharp-eyed aunt had seen and understood of her closeness to her brother after all.

'Do you speak from your own experience or someone else's?'

Lady Denham leant forward. 'My own. Not with my husband of course — it was long before that. A man called Rowleigh. Some people called him the handsomest man in Somerset; for me he was quite the handsomest in the world. Oh, and he knew it.' She smiled ruefully, her eyes far away in the past. 'My heart would pound so hard when he came into the room that I was afraid it would burst out of my chest. It was worse than influenza! Very exciting at the time, of course.'

Esther closed her mouth, which had fallen open. 'What happened?'

'Oh, he kept me dangling for a while, trembling like one of his dogs for a look or a smile, for a tender word, and then he upped and married a girl from Gloucestershire with forty thousand. He had debts, of course, and couldn't afford to marry me. It should have been obvious to me at the time, but you know what young girls are. What are you staring at? Did you think I never had a heart?'

'Well, not exactly that . . .'

'The point is, it's much better to be the one who holds the reins.'

Esther was about to protest but, to her dismay, she could think of nothing to say. To her profound surprise, she realised her aunt might be right.

Chapter Thirty-Six

It was evening, fine and soft, the air perfumed with Mary's roses, the sea and a great deal of promise. Charlotte regarded herself in the cheval glass in her room, wondering why she looked different. True, she had arranged her hair differently, and her complexion was luminous with good health, but she thought it was something more. Then it struck her: it must be happiness, lighting her from within.

When she came down the stairs, Tom and Mary were waiting – the children too, scrubbed and pink-cheeked. They had been promised that they could see everyone in their finery before they went to bed.

'Here she comes!' said Tom, looking up and spotting Charlotte first. 'You look beautiful, my dear. Quite the grown-up lady.'

'You look like a princess, Charlotte,' said little Alicia in a voice of wonder.

'Please, stop it!' she cried, feeling like nothing more than a bottle of Lady Worcester's champagne, her cork loosening dangerously. 'You'll make me nervous.'

Mary took her arm and led her to the door. 'You have nothing to be nervous about,' she said, in her comforting way. 'But, in truth, I do sense something different. Is it just your hair?' In the honeyed light cast by the evening sky, she studied Charlotte closely. 'There seems to be – I don't know – an extra sparkle about you this evening.'

Charlotte looked down, a small smile on her lips. 'I don't know what you mean.'

Mary leant in close. 'Tom asked me to marry him at a ball in Weymouth.'

'Oh. Did he?' Charlotte swallowed.

Mary laughed and stepped into the carriage. 'I've no idea what made me think of that.'

'And what are you two talking about?' said Tom, as he joined them.

'Nothing at all,' said Mary, still smiling. 'But I hope you intend to dance with me tonight, Tom.'

He took her hand up and kissed it. 'As many dances as you wish, my love.'

While the gentry were dressing and preparing for the ball, Young Stringer and his men were finishing the last details on the terrace so that everything might be ready. Potted trees were placed at elegant intervals and the last of the unsightly rubble had been cleared away.

'Coming on nicely, Fred,' said Young Stringer, nodding to his work.

'Aye, we'll make it look pretty enough for 'em.'

'Have you seen my father?' He patted the letter from London inside his pocket.

Fred grinned. 'He's inside, working on the finish, where else? Wouldn't have anyone else on it.'

Young Stringer found his father rubbing down a section of moulding which already looked finished.

'All right, Dad? You could be getting home now.'

His father didn't turn from his work. 'When it's done to my satisfaction.'

'Come on, leave it to the lads. They'll get it done. Mr

Parker wants it finished, not perfect.'

'Mr Parker's not a craftsman like you and me. If it's not right, he may not know or care, and the summer visitors may not know or care, but I will, and you will too. I'll be finished in an hour or so. You get off to the dance.'

His son hesitated. It was always the way with him at the moment, or so it seemed: two different worlds pulling him in two different directions.

'Doesn't seem right, while you're working.'

His father grunted out a laugh. 'Get on with you. I'm enjoying myself in me own way.'

Young Stringer hesitated, felt again for the letter. 'Father?'

The old man turned.

'I've had a letter.' He brought it out. The envelope was softened from the number of times he'd opened and read the contents.

'Oh ah?'

He took a breath in. 'It's about a position in London, with prospects. A chance to make something of myself.'

His father's face hardened. 'Sanditon not good enough for you now, is that it?'

He gritted his teeth. 'What are you talking about?'

'It's that Miss Charlotte, isn't it? Filled your head with a load of nonsense.'

'It's got nothing to do with her.' He was angry now. The two of them had been skirting around this for weeks. There was some relief in being honest now.

'Yes, it has,' his father said. 'And now you're off to the dance, to get more of the same. Well, off you go then!'

'Don't worry, I will go – and not just to the ball. I'll leave Sanditon too, and I shan't waste a thought on the miserable, selfish old man I left behind.'

Before his father could say anything further, Young Stringer strode away, but the all the relief had burnt away now, leaving behind in his belly a knot of misgiving that he couldn't explain, Still, he didn't turn back.

The ball that evening was a very different occasion to the one that had taken place during Charlotte's first week at Sanditon. There must have been twice the number of guests, and three times the candles. It was a neat illustration of the resort's changing fortunes, or so Tom Parker hoped.

Sidney had been one of the first to arrive and now kept glancing at the door. There was only one person he wished to see but as he looked over yet again, it was his friend Babington who arrived. Spotting Sidney, he raised a hand and made his way over.

'Sidney! Any sign of Miss Denham yet?'

'No, I'm afraid not. You've still not surrendered then, despite her best efforts?'

Babington's eyes lit up. 'I don't know what it is but I find myself quite captivated. Nothing I say seems to strike her right, and yet I prefer her sharp tongue to the simpering compliance you find with most women.'

'You want to tame her, do you?'

Babington smiled ruefully. 'I believe she has tamed me.'

Sidney looked thoughtful. 'Yes, I can just about imagine how that might feel.' He checked the door again.

'Who is it you're waiting for? Not Mrs Campion, I take it.'

'No. I don't expect we shall be seeing each other for quite some time.'

'No prospect of an engagement then?'

Sidney's eyes were still on the door. 'Not to her, no.'

Babington raised an eyebrow, most intrigued.

The room began to fill, the pitch of the throng rising as it did. Finally, Sidney saw her, entering with Tom and Mary. She looked different, though he couldn't have said why. She looked older, somehow, and more beautiful than he'd ever seen her. Without a word to Babington, he began to make his way over, but Tom beat him to it, taking the centre of the floor and raising his hands until he got everyone's attention.

'My lord, ladies and gentlemen,' he announced. 'It's my very great pleasure to invite you to this midsummer ball. I would like to thank all of you for helping us to make this first season such a success. No further words are necessary so on with the dance, and let joy be unconfined!'

The musicians struck up and, on the other side of the room from Sidney, Charlotte felt a surge of anticipation swell in her breast. There was something about tonight that she could not quite explain: a tipping sense, as though she was standing on a precipice. She didn't know if she was more excited or nervous. She knew exactly where Sidney was in the room without looking, as though they were joined by an invisible cord.

'Sidney looks happier than I've seen him in a long while,' said Mary, interrupting her thoughts.

She looked over then, finally daring to meet his eye. He smiled tenderly at her, and her blood raced in her veins.

'I wonder what can be the cause of it,' Mary was saying. 'Do you have any idea, Charlotte?'

'I expect he must be very relieved that the season turned out so well.'

Mary smiled knowingly. 'Yes, I suppose that must be it. Oh, good evening, Mr Hankins.'

The Reverend approached, beaming and perspiring in equal measure.

'Mrs Parker, Miss Heywood. What delightful and whole-some entertainment a ball is. Delightful, delightful.'

Rubbing his hands – so many young ladies to admire! – he progressed circuitously towards Mrs Griffiths, edging around and complimenting at least half a dozen of the prettiest attendees as he went.

It was Georgiana who first noticed him bearing down on them.

'Oh Lord, not him!' she said, perfectly audibly, which made the Beaufort sisters giggle.

'Ah, Mrs Griffiths,' he said, apparently oblivious, 'here you are with your bouquet of blossoms. There is nothing more pleasing to the Lord than a young girl in the first flower of her pulchritude. But we must not forget the maturer vintages, for they have a deeper and more subtle appeal to the discerning nose of the experienced connoisseur.'

Georgiana snorted.

'And you count yourself as one of those, do you, Mr Hankins?' said Mrs Griffiths.

'I do, I do, and you look particularly bewitching this evening, if I may say so.'

She turned puce with delight. 'Oh, Mr Hankins! I am here merely as chaperone to my girls.'

He leant in. 'A very lovely one, in my opinion.'

'Too kind,' she twittered.

'Perhaps it would not be wholly inappropriate to ask you for the next dance?'

'Oh, Mr Hankins! I would be delighted.'

He offered her his arm and she took it so swiftly it was as though the offer might expire. At the same time, the Beaufort girls' ostentatious preening had not gone unnoticed by two local boys who now approached, both of them smelling strongly of pomade and drink. Their offers to dance accepted, Georgiana found herself unattended. She noticed her guardian nearby and turned to see what he was looking so intently at. It was Charlotte. Georgiana approached him without hesitation.

'Georgiana,' he turned to greet her. 'I'm glad to see you enjoying yourself.'

'What are you up to with Charlotte,' she said bluntly.

He frowned. 'I don't understand your meaning.'

'You've done your best to ruin my happiness,' she retorted. 'How could I trust you not to ruin hers as well?'

They both turned, so that neither should have to bear the sight of the other for another moment. Georgiana found Arthur ambling towards her, hand raised in greeting.

'There you are, Miss L.! Care to stand up with me?'

'She would be delighted,' said Sidney over his shoulder.

The two of them made a curious pair, both of them dancing with great exuberance – one from temper and the other from general high spirits.

Sidney watched them for a moment and then found himself searching for Charlotte once again. Seeing her, his heart lifting, he began to make his way over, but Young Stringer reached her first.

Charlotte, for her part, had seen Sidney and was hoping he would approach, just as Young Stringer reached her side. He didn't look his usual cheerful self tonight and when he asked her to dance she didn't like to refuse him. In fact, they made good partners; Charlotte was surprised how comfortable she felt in his arms as he led her around the room.

'There was something I wanted to tell you, miss,' he began. 'I've been offered an excellent situation in London and, well, I plan to accept it.'

'To be an architect?'

'An apprentice to start with.'

She smiled, delighted for him. 'Oh, I'm so pleased that your talent has been recognised. You will be much missed here in Sanditon, though.'

'Thank you. And what of your plans? Do you intend to remain here?'

'I had always assumed I would be leaving at the season's end.' Her eyes took on a faraway gleam. 'But now I'm not so sure.'

Young Stringer looked across the floor to where Sidney Parker stood with Lord Babington. Charlotte followed his gaze.

'You have found a reason to stay, then?'

'Yes, I believe I have.'

He sighed, though she didn't catch it in the hubbub. 'Then I hope you'll be very happy, and I hope he'll prove worthy of you. He is a lucky man, Miss Heywood, truly.'

She smiled at him. He was the first person who had acknowledged the possibility of her and Sidney aloud except for Georgiana, but Young Stringer showed none of her scepticism. They moved off again, as the music decreed, and she was so happy she scarcely noticed how tightly Young Stringer gripped her hand, as though it was the last time he might be permitted to touch it.

Babington stood with Sidney, watching the dancers. Or rather, Babington watched Sidney watching Charlotte as she danced with Young Stringer.

'They make a handsome couple,' he said slyly.

'I think not,' returned Sidney, only half-pretending jealousy.

'Then what are you waiting for?' He raised his eyebrows at Sidney, who opened his mouth to protest and then closed it again. He could no longer see any point in denying it.

'For the dance to end,' he said, smiling now himself.

But Babington's gaze had been drawn across the room, where Lady Denham and Esther had just made their entrance, the former carving a certain path through the lesser revellers. Catching his eye, Esther gave him one of the haughty looks he found so attractive.

Babington patted Sidney on the shoulder. 'Excuse me, old friend. I hope you get a favourable answer. Indeed, I hope we both do.' With that, he walked determinedly towards the Denhams.

Hovering on the edge of the dance floor, brow knitted with anxiety and displeasure, Diana was trying to attract her brother's attention.

'Really, Arthur, what do you think you're doing?' she said when she finally caught his eye and he had obediently jigged over to her. 'And in your state of health.'

His face was a livid red but he was smiling. 'No. Am . . . perfectly well. If – I – could just . . .' He ran out of breath and collapsed into a chair.

Diana, whose fragile nerves were nothing to her protectiveness of Arthur, rounded on Georgiana.

'Miss Lambe, that was most irresponsible of you! Where is Dr Fuchs? How could you – I am so distressed! Where are my smelling salts?'

She rummaged frantically in her reticule, spilling handkerchiefs, buttons and mysterious vials as she did. The smelling salts found, she waved them under Arthur's nose for longer than was strictly necessary. He sneezed hugely and then bellowed at his sister in protest, waving her away.

'No more, no more!' He straightened up. 'If I could possibly have a bowl of ice cream? That might do the trick.'

Georgiana had been observing with amusement.

'You just need more exercise,' she said. 'Come and dance again.'

'No!' Diana's eyes flashed. She put her narrow frame between Georgiana and Arthur. 'I entirely forbid it!'

Georgiana smirked, further rousing Diana's ire. 'Avaunt, you . . . you temptress!' she cried.

But this only further amused her foe, who blew Arthur a provocative kiss. Then, abruptly bored, she gestured to a local lad who was standing nearby.

'You'll do.'

She took his hand and led him onto the dance floor. Arthur looked after her longingly.

Witnessing all this, Mrs Griffiths was horrified. 'Really, Miss Lambe!' she called out. 'Manners! Deportment!'

She turned to see if the Beaufort girls were similarly shocked but they had quite vanished. She searched the dance floor but there was no sign of them. 'Where have those two gone now! Julia? Phillida, where are you?'

Charlotte had been looking out for Sidney, even while she danced with Young Stringer. When that finished, she had continued her search, and was about to give up hope when he was suddenly there, so close that she could feel his warm breath on her neck. His voice was low and thrilling in her ear.

'Meet me on the balcony,' he said and the words made her shiver. When she turned, he had gone, as though he was never there. She threaded her way through the dancers, making sure that no one saw her leave. It was not that she was doing anything wrong; only that she wished this exchange to be private, to remain unobserved.

It was dark on the balcony. The assembly rooms were so brilliantly lit that her eyes could not immediately adjust.

'Are you there?' she murmured.

The only reply was a fit of girlish giggles.

She was about to turn back when someone opened a window and and a square of light illuminated the balcony. At one end were a collection of limbs that resolved themselves, as she peered harder, into the two Beaufort girls. They were accompanied by two local men – boys, really – whom Charlotte vaguely recognised, and all four were in disarray. She supposed that it was this her father had warned her about, on her last night in Willingden. Caught out, the girls fled, still laughing, their dubious companions lumbering after them.

Then, framed in the doorway, she saw him.

'Are you there?' he said, his eyes now struggling in the gloom.

'Over here,' she breathed.

'I *think* we are alone now.'

She laughed softly. 'Indeed I hope we are.'

He stood between her and the open window, and the light rendered him as little more than a broad-shouldered silhouette. She found that not being able to see his face calmed her nerves.

'Do you remember the last conversation we had on this balcony?' he said.

'All too well.'

'What a brute I was to you.'

'I think I may have deserved everything you said.'

He paused. 'I hope I am a different man now.'

'I wouldn't wish that.'

'What would you wish me then?' His voice was closer; he was almost touching her now. She knew he was studying her face, though she dared not look up at him – for while he was in shadow, the light shone directly on her, and would doubtless betray her every feeling.

'The same man,' she said, 'but more kindly disposed towards me.'

'Indeed I am – more than I could ever have imagined.' His voice was more eager than she had yet heard it. It made him seem younger and she was touched.

'And I have changed,' he went on, 'in no small part thanks to you. I never wanted to put myself in anyone's power before. I never wanted to care for anyone more than myself. In fact, Miss Heywood. *Charlotte*—'

She held her breath but then an enormous crash rent the air. The enchantment was shattered.

'Damn it, I will see her! Get out of my way, you blackguards!'

They were drawn to the door and saw it was Sir Edward who shouted. He was clearly drunk and swayed where he stood.

'Esther, forgive me!' he cried plaintively. 'Take me back!' To collective gasps and a few shouts of mocking laughter, he flung himself at her feet. She said nothing, apparently mute with horror and shock. The room had fallen silent, even the band had paused to better hear his pleas.

'I've been such a fool!' he wailed. 'I must have been mad, Esther. Listen to me, it was always you, I never cared for that little vixen Clara. It's you I love – you and only you. Forgive me, Esther. Say we can be together again.' He grabbed for her hands but she pulled them away, leaving him to paw at her skirts. 'Tell me you love me still – as I love you.'

She drew herself up. 'You don't know the meaning of love.'

'No, no, you don't mean that. You love me! You want me!'

Babington, who had been trying to push through the rapt crowd, came to stand between them.

'Denham, you're distressing your sister. You should leave now.'

Edward staggered to his feet and glared at him. 'Only if *she* tells me to. Esther?'

She looked away, tears glistening in her eyes. 'Just go.'

He blanched, truly shocked. 'You bitch!' he spat when he had recovered himself. 'You have just ruined my life.' Turning, he shoved his way through the crowd, who began to murmur, quietly at first, and then louder, like a swarm of bees. 'Brother or lover!' one man was heard to shout, to an answering billow of laughter.

Tom rushed to the middle of the room, gesturing frantically at the conductor.

'Ladies and gentlemen, take your partners!' he cried, and the music struck up once again.

In the newly finished house in Mr Parker's beloved crescent, which was now complete to Old Stringer's exacting standards at last, he was packing up his tools. It was late now, the moon riding high. He could just hear the music from the Assembly Rooms. His boy would be there, he supposed, mixing with the gentry he would never be. Despite what he'd said to the boy, he was proud; prouder than he'd ever know. When he discouraged him from trying to better himself, it was only to protect him from a life of dissatisfaction, and the loss of belonging. He could never seem to explain himself like that, though; all his skill was in his hands, not with words. The boy's mother had been better at all that, but she'd been gone ten years now.

He stood back to inspect the mouldings he'd been working on. From the new angle, he could see a bit he'd missed, right at the top. It wouldn't do, so he got out his sanding block, and heaved himself back up the ladder on his good leg. He was dog-tired, he thought, and wanted nothing more than his chair by the fire. Every muscle and sinew in his body hurt, his chest worst of all. He reached up with his block and the ache suddenly deepened and spread down his arm, as heavy and breath-stealing as another block of stone landing on him. He was insensible before he hit the floor, hand clutched to his heart, his last thought of his son.

The ladder he'd toppled off now teetered and fell, knocking into the candles he'd lit so he could work on, into the night. They landed, still burning, on the floor that was strewn with wood shavings. No one, including Old Stringer, heard the fierce rush of air as the first flames went up.

When Mr Parker had announced a new dance, Esther had used the distraction as an opportunity to run from the room. She thought she might collapse if she didn't. Babington caught up with her on the steps of the Assembly Rooms.

'Miss Denham! Esther.'

'Leave me alone,' she cried. 'Aren't you afraid you'll be tainted by my disgrace?'

He went to take her hands and then thought better of it. She was still trembling from head to foot. She reminded him of a cornered deer.

'Not in the least,' he said gently. 'My dear girl, don't you know that I'm in love with you?'

She covered her face with her hands. 'And what is that to me, when I don't love you?'

'I don't care. It is enough that you like me; that you trust me.'

She attempted to calm her breathing. 'I have no desire to be your property.'

'Good, because I have no desire to own you.'

That took her aback. 'But why else would you have me as a wife?'

He threw up his hands. 'Because I wish to make you happy!'

That confounded her utterly. She searched his face for guile or trickery of some sort, but could find none.

'I would never try to lead or constrain you, Esther. All I ask is to walk through life by your side.'

Esther let go a long shuddering sigh. Then she nodded, just once. 'Very well then,' she said, and waited to feel the cold fingers of regret and resignation clutch at her heart, but none came; only some measure of peace.

Babington blinked hard. 'You accept me?'

She almost smiled. 'Stop talking before I change my mind,' she said, and marvelled at the unaffected joy in Babington's face as he understood that she had relented at last.

As Babington and his newly intended left the scene, their steps were retraced by Arthur and Diana. The latter was still in a state fluctuating between tearfulness and high dudgeon.

'Really, Diana. I don't know why you should be so upset. There's no harm in dancing, surely. I'm really not *that* delicate.'

She dabbed at her eyes. 'It's not the dancing – oh, Arthur, don't you understand? Look at the Denhams! Siblings must always leave each other in the end, I suppose.'

Arthur was rather perplexed. 'We're very different from those two, sister.'

'Oh, don't try and shield me from the truth,' she exclaimed. 'I knew as soon as I saw you dancing together. You're in love with Miss Lambe, aren't you? You'll marry her and I'll be left all on my own!' A small sob escaped her and, humiliated, she walked on even faster.

Arthur was stricken. 'No, no, no! We're just pals, that's all. Love and marriage is not my style of things at all. Wouldn't have the least idea how to go about it. Don't really know how ladies work.' He patted his stomach contentedly. 'No, you've no worry on that score. I'll be a lifelong bachelor!'

'Truly?'

'Truly. Buns and cocoa once we're home?'

Diana beamed. 'Dear Arthur, of *course* buns and cocoa.'

But their contentment was short-lived. Rounding the corner to pass along Waterloo Terrace, Diana's eye was drawn by something bright in one of the windows.

'Arthur, look! Up in that window!'

They hastened closer and saw that the light was in fact flames. They had already burst the glass and were licking up the stone, turning it black. Now they were closer, they could hear its roar, louder than the crash of the sea below.

Chapter Thirty-Seven

For a terrible moment, Diana and Arthur could do nothing more than stare with profound horror as the flames leapt higher, reaching towards the evening sky. It was Arthur who acted first.

He took his sister by the shoulders. 'Hurry!' he said, with great urgency. 'Raise the alarm!'

Diana nodded and began to run back towards the Assembly Rooms.

'Fire!' Arthur bellowed at the empty street. 'Fire!' It felt as though the whole town were oblivious at the dance; that averting this disaster was in the hands of he and Diana alone. He thought of his brother Tom and his great ambitions for Sanditon and shouted again, louder this time.

Diana rushed into the Assembly Rooms and, even in her state of extreme terror, a quieter part of her mind marvelled that the scene within remained unchanged, even as disaster threatened without. She caught sight of Tom, dancing with one of the Misses Beaufort. He looked so happy and at ease after so much worry; she did not want to be the one to ruin that. But then she thought of the fire, which would be growing and spreading with every passing minute.

She tried first to wave at him, but he didn't see her and she couldn't find a way through the press of dancers. In desperation, she joined the dance herself, turning and spinning mechanically until the music brought her close enough to Tom that he noticed her at last.

'Diana! I thought you were leaving?'

Even now, she did not want to embarrass him in front of his guests. 'We were, but an – an urgent situation compelled my return.' She dropped her voice. 'You must come at once.'

Tom gave her a meaningful look. 'I'm certain it can wait till the end of the dance.'

Desperation took her over. 'It cannot!'

Somewhat exasperated, Tom made his circuitous way off the dance floor, bowing to people as he went. Mary, who had seen the exchange from where she was sitting with Lady Denham, went to him. If Tom was slow to sense trouble, she was not.

'Nothing to worry about, my dear,' he reassured her, as Charlotte joined them. 'Just a small incident at the terrace I must deal with. Can you make sure everyone continues to enjoy themselves if I slip out?'

She tried to smile but the anxiety growing inside was beginning to be insistent. Still, she nodded. 'Of course.'

Tom made for the door. Charlotte, after a moment's hesitation, followed him.

The scene that met them at the terrace was shocking enough for Diana; for Tom and Charlotte it was horrifying. The whole upper floor of the building was now ablaze, smoke billowing into the air. It was like something alive: alive and ruthless and devouring more of Tom's beloved terrace every second.

Arthur's cries had eventually brought help and men now attacked the conflagration with buckets of water in a haphazard manner, though it seemed to be making little difference to the ferocity of the fire.

'Dear God, no! How could this have happened?' said Tom.

Charlotte ran over to Arthur, who was now streaked with soot from head to toe.

'Is it not devastating?' he said desperately. 'We cannot seem to tame it. Careful!' he cried as she approached the building. 'The windows have blown out!'

But Charlotte felt peculiarly calm, just as she had when Old Stringer had fallen.

'You need to form a line!' she shouted above the din. The men, startled at the sound of a woman's voice, turned to stare. But then, quite suddenly, Sidney was there next to her. Their eyes met, understanding passing between them.

'Well, come on,' he shouted. 'You heard her!'

Soon the men were arranged into a line, along which buckets of water were passed along. A cart carrying a water pump arrived and Sidney climbed up to get it working.

'Just keep the water coming,' Charlotte cried to the men. 'You cannot let up!'

But in truth there was little to be done. Tom was paralysed as he watched the terrace burn, shock and horror rendering him helpless. Charlotte touched his arm.

'At least there was no one inside.'

He grabbed on to that like a life raft. 'Yes, you are right. It is only bricks and mortar, after all.'

At the Assembly Rooms, Mary was circulating among the guests, doing her best to appear normal. Her thoughts, though, were with Tom and what might be happening outside. Her smile was becoming increasingly strained.

'Mrs Parker! I say, Mrs Parker!' It was Lady Denham.

'Yes, my lady? I hope you're enjoying yourself.'

'Has our host absconded?' she said irritably. 'I haven't seen him in half an hour. Moreover, he seems to have taken half the party with him!'

Mary swallowed; she wouldn't be able to contain her anxiety for much longer.

'I have no doubt they will return shortly,' she managed to say.

As she did, Fred Robinson entered the room and pushed through the congregation to reach Young Stringer. At his words, unheard by anyone else over the music, all the blood drained from the foreman's face. The two of them rushed out, breaking into a run as they reached the steps.

It was a lonely dash through the dark to the only home Younger had ever known. As he approached the cottage, he could almost see his father in his usual place by the fire, Hercules at his feet. He wished with all his heart it would be so, but as he turned the door handle he could see through the window that the cottage was in complete darkness. He stepped inside, the dog running to greet him, though he hardly noticed. No fire had been lit and the air was chill. His father was not here.

Cursing himself for coming home first, when instinct had whispered that he would not be here, Young Stringer raced back towards the new part of town, to the terrace. He heard it before he saw it, like the great roar of a monster. He knew from Fred that it had caught fire but still he wasn't prepared for the sight of it when he got there. The upper floor was gone now, the clean lines of it ruined and reduced to blackened stumps like broken teeth. The fire, not yet sated, raged on, and had spread to the lower floors. The ladders propped against the facade, where men were handing up buckets of water, seemed futile. The blaze had already won. His father was inside that hell, he knew with his every fibre, and there was nothing he or anyone else could do.

Chapter Thirty-Eight

If the night was terrifying, the dawn brought only desolation. The triumphant mood of the ball seemed like a thousand years ago as Tom, Sidney and Arthur stood among the ruins of Waterloo Terrace. In places, the fire was still smouldering and all were streaked with soot.

Charlotte had already gone to the Stringers' cottage, where she found Young Stringer almost broken by grief and guilt. He was kneeling next to a trestle table where a simple coffin had been laid. Fred Robinson and some of the other men stood close by, their faces full of sorrow and their hats in their hands. They seemed afraid to approach the stricken son.

Without hesitating, Charlotte went over and laid a gentle hand on his shoulder. 'I am so sorry. No one had any idea he was there until it was too late.'

Young Stringer shook his head. 'I told him to leave but he would stay. Why did he have to be so stubborn?'

'That's who he was. That's what you loved him for.'

'I should've stayed. The last words I spoke to him were in anger. We parted on a quarrel, Charlotte!' He looked up at her, eyes rimmed with red. She could see the boy in him. He was an orphan now. Utterly at a loss for any words of comfort, she reached instead for his hand.

*

When she left him and joined the Parkers at the ruined terrace, Tom was hardly less inconsolable. His determined, occasionally delusional, optimism had finally deserted him. Like his terrace, he had been reduced to a shell of his former self.

'Take heart, Tom,' said Sidney, his encouraging words belied by his grave expression. 'We can rebuild it. We can make it even finer than it was.'

Tom looked bleak and then, in his usual way, tried to shake himself out of it. 'Yes, yes, we will. We will find a way to raise the money somehow.'

Sidney looked at him sharply. 'The money? Surely the insurance will cover that?'

His brother looked down. 'Yes. Yes, I suppose it would.'

'For God's sake, Tom, tell me the work was insured.'

He said nothing.

'Tom!' Sidney's voice was harsh.

'I – I had intended to, but the premium was so high, and there were so many other calls on my capital . . .'

'So you took a *gamble*?'

'I know. I *know*. No one could judge me more harshly than I judge myself, but never in my worst nightmares could I have anticipated . . .' He tailed off.

No one spoke for a time. It was Arthur who broke the heavy silence.

'Well, there is no point in being downhearted. We must be practical. I have barely touched my inheritance, having neither a wife nor a property to my name. Consider it yours, Tom – every last penny.'

Tom hung his head. He looked as though he might sit down in the ashes and weep.

'My dear Arthur, thank you, but with all our wealth

combined it would be a drop in the ocean compared to what I owe.'

Sidney shook his head. 'That can't be right. Forget the three thousand I gave you. However much else you need to put this right, I'm sure I can find it . . .'

'Eighty,' said Tom miserably.

Sidney absorbed the huge sum as a physical blow. '*Eighty thousand*?'

'There is no way anyone could pay such an amount. I am ruined. I am so sorry. That I should bring such shame upon my family.' He shook his head, utterly appalled.

He left them standing there in shock. He needed to be home; he needed his wife, though God knows she was well within her rights never to speak to him again. He found her in the sitting room, a shawl around her shoulders. She hadn't slept either; her beloved face pale and drawn.

At that desperate moment, Diana Parker burst into the room. Arthur and Sidney arrived out of breath a few seconds later. She gestured for her brothers to gather close, and they obeyed her as they had once heeded their mother. Their usually meek, delicate sister was almost unrecognisable, her eyes fiery and her small hands squeezed into fists. There were no smelling salts in sight.

'Arthur has told me everything and I won't have it!' she cried, eyeing each of them in turn. 'I simply won't have it! Of course this is a setback, but I refuse to let you be defeated by it. Sanditon must not be allowed to founder and fall. We are Parkers! We stand together.'

A tiny flicker of hope was just dawning on Tom's face when Lady Denham was announced.

*

'Mr Parker, you have betrayed us all!' was her opening gambit, immediately establishing the visit's theme. Charlotte, who was still removing her gloves, exchanged a look with Sidney and took Mary's hand.

'Where are your promises now?' Lady Denham went on, addressing the top of Tom's aching head, which he had lowered into his hands. 'Dust and ashes. You took my money and you gambled it away! You might as well have lost it at the gaming tables. Despicable man! I will see you in the debtor's prison. I will see you in the poorhouse!'

Mary stepped forward valiantly. 'Lady Denham—'

'I am very sorry for you, Mrs Parker, but some things can never be forgiven!'

She stood to leave but Charlotte held up a hand.

'If you pursue the debt now, Lady Denham, you may be robbing yourself. We can rebuild the terrace, better and bigger than before. Give Mr Parker a week's grace, at least.'

Lady Denham tutted her disapproval. 'Very well. *One* week.'

Tom did not – could not – answer, but Sidney nodded. 'You have my word.'

It wasn't much later that Sidney happened upon Charlotte, who had been hovering uncertainly in Tom's study. He was wearing his travelling clothes.

'I have to go to London. I must do whatever I can to help Tom, though I have no idea how I will manage it.'

'I believe you will.' There was so much encouragement and conviction in her face that it fortified him.

He reached out to cup her chin. 'When I return, we will finally have the chance to finish our conversation . . .' He stopped and they shared a long look. Both had much to say, but no time to say it in.

He bent to kiss her and then was gone from the room.

The burial of Mr Stringer, master mason, was a sad day for all of Sanditon. Tom had been fearful of attending, certain that the mourners would blame him as much as he blamed himself. He would have stayed away, had it not been for Mary and Charlotte, who insisted it would be worse if he did not go. As it was, no one accused him of anything – at least not to his face. Tom knew that the workers who attended were talking of him, and when he saw his foreman's grief-struck face, it was more than he could bear. He strode away from the mourners towards the now-empty church.

Mary gave him some minutes of solitude before she joined him, broken, on the back pew.

'I don't know what to say to you, Mary,' he began. 'We could have lived perfectly happily with what God had given us, but something made me feel I had to make a name for myself; I had to make Sanditon into a place of fashion. But why? It was all perfectly good as it was! What a silly, vainglorious fool I have been, and now I am bankrupted. What can you think of me, Mary?'

'Tom, stop that.' She reached out and stroked his face. 'I can't bear to see you punishing yourself. This is a misfortune, but somehow we'll come through it.'

'How can I face anyone after this?' He buried his face in her shoulder, more like little Henry than a man.

'I don't care what anyone else says,' said Mary staunchly. 'I absolutely believe in you, Tom. And I love you, so there.'

He looked up at her, a tiny ember of hope in his eyes. 'Oh, Mary,' he whispered. 'My dear, dear girl.'

*

It was six interminable days before Sidney returned. It might as well have been five years for the occupants of Trafalgar House. Tom had almost worn a groove in the hall tiles with his pacing, and Charlotte had spent more hours at the window of her room than she cared to count. Finally, a cry went up from little Alicia, whose sharp ears had heard his horse's shoes ring out on the street outside.

Though Charlotte had been willing his arrival, she found she could not leave her room, even as she heard the Parkers rush to greet him downstairs. She crept to the top of the stairs as the front door closed. A minute passed, her heart thudding every second of it in her chest, and then she heard Tom's cry of relief go up.

'You've done it!' His voice was lighter than it had been since the fateful night of the ball. 'You've done it! You've pulled it off and I knew you would! Well done, my boy. What a brother I have!'

Charlotte, smiling now, flew down the stairs, the sooner to hear the good news for herself.

Tom saw her first. 'Ah, Charlotte! Glorious news! Sanditon is saved, and it is all down to Sidney.'

'Oh, how wonderful!' She searched out Sidney's eyes but he was looking at his feet.

'But that's not the only good news, is it, Sidney?'

Charlotte's gaze went to Mary. Unlike Tom, she wasn't smiling. She blinked in awkwardness and confusion.

'We're just off to tell Lady Denham,' continued Tom. 'Come along, my dear.' He took Mary's arm.

'I just hope the cost was not too high,' said Mary so quietly that Charlotte only just caught it.

'Come along, Sidney!' cried Tom. He was already out of the door.

Finally Sidney looked up at Charlotte. 'In a moment,' he called after his brother.

They were abruptly alone and Charlotte's heart began to gallop once more. He was there, standing before her, just as she had pictured so many times since he had been gone. Each time, she had imagined what his face would look like if he could not secure funds for Tom, and if – what joy – he could. But the expression on his face now signalled neither. While her mind could not comprehend it at all, it seemed that her heart did. *Oh*, she thought. *Oh. It is bad news, but only for me.*

His words, when they came, were heavy with sorrow.

'Charlotte . . . dear Charlotte. I had hoped, when I returned, to be able to make you a proposal of marriage. That cannot be.'

She concentrated her gaze on a button of his coat so she didn't cry.

'The fact is,' he went on, 'I have been obliged to marry myself to . . . to Mrs Campion.'

He waited for her to say something, but when she did not – for she could not – he stumbled on.

'Please believe that if there were any other way to resolve Tom's situation . . .'

'I understand,' she interrupted him. She only wanted to leave him, nausea and tears rising in her throat. 'I – I wish you every happiness. Excuse me.'

She rushed past him and back up the stairs, pathetically grateful that Mary and Tom had gone; that the children and servants were nowhere to be seen. She closed her bedroom door quietly behind her and sat down on the bed, wishing nothing more than to pull the covers over her head like a distressed child. Only then did she allow the tears to fall.

Chapter Thirty-Nine

The weather was as fine as could be wished for a wedding, the sky above Babington Hall's chapel a rich cerulean blue, only the lightest of clouds venturing to cross it.

'Dearly beloved, we are gathered here today in the sight of God,' began the vicar. He beamed at the couple before him with approval. The groom looked particularly happy, if a little disbelieving that the woman standing up next to him had agreed to be there.

'I lent her that tiara, you know,' said Lady Denham quite audibly, nodding towards her niece at the altar, about to become Lady Babington. 'Well, it did very well for my wedding. Of course, I shall want it back after the ceremony.'

Another couple in the congregation had been separated by circumstance and both felt it keenly. Charlotte had not seen Sidney for some time and now that they were under the same roof once more, she was acutely aware of him, just across the aisle.

He caught up with her after the ceremony, when the guests had been ushered towards the hall's smooth emerald lawn, where half a dozen linen-topped tables were laden with drinks. They found themselves alone, all other eyes on the newly married couple.

'How do you do, Miss Heywood?'

'Very well, thank you.' She hated how stiff she was, but did not know how else to be.

'And your family are well?'

'Very well.'

'Ah.'

The silence yawned between them. Charlotte did not think she could bear it.

'How are your own wedding plans?' she said eventually.

'Elaborate.' He looked miserable.

She met his eye properly for the first time. There was no contentment there to be read. Mrs Campion appeared at his shoulder, having made her usual silent approach. She looked between the two of them, eyes sharp.

'Who would have thought planning a London wedding could be so exhausting?' she said merrily, though she continued to watch Charlotte like a hawk. 'Perhaps we should have a simple village affair like this one, dear.' She took Sidney's arm. 'Though I don't think that would be *quite* our sort of thing, do you?'

Sidney said nothing, his gaze now trained on the middle distance. Charlotte looked at her feet.

'Really, men – what do they know?' Mrs Campion went on, slightly too loudly. She tucked her arm in Sidney's and pulled him away. 'Good day, Miss Heywood.'

Charlotte was left quite alone, the beauty of her surroundings and the happiness of the occasion seeming to mock her.

When Esther opened her eyes on the first morning of her life as a married woman, she was disorientated for a moment.

'Good morning, Lady Babington.'

The voice, full of warmth and amusement, made her turn. Next to her in the bed was Lord Babington, who was now her husband. She might have expected regret, for this was her life now and always, but she couldn't summon the smallest misgiving. Beyond the opulent suite of rooms that were to be hers – so much lighter than poor old Denham Place, where damp stained the wallpaper and smoke yellowed the ceiling – Babington Hall seemed to lift and cradle her. It was quite the most commodious and elegant house she had ever set foot in, and a different proposition altogether to Sanditon House, with its gothic excess and tendency to vulgarity.

Quite satisfied, she turned to Babington. 'Good morning. Do you know, I had almost forgotten where I was.'

'You're not unhappy to find yourself here, I hope?'

She considered, a finger to her lips. 'Hmm, well.' Seeing his concern, she stroked his cheek. 'I am teasing. Oddly, I find I am not at all unhappy.'

'Or – disappointed?'

'Not that either, rather to my surprise. I wasn't expecting you to be quite so . . . quite so . . .' She looked down coyly at the tangled sheets.

He smiled. 'Quite so what?'

'No, I should blush to put it into words. And compliments, as you know, are not my style. Come here, Babington.'

As for Miss Lambe, she remained in Mrs Griffiths' lodging house and though she had not lately given her guardian any cause for worry, she was harbouring a new secret.

A knock at the door tore her away from the window. It was the faithful Crockett.

'Letter for you, miss.'

She almost ran to the door to snatch it.

Alone again, she tore it open, her heart lifting at the familiar hand. Otis: even saying his name under her breath made them feel closer.

He wrote:

I have been obliged to enlist in the Navy, where I hope to prosper and improve my circumstances. Wait for me, Georgiana; my love for you burns as fiercely as ever, and I promise you that I will come back and claim you, my one and only true love. I remain, your Otis.

She read it again and then clutched the missive to her breast. Sidney Parker might not know it but her feelings had not waned at all. Indeed, simmering in her dark eyes was as much determination as love. She would see her beloved again, she knew it to her marrow.

And then, quite suddenly, it seemed, it was the end of the season, and the morning of Charlotte's departure. She could not quite believe it had come. She made the walk to Young Stringer's cottage, where he now lived alone.

Despite his grief for his father, which still weighed heavily on him, he couldn't help smiling when he opened the door to Charlotte.

'Miss Heywood.'

'I just came to say goodbye.' She stooped to pat the dog, Hercules, who had bounded out to greet her.

'I appreciate you taking the trouble,' he said. 'Do you expect to return to Sanditon again?'

She gave him a pensive smile. 'I hope so, but I cannot say for certain. When do you leave for London?'

He gestured about him. 'I've decided I owe it to father's memory to stay here, at least until the new works are completed.'

They exchanged a warm look and she thought, as she had before, how much she liked him.

'I hear Mr Sidney Parker is engaged.'

She looked down. 'Yes. I hope they will be very happy.'

'She's not half the woman you are,' he said, taking her by surprise. 'If he can't see that, then he doesn't deserve you.' He had flushed with the force and passion behind the words.

She smiled again, understanding a little of what he was feeling. 'Thank you, Mr Stringer,' she said gently.

She returned to Trafalgar House, and the hour of her departure soon arrived.

At the door, she knelt to kiss the children goodbye.

'Now be good, and don't forget to write to me.'

'And you must write to us!' said Alicia, who was close to tears.

Charlotte gave her another kiss. 'Of course I will.' She straightened up and turned to Tom. 'I hope the rebuilding goes well.'

Tom flung out his arms, almost knocking little Jenny flying. 'Sanditon will rise, phoenix-like, from the ashes, sure as eggs is eggs!'

It was Mary's turn to embrace her.

'I can't thank you enough for your kindness,' said Charlotte. 'And for being such a good friend to me.'

Mary kissed her cheek. 'I'm only sorry Sidney wasn't here to say goodbye.'

A look passed between them.

'He has other commitments,' said Charlotte. 'I do understand.'

'My dear Charlotte.' Mary dabbed at her eyes with a handkerchief. 'Despite everything, I do hope you don't regret coming to Sanditon.'

Charlotte shook her head, smiling, though she too was close to tears. 'How could I? It has been the greatest adventure of my life.' It was the truth.

'Well, we will miss you. You are always welcome.'

She descended the steps and was helped into the waiting carriage. 'Goodbye,' she cried, as it moved off. 'Goodbye!'

As the Parkers retreated out of sight, Charlotte took a shaky breath, almost overcome. She watched Sanditon's houses and shops pass by the window, all of them now as familiar and dear as they had once been novel, all those weeks ago.

As they left the town behind, the road climbing to scale the cliffs ahead, a solitary figure stepped into the road. The carriage was brought to a halt and she realised with a lurch of her bruised heart that it was Sidney. She had thought never to see him again.

She stepped down to the road, her legs shaking beneath her. It was hard to look at him, knowing with certainty that he now belonged to someone else.

He moved towards her, as if to take her hand but then seemed to think better of it.

'I couldn't let you go without . . .' He sighed heavily. 'Tell me you don't think too badly of me. I don't think too well of myself.'

She shook her head. 'I don't think badly of you.'

'That is kind of you. I don't love her, you know.' There was desperation in his face and, perversely, it made Charlotte feel stronger.

'You must not speak like that. She loves you and you have agreed to marry her. You must try and make her happy.'

He looked down and nodded. 'Yes, you are right. I must fulfil my side of the bargain. Goodbye then, Charlotte. I wish you every happiness.'

'Goodbye.'

But neither one moved, not for a long moment. It was Charlotte, in the end, who broke the spell and climbed back into the carriage.

Before she shut the door, he stepped forward and this time he did take her hand. The longing in their faces was very evident.

As the carriage began to move, leaving him behind, she could not tear her eyes from his, even as he grew smaller and smaller as the horses gathered speed. When he was finally out of sight, she forced herself to look forward, though it took all her strength to do so. She was going home now, to Willingden. That other life she had glimpsed for herself, just briefly, had surely gone, carried away on the sea breeze.

Acknowledgements

I was in my early teens when Andrew Davies' classic adaptation of *Pride & Prejudice* was broadcast (and yes, that's the Colin Firth in the wet shirt one). It was my first taste of Jane Austen and I loved it so much that it inspired me to read the books that had intimidated me before. 'But she's so funny!' I said in surprised admiration to my English teacher mum, who nodded sagely.

Nearly twenty-five years on, I was commissioned to write this novelisation and immediately watched the series again. Reader, I loved it still. The books get better with every reading too, and so to find myself in this peculiar creative sandwich with *the* Jane Austen and *the* Andrew Davies is a huge and humbling privilege. Thank you to both for such an intriguing and relevant story. I so enjoyed turning it into a full-length novel.

I would also like to thank the team at Trapeze and particularly my lovely editor Phoebe Morgan, whose empathy and encouragement in the face of a necessarily challenging deadline made all the difference. Many thanks too to my brilliant agent Rebecca Ritchie, who suggested I try for the job in the first place; your faith in me to come up with the goods is something I truly treasure.

Don't miss the illustrated guide to the Masterpiece/PBS show, with behind-the-scenes photographs, interviews with the cast and crew, and insights into the making of the drama.

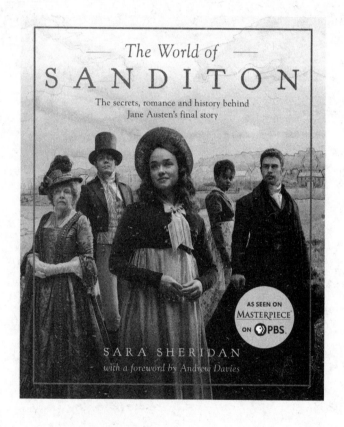

Available wherever books are sold.